ANGELA CAMERON PAGE

SECRETS THAT LIE IN THE DARK

Cover art and interior design by Louise Page at
Lobster! Lobster! Graphic Design.
Set in Bliss 11/14pt

ISBN: 978-1-0683125-3-3

Author's Note

This book contains some graphic scenes of violence,
and implied (but not depicted or described) child abuse.

For Tom, still

Acknowledgements

Possible spoiler! Skip the last paragraph till you've read the book if you don't want any hint…

I didn't put an acknowledgements page in A Fleeting Trick of the Light. I'm correcting that this time round.

Before AFTOTL came out, I was very lucky to have some great supporters who encouraged me massively. Notably: my first, accidental beta reader, Katharine Cope – accidental, because her teenage daughter was the one who was actually supposed to read the original draft, but Katharine picked it up instead, finished it over the course of a weekend, and gave me tremendous feedback – and Paula Bywater, who emailed copies of that same draft to loads of her book-reading mates who were, in turn, massively complimentary. They spurred me on to think it might have a life outside of being read by a handful of sympathetic family and friends.

Since AFTOTL was released, I've been luckier still to have had folk be super vocal about the book, which has helped so much in getting it out there, seen, bought, read, reviewed and enjoyed – some who I already knew, some who I've been grateful to meet through online communities. Thank you to Tracey Morgan, Elle Howells, Claire Bamford, Jenny Meason, Caroline Bason, Sandra Deehan, Emma McAuley, Brooke from @the_brookeshelfxx on Instagram & TikTok, and Steffi & Mel at the Silent Book Club in Birmingham, for support, shout outs and shares.

Lou Page is my amazing cover artist/insides designer, who happens to also be a member of the family. She makes the books look gorgeous whilst refusing to be paid in anything other than gin, saving me an absolute bundle of money that I don't have. I'm so lucky to have her in my corner. And her covers kick ass.

My Mom, Sheila Marion, apart from encouraging my writing since I was little, also provided me with lots of handy technical information about clearing houses, not to mention the experience as a kid of going with her to Spiritualist church, watching mediums at work, and taking part in seances of our own. Yes, she's a medium. No, she is emphatically not Grace from Book 1, as I've reminded her repeatedly.

Other family mentions to Big Sis Joanne Griffiths and her husband Cedric; Big Bruv Michael Dobson, his wife Tracey and their kids; cousins Carol Hodge and Jenny Culligan; Aunty Marg Jeffcoat; and the Extended Pages: Laura, Mat, Dan, Sarah and their respective families for encouragement and Kindle Unlimited page swipes.

To Colin and Jane Page, my lovely in-laws, not only for being such great cheerleaders but also for raising their youngest to become the exceptional man he is.

Which brings me to my last but never, ever least.

Tom Page, my amazing, wonderful husband, without whom I would never have been able to get Dot & Theo onto the page in the first place. Not only because he's supported me in every way that counts: emotionally, dealing with every meltdown, every crisis of confidence, every moody 'why bother' step of the way through the process; practically, holding my hand through over a decade of crappy health issues, having the patience of a saint when I try and fail and try again to lose weight over and over and not once making me feel anything but beautiful no matter what; financially, meaning I can work part time and for the first time ever, actually be able to focus on writing properly, like it's a proper job. He's also a super-clever Countdown finalist (check out all my gushing Insta posts).

But also, if I'd never met Tom, Theo quite literally would not exist. Tom is the love of my life – the only man I've ever loved, or been loved by – and before he came into my life, I had no concept of the depth of feeling it was possible to have for another person, never mind that anyone might feel that way about me. Dot – pre-Theo – is who I was pre-Tom: a guarded, cynical, closed off, miserable bugger, convinced she was entirely unlovable in every possible way, so why even bother to try. Dot post-Theo is a window into the way Tom being in my life changed me, how I see myself, my relationship with the world around me and the other people in it.

I'm still a (mostly) cynical, miserable bugger, but he chipped away at the rest.

I won't say everything I do is for him – I'd never be that fucking cheesy – I write for me, because I love it, it feeds me, and it's such a fundamental part of who I am that it's impossible to imagine my life without it. But it's also impossible to imagine my life without him, to the point I'm in tears if the thought ever occurs to me. Which it did, repeatedly, writing this one.

I write for me.
But this is for him.

ACP, October 2025 xxx

1

'Is there anybody there?'

Silence.

I wait for a beat.

'Will you join us here in the circle tonight?'

Another pause. To give the one I'm angling to get hold of a decent chance to show up.

'Will you communicate with us?'

My eyes are closed. Just for the minute, to help me focus a bit better while I kick things off, keep any potentially distracting client behaviour out of my eyeline. Folks living in haunted houses can be a bit on the jumpy side.

I'm sat on a highbacked chair at the head of a rectangular glass dining table, one of those modern pound-a-penny sets you see in every big chain furniture shop, where the chairs have no arms and chunky seats that are impossible to pull in properly underneath you because you can't get your hands round them, especially when you have short little arms like mine. The room is open-plan, light and airy, living, dining and kitchen all in one big ground floor space. The bifold doors leading out to what little garden the extension has left behind must've cost the previous occupants a fortune in conversion costs. No doubt those were passed onto the young, doe-eyed new owners sat at the table to my left when they bought the place, not realising they were also getting a bonus housemate in the form of a crotchety dead old git.

'We're here to receive you.'

Bless them, they look petrified. The couple – early 30s, one little kid currently shipped off to a relative while this gets sorted, another on the way – moved in less than a fortnight ago, recently enough that a jumble of half-unpacked boxes still litter one corner of the room. When we first dropped in to meet with them the other night, they explained how the place cost them a bomb – worth it, for what they planned to be their forever home, to grow into with the new baby and maybe a third kid in a couple of years – and when it fell into their Rightmove search, right at the top end of their budget, they didn't care why it'd been sitting on the market for the best part of eighteen months or had the price reduced three times. They got an inkling the first night after they moved in, when the soft-close kitchen cupboards started opening by themselves, the Quooker tap kept turning on when the room was empty and the saucepans they'd hung from the suspended feature rack above the marble breakfast bar kept clattering together for no apparent reason. When things escalated with their toddler's toys moving from room to room of their own accord, they mentioned it to a friend with a passing interest in weirdness, who knew someone who's a nurse at the hospital in Little Aston where Rob Hudson-Hicks just so happens to do his consulting work, and now here we are.

'The Guides are bringing someone.'

I nod in response to the smooth, low voice on my right. Theo's been my literal right-hand man since I started taking ghostbusting referrals after Christmas: helping with clearances, recording and making notes on the sessions, being a generally calming, steadying presence in the face of freaked-out clients.

'Thanks, Theo.'

His clerical sabbatical isn't up for another three weeks. Since it started back in November, he's been making the most of exploring his abilities in this spooky arena, before he has to make a choice about what direction he wants to go in – do the medium thing properly, and balance out the fact that it isn't exactly a money spinner by getting a day job; or ditch the spirits, go back to his parish as a Vicar and carry on doing God's work and all that. The latter option comes with a free house, which he's got comfortably used to living in for the past 20 years, and is a hell of an incentive in these challenging financial times.

Option one comes with me.

I take a slow breath and open my eyes. There's nothing visual for me to focus my attention on – no floaty apparitions, although we've had some on other jobs – but the same sense I felt over my shoulder during our initial assessment visit is immediately there. An older male presence, just hanging about, not very happy about it. There's no real sense of any threat from him, though. He's not dangerous, just hacked off about something. Our job is to find out what.

'Thank you for joining us.'

I've been finding – with Theo's encouragement – that it pays to be polite, to the dead folk as much as to the living.

'We'd like to talk with you. Can you tell me your name?'

For a second there's nothing, then on the table, my half-drunk mug of tea tremors roughly as if in response. The male half of the couple – Anthony, I think it is; Theo's much better at keeping track of the formal stuff than me – gasps audibly at the sudden movement. Four mugs to choose from, each sat neatly on its own coaster, and mine's the only one shifting about. I'll take that as an acknowledgement.

'You can't tell me your name?'

You could cut the tension around the table with a rusty butter knife. There's a distinct chill in the air, a dead giveaway – pardon the pun – of a supernatural presence if ever there was one.

Clatter.

The mug shakes again.

'Are you the spirit who occupies this house?'

When we started doing these clearances, I used to ask if they were the spirit who lived in the house. Until Theo pointed out the obvious contradiction.

Clink, clink.

Two distinct, separate movements this time. Hmm. So, is that one for no, two for yes? Or the other way around? It's so much easier when they can actually *speak*.

I cast a glance over at Theo in case he's getting any more information through than I am, but he returns my enquiring look with a slight shake of his head. Well, if this is what we're stuck with for communication, we need a definitive response to something we already know is true, or we'll be going round in circles all night.

'So we can be sure we understand you, I need to ask a simple yes or no question,' I set out slowly. 'Is the sky blue?'

Anthony and – Leila, I *think*; menopause brain has my memory for names shot to hell – exchange a puzzled look. Theo immediately leans across the table to put them back at relative ease.

'It's a control question,' he explains quietly. 'We already know the answer's yes. We just need to confirm what their yes *is*.'

As if on cue, *clink, clink* in front of us. Two for yes it is then. Theo gives the couple a quick 'there you go' shrug and sits back in his seat.

'Thank you. I know it's a silly question.'

Clink, clink.

Hmm. Our dead fella has a sense of humour.

'Did you pass in this house?

Clink.

Leila lets out a long sigh. 'Thank god for that,' she murmurs to her husband.

'Did you live here?'

Clink, clink.

Makes sense. They mostly hang around places they have a strong connection to, and those two are the strongest there is – life and death. I recall the impression I felt when Theo's Guide brought the guy through, and decide to check if it was right. The more we can learn about him, the better we can understand what he's still doing here.

And how amenable he is to leaving.

'Were you retired when you passed?'

I catch myself before blurting out 'old'. The last thing I want to do is inadvertently insult him and put his spirity knickers in a twist.

Clink, clink.

'You're a man?'

Double clink.

'In your…' I reach back to my feeling from earlier. 'Seventies? Early seventies?'

Two double clinks in quick succession.

A picture is beginning to distil around me, brush strokes gradually filling in somebody else's memory of a life.

'You wore a suit to work every day,' I go on, aware of the rattling mug affirming the words as I say them, but no longer needing it now that I have half an eye in his world with him. 'You kept it up after you retired as well, always wanted to make an effort. You and your wife lived here for a long time, raised your family here, three kids, long grown up now and moved away, two with families of their own. Then just as—'

My throat is suddenly blocked by a lump, tears stinging my eyes. This stuff hits me differently now, now that I have someone. Now that I'm with Theo.

'Just as you retired, just when you were supposed to start

enjoying this time together, your Lily got sick.'

Other people's pain, their *loss* – I feel it so much more than I ever used to. I suppose because now *I* have something to lose, I can picture myself in their shoes. The thought of what it'd do to me if, God forbid, anything ever happened to Theo… Instinctively, I look across at him for reassurance and find him frowning back at me, worry etched into the lines of his face as he sees the emotion in mine. Swallowing back tears, I give him as much of a smile as I can conjure to let him know I'm okay. Honest.

'Your lovely Lily passed away,' I go on gently as the mug clatters in sombre agreement. 'And then you were alone. I'm so, *so* sorry, Alfred.'

The clinking gradually tapers off, the couple at the table clinging noticeably closer to one another. I breathe out the emotions flowing through me before they take over completely and turn me into a blubbering mess, bringing my focus back to the matter at hand.

So, now we know why he's so connected to the place. Why is he still here?

Judging by the fashions in Alfred's post-retirement picture, this all happened a good long while ago. There's no way the recent sale was connected to him or his family.

'Alfred, is there something here you still want to do?'

Clink.

Nope. Hmm.

'Something unresolved? A message you want passing to your loved ones?'

Clink.

'Did you pass of natural causes?'

Clink, clink.

'Do you know the new owners?' I indicate the pair to my left.

Clink.

'Any problems with them?'

Clink.

I frown across at Theo, racking my brains for options. If I have to keep guessing, this is going to be a long night, and we've both got work tomorrow. As he returns my gaze, Theo raises his eyebrows, code for he has an idea. I nod at him to go for it. Whatever it is, it can't hurt to try.

'Alfred,' his low voice rumbles softly, 'do you miss Lily?'

CLINK, CLINK. Firm and clear.

Theo glances back at me, and I nod at him to go on.

'Do you want to be with her?'

CLINK, CLINK, CLINK, CLINK, CLINK, CLINK.

I'd call that a resounding yes.

'Can you find her?'

Clink. A dull, sad, stunted sound.

That's it. Theo's cracked it. He's so good at this, at *people*, at understanding them, picking up what makes them tick. Even the dead ones. Feeling a mixture of pride and love warm through my chest, I beam across at him as he nods back, indicating for me to take it from there, modest delight dancing on his face. We don't advertise our couple status when we're with clients – I'm the medium, and he's the assistant medium-in-training-slash-Vicar, depending on the potential religious leanings of the client – it's all very professional and appropriate. But it wouldn't surprise me at all if some of them pick up on it anyway. It's hard to be subtle when your head's this far over your heels.

I pick up the conversation. 'Alfred, are you stuck here?'

Clink, clink.

'Did you get lost looking for Lily?'

Clink, clink.

Now the big question. I take a breath. 'Alfred, do you want us to help you find her?'

There's the tiniest pause in history, before a cacophonous chorus breaks out around the table, all four mugs suddenly clattering in unison, the couple both scrambling swiftly out of their chairs in stunned response, stumbling backwards together away from the table.

'It's okay,' Theo reassures them gently. 'This is good.'

I nod at him. 'Sounds like enthusiastic agreement to me.'

'Definitely.'

The terrified couple look back and forth between us. 'What does that mean?' Leila asks anxiously.

'It means he *wants* to leave,' Theo replies encouragingly. 'He just doesn't know where to go, or how to get there.'

Her eyes widen hopefully, Anthony grasping her hand as she looks back at me. 'And you can... help him?'

'We can.'

We *definitely* can. It's so much easier when they actually *want* to go; it's basically just a matter of finding the door, opening it a crack and giving them a helpful nudge through. Of the dozen or so potential cases we've looked into over the last three months, half of them had perfectly natural, run of the mill, non-supernatural causes – leaky pipes, dodgy floorboards and the like – a few had varying degrees of 'unfinished business' to resolve, and one was... well, let's just say they needed some extra encouragement to sling their proverbial spiritual hook off into the light. There've only been a couple like this – spirits who'd be quite keen to do a bunk, thank you very much, if only they could find the door to the otherworldly exit – and they're a comparatively pleasant relief because they're just so *easy*. Want to cross over to the Other Side? No worries mate. One supernatural doorway coming right up, no waiting.

Theo gives me a nod. He knows this drill by now. 'You ready?'

'Yep.'

Game time. I turn back to the couple.

'Okay. So, what we're going to do is connect to the other side, and open sort of a door for him,' I explain. 'Then our Spirit Guides, who help us both do all this, will take him to the door, so whoever's waiting for him over there can meet him and get him where he needs to be.'

The pair of them stare back at me, slightly dumbstruck. I still forget how very weird that explanation is for every new client we meet.

'We're going to get him to his family,' Theo translates smoothly, leaning across the table toward them as they hover uncertainly, his voice the living embodiment of calm, steady reassurance. 'And out of your house.'

They look back at him with quiet relief. I'm sure that's basically what I just told them; he's just better at getting his point across in a way that doesn't scare the bejesus out of people.

Anthony nods. 'Okay. Do we need to do anything?'

'Well,' I start, 'if you want—'

'Not a thing,' Theo interrupts me quickly. 'We'll deal with this bit ourselves, okay? Why don't you go and sit in there and we'll let you know when we're finished.'

Leila and Anthony oblige with obvious relief and scuttle away, following Theo's gesture towards the far side of the massive open plan, where they huddle together on the l-shaped sofa, out of direct earshot.

Mildly irritated by the interference, I give Theo a look as he repositions himself, taking the empty chair directly on my left. 'Really?'

He knows why I'm snippy before he even meets my eyes. 'Come on, Dot. No way are those two up for being part of the circle. They've been like deer in headlights since before we even sat down.'

I frown, knowing he's probably right, but feeling a little put out all the same. 'Still…'

'You saw their faces when you explained what we're about to do. Those are *not* people who think helping send a ghost off into the light would be a fun story to tell their friends.'

I roll my eyes. He's right. I know he's right. I shake my head back gently. 'Three months, and he already thinks *he's* the expert.'

'With *people*,' Theo counters gleefully. 'I'm the expert with *people*. You deal with the ghosts, I handle the live ones. That's what we agreed, remember?'

He has a point. That *was* what we agreed. What with me being categorically, undeniably crap with living, breathing people, and him being all Vicar-y.

'Fine,' I sigh, adjusting my chair awkwardly until we're facing each other across the corner edge of the table. 'I bow to your superior understanding of human behaviour.'

Theo grins back at me, taking my hand in his across the glass surface. 'Thanks, Boss.'

Calm, capable, good with people, and hot. *Super* hot. Yep, that's my Vicar. 'Keep it professional, Theo,' I remind him sternly, not meaning it.

'Of *course*, Boss,' he feigns offence, then immediately outs himself by lifting my hand to his lips and kissing it gently, sneakily enough so that the clients can't see.

I roll my eyes. 'Ready?'

He nods back, letting the moment pass and taking my other hand in his. For practical reasons, this time. 'Ready.'

I call silently to my Guides to join up with us while Theo does the same with his own. Once I feel their extra energy buzzing around me, surrounding us both, ready to help get this poor lost fella to where he should be, I start the clearance.

'Alfred, are you still with us?'

Clink, clink.

'Okay. We're going to help you find Lily, okay?'

Clink, clink. Clink, clink. Clink, clink.

'Okay. I need you to listen to me, Alfred. Listen to my voice. Can you do that?'

Clink, clink.

Across from me, Theo closes his eyes, his lips moving slightly, silently, head bowed. He likes to say a little prayer as we start – that's what works for him, and I don't question it. There's a few Church bits and pieces he's brought into the process to help him adjust, and that's all fine with me, as long as he doesn't expect me to drag *my* lazy arse out of bed on a perfectly cosy Sunday morning to go to a service with him.

'Friends in spirit, guide Alfred to the light. Alfred, let our friends in spirit guide you.'

Theo nods once, eyes still closed. 'Lord, hear our prayer.'

Classic Church call and response. Sometimes I wonder what they'd think if they knew he'd adopted it for this very non-Church activity. It has helped when we've had clients who're closer to his flavour of Christian, though; I think they find it reassuring.

'Friends in spirit,' I repeat, feeling the energy in the room begin to shift. 'Friends within the Light, guide Alfred home to the Other Side.'

'Lord, hear our prayer.'

'Alfred, let yourself be guided. Cross over into the light.'

'Lord, hear our prayer.'

'Go into the light.'

'Lord, hear our prayer.'

'There is peace and serenity in the light.'

My mug starts to clatter again.

'Go into the light.'

'Lord, hear our prayer.'

'Go into the light.'

The rest of the mugs start to join in.

'Go into the light.'

I feel a sudden *pull*, as though something's passing through me, moving upwards.

I anchor myself quickly. Last thing I want is to go with him. A quick public service reminder: as a living, breathing person, should you ever find yourself in close proximity to The Light, do *not* go into it, not unless you're happy not to come back.

'Lord, hear our prayer.'

The pull is still there – *he's* still there – somewhere in me, attached, like he's holding on a bit, not sure this whole Going Into The Light business was a good idea after all.

For the briefest of moments, I see through Alfred's eyes: there's a blue sky above me, not a cloud in it, but I hear birdsong and feel the sun on my face. As I turn to my left, a woman in a spotless white dress is beside me, her dark hair pinned up in finger waves, partially hidden behind a lace veil, smiling and happy. It's Lily, and there's a crowd around us as we walk hand in hand down a path, confetti tumbling down, our wedding, our perfect, perfect day.

There's been hints of this in our last couple of proper clearances. A slight sensation of pressure, something hovering at the edges of my body that isn't me, a couple of brief flashes of somebody else's life for a moment before they finish passing over. But this is the strongest it's been so far.

I don't like it. Gives me the ick.

'*Go into the light,*' I command again firmly.

The chill in the air lifts.

The clattering stops.

The *heaviness* disappears from my shoulders.

Theo opens his eyes. 'Gone?'

I breathe for a second, feeling around with my spidey senses for any lingering traces of Alfred. No pull, no weight, no blue skies or beautiful brides.

'Gone,' I nod back, more than a touch relieved.

He smiles back, stroking my fingers gently with his thumbs. 'That was easy.'

Hmm. Easy, maybe, but weird for me, at the end. I'll tell him after though, once we're out of the house and it's just the two of us. 'Don't knock it. You want to tell them we're done?'

He shakes his head shyly.

'Go on, people person,' I egg him on. He wants to really. I know how much it means to him to tell someone we've been able to fix their problem. 'You do it. Then I can sneak off to the car.'

Theo eyes me back carefully. 'You sure? I don't want to seem like I'm...'

He doesn't say it, but I know what he's getting at. 'Taking credit?'

'Well, yeah. I mean—'

'You take all the credit you like,' I squeeze his hands back warmly. 'We're a team, remember?'

I know Theo means well. He hates to think of me not getting my dues, so to speak, with clients. He wants people to appreciate me, and what I'm doing. It's sweet, and I can't fault him for it, but I'm just as content to get done and go home. Gratitude's great, but what I really appreciate these days is a good nights' sleep. When my night sweats allow it.

Theo looks up expectantly, that familiar eager puppy expression back in his eyes. 'Really?'

'Of course. Now go tell them, so we can get going. I'm knackered.'

Theo bounds across the room as I gather up my bag and

coat, along with his phone, still recording on the table, and his meticulously kept notebook.

'Your house is clean,' I hear him tell them as I sidle out, deflecting their cries of gratitude swiftly in his direction before slipping through the front door and heading to the car parked up the road. We're in my clapped-out Fiesta tonight – a few things in my life have changed since last autumn, but this isn't one of them – I picked Theo up from his volunteering gig after I left work late, the downside of now being classed as junior management. Most of the time I bus it into work from the flat, but on the days when I do drive in, at least now I get to use the office car park, which is a handy bonus. Also, it provides me with a mild source of amusement with how uncomfortable it seems to make some of the Senior Partners when they clock my heap of junk parked up next to theirs, like they're worried my rust might be catching.

I'm not perched on the bonnet for too long before Theo appears from the house and walks down to join me.

'Gave them a card.' He plonks himself down beside me, leaning his tired head against my shoulder as he puts an arm around my waist.

I nod, planting a kiss in his wavy mop as I take his hand and pull him closer. We had business cards made – very simple, just my name and a mobile number, different to my normal one to keep things easily separated. Oh, and there's a Ghostbusters logo on the back. I only suggested it as a joke, but Theo ordered a batch with them on for a laugh, and when they got delivered, they looked so good we couldn't resist. Gets the point across, after all. We only work by referral anyway, so if someone gets that number, it's generally because a client we've helped before – or one of the very few other people who know about our ghostly shenanigans – has given them one of those cards.

Theo's name isn't on them, just in case word gets back to the Church. Until he decides for sure whether or not he's going back to full time Vicaring, there's no point taking any chances. Although, obviously, for my own selfish reasons, I'm hoping he doesn't.

'They happy?'

'Thrilled. Said something about naming the baby after me,' he mutters sheepishly.

'Poor kid.'

'Ha ha. Did you get my phone?'

'Here,' I hand it over with his notebook. 'Did you tell them—'

'—to give it a couple of weeks,' he nods, finishing my sentence. 'Then as long as there's no more incidents, send a donation if they want.'

Not for the Dot Miller Personal Retirement Fund. I have a proper job these days, I don't need cash tips any more. No, Theo's been volunteering with a homeless charity in the city centre during his sabbatical. So we tell the clients we've helped to give it a fortnight, and if they're happy there's no more bumps in the night, to donate a sum of their choice to the shelter.

I snuggle against his head, content. 'You want me to drop you home, or are you staying at mine tonight?'

Theo hesitates, and I feel him tense beside me.

'It wasn't a trick question,' I reassure him gently.

Sleepovers have been a bit of a touchy subject lately. For reasons.

He nods, head still on my shoulder, breath warm against my neck as he turns. 'I'll come to yours. If that's okay.'

'Of course.'

'I'm on afternoon shift tomorrow. I can clean the flat in the morning, get some shopping.'

'You don't have to.'

He raises back up to his full height, frowning at me. 'You never have food in.'

'You know I hate to cook.'

'You don't look after yourself. I worry.'

I remember my weird little Alfred-brain-transfer episode from earlier. I don't want to give him another reason for concern. I'll tell him about it tomorrow, after I get back from work. It's late, and we're both tired.

'You'd have *more* reason to worry if I cooked, not less.'

'You're hopeless.'

'I am.' I bat my eyelashes at him. 'Hopelessly in love with some stupid Vicar.'

That gets him. He laughs lightly and leans down for a kiss.

'Good catch with the Lily situation, by the way,' I compliment him as he pulls back. 'Did one of your Guides give you that?'

Theo shakes his head and looks down, away from me.

'What?'

'I dunno,' he shrugs, mumbling quietly. 'I just thought... if I were him, and you were, you know...*gone*. What could possibly stop me from following after you when it was my turn?'

Awwwwwwww. God, I love this man so much it's genuinely *sickening*.

I reach for him, one hand on his fuzzy cheek as I bring his face back to mine. 'I love you, Father Gregory.'

He laughs into my kiss. 'Not as much as you love Creme Eggs.'

Running joke.

'But I don't love *anything* as much as I love Creme Eggs,' I reply solemnly.

'I'm a close second, though.'

'So close.'

Theo sighs deeply, feigning disappointment. 'One day I'll make it to first.'

I raise my eyebrows. 'Tell you what. Drive us home and you might bump up the rankings.'

He frowns. 'You still that tired?'

I shrug dully as he shakes his head, eyeing me carefully.

'You're working too hard, Dot.'

'Not out of choice,' I insist.

Another touchy subject.

Theo laughs. 'Yeah, Becs has had a gun to your head for the last three months. How many times in the last six weeks has she begged you to take a day off?'

I pull a face. 'Eight.'

'So—'

'Can we talk about this later?' I deflect quickly. 'Like maybe when I'm not about to fall into a coma from exhaustion?'

'All right, drama queen.' Theo rolls his eyes, squeezing me close against him as he plants an affectionate kiss on my forehead. 'Let's get you home.'

I heave a grumbly sigh, shaking my head into my coffee. What used to be purely a Friday treat has morphed into a desperately needed regular morning pick-me-up lately. And after I necked half of Theo's latte by mistake one time and realised how comforting it tasted half filled with milk, I switched my allegiance from my old, pure black caffeine shot to his calorie-stuffed hug in a mug variant. My scales haven't been best pleased about the change.

'No good?'

Big Boss leans over from her desk beside me, squinting at the CV on my screen. Since I took over the Team Leader role after Pat left at Christmas, top priority has been trying to replace myself. Mags too, now that she's decamped upstairs for her new Technology internship. Until I can do that, I'm stuck covering the bulk of our old combined workloads, on top of supporting Becs and babysitting the two Consulting Partners who make up for only generating a days' worth of work each by being utter technology dinosaurs who need an excruciating amount of hand-holding with the most basic of tasks. Never mind managing the team as a whole, prepping for all of the secretaries' performance reviews, organising and minuting all of Becs' division meetings... there's a *lot*. And unlike Pat, I actually *do* everything that falls under my remit. I try to delegate bits out to the rest of the team when I can, if I know they've got capacity – Bonnie's a sweetheart about picking up extra dictations – but as the Line Manager, the buck stops with me and I'd rather shoulder the extra burden than I would dump it on them.

'They spelled 'secretary' wrong.'

Silly me thought the recruitment part of the job might actually be enjoyable. Hmph. Shows what I know.

Becs grimaces. 'Not an ideal start.'

'Not when that's the role you're applying for, no.'

'How many CVs is that now?'

We've been counting. 'This one makes forty-two.'

'And how many of those have you interviewed?'

I lean back hugging the coffee, rubbing my already aching temples, eyes closed. 'Seventeen.'

'Second interviews?'

'Four.'

She frowns at me sympathetically. 'And *none* of those were any good?'

'At least two of them would've been perfect as far as I'm concerned,' I remind her pointedly. 'It was your bloody lot who objected.'

Fee Earners never get any better. Stephen, ex-pain in the arse of mine, voted against one of the applicants who was up for my role. Paula, who Mags used to look after, objected to the other one. I tried to resolve it by just swapping the candidates over, but once each of them heard about the others' objection, they refused again on principle.

'I thought Izzy was supposed to be lending us the Float Secretary?' I chunter irritably. 'At least until we replace Mags. They're the one who tempted her away to the dark side, after all.'

'That was the plan,' Becs sighs, 'but then they won that massive tender last month. It's still all hands on deck up there.'

'Remind me again please why you won't just let me get a temp in?'

Becs eyes me sternly, all Big Boss mode. 'We don't have the budget left. Once we get into April...'

'I'll have drowned under a pile of files by then.'

'Dot, you're a manager now,' she points out firmly. 'You've *got* to learn to delegate.'

'I have been,' I counter quickly. 'But the whole team's stretched thin enough as it is, and Nathan's replacement hasn't even started yet. We need more people.'

'Then get us some,' she nods back at my screen. 'Look, maybe take a different approach. Instead of discounting every CV with a spelling mistake—'

'I haven't discounted *every* one of those—'

'Or every applicant who hasn't worked in law,' she continues over me, 'give someone different a chance.'

I bristle at that. 'Excuse me, I *have* been. Most of the first interviews were ex-admins from all sorts of backgrounds. We've had some decent options of people with good transferable skills. It's Fanny Adams over there who's being a dick about it.' I glare across the office in Stephen's general direction.

Becs turns back to her own desk with an airy shrug, wanting to crack on with her own stuff. 'You'll figure it out. I have complete faith in you.'

'Super helpful. Thanks.'

'Speaking of faith, has Theo made his mind up yet? Maybe he needs a new job.'

I bristle at that, too. 'Funny. And no, he hasn't.'

Becs turns back to me in surprise. '*Still?*'

I shrug noncommittally.

'Isn't he due to go back soon?'

I nod, my eyes fixed firmly on the next CV to avoid meeting hers. My voice croaks as I reply. 'Three weeks.'

'Three *weeks?*' Becs shakes her head. 'God, it's gone so fast. But – what about…'

'What about what?' I reply measuredly, focusing intently on

the candidate's job history in front of me, although I'm not really taking in any of the details.

'Well...' she frowns awkwardly. 'Won't you have to split up? If he goes back, I mean?'

And therein lies the quandary. A Church of England Vicar who may not have a direct line to God, but can definitely talk to dead people and has a medium for a girlfriend despite the existence of mediums being in direct contradiction with the teachings of said Church. A girlfriend he can't live with because Vicars can't live in sin. A girlfriend he *could* marry – it's come up – but as a Vicar, he'd have to do that in Church, before God and whoever. The same Church I used to joke would probably burn me for being a witch, given half a chance.

Turns out I was being silly. If you're familiar with Leviticus, the preferred method is actually stoning.

'Thanks for reminding me.'

Becs winces. 'Sorry.'

A girlfriend who, during his sabbatical from the stone throwing Church, he's worked alongside, using his own apparently heretical ability to help clear houses of spooks. A girlfriend whose flat he has a drawer of his belongings in for all the nights he sleeps over.

Sleep being the operative word.

There's that touchy subject again.

It wasn't a problem at first. Taking things slow, I mean. Theo means a hell of a lot more to me than a quick shag. And doing... *other* things, without that *one* thing that he absolutely *isn't* allowed to do, the thing he's supposed to reserve for marriage now that he's taken his clergy vows, has been buckets of fun to figure out. But it's been at the back of both of our minds, this stalemate situation we're stuck in.

My eyes don't leave my screen. 'Can we please not talk about it?'

'Of course,' Becs shakes her head quickly.

'Thanks.'

Out of the corner of my eye, I can just about see her, frowning over my shoulder. She's dying to say something else. The urge is coming off her in waves.

'What?'

'It's just…'

'*What*, Becs?'

'You two are *meant* to be together,' she babbles animatedly. 'That whole thing of being separated as kids, then finding each other again after all these years when you didn't even know each other *existed*—'

'I know,' I nod perfunctorily. 'I was there, remember?'

'But you're so good together, the two of you,' she insists.

'I'm not arguing.'

She's right. We are.

'I just don't – after everything else, all you've been through—' Becs lowers her voice. 'After what happened on your birthday…'

I flash her a look. I told her about that in confidence. Not so she could bring it up in casual conversation. I haven't even told Mags yet.

My forty-third birthday. Two weeks ago. All we did was go out dancing with Lisa and Penny, some sort of nostalgia night at the Nightingale where they were playing a load of old club classics. The girls got bored and did a bunk after the first hour, too young to recognise most of the tunes, but me and Theo? Nineties dance was our *era*. And as we'd missed the chance to enjoy it together the first time round, we made the most of it.

Turns out, my Theo is *smoking* hot on the dancefloor.

Honestly, the tension between us had already been hovering at boiling point for weeks by then. Going at it for three hours to some sick throwback tunes in a dark room with a bunch of other sweaty people was always going to be a risky proposition. A few minutes of grinding to a Baby D classic at the end of the night just lit the touchpaper. Big time.

I'm not sharing details, but let's just say it was the Best Birthday Ever.

Okay, I'll share one detail. He was fucking *spectacular*.

And therein lies the sore point. Because now I know exactly what I'm missing.

'How are you two not just walking off into the sunset together?'

I sigh sadly over at Becs. 'Sometimes it's different the next morning when the sun comes up.'

Yeah. The sun came up the next morning all right. And Theo – conflicted, not for the first time, between what he wants with us, and what's expected of him from his Vicar Vows – told me it couldn't happen again. Not while he's still a Vicar. Not unless we're married.

Becs shrugs simply. 'But you love each other.'

I shrug, trying to focus on someone's list of personal skills and hoping to let the conversation die. That way, I can keep pretending the situation isn't constantly on my mind, every minute of every hour of every single fucking day. 'Let's hope that's enough.'

'Pfft,' she huffs dismissively. 'If you two can't make it work, what hope is there for the rest of us?'

'Why, what's up with you and Rob?' I ask quickly, jumping at the chance to change the subject.

She shakes her head, looking down uncomfortably. 'It's just… the Hannah thing. We still can't agree on how to deal with it.'

Hmm, the Hannah thing.

So: Hannah, Becs' and Rob's ten-going-on-thirty-year-old, showed her own little glimmer of paranormal possibility after everything kicked off at their old place at Halloween, when it turned out she could see her family's demonic tormentor. Not really that unusual for a kid, so I didn't think too much of it at the time, especially as their little boy, Adam, showed a similar sense of perception. But whilst Adam's psychic twinkle seemed to be limited to the events of that week, since the new year, Hannah's been having… well. *Visitors*. Dead ones.

Not often, and not scary; the kid isn't bothered by them in the slightest. But whilst Rob is keen for her to actively explore what appears to be a slowly developing gift, Becs would rather pretend none of it's happening and hope it all just goes away by itself. Which it could, if Hannah ignores it for long enough.

'You sure you don't want me to talk to her?'

But from what I've gathered – mostly third-hand via what Rob's shared with Theo, what with Becs mostly avoiding the issue – Hannah's doing the exact opposite of ignoring it. She's well into the whole thing, regaling the family at the dinner table on a regular basis with the exploits of her latest spirit friend, much to Becs' dismay.

'I'm sure,' she replies quickly, tension evident in her voice. 'Thanks. I just worry that… if she talks to you of all people… it'll just…'

'Encourage her?' I suggest.

She grimaces. 'Yeah. Sorry.'

'Don't apologise,' I shake my head. 'I get it, really. After everything you all went through, I don't blame you.'

I can completely understand why the idea of little Hannah having any sort of supernatural talent completely freaks Becs out. Having your family possessed by a malevolent demon spirit trying to bring about chaos and damnation will do that to a person. That being said, I do worry a bit about the kid herself, and how she's dealing with it. What Hannah needs ought to come before what Becs wants, but it's not like I can say that to her. At least, not without coming off as an interfering cow.

'Just…' I go on carefully, wanting to be sensitive. I'm still trying to learn that trick, with Theo's help. 'You do know what happened with you guys was exceptionally weird and fucked up, right? Normal, run-of-the-mill medium stuff is *nothing* like that.'

'I know,' Becs smiles back tightly. It doesn't quite reach her eyes though, and I'm not that easily fooled. 'You've told me. I'd just rather she not get… *involved* with it. Okay?'

'Course,' I shrug casually, not wanting to push it. 'Think she might fancy a secretary job though?'

'Ha ha.'

The next CV draws my attention as Becs cracks back on with her mornings' jobs. Ooh, this one might actually be a goer: a couple of years at one of the smaller law firms in Brum – not on the property side, but I can live with that – a few years as a PA in manufacturing, English and Maths GCSEs both above a Grade C. I'm just about to start a quick stalk of her social media when I hear buzzing coming from under the desk.

The Batphone.

I only keep my personal phone out on my desk at work, and that's mostly just in case Theo texts needing a lift or asking if I fancy a takeaway. The spirit hotline – a cheap pay as you go job – lives permanently in my bag. After all, I'm hardly about to answer enquiries for ghostbusting services in the middle of the office, even if most everyone in the building is familiar with the rumours about me by now. So I wait for the buzzing to stop, wasting a couple of minutes scouring the current candidate's Facebook and Insta for possible recruitment red flags before I reach down and rummage through my bag to retrieve it.

One missed call.

One new voicemail.

Looks like I'm about to have a sudden urge to pop to the toilets.

The phone comes with me as I slip out to the landing, relieved to find the ladies' is empty and lock myself in the cubicle farthest from the entrance.

The message shows as just over thirty seconds long, which means they've actually left one. My outgoing message gives callers a specific instruction to leave a voicemail as I'm often unavailable, but some people call and don't bother. If it's an existing client I always try and call straight back, but depending what else Theo and I already have on, if I don't know the number and they don't leave a message, I leave it well alone. When we first started getting calls, I used to respond to everyone – I felt guilty just ignoring them, even if they didn't leave a message – but after a couple of very awkward conversations and the odd heavy breather, I stopped bothering.

'Hello.'

A man's voice. Older than me, but not *old* old. Fifties, maybe?

'This is a message for…'

Hesitation, rustling in the background. Like he's checking through papers.

'Dot… Miller, I think? Sorry, I can't read my own handwriting.'

I know that one well. Ah, the joys of aging.

'Someone I work with gave me your number. You helped a friend of theirs with a problem at their house.'

Formal, calm, steady. Whatever's happened to make him call, he doesn't sound massively rattled by it.

'I'm having a similar problem and I'm hoping you might be able to help. Erm…'

Another hesitation.

'I'm not sure what else to tell you, really. It'd be great if you could come and take a look, I suppose?'

He leaves a mobile number and an address, a place in Boldmere.

'Oh, and my name is Morrison. Owen Morrison.'

3

Once I've checked with Theo he's free tonight – sometimes the shelter ask him to help cover outreach in the evenings, going on the streets to hand out supplies, chat with folks, get some inside when they have beds free, which is painfully rare – I text the bloke back to make arrangements. By the time Theo and I pull up near the house later, after I've picked him up and we've fought the always horrendous commuter traffic on the A38 out of town, it's gone half-six and the sky's slowly darkening.

The wide suburban street we find ourselves on in Boldmere is innocuous enough. Round the corner from a train station in one of the decent parts of north Brum, the houses are a mix of big, Georgian terraces and 1940s semis, pavements on both sides interspersed with the occasional silver birch and horse chestnut trees. At the far end of the road, I can just about see the spire of the local church, and the whole area is neat, quiet and utterly unassuming. I bet they all pay a ton in Council Tax.

Theo eyes the lone detached house on the corner of a single junction halfway along the road, surrounded on two sides by a neat privet hedge taller than he is, itself dwarfed by an enormous copper beech tree in the garden, dominating the neighbourhood skyline as it rises just above the roof of the house. 'What do you think?'

I follow his gaze. 'Looks a bit out of place with the others, doesn't it.'

He nods back at me. Unlike its neighbours, this isn't a period house in the traditional sense. Its corner plot means that the front actually faces out onto the side road off the junction. With three floors, it's easily the tallest house on the street, and it's an odd shape, not fitting in with any of the other structures nearby. The pitched roof is the tiniest bit off-centre to the rest of the building, giving it a slightly lopsided feel, and although the modern double-glazed windows peep out from browny-grey pebble-dashed walls that are clearly an eighties throwback, the building itself seems much older, yet it doesn't seem to fit an immediately recognisable overall style like Victorian, postwar, or any of the other standards which usually populate the neighbourhoods of Brum.

'Got haunted house written all over it, this one,' Theo murmurs lightly.

'Yeah,' I laugh back. 'We'll see.'

'Hoping for old pipes and rotten floorboards?'

Two of the most frequent culprits behind suspected paranormal activity.

'That'd be nice,' I tip my head towards him with a weary sigh. 'I could definitely do without any more ghosts who don't want to go into the light voluntarily.'

'We could just sack it off and go home.'

Theo shrugs back at me with that gorgeous smile of his, the one that makes me fall in love with him all over again every time I see it. The orange glow from the streetlights outside frame a halo around the tip of his curls, making him appear faintly angelic.

'I'll help you relax.'

I catch his smirk and roll my eyes. Honestly, that man needs horns to keep his halo up. He's an absolute menace.

'I'm sure you would.'

And also something of a tease, given the current status of our physical relationship.

'But we can't just cancel. Not at five minutes' notice.'

Theo sighs, feigning disappointment. He'd never flake on a client. 'I suppose not. Kiss for luck?'

'You're *pushing* your luck.'

Theo leans over from the passenger seat with a grin, close enough that I can feel the heat from him as it transfers to me. 'You *are* my luck.'

Such a smoothie. His kiss is warm, welcome, so familiar to me these days. It's still home. *He's* still home.

I'm terrified of losing him.

He murmurs breathily as he pulls back. 'Let's have a look then.'

I sigh as he turns to get out of the car, already missing his closeness as I follow suit.

Theo grabs his kit bag out of the back – notebook, pen, bible, crosses of varying sizes and materials, amongst other bits and bobs he likes to keep handy, in case of a spiritual emergency, he says – before we cross over the road and approach the front gate. There's a path leading from it up to the house – neat, fresh looking paving slabs, a recent addition, I'd guess – and it splits the garden into a small section on the left where the giant tree looms imposingly, and a larger area on our right hidden by a tall, well-maintained fence. As we reach within ten feet of the house, an outdoor light floods on, and through the double glass doors in front of us I can see into the raised porch: aged terracotta floor tiles in a herringbone pattern; pairs of boots and shoes neatly stacked on one side with a long, black, closed umbrella; a wide, solid, wooden door in the centre, leading into the house proper.

Theo shrugs, casting an eye around what little we can see from the outside. 'Looks normal enough from here.'

I smile back at him. 'You say that every time.'

'And sometimes I'm even right,' he winks.

As we reach for the doorbell, a light goes on in the hall, muffled footsteps approaching from beyond the inside door. When it opens, a man steps through into the porch, unlocking the double glass doors to greet us.

For a second or two he just stares at me, looking slightly taken aback, as though he hadn't expected anyone to be out here, and I wonder if we've actually got the wrong house. Then he frowns, looking back and forth puzzledly between us until his eyes finally come to rest on me again. 'You must be Dot?'

I recognise his voice from the message, and my guess at his age was in the right area. Early fifties, I reckon. Short, dark blonde hair turning to white; an inch or two taller than Theo, maybe, brushing just over six foot; in decent shape for his age, and dressed in a smart, neatly crisped pale shirt and trousers. Decent looking, I suppose, if the older, clean-cut businessman look is your thing. A little bland for my personal taste, I have to say – I'll take Theo's scruff and jeans and perennially mussed hair that's just oh so much fun to play with any day of the week, thanks.

I nod evenly and gesture to my right. 'This is Theo, my associate.'

Theo smiles genially at the figure hovering in the doorway. 'Hi.'

'You're Owen?'

He glances back at Theo again, unsure. 'I didn't realise you'd be bringing anyone else.'

'Strength in numbers,' Theo trills back.

'We work together,' I explain. 'Some jobs are easier with two of us.'

'Hmm.' He thinks about it for a second, lines worrying his forehead. 'I just... want to make sure this stays private, you know. The fewer people know about it the better.'

We've never had anyone react so warily to the two of us showing up before. Usually they're just glad to have someone who isn't going to call them crazy for thinking their house is haunted.

'I assure you, we deal with all of our jobs discreetly. Both of us.'

Theo's using his best reassuring voice, but a little thought pops into my head.

Prick.

Technically, he's only supposed to use his mind-melding ability in case of emergencies these days; I started to get a bit icked out when he was popping in there on a regular basis and decided we needed some boundaries so I could keep at least some of my thoughts to myself. But sometimes he just can't help himself, and the urge to share is just too great. Bit of an uncharacteristic overreaction on his part though; the bloke's just a bit rattled at unexpectedly getting two of us for the price of one.

I decide to roll out Theo's clerical credentials in an effort to put the fella at ease. He seems like the straightlaced type, and they tend to respond well to it.

'Also, Theo's ordained with the church, which can be a big help in some cases.'

He looks back at Theo. 'You're a priest?'

'Vicar,' Theo replies levelly.

He raises his eyebrows. 'Hmm. Okay.'

There's an awkward pause while he takes that in. Eventually, he turns back into the hall, gesturing for us to follow. 'I suppose you'd better both come in then.'

I step up into the enclosed glass porch, Theo close behind. As I cross the threshold, everything around me suddenly *stops*.

Something's here.

Something's *off*.

It hits me immediately, like a ton of bricks, filling up my senses with an overwhelming feeling of *wrong*.

Theo's moved past me and is politely declining an offer of tea; I can just barely hear parts of the client's reply as my head fogs and the surroundings become a distant echo.

'Sorry about… bit wary…'

That instant reaction – the immediate sense that there's *something* here – has only happened twice before during our supernatural exploits together.

'All very strange…'

One of our first few cases back in January had a real bugger of a ghost – not evil per se, but disruptive, mean-spirited and utterly determined not to shuffle the rest of the way off his mortal coil – and getting shot of that one really took it out of both of us. The other was the original demonic spirit business at Becs' old house back at Halloween that brought us together in the first place.

'I'm Owen, Owen Morrison…'

Then as suddenly as it showed up, the vacuum surrounding me disappears, collapsing in on itself with a *pop* as whatever veil had begun to lift drops swiftly back down, leaving me in the hall with Theo, our new client having turned through a door on the left beside the stairs. If my zone-out was obvious, he doesn't seem to have noticed, but unsurprisingly Theo is watching me intently.

You okay?

Getting something. Don't know what yet.

He nods quickly. 'Let's find out then.'

We follow Owen into what turns out to be a living room. The furnishings are clean and minimal – it gives the feel of a showhome; nothing like my perpetually catastrophic mess of a flat – and he gestures us to a neat, boxy beige sofa on one side, sitting himself in one of two matching chairs diagonally across from it.

'So,' he shrugs amiably, his initial wariness now faded as we seat ourselves, 'where should I start?'

'If you could tell us when the first incident happened,' Theo fishes his notebook out of his rucksack as he takes the lead, conscious something's already vying for my attention elsewhere. 'And what it was.'

I keep half of my attention on the client's explanation, but what I'm really interested in is what interrupted me on our way in. Sending out a couple of feelers, I ask my Guides to poke around, see if they can coax whatever it was back out again from wherever it's gone off to hide.

'I suppose…' A deep, drawn-out sigh from Owen. 'A month ago, is when I started to think something was a little strange. I'd heard some odd noises, here and there, before that when I first moved in. Tapping, creaking when there was nobody around, that sort of thing. But, you know, it's an old house. Not that unusual, at least I didn't think so at first.'

Theo nods. 'Have you been here long?'

'Bought the place in January,' Owen shrugs, glancing at me. 'Been looking for a while, I was renting after my divorce.'

'Anything apart from the noises?'

'Yeah. Doors being open when I left them closed, chairs and bedside tables – little bits of furniture – moved out of place, things appearing in rooms when I know I never put them there.'

'Anyone else live in the house who could be messing with things?'

Owen shakes his head. 'It's just me. My kids are grown up. One of my granddaughters stays sometimes.'

Big house for just him. Theo's immediately suspicious.

I bounce his thought back. *Maybe he needs space for his train set.*

The client doesn't pick up on Theo's quickly suppressed smile, but he's not fast enough to sneak it past me.

Owen leans forward, elbows on his knees as he wrings his palms together slowly, his first sign of discomfort since he opened the front door.

'That's actually what made me call.'

Upstairs, is all I can think. Something happened upstairs—

'She came running into my room in the middle of the night,' he starts to explain, 'saying someone was in the room with her. I went in to look and there was nothing there, but it was cold – I mean, properly *freezing,* you could see your breath—'

'Was this the top bedroom?' I find myself asking. 'The one up by itself on the second floor?'

Owen looks across at me abruptly, unnerved. 'Yeah.'

I'm getting an impression of it now, in the bit behind my brain where all of this stuff floats in and out. The air hanging thick with cold, a nightlight glowing faintly in the corner, throwing shadows against the wall beside a child's small bed. Something else in the dark, though, another shadow, one with form, separate from the rest. Different.

'There was something wrong with the lightswitch.'

I'm telling, not asking.

Owen's eyes widen and he nods slowly. 'Yeah. It wouldn't work. I tried to turn it on a bunch of times but nothing happened.'

'There's a chest of drawers in there,' I go on, half in a daze. 'Against the wall where the door is. You keep finding it open, everything tossed out like someone's gone through it.'

Now he sits back, swallowing dryly. 'Yeah,' he croaks.

'And things from that room – those are what you keep finding in other places? Little toys, children's clothes, things like that?'

Owen nods slowly. 'Mmm-hmm.'

'Do they mostly end up in one room in particular? Another bedroom?'

He looks carefully back and forth between Theo and I, eyes wide. 'How could you know that?'

I shrug, a little sheepishly. I've come a long way in feeling comfortable with what I am, but I still have my moments. 'It's kind of my job.'

'I suppose so.' Owen peers over at me quizzically, like he's sizing me up. 'So you're the real thing then. I honestly thought she was imagining things, probably I was too, and it'd all turn out to be nothing. I'm only really doing this because my son said they won't bring her back over until I get it… checked out. I don't really…'

He trails off, gesturing vaguely around him as he searches for the words.

'Believe in ghosts?' I suggest helpfully.

Owen meets my eyes. 'Or psychics.'

'Good for you we're mediums then,' I reply matter-of-factly. 'We talk to the dead; psychics read peoples' minds. They also don't exist.'

Sure about that? We read each other's minds all the time.

That's different.

How?

Can we not have a philosophical debate while I'm talking to a client, please?

'Anyway,' I go on, 'you don't have to believe in what we do. We're just here to look into what's happened and let you know what we find. Then it's up to you what you want to do about it. Or not.'

'I'm sorry,' Owen replies quickly, 'I didn't mean to be rude—'

'It's really fine,' Theo holds up a placatory hand. 'Most people react the same way.'

'Yeah, we're used to it. Look,' I shrug, 'you're not the first client who's called despite thinking I'm probably full of shit, and I guarantee you won't be the last.'

I can almost feel Theo cringing beside me. I'm supposed to rein in the swearing when we're with a client – more professional, you know – but sometimes the words just pop out.

'Let's get back to what happened with your granddaughter. Did she say anything else?'

He shakes his head quickly. 'No. But she wouldn't go back in that room, not even the next day to get ready.'

Theo nods, then pulls a face, suspecting he already knows the answer. 'Do you think we might be able to talk to her?'

'*Katie?*' Owen looks taken aback at the suggestion. 'I doubt it. Like I said, they won't even bring her back to the house. She was scared to death, I can't imagine they'd be too happy for some strangers to dredge it all up.'

I shake my head. 'It's understandable. Any similar incidents, anywhere else in the house? Anything else you've seen yourself?'

'Nothing like *that*.' He looks relieved to move the subject on. 'Just the doors and things. The noises have ramped up in the last few days.'

'How?'

He shuffles uncomfortably. 'Banging. Not very loud. Probably just the pipes, but...'

'But?'

'It's very... *rhythmic*.'

Theo nods. 'Does it repeat?'

'It goes on for a few seconds, does the same a couple more times. Then it stops.'

'Does it always happen at the same time?'

Owen shakes his head no. 'Doesn't seem to.'

'Can you tell where it comes from? Is it the same room?'

'No, the banging's in the third bedroom. It's on the first floor, above the kitchen. The same one where all the stuff keeps ending up.'

So the thing with the grandkid was in the fourth bedroom. How many bedrooms does one middle-aged divorcee need? I can't resist being nosey.

'This is a big house for just one person.' I try not to sound judgmental.

He laughs heartily. 'It is. But it suits me for what I need. Now the divorce is finally sorted, it's nice to have somewhere I can spread out. I've got my office, my gym, space for guests, enough room for all my hobbies...' he trails off as he looks back at me, smiling warmly. 'And who knows, maybe one of these days I'll want to share it with someone again.'

Fair enough, I suppose.

'Besides, I couldn't resist when it came up for sale.'

'Why's that?'

Owen smiles broadly. 'I grew up here.'

4

Well. I didn't see that coming. This is why mediums never win the lottery.

'You lived here? Before?'

'You're definitely *not* psychic, then,' Owen jokes, clearly amused. 'Can't see every little thought rattling around in my brain. Probably not a bad thing,' he winks at me merrily.

The expression on my face – on *both* of our faces, actually – must be a picture.

'We lived here till I was ten,' he goes on. 'Then we moved over Coventry way. I was looking in the area, and I always loved this place, so when I saw it was up for sale…'.

Theo and I exchange a glance. It might not mean anything. It might just be a weird coincidence.

You know I don't believe in coincidence.

Theo looks over at Owen with a frown. 'Anything like this happen back then?'

Owen shrugs dismissively. 'No. I mean, I know I was just a kid, but I'm sure I'd remember.'

'No funny noises, no banging…'

'No.'

'Nothing moving around by itself—'

'No.'

'No cold spots, no issues with—'

'*No,*' Owen interrupts him curtly.

He's clearly irritated at Theo asking him to repeat himself.

'Nothing ever happened in that top bedroom?' I ask tentatively.

He turns back to me, all smiles again. 'Not a thing,' he shrugs amiably. 'And I'd definitely remember, because it was *my* room.'

Upstairs.

A sudden shiver runs down my spine, the hairs on the back of my neck standing to attention so fast I suspect a couple might've fallen off in their hurry. The Guides have done their stuff; whatever it was is back. I find myself looking upwards.

There's something upstairs. *Now.*

Theo continues to press. 'Your room was at the top? The one where your granddaughter—'

'The very same. Top was mine, parents in the master,' his eyes motion to the room directly above our heads, 'my sister had the second bedroom, across from theirs. Third bedroom was the spare.'

But… not only upstairs. Something… elsewhere. Dotted about, in different places. Almost surrounding the house itself, but from within.

Theo can tell I'm having a moment but is trying to keep focus on the client. 'Anything happen with the previous owners? Before you bought it, I mean?'

I *need* to go upstairs. I know we *should* go through our standard process – we agreed on it for good reason. We interview, take notes, then check the house for rational explanations before we try to connect with anything that might be present. But I'm suddenly *itching* to get out of my seat.

'If it did, they certainly didn't advertise it,' Owen scoffs. 'Although, they did take a lot lower offer than I thought they would.'

'How much lower?' Theo asks.

'About thirty grand.'

I barely register the double take Theo does at his response as I'm compelled to interrupt. 'We should take a look around.'

Owen shrugs and gets up from his seat as Theo frowns across at me.

I still have questions.

Ask him on the way then. I need to get up there.

Theo raises his eyebrows.

Sorry. <u>We</u> need to get up there, I mean.

Okay...

Owen hovers in the doorway as we both rise and head to join him. 'Where do you want to start?'

'Top bedroom,' I reply without a thought.

He nods, hand on the crisp white spindled banister as he turns left and starts up the staircase. 'This way.'

True to his word – or his thoughts – Theo carries on with the questions as we head after Owen. 'Is it much different? The house, I mean, from when you were little?'

'A bit. Carpets, the décor in general. New kitchen and bathroom, and the master didn't have an en-suite when we lived here. I don't think they were a thing in the seventies.'

At the top of the stairs, there's a small rectangular landing – barely even a landing, really, more just a place to pause while you decide where to go next. It's about double the width of the staircase, and from it, the house splits off in two directions. Each route starts with its own, smaller set of half a dozen stairs, one running parallel to the main staircase but heading back on itself, towards a large, full-sized landing fronting the house, and the other leading to a long corridor, which disappears around a corner further down. Owen takes the set up towards the main landing, and I can just about see the road where we parked through the half-raised venetian blind.

'What's down there?' I gesture back the other way.

'The bathroom, and the third bedroom.'

'Where the banging was coming from?'

He nods, gesturing to the other two rooms leading off the landing. The one to our left is missing a door, and through the gap, I can see an array of dust sheets, boxes and gym equipment. Owen follows my gaze.

'Second bedroom. I'm kitting that one out as my gym,' he explains. 'I like to keep myself in shape. Never know when you might need a bit of extra stamina.'

He winks brightly at me. That's the second time he's done that, and I wonder briefly if he's got something wrong with his eye, but I've been learning that people don't always like it when you ask those sorts of questions, so I just ignore it and smile back politely, nodding to the door opposite, which is firmly closed.

'And that one?'

'That's the master. My room.'

On the same side, behind where we're standing, is another staircase.

'The top bedroom's up there?'

Owen nods.

It's actually two staircases, or a double staircase in two halves. The first sits directly back parallel over the main stairs, leading to a tiny, square platform before it veers right, with the second section running flush along with what must be the back wall of the house. The same wooden banister from below, finished in matte white, continues up here, with a large post supporting it at the bottom near where we're standing, a second at the midway corner point, and a final one at the top where it meets another wall, which I assume must belong to the fourth bedroom. Owen flicks a switch and a light comes on at the very top, revealing another small, square mini-landing and a further open door directly opposite the stairs.

'That's the boxroom,' he motions toward it. 'Just storage. The bedroom's next to it.'

The tingling sensation tickles down the back of my neck again. 'Does the light in the bedroom work now?'

He nods. 'Works fine now. It only played up when… well. You know.'

'Yeah.'

'You mind if I don't come with you? I've got some work emails I need to clear down.'

'Of course.'

Owen smiles broadly back at me, turning to nod perfunctorily at Theo before he heads back downstairs.

'Emails my arse,' Theo whispers close in my ear as we start up the first set of stairs. 'Bet he's gone to hide his porn stash.'

I roll my eyes back at him. 'Like you've never had a porn stash.'

Theo shakes his head as we pass the halfway platform and turn up the second section. 'Not weird stuff. I bet he's into *weird* stuff. Like… I dunno. Pterodactyls, or something—'

'*Pterodactyls?!*'

He shrugs. 'It was on Reddit.'

I knew I should never have introduced him to that bloody site.

As we reach the small landing at the very top of the stairs, Theo steps in close behind me. The narrow, dark boxroom door stands open in front of us, while the door to the fourth bedroom sits at a right angle, tightly closed.

'Weird stuff,' he repeats with a derisive shrug.

I can practically feel the hostility coming off Theo in waves as I turn to face him.

'You don't like him.'

It's not a question.

'I don't know him,' he looks back at me levelly. 'I'm sure he's probably perfectly fine.'

I can tell he's choosing his words super carefully, and it's very out of character for Theo. I mean, he's pretty diplomatic when it comes to dealing with almost everybody else – hence why he's the people person of our little operation – but he doesn't usually mince words with me. I nod back up at him, ignoring his forced neutrality and being guided instead by the dark glare in those big brown eyes of his.

'But you don't like him,' I press.

'No,' Theo admits with a sigh. 'I don't.'

'Any particular reason?'

I mean, Owen doesn't exactly come across as Mr Personality. The house itself is kind of dull as well – almost pathologically minimalist, from the little we've seen so far – and just the act of buying such a big-arse house all to yourself after a divorce does smack somewhat of a gigantic mid-life crisis. But this is the first time I've seen Theo take such an instant dislike to someone, and I can't honestly imagine he finds any of those things grievous enough to provoke it.

Theo leans down, close to my ear. I know we're working at the moment, and being professional and all that, but it's a very small landing, and having him in such close proximity, in such a restricted space… *does* things to me. Things I can't do anything about right here and now, and can only do a tiny fraction of later, per the whole respecting his vows thing. His voice blows gently through my hair, across my face, into my ear.

'He fancies you.'

I pull back in legit surprise. '*What?!*'

He nods at me. 'Mmm-hmm.'

'Don't be daft,' I frown, immediately dismissing the suggestion.

'I'm telling you.'

'Why on *earth*—' I catch my own volume and drop it about a hundred decibels, hissing back quietly instead. 'Why on earth would you say a thing like that?'

'Oh *please.*' Theo rolls his eyes at my apparent obliviousness. 'Making a point of telling you how he might want to *share* this place with someone?'

I'm gobsmacked at the suggestion. Blokes never fancy me. That's just been an indisputable fact throughout pretty much my entire adult life. On the whole, I've generally done better with women, but if I'm honest, not by very much.

'He was just making conversation.'

'*He likes to keep himself in shape,*' Theo quotes mockingly. 'Never know when you might need extra *stamina.*'

'Come off it, Theo.'

'I saw the way he kept looking at you.'

Theo's eyes flash darkly as he steps forward, filling what little sliver of space still remains between us.

It's ridiculous, how much he affects me. How do I still find him this bloody sexy; this *intoxicating?* I mean, I know it's only been a few months, so I suppose *technically* we're still in the honeymoon period. But I've washed his scutty boxers that he's left at my flat; I've dealt with his gross morning breath, particularly heinous after we have a curry; I've cleaned up his vomit and stroked his hair when he got norovirus at New Year's, for god's sake.

'How did he look at me?' I finally manage to croak.

Theo smiles ever so slightly. 'Like he wants to…' he hesitates, his mouth barely an inch from mine. 'To… *do* things to you.'

I hum back up towards him dizzily. 'I think you're the one who wants to do things to me.'

'Like you wouldn't believe,' he purrs.

I laugh lightly, revelling in the glow of his attention, knowing that Owen – who I'm positive does *not* fancy me, and why Theo's randomly fixating on that idea I have no clue – could reappear at the bottom of the staircase any minute but not really caring.

'Aren't we supposed to be professional when we're on the job?'

'Whatever.'

Theo moves his mouth against mine, and—

Thump.

We break apart immediately, our eyes on the bedroom door, still closed beside us.

Thump.

'That doesn't sound like pipes to me,' I mutter.

Thump.

'I thought,' Theo whispers, not shifting his gaze, 'he said the banging came from the *other* bedroom.'

Thump.

I nod slowly. 'He did.'

I hear footsteps downstairs, and Owen's voice calls up from the main landing below us. 'That's it. That's the banging. But I haven't heard it there before.'

Terrific.

'Okay,' I reply levelly over Theo's shoulder. 'Stay down there please, Owen.'

He nods readily, not needing to be told twice.

I call for my Guides to link up and support me, asking Theo if he's ready as we lock eyes. When he nods back, I take a deep breath, reach out to turn the handle, and gently push the door open.

5

It's dark inside the room.

The blinds at the window opposite are closed, and if the nightlight I saw in my remote impression earlier is plugged in somewhere, it's not on at the moment. Before I step inside, I reach into the doorway, feeling against the wall to my left where I'd expect the lightswitch to be. When I find it, my expectations aren't high, but I flick it anyway. You never know.

Who am I kidding. I *always* know.

It doesn't come on.

Shocker.

'You feel it?' Theo's voice is low and measured behind me.

I nod. 'Cold. Yeah.'

There's cold, and then there's cold spots. If you've got issues with damp or mould in your house then yeah, they can make a specific room feel significantly colder than the rest of the place. Draughts, too, of course, from poor insulation, gaps in the seals of your double glazing if you have it, or basically any part of the building where something attaches to something else and the join is a crappy bodge job. But you can feel the difference. Cold – whether it's down to something being wrong with your house, or just keeping the heating off because you don't fancy selling one of your kidneys to pay the gas bill – is just cold. It's the absence of heat, simple as that.

Cold spots don't feel like the absence of heat. They're the deliberate *presence* of cold. The kind of cold that's like a living, breathing *thing*. The air in them feels pregnant with it.

They feel *heavy*.

Thump.

It's definitely coming from in here.

Thump.

Thump.

Thump.

I take a single, tentative step inside. With the landing light on behind me, I can just about make out shapes: the small child's bed against the wall near the window with a small bedside table next to it, a stack of plastic storage boxes piled up neatly on the far wall, the chest of drawers immediately to the left of where I've just come in, the ones that keep being opened by nobody. If there's anyone – any*thing* – in here at the moment, I don't see them.

Thump.

Thump.

Thump.

Thump.

But *something's* making that noise.

'What's going on up there?' Owen's voice calls up from the bottom of the stairs.

'Nothing yet,' Theo replies, as quietly as he can while still being heard. 'Just the noise.'

'And the light,' I suggest gently, still scanning the room as I take another careful step forward. 'And the cold.'

'The light doesn't work,' he relays briskly, 'and there's a cold spot in here.'

The whole *room* feels like a cold spot as I venture further, walking into the centre.

Thump. Thump. Thump. Thump.

He was right about it being rhythmic. The noise seems to repeat in sets, the sort of bang you might make on the wall if you were objecting to a neighbour making too much noise on the other side. But other than definitely being focused inside the room, it doesn't seem to be coming from any one particular spot. If anything, it's almost as though the sound is *surrounding* the room, coming from all sides, reverberating through the walls and the floor and the ceiling all at once.

I stop in the middle of the room as the chorus starts another cycle.

Thump. Thump.

'Are you in here?' I ask gently.

Thum—

The noise stops abruptly, the sudden silence deafening.

I'll take that as a yes then.

Suddenly, I feel all the hairs on the back of my neck prickle as the air thickens around me, like I'm surrounded by static electricity, then—

I *jump* as the unmistakeable sensation of fingers brushes my right hand, the world's most unprofessional shriek escaping my mouth as I turn to look down beside me.

'What is it?' Theo asks urgently.

Nothing's there.

But I hear a light, childish giggle and what sounds like the clatter of tiny feet running away.

'Did you hear that?' I spin quickly, looking all around, finding nothing but empty space.

'I didn't hear anything, Dot,' Theo sounds concerned. 'What happened?'

'Something touched me.'

'*What?*'

'My hand,' I wiggle my fingers quickly to labour the point, still looking around for something, anything. 'Then I heard a giggle and they ran off.'

'Was that—'

Thunk. Thunk. Thunk. Thunk.

The noise stops Theo before he can finish, but this time it's not in here. I look back at him as he leans down, nodding in response to something Owen's just said which I can't make out, before turning to me again. 'The third bedroom.'

There are footsteps – solid, live ones this time – across the landing below us as Owen starts off towards the sound. Theo and I hesitate only for the second it takes us to share a look of uneasy apprehension before we follow, dashing down the stairs, back across the landing and along the other corridor.

Thunk. Thunk. Thunk. Thunk.

As we round the corner past the bathroom, we find Owen standing there, hovering awkwardly.

Thunk. Thunk. Thunk. Thunk.

He points towards the slightly open door in front of him. 'In there.'

'The third bedroom?'

Owen nods back at me. 'That's where it came from before.'

'Why was it upstairs?'

For the first time, he actually looks genuinely unnerved.

'I've never heard it there before. And never this much. It's usually stopped by now.'

Thunk. Thunk. Thunk. Thunk.

It's the same pattern, all right. But there's something different about this sound, something tinnier, almost musical.

'It's not the same sound.'

Owen frowns at me. 'What? Yes it—'

'She's right,' Theo interrupts with a considered nod. 'The one upstairs was more…'

Thunk. Thunk. Thunk. Thunk.

'Solid,' I suggest after a second. 'The upstairs one sounded *heavier*, like banging on the wall or the floor or something. This one's more like...'

It takes me a second to vaguely place it.

'Metallic. It's higher pitched, lighter.'

Owen looks between us, not really taking any of it in. 'But—'

Thunk. Thunk. Thunk. Thunk.

'You going in?' Theo asks me, taking Owen's hesitation as a chance to move things along.

'Yep.'

Walking past Owen, I approach the door and push it gently open.

Thunk. Thunk. Thun—

The noise stops as soon as I cross the dark threshold. It's smaller, this room, compared to the one at the top of the house, and he must be using it for a guest room; I can just about make out the shape of some sort of folding bed in one corner, currently laid out for use. There's a brass guard in front of the fireplace – funny; I vaguely noticed a fireplace in the upstairs room as well, but it was blocked up; this one's open – and a thick, purple pile carpet, soft under my bare feet as my toes bunch into it to scrunch up the sensation—

—wait. Why do I have bare feet? I'm still in my work trousers, and I've got those stupid little pop sock things on between my ballet flats and my skin, the ones that move around all day until they end up being on your foot back to front and you have to adjust them. I look down and—

—no, definitely bare feet. Bare *legs*, in fact. It's when I notice how smooth they are – knowing that I haven't bothered shaving mine since Friday and they're well into their prickly stage by now – that's when I realise that the legs *aren't mine*.

'Shit,' I blink quickly, trying to force my eyes – are they my eyes? I'm not really sure – to adjust to the surroundings, trying to see anything that might be useful, that might make any of this make sense, but it's so dark, and everything feels sort of foggy and unclear and—

More fingers. A hand on my back now, but I'm ready for it this time and don't shriek in surprise or pull away. I do turn to look, but there's nobody behind me.

What I'm *not* ready for is a sudden, giggly voice right beside my ear.

'You're *it*.'

I freeze in sudden fear, not understanding what the hell is going on, utterly unable to be objective and use my experience to assess the situation. Hearing disembodied voices whispering in my ear isn't exactly anything new; even feeling the occasional tickle from ghostly hands is relatively pedestrian in the life of a medium. But experiencing both of these things whilst seeming to be inside *somebody else's body* is a whole new level of creepy shit.

I haven't seen anything like this before, and I don't much like it.

All I can think is that I want *out*.

And just as fast as I think it, I *am*.

'Dot?'

Theo's voice next to me, full of concern.

'Come on, Dot. Come back to me.'

I open my eyes. I'm sitting on the floor, cross-legged – hmm, didn't realise I could still do that – Theo's hands on my shoulders as he crouches in front of me, while Owen stands in the doorway, looking well and truly spooked. The light in the room is on now, and there's no sign of the foldaway bed, no heavy brass fireguard in front of the blocked fireplace, and no purple shag carpet. Just some moving boxes stacked up in a pile in one corner, storage tubs with decorating gear, plastic sheeting and gaffer tape.

'Dot.' Theo lifts my face to meet his. 'Are you with me?'

It takes me a second to remember how to breathe. As the

process kicks back in, I swallow, reaching down instinctively to touch my legs, relieved when I feel the familiar cheap material – they're only work trousers after all; I refuse to splurge – punctuated by the occasional prickle of coarse hairs underneath. 'Yeah,' I nod back at him slowly. 'I'm here.'

His dark eyes study me carefully. 'Where'd you go?'

I glance around the room briefly, making sure it's definitely all real as I carry on practicing at breathing, feeling like I'm doing it for the first time.

'Nowhere,' I tell him honestly. 'I was still here. I just wasn't here *now*.'

Theo waits quietly as I meet his eyes. He knows me well enough to tell when I'm holding something back.

'And I don't think I was *me*.'

He frowns back at me, forehead furrowed with instant alarm. '*That's* new.'

'And creepy as all fuck,' I reply, too agitated at the unpleasant recollection to check my language as I shake my head back at him. 'I didn't like it.'

'It's okay,' he soothes, one hand against the side of my face, 'you're okay. You're back now, okay? I'm with you.'

Theo leans forward and puts his arms around me, hugging me tightly to him. So much for keeping it professional in front of the client, but under the circumstances, I don't think I care.

'Erm... sorry to interrupt,' Owen's voice drifts over from where he's fixed to the spot in the doorway. 'But... what just happened?'

I break away from Theo gently, giving him the best smile I can manage to let him know I'm okay – ish – and lean out from behind his shoulder.

'Sorry, Mr Morrison. But your house is *definitely* haunted.'

We didn't bother checking out the rest of the house.

Oh, we had a wander round, just for the sake of professionalism, so Theo could tick off all of our basic checks in his neat little book. We had a nosey in the kitchen, the laundry, Owen's fancy home office setup with its plain but pricey-looking desk, snazzy tech and big bay window looking out onto the dark garden, the standard functional cupboard under the stairs used as a sort of spillover cloakroom. But we didn't look at the boiler, the pipes, potential sources of draughts, all that standard stuff. It's entirely possible some or all of those things might've been issues, entirely independently of anything else going on. But I know what I saw, and what I felt, and none of that had anything to do with pedestrian, non-supernatural explanations. Back downstairs, Theo and I spent a good three quarters of an hour talking through the situation with Owen, going over the details of the presence in the top floor bedroom with its probing fingers and creepy giggling.

Describing what happened to me in the other room was a bigger ask. I could hardly understand it myself.

I stuck to sharing what I recalled from the scene around me, but Owen's memory wasn't pricked by purple shag carpets and giant brass fireguards. It sounded as though those things must've belonged to owners who'd occupied the house either before his family bought it or after they sold up. As far as he knew, his parents moved them in when he was too little to remember, and they moved out to Coventry when he was still at middle school. If what I'd seen had been some sort of vision of a previous occupant, it likely wasn't linked to him or his family. Finally leaving close to eleven, we told Owen to stay out of both rooms while we figured out the next step, promising we'd be back in touch soon and giving him firm instructions to let us know if anything changed.

Back in the car, Theo sighs deeply, fighting back a yawn as he checks the time on his watch. I turn my head towards him as I lean my aching bones back in the drivers' seat.

'So? What do you think?'

He looks back at me, concern across his features. 'I think you should tell me what really happened in there.'

'I wish I knew,' I scoff back lightly.

'You said you weren't *you*, Dot,' he frowns. 'That's not funny.'

'I'm not laughing.'

'Well, what—'

'I don't *know* what it was,' I tell him truthfully. 'It's never happened before. I mean, I have been having these...'

I suddenly remember I haven't told him yet about my funny episode with Alfred last night, when the guy was making his way out of our plane and into the one he ought to've been in for the last thirty years via my head.

Theo frowns at my abrupt silence. 'What?'

I shrug, wanting to play it down. 'It's probably nothing.'

'Dot...'

'Okay, okay. Look, it was just... last night, when Alfred... *left*. As he went through me, it was like I could... see his memories, or something. Just for a couple of seconds.'

Theo sighs heavily. 'Why didn't you tell me?'

'Because it was late, and we were both knackered,' I explain. 'I meant to tell you when I picked you up tonight, but I just sort of forgot. And...'

He folds his arms, frowning sternly. 'Yeeeeeesssss?'

I pull a face. 'A similar thing happened on the last couple of jobs.'

'Oh, Dot…'

'Nowhere near as much,' I add quickly, hoping to minimise his reaction to the thing that I know I really probably sort of should've mentioned to my partner in ghost crime – and life – sooner. 'Literally just a second each time, tiny little glimpses. I pretty much wrote them off as nothing. Until last night.'

Theo groans. 'This doesn't sound good, Dot.'

'It didn't *feel* like anything bad,' I reason truthfully.

'Is it a possession thing? Like what happened to me?'

I shiver just thinking about that. I still haven't forgotten that feeling of utter, soul-wrenching devastation the second I realised I'd *let* it happen.

'No. I mean, I don't think so. I think I'd know.'

'How can you be sure, when you never… you don't know how it… what it…' he trails off, his voice trembling with the memory. 'How awful it felt.'

I put a reassuring hand on his arm. 'I know I didn't go through it, Theo. But I was in your head then, remember? I felt some of it.'

Theo nods gently. 'Okay. So what was this then?'

I shrug, grasping for answers that I haven't yet figured out myself. 'I don't know what to call it. But it felt like I was in somebody else's body. No,' I correct myself, 'I *was* in somebody else's body. My legs weren't mine, my hands weren't mine… it was like I was in the room, but I was looking at it in a different time, through somebody else's eyes.'

He raises his eyebrows. 'That's… *weird*.'

My fella is a master of the understatement.

'Yeah.'

'You think you were… seeing things as the ghost, somehow?

The one that's been haunting the place?'

'It's possible. Or someone who was there when whatever happened to them… *happened*, maybe. Either way, it *has* to be related.'

'Mmm. Would be a hell of a coincidence otherwise. And you know—'

'—you don't believe in coincidence,' I finish for him with a grin.

Theo pretends to glare back at me, but there's a twinkle in his eye.

'Maybe it can help us,' I suggest hopefully. 'The room definitely looked seventies. If we can find out who else lived here then, maybe we can figure out the connection to the house. Then next time we can call them.'

'I'm not sure I want you coming back here.'

His words take me utterly by surprise.

'Pardon?'

Theo's never spoken to me like that. Like he thinks it's okay to tell me what to do.

'Is that an *order*, Father Gregory?'

'I'm sorry, I'm sorry,' he holds his hands up placatingly. He's put my back up, and he knows it. 'I didn't mean it like that, I swear. I just, I mean…'

It takes a superhuman effort on my part to hold my tongue, but I wait for him to go on. He sighs deeply, turning to face me full on and taking my hands gently in his.

'You went out like a light the *second* you went in that room, Dot. I didn't know what the hell'd happened. For a minute I thought you'd had a stroke or something, except you were still standing up and walking around.'

Okay. Well, I can understand how that might bother him.

'What if we come back and it happens again? Or worse?

You said yourself, you don't know what it is. What if you can't control it?'

Hmm. He has a point.

'What if next time, you don't come back *out* of it?'

I frown. 'That's a cheery suggestion.'

'I'm just saying. Look, you're the one always pointing out how people shouldn't mess about with stuff they don't understand,' he reminds me firmly. 'Maybe this time you should take your own advice.'

I take a second to think back over what happened, the strangeness of it. It definitely shook me up – it was just so unexpected – but objectively, it didn't seem… I dunno. Hostile, I suppose.

'I don't think it's dangerous,' I consider my words, basically repeating what I've already told him. 'It didn't feel like a *bad* thing—'

'Not a bad thing?' Theo exclaims back at me like I've lost the plot. 'Seriously?'

'It didn't feel *evil*,' I clarify quickly. 'It freaked me out because I wasn't expecting it, and it's never happened before. But it didn't feel like – whatever it was – was trying to… *hurt* me.'

He holds my gaze levelly. 'Dot. Please. Try to look at this from my point of view, okay? You walk into a room, you go into some sort of trance—'

The word sparks a memory.

Something from when we were kids, working the platform at the Spiritualist Church.

'That's *it*.'

Theo hesitates. 'That's what?'

'A trance,' I lean closer to him, excitement in my voice as my brain cells kick in, wanting to spill the words out faster than my mouth can keep up. 'When we were back at the church, I must've been about eleven, so you would've been thirteen or fourteen. They had a guest medium come in from somewhere else one time. He was a trance medium, that's what he called himself, and when he worked the platform that's what'd happen, he'd go into a trance, and—'

'Dot?'

'Hmm?'

'Slow down. Take a breath.'

I do.

'I still don't have all my memories yet from back then,' he reminds me.

The hypnosis our folks put both of us through is still deeply embedded. Most of my memories are pretty much there now – well, except for the ones I've lost anyway, to middle-age and menopause – but that shit can take a long time to unravel.

'Okay.' I take another breath and start to explain. 'So, trance mediums, they allow spirits to take control of them – to a degree – so the spirit can speak directly through them. Sometimes they literally talk, sometimes they communicate through automatic writing. It's like a super-duper deep level of mediumship. I've read about cases where the medium's appearance changes to look like the spirit, and—'

Theo's face is troubled. 'That sounds like possession again.'

I shake my head quickly. 'It's not, I swear. Look, it's something that mediums usually only do if they have a really strong bond with the spirit in the first place. Most often it's one of their own Guides.'

'But this wasn't your Guides, was it. Or it wouldn't have freaked you out.'

'I know. That's what's weird—'

'*That's* what's weird?'

I roll my eyes. 'Look, it's not a simple thing to do. It takes a lot of practice. Intentional practice, I mean. That guy from years ago, he's the only one I've ever seen do it.'

Theo frowns. 'Have you been practicing it?'

'No.'

'Then how did you—'

'I don't know. And I'm not a hundred percent sure yet that it definitely *is* trance,' I add quickly. 'As far as I know, trance lets the spirit come into the *medium's* body. I've never heard of it happening the other way around.'

Theo sits silently beside me, taking it all in.

'Whatever happened in there, though,' I remind him, 'there's no denying that *something* is in that guy's house.'

'You think he's telling the truth?'

I frown at him. He *really* doesn't like this guy, does he?

'About what?'

'About whatever's in the house. What you saw. Not knowing about any of it, I mean.'

'Why on earth would he lie about that?'

'I dunno,' Theo shrugs, looking awkwardly out of the window. 'I just… I don't trust him.'

'You don't *like* him, Theo.'

'Do you?'

This is not our usual post-session conversation, and I'm at a bit of a loss as to where it's going. 'Do I what?'

'Like him.'

'I don't even know the man, Theo.'

'He likes *you*.'

I register his moody expression and realise what he's getting at.

'Are you *jealous?*' I ask incredulously.

'No,' he mumbles back. It's not very convincing.

'Theo…'

He turns back quickly to face me. 'He so *obviously* fancied you.'

I roll my eyes. 'Oh god, not this again. Is that why you don't want me coming back here?'

Theo glowers back at me. He's hot when he's in a mood.

'He was flirting with you the whole *time*—'

'He was *not*—'

'He *was*, Dot, trust me,' he sighs wearily, one hand coming to rest on my leg. 'You just don't see it because you don't know how gorgeous you are.'

Awwwwwwwwww.

I turn in my seat to look at him properly. 'Okay. First of all, I still don't think he was flirting with me. Second—'

'He *was*—'

'*Second*,' I go on over him, 'even if he was – which he wasn't – who cares? I'm not interested in anyone else. I'm with *you*, remember?'

Theo frowns, looking down sadly. 'He doesn't know that.'

'What difference does it make what he knows? Anyway, that was *your* idea,' I remind him quickly. 'Don't let on to clients we're together so we seem more professional, I believe is a direct quote.'

'I know, I know. I just...'

I search Theo's face, not understanding what's provoked this sudden bout of insecurity.

'I worry sometimes,' he says quietly. 'That's all.'

'About what?'

He shrugs. 'That you might... that you'd rather be with someone else.'

His admission shakes me to my core.

'*What?* Are you *insane?*'

Those big brown eyes meet mine, full of sadness and fear.

'Why. *Why* would I – how could you even *think* that?'

I shake my head, at a loss for words. Doesn't he know how much I love him? How happy he makes me, how amazing he is, how his being in my life has transformed it so completely, from something grey and bitter and harsh into a world of warmth, colour and comfort?

Doesn't he know how scared *I* am of losing *him?*

'I know it's hard for you.'

He holds my gaze firmly as he speaks.

'That we don't… that I won't… you know.'

Ah. The sex thing.

'I mean, I know we *did*,' he stumbles over his words as they spill out in a jumble, voice wavering as his eyes plead for understanding, 'but you know I can't, at least I *shouldn't,* and it's killing me because you know I want to, I want to *so* much, but I just—'

'Hey,' I lean up and kiss him gently, to slow him down more than anything else. 'It's okay. I knew what I was signing up for when we got together.'

It's true, I did.

Although, if I'm completely honest, I'm not sure if I really understood how it would actually *feel* to be in a relationship – a proper one – with him, but without *that*. I mean, it's not like I've ever really had a real relationship before, so my frame of reference is severely limited. Theo at least was engaged for a bit a few years before he took his vows – I still get a twinge of jealousy when I remember that, ridiculous as it is – but I carefully restricted myself to either very occasional, mostly unsatisfying casual hook-ups, or just being on my own, so I never had to put any part of myself at risk, emotional or otherwise. I'm not sure I realised how hard it would be to not share that connection with him, when we share so much else, and I love him so much, and it feels like we *should* be sharing that too.

He looks down, refusing to meet my eyes. 'I'm scared it's not enough for you.'

My heart breaks a little at his words, the desolate look on his face, how vulnerable he is. 'Theo…'

'I'm scared that if you can't get it from me, you'll get it from someone else.'

'I don't *want* it from anyone else,' I tell him, truthfully. 'I love *you*.'

'But—'

'Theo, listen to me,' I tell him firmly, his scruff tickling my skin as I take his face in my hands, forcing him to look at me properly. 'You are literally the best thing that's ever happened to me. I'm not about to fuck that up for the sake of a crappy shag with some random idiot.'

Those beautiful big brown eyes of his bore into me, welling up, and I can feel his uncertainty, his fear, his shame, his guilt, all of it.

'Is it difficult? Of course it is,' I admit. No point bullshitting a man who can see inside my head. 'Do I wish we could have that? Of course I do. But now, I *only* want it with you.'

'We can, though,' he urges suddenly. 'You *know* how we can.'

Yeah, I know. By getting married.

Which would be great. If he weren't a bloody Vicar.

I sigh sadly. 'We've had this conversation.'

'I know. But I don't want us to spend the rest of our lives together without being able to *be* together.'

We wouldn't have to. If he'd quit Vicaring.

'I wish it were that easy to do, Dot.'

'Hey,' I admonish quickly. 'No peeking in my head when we're talking about us. We agreed.'

Although, I must admit, sometimes I do miss The Voice.

'I'm sorry.' He leans close and gently kisses my forehead, pulling me close. 'Force of habit.'

We stay that way for a minute, quietly holding one another, back at the same impasse.

I *know* it isn't easy for him, I really do. His Church – for all their faults – basically saved his life, helped him turn it around, brought him back from the brink. That's how they *became* his Church in the first place. Ever since he found out that he's a medium too, he's been wrestling with that conflict, trying to find a way to reconcile these two polar opposite things together. But that's the problem; they don't *work* together. They *can't*. And he can't spend the rest of his life with one foot in two worlds; eventually, he's going to have to make a choice.

'Let's go home,' he finally sighs into my hair.

'My place?'

'Yep.'

If he decides to embrace being a medium, we can build a life together, a real one, but he won't be a Vicar anymore.

If he carries on Vicaring, he keeps hold of the liferaft that's kept him afloat for the last twenty years, but he hides what he is, and abandons his abilities.

And us. Or, more to the point, me.

I can't help but feel hurt it's not an easier choice.

7

I left Theo sat on my balcony this morning as I headed out to the bus stop round the corner, beavering away on his little laptop, coffee and toast beside him on the cheap metal garden table I picked up in the sale at B&Q, looking up from the screen every so often to scribble a note in his little book. Aside from being good with people, this is his wheelhouse, the investigation part of things: trying to find out who might have lived or died in a place, if any other supernatural incidents have been rumoured or recorded in the past, putting two and two together to compile as much solid, factual background on a case as possible. When the information's there, it helps us work out the best way to approach the situation. Of course, a big chunk of the time it's not, in which case we have to rely purely on the dead talking to us. Which is fine, except that sometimes they don't *want* to talk, sometimes they don't know *how* to talk, and sometimes they're incapable of talking anything but utter bollocks.

The balcony in question came with the flat I moved into after the New Year. Once my promotion was signed off, I started nosying at places on Rightmove – just to see what might be out there in my shiny new budget, really – so when Lisa came to me on Christmas Eve wanting Pen to move in full time, we agreed, on the basis that she'd take over my half of our lease once I found another place. I landed in a cosy one-bed in Smethwick, nestled above a car garage off the main high street. It's one of four in the building – a gorgeous old place, originally built as a bank in the 1700s – all with lovely, if slightly crumbling, period features.

There's no double glazing and the crappy storage heating is about as useful as a chocolate teapot – mmmm, chocolate teapot – but sitting so high up over the garage means it's quiet despite its proximity to the main road, it's private, and on a clear day, you can see the West Brom football ground. Assuming you'd want to.

Anyway, it's an easy bus ride to work on the days I don't take the car, and on Sunday mornings, I get to climb through the original sash window in my living room, sit on my fancy old Georgian balcony and watch grooms riding a white horse to the Sikh temple down the road for the weddings that seem to take place there on a semi-weekly basis, which is a lovely diversion. Theo's rarely here on a Sunday morning, either. Just because he's on sabbatical, doesn't mean he ignores the sabbath, and it's a trek and a half for him over to Lichfield to attend Sunday Service. I have pointed out – more than once - that there's a closer, easier alternative: there's literally an Anglican church on the high street, right opposite the flat. But he likes to catch up with his parishioners, all of whom regularly beg him to please come back soon – he's coy about it but I get the distinct impression at least half of them fancy the arse off him - plus it's a chance for him to pop in to the Vicarage, pick up his post, make sure the housekeeper hasn't killed off his plants, that sort of thing. I reckon part of him also wants to keep an eye on the competition – there's a newly qualified priest from Rugeley covering his services until his sabbatical's up – but he'd never admit to that.

After I get off the 87 and make my way through the usual morning throng up Colmore Row, I don't even bother dropping my stuff off at my desk, instead heading straight for the kitchen to get an industrial sized hit of caffeine. I'm just trying to work out if the dregs of the open four pinter of milk in the communal fridge with yesterday's date on is still drinkable when Becs' head appears around the side of the cupboard, making me jump.

'There you are,' she sighs with apparent relief.

'Jesus, Becs,' I get my breath. 'Give me a stroke for breakfast, why don't you.'

She's oblivious to my reaction. 'Can I borrow you?'

I blink back at her, open carton halfway to my nose, coat still on. 'Can I finish making my coffee first?'

Only now does Becs seem to properly register my ruffled state of not-quite-ready-for-this-yet. 'Oh. Yeah. Of course. Get yourself sorted, then meet me in the Quiet Room, okay?'

'Ok—' I start to reply, but she's already vanished.

Hmm. Not like her to be so flighty.

'Oh-*kay*,' I shrug, muttering to nobody in particular as I decide the milk just passes enough of the sniff test for coffee – it wouldn't do for tea – and finish making my drink. Detouring briefly over to our pod, I dump my bag and coat on my chair, taking the precious liquid cargo with me to go and find Becs. There's not much activity in the office yet – as Team Leader, I generally start about 8am these days, partly because as the manager, I feel like I ought to be the first secretary in, and partly because there's just so much on at the moment – and other than a couple of early bird fee earners with their heads buried in documents, I don't pass anyone on my way to the other end of the floor where the Quiet Rooms sit.

Open plan offices are great for creating the illusion that everyone working there is on a level playing field. Secretaries, grads, all the fee earners no matter what their level are all thrown in together, no fancy individual offices for anyone, nobody's more important than anyone else, aren't we a lovely shiny democracy, blah blah blah. What a load of bollocks. Becs is the only Partner – at least in our team – who I've ever known voluntarily get off her arse to do a coffee round with the rest of us mortals; the rest expect to be served, not do any serving.

Anyway, while chucking us all in one big pot might be wonderful for camaraderie – supposedly, although whenever there's a falling out between any two people who, say, cop off drunkenly on a work night out and subsequently start ignoring each other; or someone's loaned a top or a book or whatever to someone else and it's been ruined; or one person's helped another separately from work in some way but when they need the favour returning it's radio silence – believe me, the rest of us feel the tension. It's never fun, and is frequently less than ideal for concentration. Hence the existence of the Quiet Rooms. Each floor has three – two small ones, just big enough for a built-in desk surface with a phone and a chair for solo quiet working, and a larger one which gets used for one-to-ones, performance review meetings, catch ups, things like that – all with frosted glass windows and doors to give some privacy to the lucky bugger who's snagged it.

When I reach that end of the floor, Becs is pacing in the larger room with the door open, waiting for me.

'Hey,' I smile as I walk in, hoping I'm not about to get a bollocking for something I probably don't realise I've done. 'What's up—'

'Can you shut the door?' she asks urgently.

Uh-oh.

I stop where I'm standing, coffee still in hand, and take two steps back, pushing the opaque glass door closed behind me, cutting us off from any potential interruptions that might decide to wander in from the deserted open plan. As I go to take a seat at the small round conference table in the centre of the room, Becs breaks off her nervous movement, quickly grabbing the chair nearest mine, her fingers fidgeting as they pick up where her agitated pacing left off. She doesn't say anything, but it's bloody obvious that something's on her mind.

Seriously, *am* I in trouble?

'Are you… *okay?*' I ask tentatively.

'It's…' Becs looks up from the table with a deep sigh, meeting my eyes for the first time since I walked in. As she looks at me properly, she frowns suddenly. 'Are *you* okay? You look shattered.'

I wave her off, knowing the dark circles under my eyes – which I had to practically crowbar open this morning – aren't pretty. 'We had a job last night. Finished late, and I didn't sleep the best.'

Yeah, that's an understatement. I spent the first hour lying there wide awake, while Theo slept peacefully beside me – just within reach, yet so far away he might as well have been on Pluto – my overtired brain ticking over and over, analysing every word, every gesture between us since That Night for the billionth time. When I eventually did drop off, I woke up an hour later out of a nightmare where I kept walking down the same set of dusty, concrete steps over and over again, nowhere else to go but a pitch dark space below which I somehow knew was the home of something *bad* but was powerless to turn back. Wake, rinse and repeat until my alarm went off at half six.

'Thanks for reminding me that I look like shit, by the way.'

Becs looks pretty knackered herself, actually. She tries to force a smile but it doesn't really land.

'Never mind me,' I shrug, wanting to change the subject. 'What's up?'

She rubs her temples slowly, looking back down at the table as she rests her head against her palm. 'It's Hannah.'

Ah. I'm not about to get the sack then. But as Becs well knows, I have less than zero experience with – or interest in – kid stuff, so the only Hannah-related thing she'd ever be likely to approach *me* with to talk about would be the one thing I *do* have experience in, and it's not middle school politics and girly sleepovers.

'The ghost stuff?'

She nods sadly.

'Has something happened?'

'Last night.' The worry is written all over her face. 'She's already had a bunch of these – visitors, whatever you call them.'

Dead people. I call them dead people.

'Ever since we left the other house, you know. I've told you bits,' she shrugs. 'And you *know* I wasn't happy about it, Rob and I *still* can't agree on how to deal with it, but even so, it seemed sort of harmless enough, I suppose.'

I nod, waiting for her to go on.

'I kept hoping she'd just grow out of it.' She looks up at me, her expression accusatory. 'You said she would.'

'I said she might,' I correct her gently. 'She *still* might.'

'Well, she hasn't yet,' Becs huffs.

I wait quietly for her to go on. That's a trick I learned from Theo; leave the silence for long enough and people always want to fill it, he told me. Rather than just jumping straight in, which is my natural inclination, with both feet. Usually in my mouth.

'Last night she had a new one. All the others up to now, she's – it seemed like water off a duck's back to her, like all this craziness was perfectly normal.'

She rolls her eyes on the word *craziness*, and I try not to take it as a personal insult. Her craziness is my everyday normality.

'But this one – it scared the hell out of her. She came into Rob and I in the middle of the night, hysterical, shaking, in floods of tears.'

Well *that* doesn't sound good.

'What did she say happened?'

'Nothing, last night,' Becs shrugs, 'she was too upset, it took hours just to calm her down enough to get her back to sleep with us. Poor Adam didn't know what the hell was going on and then of course *he* started to get upset as well, so…'

I can see the mental picture. Two hysterical kiddiwinks having parallel meltdowns in the wee hours. And on a school night too. Not fun.

'They both slept in between us for the rest of the night – well, as much as either one of them slept, which wasn't loads. Hannah hasn't done that since she was five. But this morning, when she was calmer…'

I lean in toward her, cradling my still-steaming mug for comfort. 'What did she say?'

Becs shakes her head sadly as she recalls it. 'She said she saw a woman, standing at the foot of her bed. It didn't say anything, just stood there staring at her. I think that's what seemed to bother her the most, at first,' she adds quickly. 'From what she's told us, she can usually hear them talk, say things to her, even though their mouths don't always move, she says. But this one didn't. It just *stared*.'

I can see how that would freak her out. 'Is that when she came in to your room?'

The unsettled expression on her face tells me probably not.

'She said it reached out to her. Then came towards her, with its arms out, walked right *through* her bed up to her, then she—'

Becs shudders visibly.

'She *felt* it touch her. That's when she jumped out of bed and ran.'

Eek. Well *that's* creepy as all fuck, isn't it? Especially for a ten-year-old.

I put my free hand over Becs'. 'You want me to talk to her?'

'I want you to get whatever it is out of the fucking *house*,' Becs counters forcefully. 'You know, do your thing.'

'Becs, your house isn't haunted.'

It really isn't. Becs and Rob had Theo and I give it a once over before they even put the offer in – the estate agent was quite bemused about the appearance of another couple for the second viewing; I think they suspected we were swingers or something – while they were still staying in a rental, waiting for the sale of our last major supernatural showdown to complete. At their request, we checked it again before the movers were allowed to cross the threshold, once more right after they were moved in, and I suspect the fortnightly family dinners they've very kindly invited us to on a regular basis ever since aren't just for the pleasure of our company.

'So? What difference does that make? Just get *rid* of it.'

Of course it makes a difference, but it's a tricky thing to explain to someone who doesn't talk to dead people. When a house is haunted, it's generally because whatever's hanging about in there is stuck for whatever reason. Sometimes they get a bit lost on their way to the light and need a gentle nudge in the right direction. Sometimes they don't even *realise* they're dead, and can't understand what they're doing somewhere and why it's full of other, live people, who don't seem to be able to see them in return. But if someone appears to a medium, randomly, in their own home, *that* has nothing to do with the house itself. It *does* tend to mean one of two things. Either they've been to the Other Side already and have popped back with a message they want passing on to someone in our earthbound neck of the woods, and they need a willing medium to make contact through. Or they're making a special visit from somewhere else in the ether because they want something else.

Hannah's a natural baby medium with a wide open frequency, which can attract all sorts of different folk across that spectrum.

'If Hannah's being visited,' I start carefully, 'it's nothing to do with the house. Theo and I have checked it a million times, you know that. There's nothing there.'

'But all these others that've talked to her—'

'That's the point,' I grasp her hand gently. 'They're not *at* the house. They're visiting *her*. They're picking up that her – *channel*, so to speak – is open to getting their broadcasts. What did the other ones want?'

Becs frowns at me like she thinks I've misplaced some of my marbles.

'What do you mean?'

'She's been having visitors since you left Lichfield, right?'

She nods.

'Well, what did they all want?'

Becs frowns dismissively. 'I don't know. They're dead, why would they want anything?'

'You never asked her?'

'Oh, excuse *me*,' she sputters furiously, 'I must've missed the chapter in all the parenting books where they tell you what questions to ask when your ten-year-old starts seeing dead people.'

'Okay, I'm sorry—'

'My little girl's scared out of her wits, and you want to know if I asked if all her new dead friends came to her with side quests?'

I stifle a snort at her choice of words. Adam's got more into his gaming lately, and Becs has been trying her hand as a bonding thing. I think they play Skyrim together.

'Becs, I'm sorry,' I keep my tone steady, trying to calm her. 'I'm sorry. That was a stupid thing for me to ask, okay?'

She takes a breath, closing her eyes as she settles herself down. 'We can't go through this again, Dot. Not after what happened before.'

'It's nowhere near the same thing,' I reply quickly. 'I swear, Becs. If for a second I thought it might be anything like that, my god I'd be the first one over there kicking some spirit arse.'

Becs smiles a bit at that.

'I just want it to leave her alone, Dot. I want them *all* to leave her alone, really,' she adds wearily, 'but Rob keeps reminding me that it's not my choice to make. It's hers.'

I squeeze her hand gently, hoping it's some kind of reassurance.

'But I mean, she's just a *kid*, she's not…'

'What?'

'She's not *you*.'

Ouch.

'She's not strong like you, I mean,' Becs goes on quickly, backpedalling as she realises how what she said might've come off as insulting. 'She's not experienced. She doesn't know what she's letting herself in for, or how to deal with it.'

'Neither was I when I was her age,' I point out.

I know Becs is worried, and I totally get it – just because I'm not a parent, doesn't mean I'm a complete moron to how worried she must be feeling about all this. But I was a kid when it started for me, younger than Hannah, even. Of course, at the time I was also saddled with an exploitative, attention-seeking narcissist single parent determined to use my burgeoning abilities for the benefit of her own ego, but still.

'And look at you now,' she mutters bitterly.

Double ouch. 'What's *that* supposed to mean?'

'I'm sorry. I'm sorry,' she pulls back from me, holding her hands up in a gesture of peace. 'That was – that was uncalled for, I didn't mean to say it like that.'

I frown back at her, rattled by the remark. She's been one of Theo and my biggest supporters with the ghostbusting thing – you'd hope so, considering I rid her old house of a maniacal, psychotic, body-jumping chaos demon only a few short months ago – and despite her understandable concerns about her kid being visited by things that go bump in the night, I didn't think that meant she thought badly about me because of it.

'It's just...'

She looks at me pleadingly, wanting me to understand.

'I don't want that life for her, Dot. Everyone thinking she's mad, nobody taking her seriously, people judging her all the time without even knowing her. You've been through it for years, you know what I mean.'

Ah, I get it. And she's not wrong. I'm forty-three, and it's only recently I've been able to really start accepting what I am and not apologise for it, or feel ashamed of it, or give a shit if people think I'm a nutter. And there are moments where, *still*, none of those things are true. I sigh deeply, thinking about poor Hannah and what she'll have to go through as she grows up if she chooses to keep going with this: the teasing, the bullshit, the people laughing at her to her face, let alone behind her back. Feeling like she has to hide herself and put on a mask of something she's not, like I did for most of my adult life.

'Okay. There's two ways to sort this,' I finally reply. 'Theo and I can find out what this visitor of hers wants, and deal with whatever that is on her behalf. That should sort the current problem. But that doesn't mean she won't have more come along asking for her help.'

Becs looks unthrilled at the prospect. 'Or?'

'*Or...*' I hesitate. I don't like this alternative, but I'm also heavily biased due to my own experience, and it's only fair to make it clear that it is a possibility. 'We can make the whole thing stop for her.'

Her eyes widen. 'All of it? You can do that? No more visitors at all?'

I nod uncomfortably. 'All of it.'

'How?'

'Hypnosis. Look,' I go on quickly, 'I'll tell you now straight off, I don't like it. I'm not even comfortable suggesting it, really. But it is possible.'

Becs thinks about it for a second. 'You sure it'd work?'

I look away from her, suddenly feeling deeply ashamed. Why did I bring it up? I could've just not said anything. But she's the parent, and her kid's in pain, and she's obviously scared to death about all this. Surely it's only fair she has all the information. Right?

'It's what Theo's parents did to him. To make him stop.'

Her face falls. 'Oh. I thought that was just… you know. For the two of you. To make you forget about each other.'

I nod. 'That too. Obviously Grace never wanted *me* to stop, sacred cash cow that I was. Initially it was just to block out what happened with that demon the first time, then they did it again to block us both out for each *other*. But his parents took him back a third time after that. To shut down his… abilities. The memory only started to come back to him not long ago.'

Becs shifts awkwardly in her seat. 'I dunno. Knowing that's what happened to Theo, it seems…'

Cruel and horrible? A devastating betrayal? The reason he went from already being low-contact with his folks – mostly due to everything he put them through back years ago when he was drinking, before he joined the clergy – to cutting them out completely, after he realised that what they did to him under the guise of protection was ultimately at the core of all his problems?

'…wrong,' she finishes eventually.

'I told you,' I reply levelly, 'I don't like it.'

She meets my eyes. 'But do you think we should do it?'

I smile back at her. 'Becs, mate, I know you're not psychic or anything, but after what I've just told you, what do you *think* I think?'

Becs laughs back tightly. 'You don't think we should do it.'

'Not in a million years. Unless it's something Hannah decides she wants.'

She shakes her head. 'I doubt it. She's been adamant this whole time about how much fun it is, how much she likes her new friends. Then again, after last night…'

'Then let's park it for now.'

I wish I'd never mentioned it. I feel dirty for having even brought it up. It's not a comfortable memory for me, the knowledge that my oh-so-loving mother had me hypnotised into forgetting the existence of the only man I've ever loved. Well, technically the only *boy*, as he was at the time. But on top of that, knowing now what happened to Theo later, and how strongly he feels about it… the thought of him being forced to have that part of himself *erased* because other people thought it was best for him makes me feel sick to my stomach.

I should never have said anything.

'We'll do the other thing.'

'How do we do that?'

'It's Hannah's visitor,' I shrug apologetically. 'So it's possible she might be the one who has to. I can hold her hand through it, though.'

Becs breathes in, letting it out slowly, as though it's the first real breath she's managed to take so far this morning.

'Okay,' she replies emphatically. 'Theo, too? You know how attached she is to him.'

Like a limpet. She gets jealous if I even hold his hand when she's in the room.

'Of course. I'm meeting him for lunch. I'll talk to him about it then.'

'Okay. Okay then,' she nods slowly, mostly to herself, trying to get comfortable with the idea. 'So… do you think you could see her tonight?'

There's hope in her eyes, and I hate to burst that bubble. But god, I'm so tired after last night – whatever that weird new trance thingummy was, it sure as hell took a chunk out of me – and Theo and I have still got to decide how we're going to deal with whatever's at Owen's house, and I'm not even sure what time I'll get out of the office tonight with the way the last few weeks have been going…. I need *sleep*.

I force back a half-hearted smile and squeeze her hand tight again.

'I'll see what we can do.'

Theo already has a latte big enough to float a small island in waiting for me when I meet him at the Caffe Nero on Corporation Street. Seriously, I need to start thinking about cutting down. Maybe I should switch to decaf.

'Ordered you a panini,' he smiles, standing to kiss me on the cheek as I reach the table he's snagged for us in the corner by the window.

'Thanks, gorgeous.'

'Busy morning?' Theo asks as I settle myself into the low armchair.

'Yeah,' I shrug, wondering if I should tell him straightaway that I've obligated us to Becs and Hannah this evening or wait until the food arrives to soften the impact. 'Got a couple of interviews booked in though.'

'That's good news.'

'Hopefully.' If the fee earners don't put any more spanners in the works. 'How about you? Productive morning?'

Theo nods enthusiastically, pulling the notebook out from his old canvas messenger bag under the table. '*Oh* yeah. First of all—'

He stops as a server approaches with our plates. 'Two tuna melts?'

'Great, thanks,' Theo smiles as he takes them, setting one down in front of each of us as the server turns away. 'So, first of all, the Bloxwich case.'

The job with that couple from Sunday night.

'You found something?'

When we connect to someone during a clearance, if we haven't found out much about them before we nudge them into the light, Theo likes to go on a fact-finding mission to pull together as much information as he can track down about who they were when they were alive. Proofs are the lifeblood of being legit as a medium, and it gives Theo a huge amount of satisfaction when he digs up a detail which backs up something we've come up with in a session. Me, well, I'm not all that fussed if I'm honest, not once a job's done. But if it makes him happy, I'm all for it.

It's not only that, though. There's a part of him that still wants to prove it to himself – to prove that all of this is really *real*. Not like the Vicaring he's on sabbatical from, where he takes everything on faith. I never see him looking for traces of evidence to prove the irrefutable truth of God's existence. After everything we've been through together, everything he's seen – I'd be lying if I said that didn't rankle just a bit. But then, I haven't had a thirty-year gap in my supernatural shenanigans like he has.

Theo grins eagerly back at me over the small table, cluttered now with our lunch. 'So, it looks as though the bloke you were talking to was a man called Alfred Sargeant.'

'Oh?' I urge him to go on through a too-hot mouthful of panini, wincing as I feel my tongue burn and know it'll annoy the crap out of me for the rest of the day.

'Alfred Arthur Sargeant,' he reads proudly from his notes. 'Born in Burton in 1938. Married Lily Marion Farmer in 1959, they bought the house in '62.'

Lily. The name I picked up during the clearance. I raise my eyebrows, pleased for Theo that he's joined the dots.

'They had three kids, all long grown now. She died in '84, he went a couple of years later.'

It's amazing – and somewhat scary and disturbing – what a wealth of information you can find on the internet about complete strangers these days. Theo has subscriptions to all the genealogy sites, the Land Registry, the British Newspaper Archive… and he does get adorably enthused when he's playing detective. It's like an episode of Catfish with dead people.

'He'd been hanging about for a while then.'

'Seems like it.'

Not that it'd make a lot of difference to old Alfred – time not really existing in the spiritual plane the way it does here and all that – but still, it's nice to feel like we helped someone who needed it.

'That's good.' I sip my coffee, wary of risking the panini again for at least another couple of minutes, and turn my mind to the current job in hand. 'What about Boldmere? Anything useful?'

'Not much yet, sorry.' Theo frowns apologetically through a mouthful of food. He has what I like to call asbestos mouth; he could neck a jug of hot lava and it wouldn't affect him in the slightest. 'It took me most of the morning to track down the Bloxwich stuff.'

Bearing in mind how not keen he is on the Boldmere job, the paranoid in me wonders if he left it alone a bit accidentally on purpose. We barely learned anything from our introductory visit last night, eventful as it was – no name, no visual picture of who or what was causing all the fuss. Just my weirdarse vision of a dated purple bedroom through eyes that weren't mine.

'I did have a quick look at the archives though,' Theo goes on quickly, flicking forward through his notes in between a gulp of coffee. 'A story in one of the local papers in '95, the Sutton Observer. The family living there at the time reported some strange happenings.'

That gets my attention, and I immediately feel bad for

doubting his sincerity. It's hard, sometimes, after a lifetime of keeping people at emotional arms' length – not only to finally let someone else in, but also to genuinely believe and accept that they're sticking around voluntarily, that they might actually be here to stay, and that they care about you and want the best for you and everything they do isn't always purely for their own benefit.

'Such as?'

Theo's dark eyes flash across from me. 'Give you three guesses.'

'Banging?'

He grins cheekily over the rim of his cup.

'*Bingo*. Also,' he quotes from his notes, '*childish giggling, little feet running around upstairs*, and *doors opening and closing by themselves*.'

I swallow thickly through my foam. 'Sounds familiar.'

'Doesn't it.'

'So what happened? To the family, I mean?'

Theo shrugs. 'The reporter wrote it like they were crackpots. But it did mention they enlisted the local church to try and get rid of it.'

I can't help but be amused. 'One of yours?'

Theo shakes his head. 'United Reformed, at least they are now.'

'Now? They're still there?'

'The church is,' he shrugs. 'Who knows if it's the same clergy.'

'Could be worth checking out,' I suggest hopefully. 'See if they know anything. They might have a record.'

'Yeah. For once my proper job might actually come in useful. Professional courtesy and all that.'

His 'proper' job? Is that just a figure of speech? Or a hint he's going back to it?

'Anyway, Rightmove shows a sale of the house in '96, so it

looks as though the family didn't stick around for much longer.'

'Wow.'

'And,' he goes on through another mouthful, 'they weren't the only ones. It was sold again in '98, again in '02, in '03…'

I nod as he trails off, getting where he's going. 'So nobody stays for more than a year or two.'

'Exactly.'

'Interesting.' That's actually useful information, and I'm pretty impressed with my gorgeous hunk of a man. 'Well, Owen did say nothing spooky happened when he lived there as a kid. If it was bad enough to drive other people out, it must've started later. He wouldn't have bought the place if he knew.'

Theo makes his 'I want to say something but I'm not sure you'll like it' face.

'What?'

He squints over at me. 'Don't you think it's a bit weird?'

'What is?'

'Buying your childhood house back. In your fifties.'

I shrug back. 'Maybe he has better childhood memories than we do.'

Theo rolls his eyes, looking mildly irritated at my lack of agreement.

'It's weird to *us*,' I acknowledge, 'because neither of us would have the slightest interest in going down that memory lane, let alone taking out a mortgage on it. I'm just saying, it might not be weird to *him*.'

Theo frowns inscrutably. 'And you don't think it's odd all this stuff started happening after he moved back in?'

I pause mid-mouthful. 'Didn't you just finish telling me about at least one other, well-publicised case there? And a load of other people selling it in quick succession which *suggests* there've been problems there for a long time?'

He falters slightly. 'Yeah, but—'

'Sometimes a coincidence is just a coincidence.'

And evidently, sometimes your boyfriend is paranoid and jealous enough to try and blame paranormal happenings on a client he thinks fancies you.

'You know I don't believe in coincidence,' he mutters sullenly.

'Yeah,' I laugh gently, reaching out a hand across the table and slipping my fingers in between his. 'And I also know you don't like him.'

Theo frowns glumly into his coffee. 'Because he was flirting with you.'

I resist the urge to roll my eyes.

'I tell you what, Theo. When we go back there, I'll make it abundantly clear to the man that the two of us are a couple, despite it being the exact opposite of what you've been saying we should tell clients from day one. How's that?'

'Dot, don't be—'

'I'm not being anything,' I shrug honestly, grasping his hand that little bit tighter to labour the point. 'I mean it. I love you, and I'm happy to shout about it from the rooftops to anyone I meet who'll listen. You're the one keeping *me* a secret from everyone at your precious church, not the other way round.'

Oops. I didn't mean to say that.

I didn't even realise I *thought* that.

Theo's mouth drops open and he looks back at me, pained. 'That's what you think I'm doing?'

Is it?

I shake my head slightly, unsure, panicking. 'I don't— I don't know. I'm just…'

'Just what?'

Hurt you haven't picked me already? That you don't love me enough to just say fuck it, screw being a Vicar, I'm the one you want?

'You know you are, Dot—'

He's in my head again. This time I let it go.

'I love you *so* much. You *know* that. But it's not so easy for me to just turn away from all of that. It's been my whole life for the last twenty years. There *has* to be a way for us to be together but for me to still—'

'Have your cake and eat it? We've been through this a hundred times, Theo, you know how impossible—'

A buzzing from the floor beside my chair interrupts the thought. The Batphone.

'Go on,' he nods sadly as I hesitate to reach for it. 'Might be important.'

More important than this?

I lean down to fish it out of my bag and cringe inwardly when I see the saved contact.

'It's Owen,' I murmur dully.

Theo rolls his eyes, his hand leaving mine as he sits back in his chair. 'Well that's just fucking *perfect*.'

'He can leave a voicemail,' I shrug casually and go to put it back in my bag.

'Just answer it,' he sighs resignedly. 'Maybe something's happened. We did tell him to call.'

I meet his eyes warily. 'I don't have to—'

He forces a smile. 'It's fine. Honestly. Go on, see what he wants.'

Okay then.

I swipe the screen just before the voicemail kicks in. 'Hi, Owen, Is everything okay?'

'Something's happened.' So much for pleasantries. 'Can you come over?'

'I'm at work this afternoon,' I explain. 'Just a second.'

I lower the handset, holding it against my chest to dull the mic.

'He says something's happened,' I shrug at Theo, 'wants us to go over. Can you?'

'I'm on shift at the hostel after this,' Theo shakes his head, indicating the remains of our lunch. 'I don't finish till six.'

I go back to the phone. 'Hi Owen? We're both working until later.'

'Whenever you're free is fine,' he replies casually.

'Can you tell me what's going on?'

'A bunch of stuff got thrown around upstairs. In the top bedroom. It's stopped now, but I thought you should take a look.'

God, we're going to have a busy night. And I haven't even told Theo about Hannah yet.

'Okay,' I nod, trying to mentally calculate what time we can get there after Theo finishes his shift. 'We can probably be there about seven.'

Shit. When's Hannah's bedtime, I wonder?

'Just a second, Owen.'

I turn back to Theo. 'What time does Hannah go to bed, can you remember?'

He reads her bedtime stories sometimes on video chat.

Theo frowns at me, utterly confused. 'About eight, half-eight, around then. Why?'

'I'll tell you in a minute.'

And I'm sure you'll be thrilled.

'Owen, sorry. We might need to make it later in the evening, about nine-ish. Is that too late for you?'

'Whenever's fine, but...' I hear a pause. 'It doesn't take both of you to look. You could always just come over by yourself.'

I don't know how to respond to that.

Is Theo right? Is the man flirting?

'I mean, aren't you the one who's the proper medium anyway? What do I need you both for?'

'No, that's fine,' I reply quickly, suddenly unnerved. 'We'll be there later. Both of us. Nine or close to.'

'Okay,' I hear him sigh. 'See you later then. Bye.'

'Bye.'

As I put the phone back in my bag, Theo's regarding me quizzically. 'What was that?'

I shrug, flustered, and go back to the cooling remains of my panini. 'What?'

Theo leans over the table, crossing his arms. 'Did he just try to get you to go over there without me?'

I shake my head, eating quietly. I don't want to think about that.

'And why did you ask me about Hannah's bedtime?'

Oh shit. Yeah, that.

I pull a face. 'Er, right, yeah. Well, I'm afraid I sort of…promised Becs we'd go over tonight.'

Theo lights up. 'Dinner?'

Rob's a much better cook than I could ever be arsed to aspire to.

'Sorry, no. It's about Hannah. Although I'm sure they'll feed us while we're there if we ask nicely.'

He looks concerned. 'What's happened?'

'She had a scare last night off one of her visitors,' I explain.

He knows what I'm talking about. In fact, he likely knows more about the subject than I do. He and Rob are very close these days and I know they talk about it a bit, amongst other things. I'm surprised he hasn't already heard from Rob about last night, actually, but if he's on consult today he probably just hasn't got round to texting him yet.

'From what Becs told me, it sounds different to what she's had up to now.'

'Different how?' Theo leans forward again, the tension between us forgotten with another priority to focus on. 'Like, threatening?'

'Just… unnerving,' I think back to Becs' description this morning. 'Becs said Hannah told them this woman just stared at her, then reached out and came towards her. *Through* the bed.'

Theo's eyes widen. 'I'd definitely call that unnerving. Christ, poor kid.'

'Yeah.'

I hesitate. I know I should tell him what I said to Becs about the possibility of hypnosis, but I *so* regret even bringing it up with her in the first place, and I know he won't be pleased about it.

'Becs wants us to see if we can maybe get rid of it, or help Hannah get rid of it.

But I don't want to keep secrets from him.

'Or if not, then… erm…'

I fumble for the words.

Theo tips his head, eyeing me curiously. 'If not, what?'

He could just take the thought out of my head and he knows it. He did it a minute ago. I wonder why he doesn't this time.

Maybe he wants me to say it out loud.

I meet his eyes carefully.

'I mentioned hypnosis.'

His dark eyes flash briefly as his face turns to thunder.

It takes a lot to piss Theo off, but when it happens, my God, do you know about it.

'You did *what?*'

'Becs is desperate,' I go on quickly, suddenly feeling pretty desperate myself. 'She was panicking, scared out of her mind. I only said it was *possible.*'

'How *could* you—'

'Only as a last resort—'

Theo leans further across the table, his face close to mine now, voice low and tight in his throat, and I can tell he's trying to keep a lid on his temper. 'After what my parents did to me – after what we *both* went through,' he hisses, glaring with a mixture of outrage and disappointment in his eyes. 'How could you even *think* of that.'

It kills me that something I've done has made him feel like this. That *I've* made him feel like this. That I've hurt him.

'I told her *only* if it's what Hannah wants,' I plead vainly, reaching back across the table to take his hand again—

But he snatches it away, shaking his head, leaning back in his seat as though he's trying to put as much distance between us as possible, arms folded as he turns to stare out of the window. It's like a knife through my heart. This relationship stuff is so much harder than people advertise, especially when you've managed to reach middle age without ever having had a proper one.

We sit in silence for a minute, me pushing the last scraps of panini awkwardly round the plate while Theo refuses to look at me, his eyes fixed instead on the bustle of people making their way along Corporation Street. I watch him sadly, all curls and fluff, my gorgeous man who I'd lasso the moon for if I could. Instead, all I seem to be able to do is let him down, make him worry, hurt his feelings, at least lately. There are a few flecks of grey starting to come in at the tips of his hair, and I wonder not for the first time if it's the stress of being with me that's caused them.

'*We* didn't get a choice,' I murmur eventually. 'It was different.'

Theo sighs deeply, turning slowly back to face me. 'It's the same result. You want to brainwash her out of being who she is.'

Now *that's* a bit bloody harsh, and I won't let it go. 'I want no such thing. I don't even want to do it, and I told Becs as much.'

'Then why would you even—'

'Because she's scared,' I cut him off bluntly. 'She said Hannah was hysterical, that she had to sleep in their bed with them which she hasn't done since she was little. And Becs is my friend, and I just wanted to help, okay? I was just trying to help. I didn't think—'

'You never do.'

Now it's my turn to take a verbal punch to the gut.

'What?'

'I don't mean— dammit,' Theo looks down, shaking his head, exasperated. 'It's just – sometimes you don't stop and think for one second, you just say whatever's in your head, damn the consequences. Did it even *occur* to you how it might make me feel to hear you basically endorse what my parents did to me?'

'It did,' I admit, my voice suddenly very small. 'Just not until—'

'Until after you'd already said it,' he finishes with uncanny accuracy. 'And by then Becs was all over it already.'

He's right, of course. I didn't think. I just *reacted*.

It's what I've always done. What I always do.

And then it hits me.

Is *this* why he hasn't made his decision? Why it's so hard for him to choose *us* over the Church?

Because of me?

Am I the problem?

I wonder again if he's in my head right now, and if he is, why he doesn't answer that question.

9

We agreed to meet later at Rob and Becs' place, and as both of us had come in on the bus we'd need to cadge lifts across with each of them too. Assuming I managed to get out of work on time – which I suspected Becs would push me to do – there was no point going back to mine to pick up the car; with how long it'd take me to get back to the flat and come back into town to get Theo, he'd likely be hanging around for an hour after his shift finished at six, although he promised to get out early if he could find someone to cover the last hour or so. With neither of us having our cars, though, getting to Boldmere afterwards to check out Owen's issues could be tricky, but Theo reckoned Rob'd be happy to play taxi for the night. I'd ask Becs, but the woman drives like she's on day release from a retirement home.

As it turned out, not only was Becs more than happy to give me a lift, but she even suggested we leave early, rescheduling her last appointment of the day so we could duck out just before four, missing the worst of the traffic. Of course, that meant I was leaving another pile of work behind. But Bonnie offered to take some extra dictations, and I got an email from Izzy Ramsay in the afternoon apologising for hogging the float secretary, offering to let us borrow her for a few days from Monday while they had a brief lull. So I told myself there'd be some respite next week, and maybe even light at the end of the tunnel once my interviews were done with. All the same, the mental picture of files stacked high on my desk wouldn't stop floating around in the back of my mind the whole drive over to Solihull.

'Aunty Dot!' Adam runs out of the house as we pull up on the drive a little after half four, the childminder having already brought the kids home from school.

'All right, Adam,' I wave as I climb out of the passenger seat, letting out an involuntary *oof* as he slams into me for a hug. At seven, he's already less than a foot shorter than me, and I think sometimes he forgets that just because I'm a grown up, doesn't mean I'm big enough to withstand the full force of his weight.

'Wanna play Mario Kart?' he looks up at me eagerly. 'We can put it on the easy one.'

Because I'm crap at it.

'I'm insulted,' I exclaim in mock offence.

'Sorry, Aunty Dot,' he grins sheepishly as I ruffle his hair.

'Adam,' Becs uses her Mom voice as she walks around to our side of the car. 'Dot isn't here to play today, bug. Have you done your homework?'

His looks suspiciously guilty, eyes widening. 'Erm... *most* of it.'

She rolls her eyes. 'Come on, then,' she turns him gently back towards the house, and he walks with her, head turning to pepper me with questions.

'Aunty Dot, will you help me with my maths homework?'

'Sorry kiddo. I'm cra—' I catch myself. I've been learning to curb the swears around the kids. Most of the time, anyway. 'I'm rubbish at maths. You're better off without my help, I promise.'

'Are you staying for tea?'

'Maybe.'

Depends how long it takes to sort out your big sister's ghost problem.

As we walk into the hall, Adam runs off full speed towards the back of the house, nearly taking his sister down in the process as she wanders towards us from that direction.

'*Watch* it, sprat.'

'Sorry Han!' He sings, disappearing round a corner.

Hannah rolls her eyes. As she reaches the two of us, she looks around in apparent confusion. 'Where's Uncle Theo?'

'Manners, Han,' Becs frowns, shrugging at me as she hangs up her coat and heads off to catch up with the childminder who waves from the back.

'What am I, Mrs?' I go up to Hannah for a hug. 'Chopped liver?'

The top of her head sits comfortably against my shoulder as she clasps me back tightly. She's only a couple of inches off me now. Definitely going to take after her Mom in the height department.

'Sorry, Dot.'

Theo gets the Uncle moniker from both kids – they already knew him a bit before, because of him being their local Vicar back then, so there was a bit of a bond already established. Adam adopted the Aunty tag for me, but to Hannah, I'll always just be Dot, and that's fine with me. That's what I was when she met me, that's what I was when we got close. Truth be told, the Aunty thing makes me feel a bit weird anyway. Not exactly… uncomfortable. Just a bit… *old*. I'm kind of hoping Adam grows out of it.

'S'okay poppet,' I plonk a quick kiss on the top of her head. 'Anyway, he's coming after work.'

'He is?' Bless her, she can't hide her excitement. I think she might have a little ten-year-old crush on him.

'Yep. Will I do in the meantime?'

Hannah smirks, sighing theatrically as we let go. '*S'pose so.*'

'Cheeky mare.'

She giggles.

'You up for a chat?'

Her laughter stops, and her expression sinks a little. 'About last night.'

'Is that okay?'

The kid shrugs dully, looking down at her feet as she pokes at the hardwood floor with her slipper. 'Mom put you up to this, didn't she.'

'She told me what happened,' I reply honestly. 'But I want to help, if I can. Theo too, but he won't be here for a bit. I thought maybe we could just have a natter in the meantime.'

I hope I come off sounding as casual about it as I'm trying to.

Hannah huffs wearily. 'Okay then. But I don't want to talk about it in front of Mom. It upsets her.'

Smart kid. 'That's all right. Want to go in the front room?'

She shrugs. 'My room's fine.'

That surprises me, after what Becs told me about last night. And it must show on my face, because Hannah immediately clarifies.

'She's not in there now.'

Hmm. 'She?'

'The woman I saw.'

'You sure?'

Hannah frowns at me. '*You'd* know if she was here,' she says matter-of-factly, before turning towards the stairs.

I suppose I would.

I follow her up to her room. The house is a good deal smaller than the fancy place they had in Lichfield, but Hannah's burgeoning supernatural encounters aside, this one's not inhabited by an evil, soul-possessing demon, which is a hell of a bonus. The first floor is basically all in the eaves, with all three large bedrooms in close proximity – Becs insisted on that – and she has a smaller, separate office room up there as well, for the days she works from home. Everything else is on the ground floor, including Rob's equally small cloakroom office, the kids' playroom and the living room, all at the front of the house, with the massive, open-plan kitchen diner taking up almost the whole of the back, alongside a small guest bedroom, which Theo and I have stayed in a couple of times. The first of which prompted an amusing conversation with an outraged Hannah when she reminded us *very* sternly that Vicars weren't allowed to have girlfriends.

I've been in her room plenty of times. When Theo and I come over for dinner, she usually ends up dragging me up to see her latest Tae Kwon Do trophy, or more often, whichever of the latest rescue cats she's found on the internet that week which she wants me to talk her parents into letting her get. Usually we both sit on her trundle bed to gossip, occasionally rolling out the bottom section when she wants me to sit there below her so she can stick fifteen thousand butterfly clips in my hair, but today she makes a point of taking a seat over at the little desk she has set up for homework. There's a small armchair by the window she curls up in to read sometimes, but I'm fairly sure if I try that out either my arse'll get stuck in the seat or my weight will break the thing completely, so I head for my usual spot as she swivels her chair to face me.

'Okay if I sit here?'

Hannah shrugs. 'If you want.'

I nod back at her as I settle myself down at the end of the bed, one foot tucked under me.

'Er, *shoes*,' she admonishes quickly.

'Oops.' I flick them off and let them drop on the floor. 'Sorry Hans.'

Everyone else calls her Han for short, but Hans is our little secret. I had her at mine for a sleepover just after she turned ten last month – our birthdays are only a couple of weeks apart – and let her watch Die Hard. Rob had been banging on about what a great Christmas film it was, but of course they wouldn't let her actually *watch* it. That's what cool faux-aunts are for, right?

She's quiet for half a minute. 'I don't like talking about it when Mom's around,' she starts eventually. 'She's scared of it. You know, because of what happened at the old house. She thinks it's the same.'

'It's not, you know.'

'I know,' she shrugs.

'You mind talking about it with me?'

'No. You and Uncle Theo understand.'

I nod back at her. 'I'm sorry neither of us've talked to you about it before now.'

'S'okay,' she smiles at me awkwardly. 'I know Mom wouldn't let you.'

She's not wrong about that. But I feel bad letting Becs completely take the fall for that. 'She's just worried about you, that's all.'

'Because she's scared of it,' she repeats simply.

It's hard to argue with that.

'Can you blame her?' I ask gently.

'S'pose not. Dad isn't scared of it though.'

'But he's still worried about you.'

'Only after last night,' she protests. 'He wasn't before.'

'You want to tell me about last night?'

Hannah frowns, cautiously eyeing the spot where I'm sitting. 'Hasn't Mom already told you?'

'Yeah,' I nod back. 'She's told me her version. I want to hear yours.'

She looks up at me quickly, searching my eyes closely.

'Are you going to make it go away?'

I don't know if she means the thing from last night, or... *everything*.

I take a breath, not sure what I'm hoping her next answer will be.

'Do you want me to?'

Hannah shakes her head fiercely. '*No.*'

'Not even the thing from last night?' I ask carefully.

'Not *any* of it,' she answers firmly.

'Didn't last night scare you?'

'Yeah,' she admits. 'It did *then*.'

'Not anymore?'

'No,' she shakes her head again. 'It was just scary because it was *different*, you know? To what normally happens. It wasn't *threatening*.'

I have a moment of déjà vu, and I'm suddenly struck by the parallel – the scary, different ghosty thing that happened to her last night, and the scary, different trancey thing that happened to me.

'What *does* normally happen?'

I'm curious. This is the first chance I've been allowed to properly talk to her about it, and I really do want to understand what she's been dealing with. I want to help her, if I can.

'I just – I *see* people sometimes,' she muses, utterly unaffected by the idea of it all. 'And they talk to me. They tell me things, and sometimes they ask me things.'

'You hear them?'

'Not out loud like you or Uncle Theo. Just… I dunno,' she shrugs. 'Inside my head, I s'pose.'

'And do you always see them? Or sometimes do you just hear them?'

She thinks about it for a second. 'I see them too. When they talk to me though, their mouths don't move.'

Visual *and* auditory. Shit. The kid's definitely got a gift and a half.

'What do they say?'

'They tell me about their families. People they've left behind, you know. They want me to tell them they're okay,' she sighs, shaking her head. 'I keep having to explain that I'm just a kid, so I can't help them.'

'Hmm.' It sounds so odd coming out of her ten-year-old mouth. I wonder if this is what I sounded like when I talked about it at her age. 'Does that upset them? That you can't help them?'

'No. They just say thank you for listening to them and off they go.'

'Okay.'

'That's why I think she was different, though,' Hannah goes on with sudden urgency. 'The woman last night. I think she wanted something but she couldn't tell me.'

'You couldn't hear her?'

'No, not her *or* her friend.'

Friend?

I frown at her. 'Your Mom didn't tell me she had a friend.'

Hannah looks back at me like I've lost the plot. 'She doesn't *know*,' she replies firmly. 'She's freaked out enough already and she only thinks there's one of them.'

'D'you tell your Dad?'

'Not yet. It all happened so fast last night, and then this morning he was busy and I just… didn't,' she sighs sadly.

'What about your friends at school? Tell any of them?'

Hannah's eyes widen. 'Are you mad? They don't know about *any* of it, and I'm not telling. I'm not stupid, you know,' she shakes her head at me with a frown. 'They'd all think I was mad. And Mom'd *kill* me.'

Poor kid, sitting with this by herself, having to put a brave face over it to get through all day at school, pretending everything in her life is normal. Sounds familiar. In fact, it sounds so familiar that I have to remind myself that she isn't actually me, visiting from some parallel, alternate time-travel universe to get advice on how to grow up sane while harbouring a special, non-returnable gift. Not that I'd be much help with that. She already seems to have a much better handle on how to deal with it all than I ever did. Like I said, she's a smart kid.

'Can you talk me through what happened?'

Hannah shrugs. 'I woke up and she was just standing there.'

She nods towards where I'm sitting, at the end of the bed.

'Where was her friend?'

'In the corner, by the door. I didn't see her at first though, I only noticed her when I ran out. She looked upset, like she was crying.'

'Could you *hear* her crying?'

'Yeah. And she had her head in her hands, you know, like…' she trails off, bowing her head into her palms and shaking her shoulders up and down by way of creepy demonstration.

'Did you talk to them?'

Hannah lifts her head, nodding. 'The first one. I tried to. I was tired though, I didn't want them to bother me, I wanted to sleep. So I said hello, but please not now, I'm really tired.'

'But she didn't go away.'

'No. She just stood there, staring at me like a statue. With these big, weird eyes. *Soooo* creepy.'

I frown. 'Weird how?'

Her face twists in a grimace as she recalls the memory. 'Like… saucers. They were all flat and black, like… we learned in science at school about eyes, and irises and pupils and all that stuff. She looked like she had no irises, just huge, black pupils that took up all of her eyes.'

That *is* creepy.

'*That's* what scared me, because she just *stared* at me with her big black *bug* eyes—'

I stifle a giggle, suddenly assaulted by the mental picture

of a giant bug-eyed ghost. A little snort busts its way out, and Hannah glares at me, folding her arms.

'It's not funny, Dot.'

'Sorry.' I cough it back, clamping my lips together to try and stop anything else escaping. Of course that makes it worse.

Hannah's indignant. 'If you're not going to take this seriously—'

'I am, Hans,' I plead. 'I swear. I just… I keep picturing a giant ghost bug making that weird buzzy noise like a cricket, and…'

Her eyes drift upwards as she conjures the image, and she starts to giggle herself.

'You see!' I lean over past the footboard at the bottom of the bed and nudge her shoulder gently. 'It *is* funny.'

'She was *not* a giant ghost bug,' she informs me smartly, choking back her own laughter. 'She was a giant *human* ghost bug – no, wait—'

She giggles again at her own confusion, drooping her head on the desk in mock defeat.

'Okay, so, Bug Lady is at the end of the bed,' I go on, steering us gently back to last night. 'Then what?'

Hannah straightens up with a weary sigh. 'She reached out to me, like this.'

Another demo as she puts her right arm out towards me.

'I told her sorry, but I don't know what you want. Then she started walking towards me, and she came right through the bed, and got really close and that's when I panicked and ran.' She shakes her head, looking away. When she eventually turns back, she eyes me sheepishly. 'I'm sorry, Dot.'

That takes me by surprise. 'What on earth are you sorry for?'

'I shouldn't've run away like that.'

'Hans, you were *scared*.'

'*You* wouldn't've run away,' she pouts.

'From a speechless giant Bug Lady walking through my bed? I bloody would,' I tell her. 'That sounds terrifying.'

Hannah frowns. 'Really?'

'*Really*,' I reply firmly. 'And I probably would've wet myself as well.'

It's happened for less. Menopause is shit.

She giggles again. 'No you wouldn't.'

'I bet I would. Can you remember anything else? What either of them looked like, maybe?'

'A bit. I saw more of Bug Lady. She was older, not like *you* old—'

'Thanks, Hans.'

'Sorry. Like *Mom* old.'

So, mid-thirties.

'The other one was like… teenage, I think. Maybe a bit older.'

'Anything else?'

'It was dark, it was hard to tell,' she shrugs. 'I think they both had brown hair.'

'Like yours?' Hers is dark brown, almost black.

'More like yours,' she nods at me.

On the mousier end of the spectrum.

'They were both short like you, as well.'

Subtle as a brick, this kid is.

'And…'

'And what?'

Hannah screws up her face in discomfort. 'I don't want to upset you.'

This should be good.

I shrug back at her. 'Don't worry about that. Go for it.'

'Well, with the hair and being short and… they were both a little…' she shifts awkwardly in her seat as she searches for something close to diplomacy. 'Not *skinny*, as well, you know.

So they both sort of reminded me of you.'

Not skinny? Terrific, thanks Hans. At least she didn't use the f-word.

'Oh, and I think there was something wrong with Bug Lady,' she adds suddenly. 'Apart from her bug eyes. Something wrong with her mouth. Maybe that's why she couldn't talk to me.'

'Wrong how?'

Hannah shakes her head. 'Like, maybe she was in an accident or something. It looked all messed up, like it'd been cut up a bunch of times. There were marks all on her face.'

Hmm. If she had an injury, and that had something to do with her death, it's possible that the limitations of that could follow her into spiritual limbo.

'That might just've been 'cos she was dead though,' Hannah speculates. 'I dunno, like she was rotting or something.'

Nice mental picture.

'Will they come back, Dot?'

The million quid question. In my experience, when they want something and they know you can help, they don't tend to bugger off until you sort it out for them. Of course, Hannah's not in much of a position to go hunting for old keepsakes or disturbed remains to send the restless to their eternal slumber. And from what she's told me, it sounds like all the dead people she's seen – up to last night, anyway – have accepted that without issue and been chill, moving on when they realise she's not the most practical channel for communicating with their earthbound loved ones.

But from her description, this one – Bug Lady, at least; I'm not sure about her teary companion – has a different feel to it.

'I'm not sure, poppet,' I reply honestly. 'They might.'

'Can we *make* them come back?'

She's full of surprises today, this one. 'You want them to?'

'Well *yeah*,' she almost whines at me. 'I feel bad for them. Especially Bug Lady. I want to *help* them.'

Bless her. She's a sweet kid, when she's not being a sulky preteen know-it-all. 'Hans, you don't know what's the matter with them. You might not be able to help even if you did.'

'You and Uncle Theo could though, couldn't you?'

Ah. Now I see where she's going.

'*You* can find out what's wrong and fix it for them,' she informs me eagerly. 'And maybe then I can help too.'

'Hans love,' I tell her gently, 'it might not work. They came to you, so they might not want to talk to me and Theo.'

'But you can try though, right?'

I sigh. I promised Becs I'd get rid of the visitors, not add them to my and Theo's troubled spirit outreach programme. 'You sure you don't want Uncle Theo and I to just send them away, if they're scary?'

'I *told* you,' she huffs, 'I was only scared because they were different, and they woke me up, and I was confused. I'm not scared now.'

'But—'

'You won't send them away without helping them, will you Dot?'

Hannah looks genuinely pained at the idea.

'No, poppet, of course not.'

What else can I say?

'And I can help? You'll let me?'

That might be a step too far. '*Hans…*'

'*Pleeeeease*, Dot,' Hannah leans over toward me from her seat, putting on her best sad begging face, the one she normally uses to get sweets out of me at the pictures behind her parents' backs.

I roll my eyes. 'Ugh. You're such a pain.'

'Please please pretty *pleeeease*,' she begs again, reaching to grab at my hands in a theatrical display of desperation.

'All right, all right, get yours paws off me, you big germ factory,' I tease her as she bounds out of the chair with glee and jumps on the bed beside me for a grateful cuddle. 'Let me talk to Theo and see what we can figure out.'

'Thanks, Dot.'

She mumbles into my hair as she hugs me.

'And you'll talk to Mom and Dad? About letting me help?'

My insides start to crumple at the thought of Becs' reaction.

'Yeah, I'll talk to them.'

That'll be a fun conversation.

10

Hannah and I wander back downstairs together, arm in arm. The prospect of explaining the outcome of our chat to Becs doesn't exactly fill me with joy, but with a bit of luck I can at least put it off until Theo gets here, then he can back me up. Rob I don't know about – just because he's been okay with the idea of his little girl being able to talk to dead people, doesn't necessarily mean he'll be cool about the prospect of her taking an active part in dealing with a pair.

I'm not entirely thrilled about it myself. I probably should've just told her no.

You just say whatever's in your head, damn the consequences.

Theo's words from earlier echo in my head.

I've gone and done it *again*, haven't I? Shit.

Why didn't I stop and *think*? Or at least say something *neutral*. Why did I have to say *yes*?

'Well?'

I realise the futility of my plan to wait for Theo as we get halfway down the stairs and are immediately met with Becs, hovering in the hall.

'Can I go play now?'

Hannah looks up at her Mom as we descend the last few steps.

'Homework first,' Becs instructs.

'*Mom*,' the girl groans.

'Homework,' Becs repeats firmly. 'Go on.'

Hannah rolls her eyes but scampers dutifully off towards the kitchen. The second she's out of earshot, Becs turns back to me.

'Well? How did you get on? Can you get rid of it?'

Getting right to it, then. I glance around uncomfortably, wondering if Theo managed to get out early or not, and decide to try and stall.

'We should probably wait until the boys get here. Theo wasn't due to finish until six though—'

'Rob's picking him up from the station on his way,' Becs shrugs dismissively. 'He called while you were upstairs to see if you were here, he managed to get off his shift.'

'Oh,' I reply cheerily, 'great.'

'They should be here in a few minutes.'

'Right, well,' I stammer awkwardly. 'Let's wait then—'

'I'd rather not,' Becs frowns at me, crossing her arms.

'Becs, I kind of need to talk to Theo first—'

'Dot, would you please just tell me?'

I pull a face. 'Erm... maybe we should sit. How about a cup of tea?'

She can't kill me if we go in the kitchen. There's at least one kid in there.

'Oh god,' she catches her breath, rubbing her forehead, one of her stress tells. 'Is it bad? It's bad, isn't it.'

'It's fine,' I tell her, trying to sound reassuring. 'It's not bad, it's just...'

'Just what?'

I hesitate, tensing as I try to figure out how to explain it all. 'I really think we should wait until the—'

'Sod that,' she hisses angrily. 'Just bloody *tell* me, Dot.'

Oh dear. Well, if she's pissed off now, this isn't going to make things any better.

All right. Rip off the plaster.

'It's not bad. It's just not what you wanted. Not exactly.'

Becs frowns, looking at me suspiciously. 'What does *that* mean?'

I make another beeline towards the kitchen. 'Why don't we go and—'

'*No, Dot,*' she grabs my arm, practically yanking me back. 'Tell me what's going on.'

I shuffle uncomfortably. 'Okay,' I relent, 'but please don't get upset.'

She just folds her arms again, glaring at me. I'm not reassured.

'Hannah doesn't want us to get rid of them. She wants us to help them.'

'*Them?*'

'There are two of them,' I start to explain. 'She wants Theo and I to call them back.'

'*What?*' Becs exclaims, aghast. I'm not sure if she's reacting to the news that there's two of them, that Hannah wants us to actively invite their presence, or both.

'Yeah, so she says she's not scared—'

'Not *scared?!*'

'And she wants to help these women. Well,' I prattle on, talking at lightning speed, 'she wants Theo and I to help them. But she wants to *help* us help them.'

Becs just blinks at me.

'She really didn't sound scared, Becs,' I try to grasp onto something she might feel better about. 'She said she was last night, because it was so different from—'

I hesitate as Becs starts shaking her head, glancing around quickly as though she's looking for someone to give her an alternative explanation, one that fits more comfortably into her neat little world.

'—from when she's had visitors before. But now she really just wants to find out why they were here.'

'No,' she mutters eventually, still shaking her head. 'No. This is wrong. This is all wrong.'

'Becs—'

'*No,*' her eyes snap back onto me like a laser sight. 'You *told* me you'd just get rid of it, you promised me—'

'I did say we might have to figure out what it wants first,' I remind her quickly.

'Then just do the other thing,' she hisses. 'Get rid of *all* of it. You know what I mean.'

Not on your bloody life. Not after what Hannah told me.

Not after everything Theo said.

'Hannah doesn't want that,' I reply firmly. 'She was very clear. Look, I know it's scary for you and don't get me wrong, I completely understand why after what happened before, but that was different.'

'Don't patronise me,' she splutters indignantly.

'I'm not, Becs.'

'Just because all of this – this – *craziness* – is normal for you, doesn't make it okay for my daughter.'

'What's all the commotion?'

Rob's steady tone interrupts her as he wanders in through the front door a few feet behind us. 'Christ, Becs, we could hear you from the car. Did the world almost end again?'

I fight a smile at that, grateful for Rob's unexpected intervention. Then Theo appears through the doorway behind him, one cheeky, quizzical eyebrow raised in mild bemusement at the tense scene. As he catches my eye, he gives me a sneaky wink, and my body floods with equal parts dopamine and relief.

Rob gives Becs a reassuring peck on the head as he reaches her. 'Hey, Dot. You met the new ghost yet?'

'Ghosts,' she corrects him wearily, her temper diffusing slightly as she welcomes his arm around her. 'Plural.'

'Really?' He looks curiously from her to me and back, as she nods in response. 'A whole herd?'

'No. Just the two,' I sigh as Theo plants himself close behind me, slipping his arms around my waist, and I automatically lean into the reassuring warmth of him. I could do with some comfort right now.

'Oh, okay. Does that *include* the one we know about?'

'Yeah. I was just explaining to Becs—'

'Apparently,' she announces over me, 'our daughter wants to summon them back.'

'That sounds like fun.'

'*Rob,*' Becs chides grumpily. But she's calmer now.

'Well, it does,' he shrugs. 'Do we need to clear out the front room and draw a pentagon on the floor or something?'

I told you he was pretty chill about Hannah's emerging gifts. Relaxed to the point of horizontal is more like it. Ever since she first told them about it, he's made a point of playing it down – not so much making a joke *of* it as joking *around* it, trying to help it sit easier with Becs more than anything, is what I gather from Theo – but also so that Hannah doesn't panic about it herself.

Theo scoffs. 'Not unless you want to summon something less pleasant.'

Rob grins back at him. 'Rather not.'

They've forged quite the bond since last year, the ex-Sceptic and the sort-of-Vicar. No weirder of a combo than Theo being halfway to shacked up with a medium, I suppose.

'Nothing quite so dramatic,' I shake my head quickly, glancing at Theo over my shoulder. I really *do* want to talk to him about it all before we get any deeper into the conversation.

'I guess we should have a chat then,' Rob leans in to give Becs another peck. 'Shall I put the kettle on? Or does this call for something stronger?'

'Tea'll be fine, thanks Rob.'

'Right then. Give us a hand Becs, yeah?'

He smiles at me genially, a look of – something, I'm not sure what – passing between him and Theo, as the couple walk each other towards the kitchen. 'Come and find us when you're ready.'

Theo nods after them. 'Thanks, Rob.'

Rob throws back a wave, already halfway down the corridor.

'I'm sorry,' I start quickly as he turns me around to face him. 'I'm *so* sorry. I didn't want to discuss any of it with her without talking to you first, I told her that, but she was just so—'

'It's okay, Dot.'

'And I went and told Hannah that she could help us with it and I *know* I shouldn't've, I *know* I should've stopped and thought before I said *anything*, like you told me before, and I don't know why I can't just shut up and think before I speak and—'

'Shhh,' he immediately envelops me in a massive, full body hug, breathing into my hair as he kisses my head gently. 'Forget about that, I never should have said it, I hate that I did. I love that you always say what's on your mind, Dot, I do. I'm sorry.'

It's such a 180 from lunchtime. It feels like *him* again, like *us*. I allow myself to drink it in, the warmth and reassurance of having him this close to me, just holding me, calming me.

'Are you okay? Becs sounded pretty heated when we pulled up.'

'I'm fine,' my voice cracks as I lie blatantly into his chest, nuzzling up against it contentedly.

'Liar,' he purrs gently. 'You're shaking.'

He holds me tighter then, if that's possible.

'She's just – you know how touchy she is about Hannah and all this.'

'Yeah. Rob filled in some gaps on the way here about what happened last night.'

His voice is low and soft above my ear, and I can feel the tension from the last few minutes with Becs starting to melt out of my body. This is Theo and the effect he has on me: it doesn't matter where we are, or what chaos might be going on around us. When he holds me like this, I'm *home.* That's all there is to it.

As he starts to pull away gently, I refuse to let him go, snuggling back up against him, my arms around his neck.

'No, just a bit longer.'

Theo chuckles into the top of my head, sighing as he relaxes back against me. 'Okay.'

Basking in his closeness, feeling the soothing balm of his incomparable embrace, my stupid overthinking brain can't help but think back to our conversation at lunchtime, and the one we had in the car last night. It niggles and claws at my insides until the seed of doubt takes root, telling me that I ought to make the most of the moment, because who knows when it'll happen again… or worse, that this could be the last time it does.

Don't cry, I tell myself. *Don't. Cry.*

So naturally I well up immediately.

My emotions have been so much closer to the surface since Theo and I have been together. And I *hate* it. It makes me feel like a hysterical, idiotic, out of control sap. Anything can set me off, and I'm just not used to it, not used to *feeling* so much. I don't know how to deal with being so overwhelmed with my emotions, most of which I didn't release I had in the first place. Of course, the slightest, most barely perceptible shift in my otherwise completely still, silent demeanour, and Theo immediately picks up on it.

'Hey, it's okay,' he soothes, gently drawing back. When he does, he sees my eyes, full and rimmed with sudden tears, and his face falls as he pulls me in tightly again. 'Oh Dot, lovely, please don't cry. We'll figure it all out, I promise.'

I'm not sure if he's talking about Hannah, or us.

'I know,' I sniff, choking the tears back where they came from as I pull away from him, wiping my face with my hand. 'I'm okay. It'll be fine.'

Will it?

'You sure?'

He searches my face for the truth, but I daren't let him see it. Not now.

I hope he's not in my head.

'Of course,' I smile back as warmly as I can manage. 'It's all just – I'm so tired. I think it's getting to me a bit.'

'You *have* to get a break,' Theo frowns, concern clear as day across his face.

'I wish,' I shrug.

'I mean it.'

I look back up into those deep brown eyes, and see nothing but love. It warms my heart.

'I know. But it's not going to happen tonight,' I shrug. 'Look, I have half an idea about all this.'

Theo nods. 'What's the plan?'

'Well, Hannah does want the ghosts to come back. She thinks they need help, and she wants us to help them.'

'Makes sense,' he shrugs.

'So,' I go on, 'I was going to suggest… now I know a bit more of what's going on with her, if we can get over to Boldmere earlier, maybe we can come back *here* again after and stay the night…'

He catches on immediately. 'And see if we can talk to Hannah's new friends.'

'Exactly.'

He frowns down at me. 'Where exactly does you getting a break factor into this plan?'

'Ah, well. The caveat is that if we deal with this for them

tonight, Becs has to let me take tomorrow afternoon off.'

'Just the afternoon?' He's not impressed. 'How about all *day*, Dot.'

I shake my head. 'Can't. Interviews.'

Theo groans.

'I don't have a change of clothes, and we know Becs' stuff doesn't fit me, so I'll have to go in tomorrow looking like a dirty stopout.'

Theo looks me up and down, raising his eyebrows suggestively.

Yeah, he's *definitely* feeling better about us. That's a good sign.

'But I should be done interviewing by lunchtime at the latest, so I could go home for a nap, and I thought then maybe *we* could go back to Boldmere, but this time have a nosey with that church you found out about. You know, the one who dealt with the family who lived there before.'

Theo smiles slightly as he gazes back at me. 'You've got it all figured out.'

I *am* quite pleased with myself. 'Except I wasn't sure if you'd got a shift tomorrow.'

'Nope,' he sighs, shaking his head, stepping closer to put his arms back around me. 'I'm all yours.'

God, I hope that's true.

'I told Rob about the Boldmere job tonight,' he goes on quickly, 'and he's already said he'll drop us. If we're coming back here anyway, he'll probably just hang about and wait.'

'That'd make things easier.'

'You think you can talk to them? These ghosts of Hannah's, I mean?'

I falter slightly. 'Well, Hannah seems to think they can't actually speak. But that might not matter.'

Theo nods understandingly. 'Not if they talk to *you*.'

Bless her, Hannah. She understands enough to get that she

only hears her visitors talking inside her head, that it's not like a normal conversation. But she doesn't know enough yet to understand that there are other ways they can communicate, even if they *do* have issues with traditional speech that they've brought with them from their physical bodies. This is the problem with Becs and Rob leaving her to feel it out, with no guidance or support – from someone who shares her experiences, I mean. If it keeps developing, she'll come across other things like this that she's just not equipped to deal with.

And some of her visitors might not be as understanding as they have up to now.

'Once we get this squared away though, we *have* to sit them down and have a proper conversation about it all,' I urge. 'They *have* to decide how they want to manage this thing of Hannah's. They can't keep ignoring it and just hoping it'll go away by itself.'

'I don't think Rob *does* ignore it.'

'Becs does,' I point out. 'And she dodges the subject with me any time it comes up.'

'She thinks Hannah'll just grow out of it.'

It's still possible. 'And she might. But in the meantime, it's not fair for her to have to keep dealing with it all by herself. What if next time it's something… not so friendly? She's just a kid, for god's sake.'

Theo smiles sympathetically. 'Feeling some déjà vu, are we?'

'Yeah,' I laugh. 'I mean, Grace went way too far in the opposite direction with me, but… at least you and I had people around us – sort of – who could show us how to manage it.'

He nods slowly. 'So, no… no wiping it out of her, then?'

It hurts to even hear him mention it again. 'God, no. She doesn't want that. *I* don't want that.'

'Becs'd still do it if she could.' His voice is tinged with well-suppressed anger.

'Well, she can't. Look, Hannah is *up* for this. Oh.' I break off as that reminds me that I haven't mentioned the *really* tricky part yet. 'And… she wants to help us. To deal with it, I mean.'

Theo frowns. 'Is that a good idea?'

'She's already up to her neck in it,' I shrug. 'I don't love it, but maybe at least this way she can learn how to control some of it. How to *use* it. Safely.'

He looks back at me, faintly amused.

'You volunteering to mentor her?'

I can't resist a smile as I run my fingers gently up the nape of his neck, burying them in the softness of his curls.

'I think she'd rather have you, Uncle Theo.'

'Rubbish.'

He reaches out softly to me in return, pushing a loose strand of hair back behind my ear. 'You're still the master. I'm just… trying to catch the stars in your wake.'

Theo looks away, but not before I see the shadow of sadness and conflict pass across his face.

'It's not a competition, Theo,' I reply gently.

'I know,' he nods. 'Sometimes it just feels like… you don't really *need* me there, that's all. Like I'm not any use.'

How can he think that?

'I *do*, Theo. You *are*.'

'Mmm.' He forces an unconvincing smile.

'Hey, look at me,' I duck into his line of sight to catch his eyes again and lock them with mine. 'I *need* you, Theo. And I don't just mean professionally. You think I'd want to do any of this without you?'

'But you could.'

I shake my head firmly. 'No. No, I couldn't. And I wouldn't. It'd all be pointless without—'

I break off as the sting of unbidden tears hits my eyes again.

'If you weren't – if we weren't—'

I can't get the words out, and my heart suddenly floods with panic, the seed of doubt from earlier blossoming into a fully grown ornamental hedge. Is this it? Is this what he's been dancing around these last few weeks? Is this the moment he finally tells me that he's made his choice, and I'm not it?

Then suddenly he's holding me tight again, apologising over and over, telling me it's okay, trying to soothe me as I fight to not break down and sob into his shoulder. Eventually the moment passes and we separate ourselves hesitantly, knowing there are more pressing issues to deal with right now as we head slowly down to the kitchen to join the others.

But in my heart, I know that's not the end of it. The conversation isn't over.

It's just a temporary stay of execution.

11

Becs grudgingly agreed to go along with the idea of 'inviting' Hannah's nocturnal guests back late tonight, on the basis that doing so – with the aim of finding out what they'd rocked up for in the first place – was the best way to guarantee them not showing up again in the future. Failing that, Theo and I said we'd *try* and force them into the light, but I wasn't keen. Bug Lady and her mate hadn't done anything wrong and didn't appear to be any kind of threat. At Rob's request that she should have a say, we brought Hannah into the conversation and she continued to insist that her scare was due only to the shock at their initial strange appearance last night and how unprepared she was for it. And strong-arming folk over to the Other Side who, for whatever reason, aren't ready to complete that particular trip, when they otherwise have no ill intentions, is just not okay with me. I agreed to it as a back-up option, but only to get Becs on board with the main plan in the first place. When she's got a bug up her arse about something, there's just no point arguing with her.

In the meantime, I took Hannah's usual spot in the back of Rob's car for the drive to Boldmere, ignoring his familiar jokes about me needing Adam's booster seat. Becs stayed behind sorting dinner with the kids and got the airbed out for Theo, as the plan was for both of us to spend the night in Hannah's room. Hannah ran off excitedly to kit up the wheeled pull-out under the trundle for me – yes, I can fit in a child's bed, and my feet don't even hang off the end – but Theo's frame needs something more adult-sized.

The boys chatted amiably up front, while I was content being left to zone out with my own thoughts in the back of the car. But my current, constant state of knackeredness, combined with the steady purr of the engine and the gentle glow of the streetlights outside led inevitably to me nodding off while we were somewhere along the M42.

I wake to Theo's voice, lulling me into consciousness as he shakes my knee gently.

'Dot? We're here.'

As I open my eyes, he's smiling at me as he reaches back from the passenger seat, while Rob is giving the house a once over, having parked us alongside the front gate.

'Nice looking place,' he muses. 'We thought about moving back over this way after we left the Hellmouth. Something like this would've suited us down to the ground.'

'I wouldn't recommend it in its current situation.'

He laughs. 'I suppose not. Any idea how long you'll be?'

'Hopefully not too long,' Theo shrugs. 'We're just here to look at this damage he says there is, right?' He glances pointedly towards me over his shoulder.

'That's the plan.'

'Okay then.' Rob leans past Theo and opens the glove compartment, pulling out a handheld console case with a big grin on his face. 'I'll be right here, enjoying this without sticky little hands trying to steal it off me every five minutes.'

Theo chuckles, shaking his head on his way out of the passenger seat.

'Make the most of it while you can,' I smile as I move to follow suit, finding that I can't open the door. 'Rob?'

He's already engrossed in the home screen, scrolling as he looks for a game. 'Hmm?'

'Childlock?'

Rob looks up, bemused. 'Oh. Sorry,' he shrugs sheepishly, pressing a magic button to disengage it. 'Force of habit.'

I climb out, leaning my head back toward him. 'We'll try not to take too long.'

'Take your time,' he grins, happily wiggling the controller. 'I'm begging you.'

I roll my eyes, laughing quietly as I close the door.

Theo walks round to join me from the passenger side. 'Just check on the damage and go, right?'

I nod. 'Assuming it's otherwise quiet. Hopefully it's nothing too drastic.'

'Hmm.'

He's holding back again. It's so frustrating when he does that – and also an unfair double standard, as I can't just nip into his head to check what's up the same way he can into mine. The trip I took in there to get him back from Psycho Demon seems to've been a one-off extravaganza, because I haven't been able to replicate anything close to it since – likely due to the particularly unusual circumstance that prompted it in the first place. And The Voice that used to link us is long gone now; I guess now we're together all the time, we don't really have any need for it anymore. Anyway, we can manage the odd quick conversation remotely, but the rest of it's a skill only he seems to have. He says it's to make up for all the other magic medium shit I have in spades which he doesn't, but I'm still convinced the only real difference between us with that is down to me having been doing it longer.

'What?'

Theo shakes his head as he turns to start down the path. 'No. It'll just piss you off.'

'Doesn't usually stop you,' I tease.

'Dot, I don't want another argument.'

'I was *joking*,' I frown, exasperated. 'Jesus.'

'Fine.'

Halfway to the front door, he stops abruptly and I nearly walk into him.

'I was *going* to say that whatever damage there is, he probably did it himself, to have an excuse to get you back here. Satisfied?'

Wow. He is *so* paranoid about this guy.

'Anything's possible,' I shrug noncommittally, hoping to defuse his irritation. 'Not that it matters, because I'm going to make sure it's abundantly clear to him that I am *not* available for anything other than professional ghost-related services.'

I'm still not convinced Owen genuinely has any sort of romantic interest in me, despite Theo's assertions. But when I spoke to him at lunchtime, he definitely did hint – okay, suggest – I could come over without Theo, and if I'm not mistaken, he might've sounded mildly disappointed when I made it clear we'd both be showing up.

Which I still think means less than nothing, though.

Theo smiles back at me awkwardly. 'You don't have to do that, you know. Look, I know it's a stupid thing for me to think, I *know* I'm being paranoid—'

Does he? Or did he pluck that one out of my head again?

'—I just… I don't like him. Something feels *off* about him, and I know I probably only think that because I'm jealous. And I know I shouldn't be,' he adds before I can respond, 'because you would never, and it's not that I don't trust you, of course I do, I just don't trust *him*.'

He finally takes a breath, and I step up close to him, a hand on his neck, stroking the side of it gently, wanting to soothe him.

'I just…' he shakes his head. 'I love you *so* much.'

I know he does, of course – all recent tension aside – but it still gets me right in the feels.

'I love you too. So, so much.'

Theo grins crookedly, his eyes sparkling as he tips his head slightly and I move my hand to the side of his face. It's become so automatic, this gesture of affection. 'As much as Creme Eggs?'

'I don't love anything as much as I love Creme Eggs. You'd think you'd know that by now.'

'I'm a close second though, right?'

'Of course.'

'Even though I'm paranoid and jealous?'

I nod. 'And hog all the bedcovers.'

He laughs gently. 'And put the empty cereal box back in the cupboard.'

'Yeah, why *do* you do that, again?'

'I forget it's empty.'

I feign annoyance. 'How is that possible when you've just tipped the last of my Special K into your bowl?'

'It still *feels* full.'

I shake my head, smiling. It's funny, the little habits someone has that weave themselves into your life, become part of the fabric of it. 'Boys are weird.'

'Can't argue with that.'

I glance down briefly as I remember again why we're here, and Theo immediately catches my troubled expression, even though it only crosses my face for less than a moment.

'What's wrong?'

I meet his eyes again, hesitant. 'Are you really okay with us doing this job?

Theo shrugs. 'I'll be fine.'

'I mean it, Theo,' I urge, wanting him to be honest with me. I know sometimes he says what he thinks I want to hear, instead of telling me what he actually thinks, and I hate it. I'd rather him just tell me the truth, no matter how much he thinks I might not like it. 'If you're not comfortable being here, we need to have a conversation about it. Apart from anything else, you know how much any negative vibes can affect—'

'Honestly, Dot,' he puts an arm round my waist, kissing my palm against the scruff of his face. 'I can deal with it. Look, we know there's something here. And for my own curiosity I'd like to find out what this mysterious history is all about. The job's fine, I just wish the client didn't rub me up the wrong way so much.'

He *sounds* like he means it.

'I don't want you to feel like I'm *making* you do it, not if you don't want to.'

I didn't want him to feel that way about the other, much lovelier thing we did on my birthday either, but sometimes I worry that he does.

'I don't. I promise. But I want you to promise *me*,' he holds my gaze, 'that you'll be careful. No transcendental thingumajigging—'

'Trance, gorgeous, just trance.'

'Whatever. Don't go jumping into some dead ghost's body without at least giving me some warning first.'

I blink back at him. 'It's not like I did it on purpose the last time.'

Theo sighs. 'Okay, I know. But – just – we're not here for that, not tonight. Right? Not until we find out more about what we're dealing with.'

I nod in agreement. 'I promise. We're just here to look at the damage.'

'Good. Okay then.'

He turns back to the path. As we walk on, I take his hand and squeeze it, holding on tightly as we reach the house.

Owen's already opening the porch before we reach it, a chunky, industrial torch in his hand. 'There you are. I was wondering when you'd get here.'

'Evening, Owen,' I nod genially. 'So, what's the damage?'

'Well, like I said on the phone… erm…'

His eyes drift down to our clasped hands as he hesitates, clearing his throat.

'It's all in the upstairs bedroom.' His eyes snap back up abruptly, not quite looking either one of us straight on. 'The one at the top.'

Owen turns away with a frown, tipping his head to indicate for us to follow. Theo and I exchange a glance, and he pulls an *I told you so* face as we head in.

'What happened?' I ask as we follow him up the stairs.

'That bloody banging started again this morning. I was on a call with a client in Qatar,' he goes on, clearly annoyed, 'but it was so loud they thought someone'd driven a wrecking ball into the house.'

'Qatar?'

Owen waves dismissively. 'I'm designing a building in Doha. Anyway, I came off the call and there was a load of commotion, it sounded like someone was throwing things around. I got as far as here.' He indicates the main landing as we reach it.

'All I could hear was things smashing about, breaking. It was all so *loud*. The neighbours called the *police*, for Christ's sake,' he goes on, exasperated, before glancing at Theo. 'Sorry. Didn't mean to take his name in vain.'

'Not a problem,' Theo shrugs amiably. 'Do it all the time myself.'

'Did the police look at the room?'

'Nah,' he shrugs. 'They didn't turn up until after I'd spoken to you, and it'd all stopped by then. Didn't even come inside. I just told them some shelves had fallen down, that seemed to satisfy them. I don't think they were really interested.'

'Have *you* looked at the room?'

Owen frowns, his face darkening. 'I tried. It wouldn't let me.'

Theo and I exchange an uncomfortable look.

'What do you mean?' Theo asks. 'It wouldn't let you?'

'I went to go in there and it slammed the door in my face,' Owen replies simply. 'The boxroom door too. If I try and open either door, they don't give. It's like they're barred from the inside.'

Theo raises his eyebrows. 'That's curious.'

Again, the King of understatement.

'Has anything else happened since?'

'If it has, I haven't heard it.'

'Okay,' I nod politely, 'let's see if we pick anything up.'

I look at Theo who nods in agreement.

'You stay down here for now, we'll shout you if we need you.'

'Happily.' Owen hands me the torch. 'The lights are out at the top. Bulb's broken up there, be careful of the glass.'

That bodes well.

Theo and I start up the staircase to the top floor. Everything looks normal enough, until we reach the little mini-landing halfway up where the stairs branch to the right, and then we see it.

Whatever's happened, it's not only the broken lightbulb that's spilled out beyond the bedroom. The top few stairs are littered with debris – chunks of something ceramic, large strips of what looks like torn material, little pieces of glass which glint in the light of the torch, a pile of what looks like tiny feathers, scraps of general detritus – a preview of what might be to come. I glance back at Theo who's studying the scene intently as he takes it all in. The further up we get, the harder the mess is to avoid as the crumbs become heaps, covering the ribbed beige carpet like some abstract art piece. Avoiding the bits of glass and sharp edges, I gently nudge away bits of the wreckage with my feet, until I make enough space to stand just about comfortably on the small square landing, the two closed doors at diagonals on either side of me as I stand at an angle between them.

It's weird. I can feel… *shaking.*

That makes me nervous.

I breathe out deeply to steady myself, looking over my shoulder at Theo as he hovers behind me on the next step down.

'Can you feel that?'

He shakes his head. 'What is it?'

'It's like…' I raise a hand towards the bedroom door to test it. The closer my hand gets to the surface of the wood, the more I can feel it; as I pull back, it retreats into the background. 'Like an electrical hum, almost. Like the doors are giving off a charge. It feels like they're shaking, but it doesn't look like there's any actual movement.'

Theo leans forward, reaching past me toward the bedroom door to check for himself. As his hand gets within a couple of inches, he flinches back, frowning in concern as he looks back up at me. 'I feel it. You ever come across this before?'

Er, *nope.* I shake my head.

'Hmm,' he muses uncomfortably. 'So should we be worried?'

'I have no idea. But let's not take any chances.'

'Call my Guides?'

'Yep.' I think briefly back to the last major supernatural incident we got caught up in at Becs' old place, where we met. Well, where we… *re*-met. 'Put up your wall as well.'

Theo's eyebrows go up in surprise at the suggestion of using the psychic barrier. Neither of us have needed to since that whole awful business was over and done with. 'Seriously?'

'Just in case,' I shrug. 'Like you said, we don't know exactly what we're dealing with yet, and if it's strong enough to trash a room, hold a pair of doors closed and make them vibrate, I reckon better safe than sorry.'

'Fair point.'

As Theo prepares himself, I summon my own protective blockade into place, at the same time calling Grandma and Norman to join me and give me strength.

'You ready?'

Theo nods solemnly.

Slowly, I reach for the bedroom door handle, steeling myself ready to force it open, half expecting to be on the receiving end of some sort of electric shock as soon as I touch it, wondering how strong a resistance there'll be when I try to turn the knob—

—and it opens immediately.

Like an entirely normal bedroom door.

The sight inside, though, is decidedly *not* normal. As I gingerly push it open the rest of the way, Theo and I sharing a confused, tentative glance, the wood scrapes against more debris inside, piling it behind the door until the point where it won't move any further. Shining the torch inside, the room looks as though it's fallen victim to a suspiciously localised tornado. The previously neatly stacked, organised storage boxes have been upended, lids removed, meticulously tidied-away contents spilled across the floor. The chest of drawers is now just a chest – an upside-down one, no less – as its drawers and their contents have all been strewn around the room, sheets and pillowcases in pieces, ripped to shreds.

I start across the threshold to get a better look inside but Theo grabs my arm. 'Dot, wait. Are you sure that's a good idea?'

'Got any better ones?'

He looks around for a second, as though hoping divine inspiration might kick in and give him one, and sighs in muted frustration.

'I just want to look around for a second, okay? I can barely see inside from here. You stay out here if you'd rather.'

'You're not going in there by yourself,' he hisses forcefully.

'Well then,' I reply matter-of-factly, 'you'd better come with me, hadn't you.'

Turning away before I can see Theo roll his eyes, I take a couple of exploratory steps inside, tiptoeing carefully amongst the mess and shine the torch around slowly, taking in the broken ceiling light, the ripped blinds at the window, the small chunks of plaster gouged out of the wall where things have smashed and dented—

'Oh *shit.*'

I stop in my tracks as I move the light across the wall to my left, and see a pile of chaos where the bed used to be.

'What is it?' Theo peers over my shoulder, squinting through the limited light.

I nod toward the scene.

The little child's bed has been roughly dismantled.

Actually, that's a little too neat of a description. *Ripped apart* would be more accurate.

Chunks of wood and screws have been torn from the parts where they were previously joined, the headboard now lying upended across the room, the mattress dislodged, crisp bedding torn away, pillow ripped and spilling a cascade of little downy feathers like the ones we saw on the landing.

Bloody hell.

'Still think he did it himself?' I whisper quietly.

Theo laughs anxiously. 'Not so much.'

He steps carefully past me into the path of the torch, casting an eerily oversized shadow on the opposite wall as he approaches the heap, crouching for a closer look. 'You see this?' he frowns.

I move the light again, focusing on the spot he indicates on the flat side of the mattress as it leans balanced on its long edge, parked against the wall. There are huge, deep tears in the material, diagonally across from edge to edge, severe enough for crumbs of the sponge stuffing inside to have spilled out across the surrounding carpet.

'Looks like it's been slashed with something,' I muse uneasily.

Something really bloody sharp.

'There are four of them,' Theo murmurs as he studies the surface carefully. 'Almost like—'

'Like what?'

He looks back at me apologetically, swallowing. 'Claws.'

Shit. *Shit.*

'The pillow too,' he climbs back up to his feet, leaning on a nearby chunk of bedframe to steady his knees.

I don't understand it. Claws imply demon, but we've met one of those before, and it felt *nothing* like this.

'Theo,' I shake my head, 'I haven't had *any* hint that it's demonic. I can't believe—'

A slow creak from behind me makes me jump and I turn quickly, stumbling slightly on the uneven floor full of crap, the light from the torch floundering wildly. Theo's immediately there to steady me and we both look towards the dark top step for the source of the sound as I grab him for support, trying to catch my breath as I steady the torch.

The boxroom door is cracked open.

Shit. Shit. *Shit.*

'You have to be *fucking* kidding me,' I growl in disbelief, irritated at my own jitters.

Theo leans down to whisper in my ear. 'Should we go in there?'

He doesn't sound particularly enthusiastic.

'I guess that's the general idea.'

'Yeah. But *should* we?'

I shake my head, at a loss to explain what on earth is going on. Something's clearly nearby – that tightly closed door definitely did *not* open itself – but whatever it is, it hasn't interacted with us directly yet, and it seems to be keeping its distance. But why?

Because it's shy?

Or because it's a trap?

'I still don't feel anything…*bad*,' I shrug honestly.

'You won't say that if it drops a broken bed on your head.'

'I don't think there are any beds in that boxroom.'

'You know what I mean.'

'I do.'

'What if it locks the door shut again? With us inside?'

I turn to look at him. 'It could've done that in here. Why let us in here and do nothing, then invite us in *there* and fuck about?'

'For shits and giggles,' Theo mutters, troubled. 'Hey, that's a point.'

'What is?'

'Why *did* it open up for us? When it wouldn't for whatsisface?'

I frown at him. 'Maybe because he's not a medium, and he can't help whatever it is?'

Theo shrugs. 'Or maybe *it* doesn't like him either.'

'Maybe it doesn't. Are you coming with me or not?'

He pulls a face. 'Of course I am.'

'Well come on then.'

With the torch shining a path ahead of us, I walk back out of the bedroom and turn towards the other, smaller room. The door is fully open now, flat back against the wall beyond, and the dark space gives little clue to what we should expect. I shine the torch briefly around the room to get an idea of it, but as you'd expect for a boxroom, there's not much of it to see. Only slightly wider than the doorway itself, it stretches back in line with the wall of the bedroom beside it, the back of the room maybe ten or twelve feet from where we're standing. As the light passes over the various flattened moving boxes stacked against a set of old, wall mounted shelves on the right, I see other household bits and bobs – more decorating stuff mostly, by the look of it, just plastic sheets and various tools – and it's clear the tornado didn't have too much effect in here. Only minor crumbs of mess litter the floor, just whatever bits managed to slip through the crack of space under the previously closed door. But there doesn't seem to be any direct damage.

On a whim, I swing the torch up to check the light. The long strip bulb in the fitting above us is intact.

I try the switch on the wall, hoping for a stroke of luck, and the light immediately comes on, the abrupt brilliance of the fluorescent glare blinding against the darkness. Theo and I both squint as I turn off the torch, crouching to put it on the floor as our eyes adjust.

'Thought those things were obsolete,' Theo nods up at the light. 'Looks like it's an old one.'

I nod. 'They were everywhere when we were kids.'

'Mmm.'

We both look around the room, searching for a reason for our creepy invitation.

Theo shakes his head. 'I don't see anything.'

I look around, stepping further inside, my steps echoing around us. Unlike the rest of the house, the boxroom has bare floorboards, bare plaster, no skirting board. It's a shell of a room, ignored and overlooked save for the shallow wooden shelves running almost the length of the right-hand wall.

'Nothing obvious.'

Then I feel it.

A prickle at the base of my neck.

The hairs there stand abruptly on end as the temperature suddenly drops by about twenty degrees. '*Theo.*'

He nods. 'I feel it.'

The tiniest breeze moves past me, across my shoulders from left to right, almost in a caress. I swallow thickly, waiting, keeping my composure.

'Something's here.'

Then I hear a noise, faint and fuzzy at first, then clearer.

Breathing.

Light, shallow breathing.

And it's not ours. It's coming from about two feet in front of me, right at the end of the small, narrow room.

I take a tentative step towards it and reach out slowly ahead of me.

My fingers can feel that *vibration* again. That *electricity*.

I take a breath of my own.

'Can you tell us who you are? Can you talk?'

Nothing.

It seems to stretch out forever, the tension in the room growing with the cold around us.

Clatter.

Both of us jump as the flat-packed moving boxes fall down abruptly from their position propped up against the shelves, landing in a heap on the floor.

'*Jesus.*' Theo breathes out like he's been holding it for an hour.

I walk over to the now empty spot to inspect it more closely. There doesn't seem to be anything unusual there: the long, not-quite-straight row of shelves are built from lengths of bare timber, rough and worn by age, the metal fittings which fix each one to the wall long rusted. There are six in total, running in parallel from floor to ceiling, empty except for a few boxes of corroded screws that look like they've been here as long as the shelves themselves, but—

My eyes do a double take.

Between the middle two shelves, on the wall at about waist height to me, there's an odd bump sticking out. It protrudes by a couple of inches, smooth and round, and looks so much like it doesn't belong *where* it is that it takes my brain a minute to accept *what* it is.

'Theo?'

'What is it?'

I point towards the bump on the wall behind the shelves.

The bump that looks suspiciously like a doorknob.

'Is that a *door?*'

12

'That's definitely a door, right?'

Theo looks back up at me from where he's crouched down to inspect it more closely.

'Looks like a door.'

Behind the shelves, in the middle of the otherwise bare plaster wall, is a panel. It's just a plain, pale, worn, wide section of wood, slightly narrower than a proper door would be, and maybe three or four inches taller than me. The lightness of the wood and the faintness of the aged grain make it resemble the pattern of the bare, crackled plaster around it, camouflaging it neatly into its surroundings. No wonder I didn't see it until I was looking right up close.

I shake my head in disbelief at the discovery. 'Is there another *room* back there?'

Theo's eyes sparkle. 'Let's find out,' he suggests gleefully as he gets back to his feet.

I scoff lightly at his sudden sense of adventure. 'You've changed your tune.'

'This is getting interesting,' he grins back.

I fold my arms, mildly amused. 'I thought you didn't want to take any chances tonight.'

'Well,' he shrugs nonchalantly, 'you were right. Nothing bad happened.'

I feign shock. 'I'm sorry. Did you just say I was *right?*'

'Besides,' Theo ignores my sarcasm and leans down to whisper in my ear. 'We were invited. Be rude to say no.'

He walks back to the open boxroom door and leans out into the landing, leaving me shaking my head in disbelief.

'Owen, could you come up here a minute?'

He calls back down the stairs, adding a slightly sarcastic *watch the glass* as I flash him a warning look, hoping he's going to behave.

Owen's voice drifts closer as he picks his way through the mess and wanders into the boxroom. 'Any idea what it is yet?'

Theo points – a little smugly – to the revelation in the wall.

'Is there another room in the house you haven't told us about?'

Owen follows his gesture, frowning in apparent confusion. 'Another *room?* Of course not, why on earth would you think—'

His eyes go wide as he sees it, his face a picture of shock.

'Is that a *door?*'

Theo frowns at him dubiously. 'You didn't know about it?'

'I've never seen it before,' he frowns with a shake of his head, leaning down to inspect it in a mirror of Theo's action from a minute ago. 'How have I never *seen* it before?'

Theo and I exchange glances. He certainly *sounds* every bit as shocked to find it as we both were.

'We didn't notice it when we first came in,' I tell him, 'and I had a good look round. It's pretty well camouflaged in the wall. You don't remember it being here when you were a kid?'

Owen straightens up, shaking his head again as he looks back and forth between us. 'I wasn't allowed in this room when I was a kid. There was always all sorts of junk piled in here, my parents said it was dangerous. I tried to come in once because I was curious and got a right walloping from my dad for the pleasure,' he muses. 'He was super strict, ex-Army, you know. Served in Oman and Northern Ireland in the sixties. He could be... *turbulent.*'

Fun story.

'The shelves have always been there, though. I think Dad put them up.'

Aha. *That's* interesting.

'So he must've known about the door,' I think aloud.

Theo nods. 'It's easy to miss, but not if you're stood here screwing shelves into the wall for hours on end.'

'But why put them up in front of it?'

My mind's racing with the possibilities of what could be back there.

'Maybe that's why I wasn't allowed in here,' Owen suggests as he eyes the concealed panel. 'Maybe *that's* what they thought was dangerous.'

'So they blocked it off,' Theo murmurs.

Owen looks at me. 'You think this has something to do with what's been going on?'

Considering his furniture-trashing guest is the one who showed us it was here...

'I think there's a strong chance it's connected,' I reply politely.

'Hmm.' Owen frowns and turns to leave the room.

I look at Theo, the question of where he's off to written across my face. Theo rolls his eyes with a shrug, before Owen's voice floats back up towards us as he heads down the stairs. 'I've got a drill that'll get those screws out.'

Okay then.

'Well, this might explain some things,' Theo sighs as he looks at our mysterious find 'You think whoever it is, is... *in* there?'

'Blocked off hidden room with old human remains?' I shiver anxiously at the idea. 'It actually could be. Kind of hope not though.'

Theo chuckles. 'You're not usually squeamish.'

'I'm not usually worried I might see a dead body.'

'What are you talking about? You see dead people all the time.'

'Dead people, Theo. Not dead *bodies*.'

'Wow. Imagine that,' he shakes his head, feigning disbelief. 'My amazing Dot, fearless champion of the spirits, freaked out by the idea of a harmless old corpse. Come here.'

He pulls me into a soothing hug, kissing the top of my head gently.

'What if there really *is* something in there, though?' I mutter into his chest. 'What if it's all…'

'What?'

'Rotting and putrefied and gross?'

I hear Theo snigger gently above me. 'Aww, don't worry. I'll protect you. Besides, if something really *has* been in there all these years, it'll probably just be bones by now.'

'Eeeeeww.' A chill runs through me as I lean back, his arms snug around me as I look up at him. 'I'm not sure that's any better.'

'Found it—' Owen reappears suddenly at the top of the stairs, drill in hand, eyebrows raised as he clocks our embrace. 'Sorry. Am I interrupting?'

Theo shrugs, still holding me. 'Just a bit of pre-investigation encouragement.'

'You're very…' he frowns back, studying Theo carefully. 'Tactile. For a priest. Wouldn't've thought they'd encourage that sort of thing.'

'Vicar,' Theo corrects, the slightest undertone in his voice belying his narrow smile.

Uh-oh. I sense a pissing contest. Detaching myself gently from Theo's grasp, I stand beside him instead, one arm round his waist. 'He's allowed. We're together.'

I feel the slightest squeeze of Theo's hand on my arm, thanking me for saying it aloud.

'Oh.' Owen looks surprised. 'You two are married?'

Theo and I exchange a slightly awkward glance before he grins back at Owen. 'More or less,' he grins back at Owen.

I keep my mouth diplomatically shut.

'Hmm,' Owen muses. 'Didn't realise the church let you sort marry outside of your own.'

'Oh,' Theo trills lightly, 'you'd be surprised what they let us get away with these days.'

'But… a spiritualist?'

I shake my head. 'I'm not a spiritualist.'

'But you *are* a medium.'

I shrug quietly in reply.

'Didn't think talking to spooks and spirits was compatible with eternal life.'

He's right, of course, and that's exactly the source of mine and Theo's current stalemate. I can see Theo out of the corner of my eye, his expression troubled, uncomfortable with the direction the conversation is going.

'It's getting late,' I redirect quickly, having no intention of going into the nitty gritty of our personal issues with some stranger. 'Shall we see what this door's all about?

Owen frowns, but turns towards the shelves regardless. The second his back's turned, Theo rolls his eyes in frustration, his face like thunder. It's not often he shows his temper – it takes a hell of a lot to provoke it in the first place – but I can tell dealing with this bloke is clearly trying his last nerve.

While Owen uses the reverse setting on the drill to unscrew the wall brackets, Theo and I steady the planks between us as they come loose, leaning them upright against the opposite wall out of the way, Owen stacking the rusting fittings neatly in the far corner. With the shelves removed, the panel in the wall is much more obvious. Now there's a clear view, I can see a thin, extra strip of wood down one side, sandwiched between the panel and the wall itself.

'The hinges are on this side,' I point out as I spot the rusting metal attached to the narrow fringe. 'It must open *this* way, into the boxroom, instead of into whatever's behind it.'

'Who wants to do the honours?' Owen asks.

'It's your house,' Theo replies with a shrug.

Owen shakes his head quickly. 'Not a chance. Whatever's in there, it doesn't seem to get half as violent when you two are around. One of you do it.'

I roll my eyes wearily. 'I'll do it.'

Forcing thoughts of rotting things and bones and eyeless skull sockets out of my head, I approach the door and reach for the small round knob. As I twist it, it moves – a little stiffly at first – but then there's resistance when I try and pull the door open.

'It's stuck.'

I try grasping the knob with my left hand as well. There's a little give at the bottom as I continue to tug at it.

'It must've been shut up for what, fifty years at least?' Owen shakes his head. 'God knows how much dust and—'

'Maybe there's a lock on the inside,' Theo suggests.

'There's not,' I hear myself mutter firmly as I pull at it, suddenly certain of that.

'How would you know?' Owen asks.

Theo looks at him disapprovingly. 'How do you think?'

Owen's face falls at the obvious suggestion, like in all the excitement he'd forgotten for a second what we were doing here in the first place. 'Oh. Yeah. Right.'

I brace myself, one foot up against the wall beside the little door so I can put all my strength into the next pull.

'Dot, why don't I have a go—'

But as I pour everything I have in front of me and give it one more solid *yank*, it gives, almost hitting me in the face as it opens towards me. There's fifty years' worth of dust all right, and half of it goes straight up my nose as the door opens, making me cough hoarsely as I wave the rest of it away. As it settles, I start to just about make out what's on the other side, and...

Wow.

Secret passageway alert.

'It's not a room,' I announce as Theo and Owen both peer inside, one over each of my shoulders.

It's a staircase.

I grab the big torch back up off the floor where I left it and shine it through into the dark, narrow space. There are shallow steps leading down, below the line of the adjacent bedroom wall, through the dark to god knows where.

Theo turns back to Owen. 'You never knew about *any* of this?'

Owen shakes his head vehemently, eyes as wide with shock as ours. 'I had no idea. I swear on my kids, on my *grandkids*, I've never seen *any* of this before.'

With no immediate jump scares or putrefying corpses in sight, my curiosity wins out over my trepidation. 'I wonder where it goes,' I muse as I shine the torch around, poking my head inside. Though the door itself is really only about the right height for me – both of the guys would have to stoop to get through it – the passage itself opens up to full adult height, although it's barely the width of the door across. 'Where are we now, relative to downstairs?'

'Over the bathroom,' Owen explains, pointing to the back wall to our left. 'That's the side wall of the house.'

I nod. 'The same side the Purple Room's on?'

Owen frowns. 'What?'

I realise I can only think about it the way I saw it last night.

'Sorry. The other bedroom, I mean, the one we went in yesterday.'

'Oh, of course,' Owen nods quickly. 'Where you had your little… episode. Yeah, you'd end up directly over it… somewhere in *that* direction.'

He points towards the passage.

Theo leans down past me to take a closer look. 'So where do we think this leads then?'

'Only one way to find out.'

I've always wanted to say that.

Theo's eyes gleam with curious delight as he nudges me. 'After you, then.'

I nod back, looking briefly at Owen. 'I think you should stay here. Like you said, whatever led us here is less violent with us around, and it actively stopped you from getting into this room earlier. It might be safer if you hang back for now.'

'Fine with me.' He holds up his hands, clearly relieved. 'Should I… I dunno. Do anything?'

'Just keep an ear out in case we call you,' I tell him. 'We'll see how far this goes and hopefully it'll give us some idea as to why it's been shown to us in the first place.'

Turning back to the passage, I step carefully through the small door, shining the torch around as Theo ducks through behind me. The left wall of the passage is all solid brick, cool to the touch when I put a hand on it – the outside wall of the house, just like Owen said – but opposite, along the back of the top bedroom, is just wood and plaster. Thick, upright timbers are placed every few feet, and embedded between each one are row upon row of narrow, horizontal wooden strips, interlaced with crumbling plaster.

'It's just a stud wall,' I remark as I look it over.

Theo nods. 'An old one, too. They stopped doing lath and plaster in the thirties.'

Him and his house-age assessing detective knowledge.

'So this might be an original feature?' I ask. 'From when it was built?'

'Maybe. It's possible. This is *wild*,' he babbles excitedly. 'It's like we're in the Cluedo house.'

I laugh lightly. 'Mrs Peacock did it with the lead pipe in the secret passageway.'

'Exactly.' He pulls his phone out of his back pocket, swiping the torch into life. 'Should've thought of this earlier.'

As I shine the larger torch around us, I see we're standing directly beneath the slope of the roof – the tips of bare beams stick out above us, more wood strips between them – and below us are floorboards, littered with years of accumulated plaster dust, splinters, cobwebs. There's only about a foot or so of level floor before the steps drop down in front of us, each one very shallow, maybe about a third of the depth of a standard stair.

'Well, I don't *smell* any rotting corpses.'

Theo shrugs behind me in reply as he gives the scene a once over. 'Bones don't smell after about ten years,' he informs me casually.

I turn back to face him, surprised at his casual reveal of such gruesome knowledge. 'How in the *world* would you know that?'

'There's a cemetery in the churchyard. The vicarage is right next door, remember? I've lived there nearly twenty years, it's only natural to be curious about your neighbours.'

Of course. I've dropped Theo home plenty of times, but I've never been *into* the vicarage, what with our whole thing of wanting to avoid any potential prying eyes and gossip about the attractive local Vicar and his mysterious female companion. And I certainly haven't been into the church itself, lest it burst into flames at the intrusion of my heathen presence.

'You're weird.'

'Takes one to know one.'

Fair point.

'Watch these steps,' I warn him. 'They're tiny.'

'Perfect for you then,' he teases.

'Funny.'

'Maybe the Borrowers live down here? You could get some tips.'

'Hardy har har.'

The passageway is wide enough – just – for us to face straight on as we descend the steps, both watching our footing carefully, but I sidle my way down crab-style anyway, keen to avoid any part of my body coming into even the slightest contact with anything which might've been making its home here for the last god knows how many years.

'You see anything yet?'

'Nothing,' I tell Theo as I keep shining the torch, looking around for signs of anything unusual, not counting the existence of the secret stairs in the first place, of course. 'Just more steps and dust.'

'How far down do you think we are?'

'We must be near the first floor by now, I think—'

I break off as I spot flat brick directly facing us, only a few feet ahead.

'Wait. This might be the bottom. I can see another wall up ahead—'

A sudden rustle nearby stops me dead in my tracks and I lean back close to Theo.

'Did you hear that?' I whisper.

He nods slowly as we look around. The hackles are rising on the back of my neck.

Rustle.

'There it is again.' He shines his phone torch back and forth, up above us, trying to pinpoint the source.

Rustle.

We both jump, grabbing for each other. 'What *is* that?'

'Probably just a pigeon.'

'You sound completely convinced—'

Rustle rustle rustle rustle—

Something brushes past my head and I squeal in terror.

'What the *hell* is that Theo, Jesus *Christ*—'

An equally high-pitched, eerie squeak calls out in response.

There's a second of quiet, both of us standing stock-still with tension, before another *screech* barrels in my direction, wings flapping suddenly against my head and there are claws in my hair and I'm screaming and trying to shake it off and *it's* screaming and trying to burrow further—

'Shit,' Theo exclaims, reaching into my hair, fighting against the onslaught, while I duck and move and shake my head frantically, panicking and scared to death—

'It's a bat, Dot,' I hear him say as he tries to dislodge it from where it's caught up in my hair, 'just a bat, keep still, let me—'

'Get it off me,' I plead desperately, 'get it *off*—'

'Almost—'

There's a *pull* against my hair, something ripping away, then it's gone.

'Ow, *shit* that hurt.'

'Are you okay?'

I frown, rubbing the side of my head. 'Felt like it took a chunk out of me.'

Theo leans over, parting my hair gently to look. 'Maybe it was building a nest.'

I elbow him. 'Thanks a lot.'

He laughs gently. 'It looks okay. I don't think it did any major damage.'

'You sure?'

'Other than putting bats in your belfry, lovely, but we knew about those already.'

'Oh, you are on *fire* with the sarky jokes tonight.'

Theo kisses the spot the bat left behind, his free arm pulling me close. 'You love it.'

He's not wrong.

'You okay? Want to go back?'

'Bugger *that*,' I look up at him like he's lost it, my run-in with the evil screechy one forgotten. 'I want to see where the hell this goes.'

'Come on then, batgirl.'

At the bottom of the steps, where the brick wall faces us, is a small landing. But as I step onto it, that seems to be as far as it goes.

'Dead end.'

'What?' Theo sounds beyond disappointed. 'Really?'

'Just the wall,' I shrug, feeling the same myself as I reach out to check, just in case. I run my free hand across the surface of the brick, back and forth in front of me, then across to the right and along the stud wall.

Something on that side gives slightly under my hand.

'This *moves*.'

'The wall?'

'The stud wall, on the right.' I push gently against the last two feet of it with my hand, both of us watching in fascination as the thin strips of wood on the surface spring softly back and forth. 'See?'

I bring the torch up fully to take a closer look.

'Maybe it's just damaged,' Theo suggests.

As I run the light across it, I see two things: there's no solid, upright timber at the end of the stud wall where it meets the brick wall in front of us, nothing connecting those two sections to one another. And, alongside the last timber in place, a couple of feet before the end, is a break in the wooden slats. A gap, top to bottom, floor to ceiling, like the strips of wood have all been cut through on one side.

Is this another door?

I give it a heftier push and—

'Oh wow.'

Yeah. Another door. It doesn't quite open all the way – too many chunks of broken brick and rotten wood piled up behind for it to give very far – but it's enough that we can squeeze through it.

'What *is* this?'

On the other side of the movable section is a tiny room.

I'd barely call it a room, even. It's just a void behind the stud wall, a few feet long, barely deep enough to stand in as we squeeze our way carefully into it. The half where I end up standing is slightly deeper than the entrance, giving the space a shape like a loose piano key, the wider part jutting slightly further out.

'Where are we?'

Theo works out the route. 'Well, if the boxroom's over the bathroom, the steps must've come down past that, like he said,' he nods back up in the direction where we left Owen. 'Assuming we're down on the first floor, the bathroom should be somewhere behind us. I think.'

'So we're between the bathroom and the Purple Room.'

'I think so.'

I shine the torch around, still not seeing any indication of why this whole weird area is anything more than just a curious architectural oddity.

Until I do.

Something glints in the torchlight to my right. Metal hinges, lined up vertically down the edge of the wall.

Another camouflaged panel. The exit from the secret passage maybe?

Only when I try to push this one, it's stuck firmly shut.

'*Another* door?'

I nod. 'It must go into the Purple Room, but I think it's blocked off.'

My heart seizes in my mouth as I notice something else on the surface in front of me and my blood suddenly runs cold.

Even in the dark, Theo picks up on my reaction. 'What? Dot, what is it?'

At head height – *my* head height, anyway – two holes have been carved out. Small, oval, the long side of the shape positioned horizontally, like two tiny bird eggs lying on their sides, spaced maybe an inch and a half apart. No light passes through them from the other side of the structure – there's some other material across them on that side, covering them up – but the shapes are too perfect to be accidental.

'Dot?'

I lean my face closer, feeling myself tremble as I test the suspicion in my gut.

It's a perfect fit.

I swallow as I turn to look at Theo, my skin creeping as it prickles in grim realisation.

'They're *eyeholes*.'

13

Theo tried to take a picture on his phone, but even with the flash and the extra light from the torch I was carrying, it barely came out. Instead, after we made our way back up the narrow, dusty staircase and reported our findings to Owen, he insisted on taking the torch to go and see for himself. A few minutes later when he clambers back out through the little door, he looks dazed.

'I don't…' he shakes his head dully, turning off the torch. 'I don't understand. What is… I mean, *why* would that…'

He trails off with a lost little sigh.

'It's just so… *strange*.'

That's a fair assessment.

I look from him to Theo. 'Something *had* to've happened in that Purple Room. Somebody must've used the passage and those holes to spy on someone, and if that *is* another blocked off door…'

Theo nods. 'We have to assume that at some point it *wasn't* blocked off.'

'And it was used to get in that room.'

'But why?' Owen frowns.

'Not for anything good,' Theo murmurs.

'Yeah,' I agree quickly. 'I can't imagine anyone who puts secret passages and creepy weird peepholes in their house does it with the best of intentions.'

Owen considers the point. 'And you think this is all connected to the…' he searches for the word. 'Disruption?'

'It has to be. Whoever – *whatever* – they are they *led* us to this.

We'd never have found that blocked off door if they hadn't—'

An unpleasant spark of inspiration fires suddenly into my brain. Theo knows that look well and frowns at me, concerned.

'What is it, Dot?'

This is a delicate one.

'You said before,' I start carefully, 'that your dad was the one who put the shelves up. So, he must've known about the door. Do you think… do you think he maybe knew about the spyhole as well?'

Owen lets out a deep breath. 'I suppose. I mean, I can't imagine if he found the door that he wouldn't've gone in to have a look down there.'

I also remember him saying his dad had been… what was the word he used?

Turbulent.

Hmm.

'Maybe that's why he put the shelves up in the first place,' he suggests. 'Maybe he found it after they moved in and did it to block it all off. That creepy door into the spare bedroom has been long covered over, so…'

'Whose bedroom was the Purple Room again? When you were little?'

'Nobody's,' he shrugs. 'It was just a spare room, for guests. But it wasn't purple, I told you that.'

'You did,' I nod politely.

'It makes so much more sense to me now,' Owen muses. 'If he did block it off up here, I mean.'

Maybe.

Or maybe…

Could Owen's dad have been the one who put it there in the first place?

'Could we ask him, do you think?'

Owen laughs. 'You'd have to use your special powers. He died… god, ten years ago it must be. Mom too. Car crash.'

Oops. I remind myself to extract my foot from my mouth *before* piping up next time.

'Sorry.'

He shrugs. 'He'd have been in his nineties by now, Mom in her eighties. Probably both senile and God knows what else. Better they never had to deal with that.'

'What about your sister? Might she remember anything about it?'

Owen looks down now, arms folded, shaking his head. 'Erica passed when we were teenagers.'

Bloody hell. Death really follows this bloke around. I pull a mortified face at Theo, who looks back at me, eyebrows raised. 'I'm *so* sorry.'

He doesn't look up. 'Long, long time ago.'

There's an awkward silence for a minute, before I breathe out again and turn to Theo. 'We need to look at the Purple Room again. That seems to be the key to all of this.'

Theo flinches. 'What about – what happened to you in there before?'

'I know. But we tried to make contact the normal way, and they didn't respond. Maybe that's why that happened in the Purple Room last night.'

'I wish you'd stop calling it that,' Owen mumbles gruffly. 'It's not purple. It's never *been* purple.'

'Oh, it was purple once all right,' I tell him smartly. 'Maybe not for you, but for someone. For whoever it is who's been doing all of this, most likely.' I turn back to Theo. 'Look, it was only when that – trance, whatever it was – happened in that room that I actually heard a *proper* voice, not just heavy breathing and giggles. Maybe the only way they can communicate direct is if

I'm literally there, in it, with them.'

Theo frowns unhappily. 'I still don't think we know enough about what happened for you to jump back in there voluntarily. I don't like it. It feels…'

He hesitates.

'It feels like Lichfield all over again.'

I put a reassuring hand on his arm. 'It is *not* Lichfield. Not *anything* like it. I'm positive.'

Okay, so being in somebody else's body was creepy, and whoever they are, they certainly do like to rip up bedsheets and throw shit around. But they've also led us to a giant clue, they haven't put anyone in a coma, and they haven't thrown a Ouija board at Theo's head. Doesn't sound like the behaviour of a sadistic soul-possessing demon to me.

'What happened in Lichfield?' Owen pipes up curiously.

'Our first job together, long story,' I wave him off, focused on setting Theo's mind at rest as I turn back to him. 'Look, nothing's tried to decapitate you, possess you or otherwise fuck with you in general.'

Theo smiles dully at my weak attempt at humour. 'You know it's not me I'm worried about.'

'You're here to back me up, right? I'll be fine.'

He laughs bitterly. 'Yeah.'

I take a step closer to him. 'Whatever happened to me in that room, happened for a reason. For it to happen out of nowhere like that, when I've never done it before, never even had any inkling that I *could* do it…'

Of course, Theo and I both know I jumped into *his* subconscious back in Lichfield, but that was very, *very* different. Although I got to feel my way through some of his most beautiful memories in order to reach the core of him, I wasn't – in a technical sense – inside his actual body and viewing them through his eyes, like I did in the Purple Room.

'Okay,' Theo eventually sighs. 'Let's see how it goes.'

I squeeze his arm then turn back to Owen, all business. 'Owen, could we get a couple of chairs down there to use please? Just outside the door, we don't know if I'll drop straight into a trance again as soon as I walk inside.'

Owen nods as the three of us head out of the room, picking our way carefully down through the staircase debris. 'I'll fetch some.'

'Thanks.'

As we reach the main landing, we split up, Theo and I heading along the corridor towards the Purple Room while Owen disappears off to the ground floor. Once the two of us round the corner at the end of the passage – out of sight of Owen should he pop back up too quickly – Theo stops me gently, a hand on my shoulder.

'Are you sure you know what you're getting into?'

I take a breath before I reply, choosing my words carefully. I understand completely why he's so concerned, and why he keeps pushing it, but every instinct in me keeps telling me that this is the right thing to do. Not just that, but the *only* thing to do.

That being said – I think I've just remembered something. Something from before, from years ago, back at Grace's church.

'I told you before that I thought it was trance mediumship, what happened last night.'

Theo looks back at me questioningly. 'You don't think so?'

I shake my head.

'So? What do you think it was then?'

I start slowly, wanting to explain, but in a way that won't make him completely freak out.

'Grace was talking to one of her disciples once, about a clearance they'd worked on. I was probably about seven or eight, it was a couple of years before your parents joined the church. I was just eavesdropping, you know. Bored, hanging about, trying not to get in anybody's way… it'd been a tricky job. They struggled to connect properly with the one who'd passed.'

Theo waits for me to go on.

'Turned out they didn't know they were dead.'

The surprise is evident on his face. 'What happened?'

'Grace led the clearance,' I recall, the memory coming fully into focus, 'but it was one of the other mediums who ended up getting them to cross over. He did something she called… transference.'

Theo's expression darkens. 'Why do I feel like I'm not going to like this?'

'It gets better. So, they couldn't talk him over into the light like they would normally, because the bloke wouldn't accept he was dead. Instead, with this transference thing, the medium who did it… sort of had to… guide him there. Personally.'

He looks dubious. 'What do you mean, *personally?*'

If he didn't like what I've told him so far, he's *really* not going to like this.

'The medium kind of… had a piggyback.'

Theo breathes out deeply, and I can tell he's back at the edge of his patience. 'Will you please stop dancing around it and just tell me what you mean?'

I let out a breath of my own, looking him firmly in the eye. 'He mind-melded with the dead guy and took him back through his death to make him understand. Then led him into the light by hand. Literally.'

Theo's face reaches a whole new level of shocked. 'Mind-melded?'

'Went into the dead bloke's consciousness. Sort of an out of body experience, except he was in someone else's body, but the body itself wasn't there, so really—'

I realise I'm rambling and need to make it clearer.

'He experienced – mentally, anyway – what the dead bloke experienced. To show him, to make him see that he was actually dead, so he could leave.'

Theo's eyes are almost comically wide. 'He *experienced*—'

'Once he went back through his death, he could cross over—'

'—his *death?!*'

'Only mentally,' I point out quickly. 'Transference.'

'Transference,' Theo repeats in dull disbelief. 'And that's what you think happened to you in there?'

'It fits better than the trance thing,' I shrug, trying to appear casually confident, but I suspect it's not all that convincing.

Theo locks his eyes with mine, hands on my shoulders. 'Dot. *None* of what you just said makes me feel *any* better about you doing this.'

I sigh as footsteps start towards us from the other end of the corridor.

'I've got chairs,' Owen rounds the corner, dragging two modern-looking, Scandi-style dining chairs along with him, one in each hand. He stops abruptly as he catches sight of our faces. 'Something wrong?'

Theo turns to face him, regarding him steadily. He sounds polite as anything, and neither Owen nor anyone else would guess his intention was anything different, but I can feel the annoyance coming off him in bloody great waves.

'Just discussing how best to approach this.' He nods at the contents of Owen's hands. 'You'll need a third chair for yourself.'

Owen sets them down beside us and nods toward the closed bedroom door.

The Purple Room, is all I can think of it as.

'There's one in there.'

Theo shakes his head. 'Probably not a good idea to bank on that one. Just in case.'

Owen weighs it up for a second before he shrugs, sloping back off the way he came. The moment he's back out of sight, Theo steps closer to me, leaning down to whisper.

'What if something goes wrong?'

'Then you'll snap me back out of it,' I tell him firmly, one hand on his to labour the point. 'Just like you did last night.'

He doesn't look convinced. 'What are the chances of me talking you out of this?'

I smile gently back up at him, moving my hand to brush his hair out of his eyes, knowing he already knows the answer. 'Slim to none.'

Theo tips his head back, sighing in resigned frustration. 'Arrgh.'

'But Theo,' I go on quickly, 'whatever's in there, whatever's been doing all this, it doesn't want to hurt me. I'm positive.'

'I hope to God you're right.'

I nod confidently. 'You better let Rob know what's going on. We might be a while.'

14

'Is there anybody there?'

Theo gets us started as we sit in the light corridor outside the bedroom, the two of us directly across from the door, barely ajar. Owen sits back a little way down the corridor, close enough in case we need him but not so close he's going to piss off the ghosts, if they really *don't* like him being around. Our plan is to try and open up the channels of communication just like we would normally in the first instance, and if that doesn't get us anywhere…

We'll try a bit of transference.

Or at least, I will.

Theo tries again. 'Is there anybody there?'

No response.

'We want to talk to the one whose presence Dot felt last night.'

I asked him to take the lead. It felt important to give him a strong hand in the session from the start, in case he *does* end up needing to pull me back out of anything untoward. And so he can feel some semblance of agency in what's going on, so he doesn't feel like he's just a useless bystander, like he said earlier.

Still nothing.

'Are you with us?'

After another couple of seconds of silence, he frowns over at me. 'I don't think I'm getting anything. Do you want to—'

A gentle thump from inside the bedroom grabs both of our attention.

'Sounds like one of the packing boxes fell down,' Owen shrugs, nonplussed.

I wouldn't bloody bet on it.

'Keep trying,' I nudge Theo.

'Did you do that?' he asks the air.

A second passes, then an unmistakeable, metallic *thunk*, louder this time and very obviously deliberate. The same noise we heard last night, the one that brought us down here in the first place.

'Can you talk to us?'

Thunk.

'We want to help you.'

Thunk.

Theo turns to me again. 'I'm not picking anything else up, apart from those noises. Do you feel anyone with us out here?'

I shake my head. 'Not yet.'

There's clearly something in the bedroom though, responding directly to Theo every time he speaks. But out here, not a sausage – no feeling of any kind of presence, no cold spot, nothing. Then I remember: when we got here last night, apart from a hint when we came in that something was elsewhere in the house, the presence only *directly* made itself known once we were in each of the two bedrooms.

'Maybe it's trapped in there,' I suggest tentatively. 'Maybe it can't come *out* to talk to us.'

Which can happen. If something… very *bad*… happened in that room, whatever's been left behind from that could be stuck there from the sheer force of that experience.

Theo shakes his head. 'Can't be. What about when you felt it in the upstairs room? What about what happened in the boxroom?'

I shrug. 'Maybe it can use the passageway?'

Theo takes a second to consider before he turns back to face the Purple Room. 'Are you trapped in there?'

Thunk. Thunk. Thunk. Thunk.

We exchange glances. Result.

'Did something happen to you in there?'

Thunk-thunk-thunk-thunk-thunk-thunk-thunk-thunk.

Even Owen looks nervous now.

'I think we have to go in there,' I tell Theo gently as I start to stand. A feeling of nervous urgency is starting to creep its way around my body, settling in nauseatingly just under my shoulders.

Theo looks torn. I know he doesn't want to – doesn't want *me* to, more specifically – but at the same time, he wants to figure this out, he wants to fix it, help whoever it is that's lost in there. And ultimately, complete a neat and tidy job for our client, despite the fact that he's taken the biggest personal dislike of his life to the man.

'Okay. But hold onto me.' He stands up beside me.

We've so much more strength together.

I take his hand firmly in mine and reach forward to push the door open the rest of the way. This time, Theo crosses the threshold first, his warm hand around mine, and it all seems fine as I follow him through the open doorway—

Oh crap.

Purple.

Purple carpet, and this time there's a tiny shred of light coming from somewhere, so I see purple curtains as well. I look around me and Theo's nowhere to be seen, although I can still feel a faint pressure on my hand where his is encased around it, back in our reality. The sensation floats somewhere in the background, almost as though my hand is in two pieces – half here, half there – somehow existing in both places at once, Theo my only anchor back to the one I actually belong in.

Except, it's *not* two different places, is it? I'm still here, in the same room. The physical part of me is right there beside Theo, it's just that some other part of me is in another version of the Purple Room, an older version, one from years before.

And it's in somebody else's body. Again. Bare feet, again. Bare legs.

I breathe slowly to steady myself. Come on, don't panic. You knew this would probably happen, you signed up for it. At least this time, use it to find out something *useful*.

Look around. Get a clearer picture. Figure this out.

Above my bare legs, the hem of a nightie at my knees. My hair – *someone's* hair – long as it hangs down low in front of me, a similar mousy brown colour to my own, but not mine. I reach down to touch the dainty pink ruffles along the edge of the nightdress, feeling the unmistakeable crunch of polyester, and that's when I notice my hands.

They're *small*.

I'm not an adult. I'm a little kid.

My eye view isn't far off the level of my usual one, though, so I can't be a *really* little kid. Eight or nine, maybe? Bigger than a toddler but not a teenager, I'd guess. I take a couple of steps across the deep pile underneath my feet, looking around some more. Maybe there's a mirror in the room somewhere, maybe I can see her face—

A slow creak behind me sends a cold shiver up my spine.

I almost daren't turn to look, but I have to, I *have* to see. I swallow thickly and slowly start to turn, reminding myself that none of this is real, whatever it is, it's already happened. As I turn, I back up towards the opposite wall, putting as much distance behind me and the source of the noise as I can.

The door.

The door. The one in the wall, the one to the hidden passage. It's open.

Barely a crack, and it's hard to make out, but it's definitely open. On the purple wall where the door hides, there's a clock, one of those old black and white Kit-Kat clocks with the creepy shifting cat eyes, and the clock is at a slight angle from me now.

An angle it could only be at if the door in the wall had moved.

The eyes. Those big, creepy, ticking eyes.

They're right at the height of the spyhole, and as I look closer, I realise that I'm not looking at the clock eyes at all. In the middle of the cat's face, where they should be, instead there are two dark shadows, as though the big plastic eyes have been popped out of the clock face.

Then something moves behind them.

Flutters.

Blinks.

Is that – are those—

—*human* eyes?

The hidden door creaks again.

And this time it doesn't stop; the gap widens as the panel is pushed all the way open into the room and a shadowy figure steps out. Reflexively I step back, away from it, but in the dim light of the room my footing is off and I stumble against the fireguard behind me, the metal clanging loudly against the fireplace, ringing in my ears as I stumble to the floor in a daze. The figure moves slowly closer, too dark for me to make out, and I want to get up and I *try* to get up but my arms and legs won't work together properly; every time I go to push myself up I just slip against the fireguard again, the narrow brass lines of metal pressing into my back, the frame boxed in tightly between me and the fireplace, leaving me no room to manoeuvre; so I try to shuffle to one side instead, anything, as long as it's away from the advancing figure, already almost at my feet. The dark shape stands over me, looming, featureless and indistinct, and then it crouches down, holding me in place as I flail my arms wildly, trying to hit it, get it off me, get myself free. Before I can, its hands – it's *human*, my mind registers, it has *hands*, clammy, sticky ones – are on my throat, pushing, squeezing, and I try to pull them off me but I can't, whatever it is, *whoever* it is, it's bigger than me, stronger, and it's sitting on my chest, keeping me solidly in place, crushing me as I gasp desperately for air now, panicking, the dark room around me starting to spin, little pinpricks of light appearing behind my eyes somehow, everything in front of me drifting into a cloudy blur as I feel the life slip out of me—

'Come on, I said you were *it*—'

A female voice rips suddenly through the haze.

The voice is young, light, high.

Another kid.

'What the – what are you – oh my *god*—'

The weight on my chest vanishes abruptly and I hear rushing footsteps clatter into the distance as I try desperately to gasp for air, forgetting how, thinking it might already be too late; there are dull shouts and screams somewhere in the house, heading upstairs, getting fainter quickly, and not just because they're getting further away; *everything* is getting fainter now, drifting away from me as I drift away myself, slowly slipping from my last grasp on the world around me—

No, I remember. *Not* me. *Her*.

Not me.

Me is back in the room that's no longer purple, the room that's beige and magnolia in personality as well as décor, Theo somewhere beside me, my anchor, holding me steady, waiting for me to come back, and as that realisation hits me, I *fight*, not to live, but to get out, out of where I am, to go back, back to *myself*—

'Dot?'

Theo's voice, warm, steady, concerned.

'You with us?'

It takes me a few seconds to adjust, the transition is so sudden. My immediate instinct before I even open my eyes is to cough, breathing air back desperately into my lungs again as I reach for my neck, wondering for a second how badly bruised it must be before I remember again that it wasn't my neck, it wasn't *me*.

'Are you okay? Dot?'

Theo's hand is holding mine, his other one at my back, helping me sit up as I rub my neck repeatedly, trying to wipe away the residual memory of the sensation, that horrible pressure. That *fear*. I breathe in deeply and open my eyes, taking in the sight of Theo crouched down beside me, the nondescript room, fully lit around us, no eyeless Kit-Kat clock on the blocked-up wall, no open panel. Owen hovers nervously in the corridor near the chairs.

'There were two of them,' I breathe finally. 'I think there are two of them.'

'Two? Two what?'

'Two girls,' I sigh. 'Little girls. I dunno, eight, nine-ish maybe?'

Owen frowns across from his spot outside the room, arms folded, his expression troubled.

'Walk me through it, Dot,' Theo tries to steady me. 'What happened?'

I shake my head. 'I was… one of them. A little kid, in a nightie, it had pink ruffles on it. It was dark… there was someone in the passage.'

I point shakily to the sealed-up panel in the wall across the room, rubbing my neck absentmindedly.

'What's wrong with your neck?'

'Huh?'

Theo looks pointedly at my hand. 'You keep rubbing your neck.'

'Oh.' I lower my hand. 'They killed her. The person in the passage, they... strangled her. I felt it,' I swallow thickly, the unpleasant memory still a little too close for comfort, 'as if I *was* her.'

'You... *felt* it?' Owen takes a step closer to the room, not quite inside the doorway, looking at me sceptically. 'You felt her die?'

I nod dully.

'What did it feel like?'

'*Jesus.*' This time, Theo doesn't hide his displeasure as he whips his head around, glaring at him.

'Fucking horrible,' I frown darkly.

'What the *hell* sort of question is that?' Theo barks at him, that rarely-seen temper of his flashing abruptly in Owen's direction.

Owen shrugs harmlessly, quite unbothered by his reaction. 'Sorry. Just curious.'

Theo shakes his head angrily and turns back to me. 'You said there were two? What about the other one?'

'I'm not sure exactly what happened to her, but she must've walked in and caught them. She ran off, but they chased her somewhere else in the house. Upstairs, I think, I heard screams, but by then I was already – *she* was already... dying.'

'That's...' Owen's eyes are wide as he watches me carefully. 'Wow.'

'Dot. Did you see who killed her?'

I shake my head at Theo sadly. 'No. The room was still dark. All I saw was a figure, everything was shadows.'

'A figure?' Owen leans forward, interested. 'Is that what's been doing all this stuff in the house?'

I frown back at him, wondering if I'm not being clear enough or he's just a bit obtuse. 'No. It's the girls.'

'But—' he hesitates. 'I thought you said they were just kids?'

'Kids can be ghosts too,' I shrug, turning back to Theo. 'That could be why it seems to be focused in two places. If one of them was killed in here, maybe the other one—'

'Was killed in the upstairs room.' Theo nods sombrely, immediately getting where I'm going.

Another memory flashes into my head. 'The noise. Of course, that's *it*.'

'What about it?'

'The banging,' I remind him. 'We heard two distinct noises. When I – *she* – was killed, there was an old fireguard here, by the fireplace, one of those old brass ones. She fell into it, knocked against it more than once, trying to get away, which would account for that metallic banging noise we heard down here. But the banging upstairs was different, remember? It was lower, not a light noise like metal at all.'

'If there was a separate incident upstairs, that would explain the two different noises.'

'Two girls,' I set it out. 'Two rooms.'

I nod slowly as the realisation finally fully hits me.

'Two *murders*.'

15

'Did you ever hear stories of anyone having died here?' I ask Owen as we regroup downstairs with a comforting cuppa. 'When you were a kid, I mean?'

'God, no,' he looks shocked at the suggestion. 'I can't imagine my parents would've bought the house in the first place if they'd known about anything like that. My Dad might not've cared too much one way or the other – he probably would've used it to try and knock the sellers down on price, maybe, that's the sort of thing he'd do – but my Mom was pretty superstitious.'

Of all the circumstances that can lead to someone who's shuffled off this mortal coil to still be hanging about in our earthly neck of the woods, being murdered – suffering any kind of extreme, violent end – is the one that can create a hell of a capacity for them to cause major physical disruption on our side of the plane. Think about it: you'd probably throw your toys out of the pram a bit if somebody killed you horribly. And those who go through that – who suffer that level of injustice at somebody else's hands – can often carry all of that outrage, that pent-up anger, with them after they go. Technically, there's nothing to actually stop them from carrying on to the Other Side, but if they get distracted on their way to the light – or worse, fight deliberately against it – the potential energy they hold onto from all their entirely reasonable rage can be redirected to create a whole smorgasbord of physical destruction back here.

'We need to find out who these girls were,' I tell Theo. 'What happened to them.'

'And why they're still here.'

'Yeah. What do they want.'

Apart from giving me a piggyback to witness their dying moments first hand, of course.

Theo sighs wearily. 'Sometimes it'd be so much easier if they'd just tell us.'

I smirk back at him. 'Then you wouldn't get to use your ace detective skills.'

He rolls his eyes with a smile, necking the last dregs of his tea before he gets up to leave. 'We've got some work to do.'

'Mmm-hmm,' I reply as I follow suit.

'So what does all this mean?' Owen hovers anxiously as we gather our belongings. 'What do I do now?'

'You've got a couple of very pissed off ghosts,' Theo shrugs, sounding a little too pleased about it as he heads into the hall.

'What we have to do now,' I explain, 'is figure out what's keeping them here. Then we can help them get to where they need to go.'

Owen frowns, looking unimpressed with this assessment. 'Can't you just... get *rid* of them? I mean, I thought that was what I asked you here for in the first place?'

It still surprises me when people think it's that simple. If it were, everyone could do it.

'It's not like turning off a tap, Owen. If they're still lingering over here causing all this havoc, there's a reason. If you want rid of them... that's the key to doing it.'

'You can't just kick them out?'

He sounds like Becs. But more irritated.

I shake my head, turning after Theo. 'No. We can't. Especially under these circumstances. Whatever they're here for, that closure is what they need to be at peace. We can't disrupt that.' I walk into the hall, Owen close at my heels.

Theo's already out of the front door, waiting for me outside.

'Look, we'll probably need a couple of days to get more information. Can you go to a hotel maybe, or stay with one of your kids?'

'Well, I mean, I *could*, but…' Owen huffs irritably behind me. 'All of my work's here, my clothes, my gym stuff. It wouldn't be very convenient.'

I hesitate in the porch, turning back to him with a shrug. 'Well, it's up to you. But it might be sensible to get out of the way for a day or two, just in case anything else like today happens again.'

'You think it might?'

'Rob's waiting, Dot.'

Theo calls to me from the path, a *hurry up* expression on his face.

'All right,' I nod back before turning briefly to Owen once more. 'We can't guarantee it won't. But like I said, it's up to you. If you're going to stay here, at the very least keep out of both of those rooms. I wouldn't go near the top floor at all, in fact. We'll let you know when we find out more.'

Owen looks concerned. 'If anything else *does* happen—'

'Call us straightaway.'

He shrugs, dissatisfied. 'I suppose that's the best I can expect.'

Ooh, he's a bit prickly. Although, he is currently living in a haunted house where the episodes seem to be escalating, so I can't really blame him for being a touch on edge.

'We'll be in touch soon.'

'Okay,' Owen shrugs gruffly.

'Just as soon as we can,' Theo parrots brightly as he leans back into the porch with a thumbs up, a hand on my waist to guide me out. '*Soon* as we can.'

He doesn't usually rush us away. If anything, I'm the one always trying to get us off home while Theo practices his extensive customer service skills chatting away with clients like we've nowhere else to be. I've a feeling I know why he was so keen to get out of this one, but I wait until the front door's closed and we're halfway down the path before I ask the question.

'What was that about?'

Theo pretends not to know what I mean as we pass through the front gate and head to the car, the inside illuminated with the light from whatever game it is Rob's playing.

'Hmm?'

He opens the back door for me and carries on around to the other side.

'Come on, you never rush out like that. You're not still jealous are you?'

Theo stops, passenger door half way open under his hand as he sighs. 'No. Well, yes, but – that's not why.'

'Then what?'

'I wanted to get you out of there, Dot,' he replies plaintively. 'That – whatever the hell it was in there – nearly *killed* you, for fuck's sake.'

Rob looks up from his console, eyebrows raised as he looks at Theo over his left shoulder, then swivels to look at me over his right.

'It wasn't *me*,' I explain for what feels like the billionth time. '*I* wasn't dying. It was the little girl.'

Theo frowns as he drops into the passenger seat, waiting as I settle in the back.

'You said you felt her die, Dot.'

Rob turns all the way around in his seat now, wide-eyed as he stares at me. 'You felt somebody die? Ew.'

'It wasn't that dramatic,' I lie blatantly, fastening my seatbelt.

Theo scoffs. 'And what the hell was with that *psycho* asking you how it felt?'

Now Rob turns to him. 'How it felt to die?' Back to me again. 'Someone asked you how it felt to *die?*'

'The client,' I sigh wearily.

'Creepy fucker,' Theo rages sullenly.

'That *is* pretty creepy, Dot,' Rob shrugs in amiable agreement as he starts the car. 'I mean, I hate to take sides between you two, but I'm gonna have to go with Theo on this one.'

'I'm sure it was just… he was just…'

'What?' Theo frowns back at me.

I shrug weakly. 'Being weird?'

He rolls his eyes, shaking his head as he turns to look out of the window.

'Well, sounds like this job's shaping up to be almost as much fun as the one you did for us,' Rob chirps perkily as he pulls the car out. 'I hope what you're doing with Hannah when we get back won't be quite so eventful.'

Me too.

'Let's talk about something less grim, shall we?' he suggests. 'Dot, how's the day job going? Becs driven you over the edge yet?'

I have to suppress a laugh. 'Nearly.'

'Understandable,' he nods in mock seriousness. 'What about the flat? You still enjoying not tripping over Penny and Lisa with their tongues down each other's throats every five minutes, or has the novelty of paying an arm and a leg in rent by yourself worn off already?'

Rob has such a way with words. 'First place without roommates in the whole of my adult life? I'm not sure that novelty'll *ever* wear off.'

'Space for one more though, right?'

Rob nudges Theo cheekily across the centre console, flashing me a knowing wink through the rearview mirror.

'Plenty,' I agree.

If only Theo *would* actually move in with me, I'd bloody love it. Having my own place is fantastic, especially after so many years of housemates and shitholes, but he spends so much time there anyway, I feel like I'd barely notice the difference. And it's not like I haven't offered him the option already. Of course, he said no: Vicars can't live in sin.

For a couple of seconds Theo doesn't respond, and I wonder if Rob's touched too much of a raw nerve in his attempt to lighten the mood.

'Don't encourage him,' Theo murmurs finally, the slightest hint of a smile in his voice.

I laugh back. 'As if I could make him any worse.'

'Hah,' Rob scoffs. 'I love how the two of you say that like *I'm* the problem. Bloody hell, why the two of you can't just put us all out of our misery and get married already—'

'*Rob*—'

'*Rob!*'

'—I'll never understand,' Rob ignores us both, continuing his thought. 'God, you two. Honestly, neither one of you'd realise what a good thing you've got if it came up and bit you in the arse.'

I lean forward quickly in the gap between the front seats. 'Okay, Rob, you know it's not as simple as that—'

'You love each other,' he counters. 'Everyone else in the world can see you're *supposed* to be together. What could *possibly* be simpler?'

I look to Theo, expecting he might jump in with a counter argument, but he's staring out of the window, refusing point blank to engage. So I sit back quietly, honestly not having anything to refute Rob's words. I mean, it's not like I disagree with him.

After a few seconds of quiet, Theo finally pipes up.

'It's none of your bloody business,' he mutters, still looking out of the window.

'Then don't *make* it my business,' Rob retorts sharply, shooting him a loaded look.

I'm reminded suddenly of the moment they shared earlier after they arrived at the house – to the strains of Becs giving me a massive bollocking – and I wonder if the two of them were talking about *us* before they got there. I glance back and forth at the two of them. Rob was doing such a good job of diffusing the sliver of tension Theo and I brought into the car, and now the boys seem to have even more of it between them than we had to start with.

'Anything you want to share with the rest of the class?' I ask curiously. 'Either of you?'

Rob glances expectantly over at Theo, who shakes his head in irritation, eyes fixed on the window beside him.

'Fine.' I sigh wearily, deciding to leave them to it as I lean backwards against the seat, feeling the toll of our spiritual shenanigans catching up with me. 'Wake me up when we get back.'

Then there's nothing.

16

'Dot?'

Theo's voice barely registers in my brain.

'Come on, lovely.'

His hand is on my arm.

'Wake up. We're back.'

My eyes flutter open, barely able to focus. Theo's crouched beside me in the open doorway of the car. I blink slowly, just about managing to take in that we're parked on the drive back at the house, Rob is nowhere to be seen, and all I want to do in the world is go straight back to sleep.

'Dot?'

I catch myself with a start and look back at him dozily. 'Hmm?'

'You're exhausted,' Theo shakes his head. 'You can't do this thing with Hannah tonight.'

'Promised,' I shrug dazedly through a yawn.

'You're pushing yourself too hard,' he tells me, that concerned frown of his I fell so much in love with creasing across his handsome face. 'All the extra hours and stress at work, the job last week, what happened last night and tonight...'

Theo trails off, and through my heavy lids I can just make out the beginnings of tears pricking the corners of his eyes.

'I was so scared earlier, Dot,' his voice cracks as he hangs his head. 'Seeing you like that, and then when you came out of it and told me what happened, I just...'

'S'okay,' I murmur gently, trying so hard to wake up properly for whatever conversation this is that he wants to have now. I reach out and stroke his hair, coaxing his head up to look back at me.

He does, and now his eyes are wet. 'It's not okay. I've not been fair to you, Dot, I know that,' he shakes his head, wiping his eyes with his sleeve. 'Ever since we – ever since your birthday—'

Theo halts abruptly, but he doesn't need to spell it out. I know exactly what he's talking about. Since *that* night.

'I know I need to – *we* need to—'

He stumbles over the words.

I put him out of his misery. It's not like I didn't know this was coming.

'Talk,' I nod glumly. 'Properly.'

'Yeah.'

The sadness in his eyes is already making my heart worry that I know exactly how this talk is going to end up.

'But not now. You're so *tired*, Dot. Look,' he goes on quickly, pivoting away from the elephant in the space between us, 'I've already told Rob I don't think this is a good idea, not when you're like this. He's gone in to talk to Becs—'

I frown. 'No. *No*, Theo, I promised Hannah.'

'Dot, no. You *can't*. You've got nothing left in you to *do* it with.'

'I've got you,' I point out. 'You can do it.'

That stops him in his tracks. 'Me?'

'Yeah. You. Don't look so shocked, Theo,' I add. 'What else have you been doing all this training with me for in the first place?'

He shrugs uncertainly. 'To keep you company?'

'Funny. Look, gorgeous,' I reach out again, stroking his hesitant face, my other hand on his own, 'you wanted to learn how to control it, how to use it, to do what you could do before our collective shitty parents wiped it all out of your brain, remember?'

'Mmmm,' he replies noncommittally.

'Well, you *have*,' I tell him firmly. 'You *can*. If you don't want me to work Hannah's thing tonight, fine. You do it. I'll just be support.'

Theo starts to shake his head, doubting himself. 'But I can't.'

'Of course you can. You've *been* doing it. You led at the Bloxwich job, you led us in tonight. And I'll still be there to back you up,' I add quickly, sensing his reticence, 'I just won't be the primary. I've got enough left in the tank to assist.'

And I'll have to, because I'm not letting Hannah deal with this alone one more night.

'Guys?'

I look up as Rob appears at the front door.

'Sorry to interrupt. Dot, mate, I know you're knackered, but Becs is freaking out.'

Theo hesitates for a second.

Until he doesn't.

'It's okay,' he tells Rob, not taking his eyes from mine. 'We'll do it tonight.'

Rob's relief is obvious as Theo takes my hand to help me from the car. 'You sure? You're not too tired?'

I shut the car door behind me as Theo and I walk slowly up the drive together. 'I am. But I can get away with it. Father Gregory here will be taking the lead.'

Rob looks surprised for a second. 'Oh. Okay.'

Theo eyes him cautiously. 'Are you okay with that? I know I'm not quite at Dot's level—'

'Theo's more than capable,' I tell both of them, in a tone that suggests neither one of them should try and argue with me.

'Of course. I know that.' Rob shrugs at Theo. 'Never doubted you for a moment, mate.'

'Besides,' I add, brushing past him into the house, 'you know how much Hannah adores him. She'll be thrilled.'

'I'll probably never hear the end of it,' Theo mutters as he follows me.

Rob shuts the front door behind us. 'I'll go and tell Becs we're still on. Do you need us up there, or is this better just between you two and Han?'

Theo looks to me for guidance.

'I think Becs is too wound up about it. Having her there might be counterproductive. How about you come in,' I suggest, 'and she goes to sit with Adam, keeps an eye on him?'

'Sounds like a plan to me,' Rob nods and heads down to the kitchen.

Once he's out of eyeline, Theo turns and puts his arms around me. 'You sure this is all okay?'

'Absolutely.' I nod back up at him, smiling confidently. He may not have complete faith in his abilities, but I bloody do. 'Not a doubt in my mind, Father.'

He looks back at me, so warm and full of love. Which is great, but then… at some point after this, like he said, we need to *talk*, don't we. I suspect that'll be less great.

'I love you, Dot Miller.'

For now, that's enough.

'I love you, Theo Gregory.'

'Not as much as Creme Eggs.'

I shrug. 'But more than Wispa Golds.'

Theo smiles mutedly and takes a deep breath, nodding up the staircase. 'Shall we crack on?'

As we make it up to Hannah's room, of course she's not asleep, even though it's definitely past her bedtime.

'Uncle Theo!' she exclaims as we walk in, bounding off her bed and flying across the room to hug him. 'I knew you'd come back.'

'Only 'cos Dot made me,' he teases her.

She laughs, smiling at me behind him. 'Liar.'

'You still want to do this tonight, poppet?'

'Oh yeah,' Hannah grabs his hands in hers, flailing them around enthusiastically as she jumps up and down in her excitement. 'You can help them, right?'

Theo's smile falters. 'I hope so, Han. No promises, though, okay?'

Hannah stills, shoulders sagging a little. 'Oh-*kay*, Uncle Theo.'

'Hans, love,' I nudge my way into the room, 'have a seat on the bed, okay? We'll start once your Dad gets up here.'

'What about Mom?'

'She's going to stay with Adam.'

Hannah shrugs, satisfied, and crosses the room to perch back on the end of her bed. As she gets there, Becs and Rob arrive at the top of the stairs, and Becs flashes me a quick thumbs up with a pained expression of thanks as she heads off into Adam's room.

Rob walks up to me. 'All ready?'

I look to Theo, who nods on his way to sit beside Hannah, taking care to avoid the already-inflated airbed laid out for his sleeping arrangements on the floor. Bedclothes poke out from the gap beneath Hannah's trundle bed, where the pull-out is made up for me.

'Ready.'

'Where'd you want me?'

'With me.' I walk over to Hannah's desk and pull out her swivel chair, which is just big enough for me to sit on, and set it facing the spot on the end of the bed where Hannah's chosen to sit, leaving a few feet's gap between us. 'Can you grab yourself a chair?'

'Be right back.'

A few minutes later, after Theo's done a bang-up job of explaining to Hannah exactly what's going to happen, Rob's sat beside me on a chair from the landing, all of us quiet now, giving ourselves a minute to breathe and relax. Across from him, sat beside Hannah on the bed, Theo starts us off.

'Is there anybody there?'

Nothing. They never turn up straight away, even when you invite them.

'We'd like to connect with the visitors who were here with Hannah last night.'

Hannah concentrates on nothing but breathing steadily, her eyes closed, emptying her mind per her instructions from Theo, which she's dutifully following to the letter.

'Will you join us?'

Hannah being the person the pair both appeared to in the first place suggests they've established some sort of connection with her, so keeping her with us through the session is our best chance of getting them back. Theo took her step by step back through how to use the psychological wall barrier to protect herself, in case she'd forgotten from when I taught it to all of them at Halloween, and the main thing we needed from her, which is to basically try and stay calm, keep focused, and tell us if she sees or hears anything. If they've linked to her for a particular reason, it's always possible – unlikely, but possible – she might even be the only one who does.

'Are you with us?'

There's the tiniest movement in the corner of my eyeline, and I see Hannah flinch ever-so-slightly, her eyes still closed.

'Hannah? You feel something?'

She nods back at me carefully, squinting, one eye open. 'Someone's here.'

That's exactly why we need her. I haven't picked up anything yet – okay, so maybe the tiredness might be interfering more than I expected – and yet here she is, already aware, way ahead of either me or Theo, years of experience be damned.

Theo opens his eyes, giving her a reassuring smile. 'That's good, Hannah, thanks.' He looks across at me. 'Anything?'

I shrug uncertainly, wondering if our earlier escapade has taken so much out of me that I don't have anything left. 'Nothing. I don't—'

Another movement catches my eye, this time from the opposite direction, near the open doorway. As I turn my head to look, frowning into the shadows of my peripheral vision, a hazy shape fades into being and I realise I might've spoken too soon.

'Something,' I correct carefully, whispering as I nod towards the figure. 'By the door.'

Three heads turn to follow my gaze and Hannah gasps. 'It's *her.*'

Now I see her too.

'Hannah, I only see one. Is the other one here?'

'I— I don't think so,' she falters. 'I only see *her.*'

'Is she the one that—'

'*Yeah.*'

The one that reached out for her.

The description she gave me before of the woman is pretty accurate: short, brown-haired grown-up woman with a scarred mouth and empty, dead shark's eyes. Bug Lady. To me, she looks a little younger than Hannah thought; I'd put her somewhere in her twenties. The brown hair is on the lighter side, just brushing her shoulders, a bit over average build leaning towards curvy. If it wasn't for her creepy, blown-out eyes and the vertical lines of scars criss-crossing her tightly closed lips, she could be my long-lost second cousin, twice removed.

The vague similarity between her and me isn't lost on Theo.

'Dot, do you see her?' he whispers, confusion and concern threaded evenly through his low voice. 'She looks – she looks... sort of...'

I don't think he wants to say it out loud, so I put him out of his misery. 'She looks a little bit like me. Just twenty years younger and a whole lot deader.'

Poor Rob, the only one in the room without the benefit of supernatural sight, has no clue what's going on. 'The ghost looks like you? What?'

'Not exactly,' I clarify quickly, steadying my voice as I keep my eyes carefully on my shadowy dead counterpart, not wanting to spook her. Pardon the pun. 'She's not my evil twin or anything. But there's… a bit of a resemblance.'

'A bit of a *resemblance?*' Theo murmurs tightly, his eyes fixed on her. 'You could be sisters.'

I shake my head dismissively, playing it down. 'Cousins, at most.'

'I did say they looked sort of like you,' Hannah whispers urgently.

'They *both* do?' Theo hisses.

I do remember her saying they reminded her of me, because they were short and – what was it again – *'not skinny'*. Thanks Hans. But I didn't realise she meant they *properly* looked like me. I frown back uncomfortably. 'So they both look this much like me?'

Hannah shrugs back at me. *Duh.*

All the while, the ghostly shape is just standing – sorry, hovering is probably more accurate – over by the door. Finally, Theo turns to Hannah.

'Go on,' he urges. 'Like I told you, okay?'

Hannah nods back up at him trustingly before turning back to face the apparition.

'We're here to help you,' she recites, clear and steady, repeating the instructions Theo gave her before we all sat down. 'Can you talk to us? Can you tell us how to help you?'

Bug Lady just stares back at us with her dead, empty eyes for a while. Then she slowly raises her right hand and puts it over her mouth.

'See,' Hannah turns to me, 'I told you. She can't *talk*.'

Hmm. Helpful.

Then I remember something else Hannah told me before. 'What about her friend? You heard her crying, right?'

'Yeah,' Hannah agrees.

'So maybe *she* can talk. Ask.'

Rob shoots Theo a mildly panicked look and Theo replies with a calming gesture.

Hannah turns back to Bug Lady, who waits patiently on the other side of the room.

'Can your friend talk to us? Can she come back?'

Bug Lady's head drops, her already hazy appearance dimming even more for a few seconds, as though the signal from whatever bandwidth she occupies is dipping in and out. As she brightens back into focus, another shadow appears beside her, vague at first then slowly taking form. Lo and behold, it's short, brown-haired, not skinny lady ghost number two, teenage version.

Theo's voice is tenser than it ought to be, considering he's in charge of this situation. 'Dot, do you see—'

'I see her.'

What he *means* is do I see just how much this one looks like me as well.

She's crying, like Hannah told me before. The sound is soft and muffled, like she's trying to hold back her cries. She looks up from where her head was in her hands with wide, teary eyes, and those are what really sell it. They're not dark and blown out like Bug Lady's beside her, but a bright, deep blue.

Just like mine.

This one could practically be my twin, if I were still about nineteen.

Okay, so it's a *little* creepy.

But I mean, come on. My looks aren't exactly exceptional. Shortarse, blue-eyed, slightly chubby, mousy brunettes are ten a penny in the Midlands. Just because not one, but *two* ghosts, who happen to have a few *very* generic physical traits in common with me, have come to visit Hannah, I'm sure it doesn't mean anything.

At least, I mean, I'm *pretty* sure it doesn't mean anything.

Right?

Theo breaks out of his unnerved paralysis and gives Hannah a nudge, his gaze fixed on the not-quite-twins across the room, eyes darting occasionally back in my direction as he tries to compare our striking yet not-quite-perfect similarities. 'Go on. Try again.'

Hannah turns to the new arrival, invoking her best big girl voice. 'Tell us how to help you.'

The figure looks back over at her, still stifling quiet sobs.

Help us, she says.

Her voice is brittle and thin, but it's clear from the quickly exchanged glances that we all heard it. All but Rob, of course, who's sat beside me in quiet, wide-eyed trepidation at the invisibly unfolding scene.

'*Yes!*' Hannah exclaims, a little too enthusiastically.

'Calm and steady, remember?' Theo whispers to her.

'Sorry,' she replies sheepishly. 'Can I carry on?'

Theo nods carefully.

Hannah's eyes sparkle as she turns back to the spectral figure. 'We want to help you. Can you tell us how? Can you tell us who you are?' She gestures at Bug Lady. 'Who she is?'

'Not too many questions at once,' Theo cautions. 'Give her time to respond.'

'Sorry. What should I ask first?'

Theo shrugs back at her. 'What do you think's most important?'

She screws up her face in thought for a second, then looks back across the room. 'Tell us how to help you,' she repeats solemnly.

The figure moves forward slightly, one arm raised as she reaches out in a strikingly similar display to Hannah's description of Bug Lady's actions from last night.

Help us, she says again.

Hannah moves to interject but Theo gestures for her to hang fire. 'Wait. Give her a chance.'

Help us, the girl repeats, her crying picking back up a gear. *Killed us.*

Uh-oh. Theo and I exchange a look. That's not good. More violent deaths. What with the business on the Boldmere job, it's starting to feel like a bit of an epidemic.

Hannah's eyes look like they're about to pop out of her head. 'Someone killed you? Who killed you?'

Killed us. Killed both of us.

Rob leans over to me, his eyes on his daughter as he reacts to her words, shared with an unseen – to him – audience. 'Dot, I'm not sure I'm okay with whatever this is.'

'We're okay,' I reassure him quickly. 'Just let it take its course. It's under control.'

He looks pleadingly over at Theo, who nods back at him. 'Dot's right. They're just talking, okay? We'll step in if there's any hint it'll escalate.'

Rob frowns, unconvinced, but sits back in his chair for the moment. In the meantime, his ten-year-old and her new bestie continue their conversation.

Killed us, the shadowy girl repeats. *Killed ALL of us.*

All? That's an unsettling step up from *both*.

'*Who* did?' Hannah asks plaintively.

HE did, is the only response.

You might think that when talking to dead people – especially *directly* talking, like Hannah is now – they'd be more forthcoming with specifics. Unfortunately, it doesn't always work like that. In fact, if I'm honest, it rarely ever does. The first thing to bear in mind is that, although superficially it might oddly resemble it, this is *not* like having a normal conversation. Not only does it take a colossal amount of energy on their part to audibly 'speak' like this, which limits the number of words they can force out for us to hear, but they're also doing it whilst 'beaming in', so to speak, from a whole other place, one beyond our normal level of consciousness. Add to that the fact that this particular pair are also using yet more from that limited pot of energy to make themselves visible to us at the same time, and that doesn't leave a whole lot left to *also* be able to go into detail. You get basic words and phrases – and that's if *you're* incredibly lucky, and *they're* working incredibly hard. You can't just chat away at normal speed like you're having brunch in Costa.

From our perspective, it's inconvenient as hell.

Hannah keeps trying, though. 'Who's *he?*'

I turn to Theo. 'We checked before they moved in, right? Nobody died here?'

He shakes his head quickly. 'No record of anything. And it's a new build, it's not even five years old—'

'Becs insisted on that,' Rob chimes in. 'After what happened at the other place.'

'Nothing untoward anywhere else on the estate? No iffy history before it was developed or anything?'

'It's not built on an old burial ground if that's what you're wondering,' Theo replies firmly. 'I checked all the development stuff. It was only ever farmland before, no record of any deaths or burials nearby. They only built ten houses on the estate when it went up a few years ago, and the other nine are still occupied by the original owners.'

So the visitors are definitely connected to Hannah herself, not the house. Which is the assumption we've been working on anyway, of course, but it always helps to be sure.

Rob frowns at me. 'What are you thinking?'

I shake my head. 'Just being sure it's nothing to do with the house.'

'You said before they weren't—'

'I'm just thinking out loud, Rob.'

He...

'Shhhhhh,' Hannah hisses at us indignantly, leaning forward from her perch on the bed with a frown. 'She can't talk to us if you two don't shut up.'

Rob straightens back up in his chair, bemused. 'That's us told.'

Hannah glowers, nodding back at the two figures as she directs us to pay appropriate respect and attention.

...EVIL, the young woman finishes.

Looking between me and Theo now, Hannah looks lost.

'Uncle Theo,' she whispers. 'I don't know what to ask.'

'Want me to take over?'

She nods plaintively, relief in her eyes. Poor kid, she was doing really well. Knowing a bit more of how to interact with them, how to stay calm and focused, will stand her in good stead for any future run-ins. But when you've got a spirit telling you how she and her ethereal almost-lookalike were killed by an evil man, it's no surprise that a ten-year-old might start feeling a bit out of her depth.

Theo turns to The Cryer, her arm still raised in a pleading gesture. 'We want to help you. Tell us what you need.'

Now Bug Lady decides to get in on the action. She moves

forward alongside her friend, raising her own hand in an eerie, ghostly parallel.

Find…

Theo gives her some time to go on. When she doesn't after a few seconds, he gives her another verbal nudge. 'What do you want us to find?'

Find… them… HIM… evil…

Find the evil man? The one who killed them? I flash Theo a quick *'can I?'* look and as he nods back to encourage me, I turn to face the two women.

'Do you want us to find who killed you?' I ask. 'Is he still out there?'

At the sound of my voice addressing them, both women turn to look directly at me, their heads moving in perfect synch. Then, possibly the creepiest thing ever happens: they swing their matching outstretched arms around in my direction, close each of their hands into fists, then slowly straighten their index fingers and *point*.

Towards *me*.

FIND, The Cryer says again.

Bug Lady's head tips forward, an urging on her damaged face, as though she's trying to say it too, but because of whatever happened to her, just *can't*.

Then they start walking towards us.

Well, actually, towards *me*.

'Aunty Dot…'

There's tension in Hannah's voice. Also, she just called me Aunty, which she *never* does.

She doesn't like this.

'It's okay, Hannah,' I reassure her steadily, fighting my own unsettled reaction in my desire to keep her calm. 'They won't hurt me.'

I'm mostly pretty confident about that.

Mostly.

After all, they're not dangerous. They just want help, right?

'We'll help you,' I get to my feet to face them as they continue to pace gradually in my direction. '*I'll* help you.'

I thought confirming that might give them pause, but they're still coming.

Him…

'Tell us who he is,' I reply, backing up instinctively.

'What's going on?' Rob asks.

'Not now,' Theo urges.

They're still coming.

Evil…

I decide to hold my ground. 'I'll help you,' I repeat firmly. 'I'll find him.'

Five feet away. Four feet.

'Dot,' Theo warns.

'I know.'

Three feet.

Two.

Face to face – close enough for me to see every line of the scars on Bug Lady's mouth, to make out the flecks of grey in The Cryer's blue eyes, such a mirror to my own – they stop, their raised, pointed fingers both almost touching my nose. Then, in perfect harmony, they both reach forward towards me, one of each of their hands moving towards each of my shoulders.

'*Dot.*' Theo again.

I put my own hand out to the side to reassure him. 'It's okay.'

It is. It's weird, and a bit creepy, and I'm trembling, but it's okay. Instinctively, some part of me knows they don't mean me any harm. As their vaporous fingers grasp me, there's no sensation as such, other than a feeling of *cold*; I'd hardly even call it touching, as they have no solid, physical presence; there's the barest hint of pressure against my skin, like the memory of what a hand once felt like, as though it rested there for a while and then disappeared.

But it quickly becomes clear that the touch itself is not the point.

With the touch, comes an image. A bunch of them, in fact, flashing so quickly that I can barely keep up. My eyes are open, but somehow what they're showing me is interwoven with the room around me, like a layer of tracing paper.

I see a path alongside a housing estate, late at night, badly lit; a car park by an office building, not completely empty; a sweet smell coupled with a muffled sensation; a male voice, familiar to at least one of them I guess; a dark, cramped space, bumping with vibration and noise, and I don't know which image belongs to which one of them and then—

Nothing.

They're gone.

17

Becs was *not* impressed.

After Rob ducked out to let her know we were done, she stormed into Hannah's room while Theo and I were fixing our respective beds for the night, thunder on her face.

'You were supposed to get rid of them,' she fumes at me as she walks in, wasting no time in making her displeasure abundantly clear.

'Becs…' Rob trails in wearily after her.

Theo steps forward immediately to put himself between us as he holds up a placatory hand, Hannah scurrying down off her bed hot on his heels.

'I know it's not exactly what you wanted.'

Becs scoffs, wide-eyed. 'Not *exactly* what I wanted?!'

'It's not an exorcism, Becs,' Theo counters sharply. 'We can't just cast them out. Trying to force them to go when they're not ready is risky. It'd be different if they were a threat.'

'They *are* a threat!'

'They don't want to hurt her,' he shakes his head. 'They're just here for help, that's all.'

'Uncle Theo's right, Mom,' Hannah chimes in, pulling on Becs' arm. 'They just want us to help them.'

'Help them *how?!*'

'I think they were both murdered,' I start to explain with a heavy sigh. 'By the same man. They want us to find him.'

Becs frowns uneasily. 'These ghosts want you to find a murderer? What on earth for?'

I shrug wearily. 'I'd guess he's never been caught.'

Becs looks around at the three of us like we've all gone mad. '*They* want you to track down a murderer? Oh, well then, in that case I suppose it's all perfectly fine,' she shrugs sarcastically.

'Look,' Rob steps in, 'it's late, we're all tired, and this one should've been in bed a couple of hours ago.' He gives Hannah's shoulder a gentle squeeze. 'Maybe we can deal with this tomorrow?'

Becs wheels on him irritably. 'The whole point of them doing this tonight was to fix it so we don't *have* to deal with it tomorrow. Or the day after that. Now we've got another night worrying about Hannah—'

'Don't blame your mardy on me,' Hannah replies indignantly.

Becs and Rob both look down at her, shocked, while Theo and I exchange an uncomfortable glance. Don't get me wrong, much as I love Hannah, I'm well aware that she can be a little bratty at times. But… *oof.*

'*What* did you say, young lady?'

Becs is, again, unimpressed.

'You don't need to be worried about me,' Hannah goes on firmly. 'I can look after myself now if they come back, Uncle Theo showed me how. And you're not *really* worried about me anyway.'

'Hannah!' Becs' face falls. 'How can you *say* that—'

'You're not worried I won't be *safe*,' Hannah goes on slowly, picking her words with care. 'You just don't want me to be different.'

'What— but—' Becs stumbles over her words, suddenly flustered.

'But I *am* different, Mom,' Hannah urges wearily, the weight of the world – of feeling like something *other* – suddenly drawn across her young face. 'I *am*. I know you don't like it.'

'Oh, sweetheart,' Becs shakes her head, pained. 'It's not that I don't— I just—'

Tumbling over her words, she turns back to me, eyes damp and pleading.

I face Hannah gently, catching her eye. 'Hans love, she's scared. That's all it is.'

'But it's not scary.'

'Not now. But you were scared before when they first visited, right?' I remind her quickly. 'And you will be again, sooner or later. This – it's not always *easy*, being like this.'

That's the understatement of the century.

'And it's not just that. She's scared of what it might mean for you,' I go on sadly, finding it impossible not to think of my younger self, everything I missed out on because I was so involved in doing this, every unkind word from someone who didn't understand it or was scared of it, every time *I* felt *other*. 'As you get older. She's scared of what else might happen, how it might affect you, how other people might treat you.'

Hannah listens patiently to every word then looks down, shaking her head.

'I know that, Aunty Dot.'

Invoking the A-word again. She's serious.

Hannah sighs as she raises her eyes back up to mine, turning to look at Theo, then her parents. 'But I can't change what I am,' she shrugs. 'It just *is*. This is what I am.'

Pretty damned insightful for a ten-year-old. Good for her. I wish I'd been self-possessed enough to have such conviction at her age.

Becs is staring at her, tears rolling quietly down her face, shellshocked. She looks paralysed, like the foundation of her entire world view has been shattered to its core. I don't think I've ever seen her so lost. Rob takes her frozen hand in his, then crouches down to his daughter's level.

'And neither one of us would have you any differently,' he tells her.

Becs breaks down completely at that, falling to her knees as she reaches for Hannah to pull her in for a hug. 'Oh, Han, I'm so sorry,' she blubs shakily.

The little girl clasps her hands around her Mom's neck, stroking her hair gently, suddenly seeming so much older than her years. 'It's okay, Mom. I just wish you wouldn't be scared of it. That makes me worry you're scared of *me*.'

Becs sobs, shaking her head fiercely. 'I could *never*, I would *never*...' she objects, pulling back to look at her daughter as she chokes the tears away. 'Of *course* I'm not scared of you, my angel. Of *course* not. I *love* you, more than anything in the world—'

'More than Adam?' Hannah asks cheekily.

Becs and Rob both laugh.

'Sometimes,' Becs nods.

'Yeah,' Rob agrees. 'And sometimes you're *both* a pain in the arse.'

Hannah grins back mischievously.

'Now, I know you'll do anything to get out of bedtime,' he goes on with mock sternness, 'but this is pushing it a bit, don't you think?'

She groans, back to the eyerolls. '*Dad*...'

Rob ruffles her hair gently as Becs gets back to her feet, giving Hannah one last hug.

'C'mon, kiddo. This is far too late for a school night as it is.'

'But...' she whines, looking to Theo and me for support. 'Dot and Uncle Theo came all the way here to stay over.'

She's dropped the 'Aunty' again, I notice. Normal service is clearly resumed.

'Don't drag us into this,' I shake my head. 'Anyway, it's a school night for both of us as well.'

'Awwwww, but—'

'Bedtime, Han,' Becs instructs wearily.

Once teeth are brushed and pyjamas picked out and everyone drifts to their assigned sleeping area, the kid's barely in bed five minutes before she's out like a light.

'Wish I could still go under that fast,' I muse from the trundle on the floor beside her as she breathes steadily.

Theo yawns from the airbed a few feet away. 'It's not the going under. It's the *staying* under.'

'That too.'

'You can take the guest bedroom if you want, you know,' he suggests gently. 'If you'll sleep better. We don't both have to sleep up here.'

'I'll be fine,' I murmur sleepily. 'I'm so tired. I'm surprised I haven't conked straight out already.'

And then I do.

It's dark.

I'm in some sort of building, I don't know where; there are rooms, so many rooms, ones I don't expect, even in my dream. As I walk along, the darkness surrounds me, hemming me in; my hands use the walls beside me as a guide and I can feel the rough coolness of old brick; occasional specks of light break randomly through the gloom and provide flashes of the floor beneath me, dusty, rough concrete going down, further and further. I'm not sure where I'm going but all I can do is keep moving forward, from one room to another, *so* many rooms in this place and each one darker than the one before, each one a surprise, rooms leading to rooms upon rooms that nobody ever knew existed. Somehow I know that at the core of it all is something dark; that if I keep going, I'm going to run into *something dark* and I won't be able to get away from it, but I can't stop, all I can do is keep walking, keep blindly feeling my way through a seemingly never-ending parade of room after room after room.

Then suddenly, I'm not walking anymore.

I'm in one of the rooms, lying down, flat on my back.

As my eyes start to adjust, I realise I'm not in complete darkness anymore. There's light, but it's faint, and I can't quite pinpoint where it's coming from. I look around and see the floor of bare, old tile – hard, cold, dusty with age – a couple of feet below me, walls of damp, exposed brick. Whatever I'm lying on, it's hard, unyielding, uncomfortable, and as I move my fingers against it I feel the knobbly edges of grain.

Ow!

A splinter pricks my finger. It's wood. A table, maybe?

I try to reach around more, finding it a struggle to wiggle my fingers more than an inch or two. They brush a small patch of metal, and as my eyes frown to identify it, they see another flash of it glinting in the dim light, further along, close to my feet.

Hinges.

A drop leaf table?

As I try and reach up towards what feels like my very woozy head, I realise I can't move my fingers any further. Something's in the way.

What?

That's when I realise.

I'm *restrained.*

My arm and my hand can shuffle down my body a bit, but when I try to move them up, there's a barrier. Some sort of binding across me, just below shoulder level, holding my top half securely in place. I go to shift and there's another; lower down this one, across my hips, a third one just below my knees; my right knee is *killing* me, and I don't know if it's because of what's holding me in place or because I'm hurt in some way. Then the smell of it hits me: leather, metal, rust.

They're straps. Buckled across me.

I'm overwhelmed with panic. I reach up with my free hand, feeling my way along the strap across my hips for the buckle, thinking maybe I can unfasten it, set myself free, breathe. But my fingers barely cooperate, and when they do, all I can touch is the frayed, aged end of the strap itself. I go to lift my other hand, figuring if I can use both, I have a better chance of—

It doesn't move.

I'm willing it, I'm sending all the instructions from my brain in clear and precise language: *MOVE MOVE HAND ARM FUCKING MOVE* – but it just lies there at my side, limp and heavy and useless.

In my dazed awakening, I hadn't noticed.

It's not just my hand and my arm.

Below me, my legs are leaden and stiff as well. My head didn't turn to look around me at the floor, the wall, the wooden surface below me; only my eyes did.

The rest of my face is frozen. But it *aches*. Why does my face ache?

I can't move. At all. And not just because I'm strapped to a table.

I remember then that this is all just a dream anyway – crossing into nightmare territory, admittedly – so it's okay. I can wake myself up any time I like. I've always had super-vivid dreams, and it's not unusual for them to be unpleasant or threatening in some way, but I've always been able to snap myself back out of them. The hardest part is not falling back asleep straight away again afterwards and dropping right back in where I left off.

Then there's a noise.

Above me. A creak.

Footsteps.

Someone's coming.

In the dream, I know who they are – but *I* don't know who they are, if that makes sense – and my panic spikes dramatically. Apparently this development is a *bad* thing.

Okay then. Time to wake up, in that case.

Time to wake up.

Dot. Come on. Have a word with yourself.

Wake up.

But I can't.

I *can't*.

The footsteps above me are on the move. As they hesitate somewhere nearby, fear and doubt suddenly fills my chest – is this really just a dream? Or is this *happening?*

There's noise from across the room, a clatter as something shifts and moves, then more footsteps. Close now, in here with me, no wall or floor or ceiling to separate me from them, whoever they are.

'Oh, no. This is no good. No good at *all*.'

In the dream, I know the voice. But again, *I* don't know it.

I agree with it, though. This is no good at all.

Wake up, Dot.

The owner of the voice approaches, but in typical dream fashion, I can't make them out. I'm sure they *have* a face, but for the purposes of my dream, it doesn't exist; the person moving toward me is nothing but a groggy blur. As they reach my side, they take my marginally able hand in theirs, probing and testing each finger as I lie there, too terrified to shake them off, somehow knowing it'd be pointless to even try. They – *he*, it's a man, that much I'm sure of from the cadence of their voice – move their fingers along my wrist, my arm, testing for feeling, before reaching across my prone body to do the same to the opposite hand.

'Hmm.'

He leans over me, forcing each eyelid open wide one at a time as he peers into my eyes.

I can't see his. In my dream they're masked, hidden beside a thin film of shadow.

'Time for a top up.'

My regular brain doesn't know what that means, but my *dream* brain does, and as a tiny glint of metal flashes in his hand, my regular brain catches on.

A needle. It's a hypodermic needle

He's going to inject me with something.

He already did; that's why I'm like this.

No no no no no no—

Wake *up*, Dot.

He swabs my live arm with something that appears from his pocket, the needle poised against the crook of my elbow.

Wake up, Dot.

He pulls the plunger back.

WAKE UP WAKE UP DOT FOR THE LOVE OF GOD PLEASE WAKE YOURSELF UP JESUS CHRIST—

18

I'm on the pullout bed in Hannah's room.

Shit. Even by the standard of my usual nightmares, that was intense.

I do *not* want to go back there.

Turning over, I squint up through the dark at the clock on Hannah's bedside table, a cute capybara with glowing digits on its tummy.

2.27am. Not even time for my usual semi-regular 4am toilet visit, courtesy of menopause.

God. I'm so tired still, but I daren't risk kicking that bloody dream off again. If I get up and clear my head for half an hour, that should shift enough of the memory to make the prospect of sleeping seem safe – *ish* – so I still have time for at least a bit of decent shuteye before I have to get back up for work. Lifting the covers, I climb awkwardly onto my feet, trying to be quiet so as not to wake either Hannah or Theo as I tiptoe across to the door.

But the airbed's empty. Theo's not there.

I've never known him be up in the night, not once since we've been together. The zombie apocalypse could be in full swing outside and that man would sleep straight through it. And he wouldn't have just done a bunk to the relative comfort of the guestroom, either, not without checking in first. Maybe I'm not the only one with bad dreams tonight?

I figure it's been quiet long enough that Hannah's safe to be left alone for a little while at least, and creep out of the room, heading past the closed door of the master bedroom and the cracked open one of Adam's, towards the stairs to make my way down. As I reach the hall, there's a faint glow coming from the back of the house, and I turn down the corridor towards the kitchen diner.

Theo's there, of course. Sat at the main dining table by the massive bifold doors which lead to the garden, a mug of something steaming up beside him, his head bowed, reading something, I can't see what. It's not unusual for him to have his head in a book – weekend afternoons at my place, he'll often be sat beside me on the sofa, engrossed, the tip of his tongue peeking out of the corner of his mouth in concentration, a gorgeous distraction from whatever game I'm frustratedly button mashing the controller over – he'll always be an English teacher at heart. But the last time I found him like this in the middle of the night was when the two of us were on demon watch at Becs and Robs' old house – the night the two of us first admitted how we felt about each other, properly, I mean – and the eerie parallel isn't lost on me.

As I approach, Theo looks up, startled. 'Hey.'

'Hey. Can't sleep?'

'Not really.'

I frown, concerned. 'That's not like you.'

'Airbed's too bouncy.'

He smiles back at me, but there's sadness in it, and neither it nor his pat explanation ring quite true. Whatever's put that sadness there, I want nothing more in the world than to fix it. But more and more, I'm worried that 'it' might just be me.

'You?'

I brush his shoulder affectionately, taking the seat beside him while he adjusts to face me. 'Bad dreams.'

'About tonight?'

'No. Just… *bad.*'

I shrug, not keen to relive it. I don't want to solidify any part of the mental picture in my mind in case it reappears when I *do* go back to sleep in a bit. *If* I do, of course. With the whole menopause hormone nonsense lately, once I'm awake, the chances of dropping back off without medicinal interference are roughly 60/40 against. But I need sleep desperately, so four times the recommended dose of gummies from the stash in the back pocket of my handbag and a secular prayer for no more bad dreams will have to do.

Theo doesn't press the issue. He knows me well enough to tell when to leave well alone. 'Still quiet up there?'

I nod. 'Yeah. I don't think anything else is going to happen tonight.'

'I figured as much.'

He straightens up, stretching as he yawns lightly, and I spy the book splayed open in front of him.

It's his Bible.

I raise my eyebrows, surprised. 'Bit of light reading?'

'Hmm? Oh,' he registers my gaze. 'Yeah.'

'Looking for inspiration?'

Theo shrugs. 'Something like that.'

He always has it with him when we're on a job, of course. It's part of his kit. It's just not often since we've been together that I've seen him actually *read* it; it's enough of a rarity for me to mostly kind of forget it exists. It's the same with his clerical collar, and the shirt with the funny neck that it fits into; he only wears it these days when he goes back to his church to attend Sunday service, and he never changes into it at mine; he always stops back off at the vicarage first. I haven't even seen him in his penguin suit since – well, since the day we fought the demon who possessed him to get to me because it wanted to take over the world, or whatever. The day Jackie died.

That was four months ago, and the priest – sorry, Vicar – part of his life has felt completely removed from all of the day-to-day we spend together. What little clerical pie he's still kept a finger in during his sabbatical, he's made a point of keeping it separate from us, and that's made it easy for me to pretty much forget it's even still there most of the time.

It's jarring to suddenly realise how much it really, really *is*.

I almost don't want to ask.

'Find any?' I croak tentatively. 'Inspiration, I mean?'

Theo nods slowly, avoiding my eyes. 'Some.'

The silence stretches out as he chooses not to expand on his answer.

But I can't just leave it alone.

'Anything you want to share?'

Theo looks back at me carefully, holding my gaze. 'You really want to have this conversation now?'

What does he mean, *this* conversat—

Oh.

This conversation.

The one we've both been avoiding.

I smile back ruefully, fighting a sudden rush of nausea from the pit of my stomach. 'When you put it like that, I'm not sure we even need to.'

He's decided. He's made his choice, between us and the Church.

And he hasn't picked us.

'You're going back, then. When your sabbatical's up at the end of the month?'

I hear the tightness in my voice, the effort to not show him just how much this hurts, and I hate it. It's not me. It's not *us*. We've always been so honest with each other, so open.

But there is no more *us*. This is it. I can't think that way anymore. I have to go back to just *me*.

Theo quickly takes my hand in his, holding it tightly as he pleads with his eyes. 'I know it's not what you wanted.'

I shake my head, jaw fixed as I fight back tears.

'I want you to be happy,' I reply truthfully.

But I wanted him to be happy with *me*.

'If this is what makes you happy…'

'Being with *you* makes me happy,' he tells me, grabbing my other hand as well, holding both of them so hard that for a second I think he might break something. 'You *know* that.'

'Not that happy, obviously.'

'Don't say that,' Theo wells up himself. 'You've made me happier than I ever thought I could be.'

'How can I believe that when this is what you've chosen? You *know* what this means for us.'

It means the end. It means we're over.

'It doesn't have to,' he urges.

There were always two options. He leaves the Church, we stay together; he goes back, we're done. That's it. That's all we've got. We've been over and over why he can't have it both ways about a billion times by now. Don't get me wrong, I'd love for both us to be able to have our cake and eat it – I do love cake – but there's just no way to make that work.

'Dot, I love you.'

'Obviously not enough,' I reply quietly.

It's a low blow, and I know it.

Theo looks pained. 'That's not fair, Dot.'

'None of this is *fair*, Theo.'

I hear the edge creeping into my voice, the urge to immediately harden my heart and shut down all the swirling emotions of hurt and disappointment and betrayal almost overwhelming. Just put that wall back up, plaster over it, go back to being numb and cold and empty like I did before he fell back into my life out of nowhere after thirty years. I only opened it up for business in the first place because I couldn't help but let him in there; with him gone I don't need the stupid thing anymore. Suddenly, Theo's hands feel far too warm on mine: too much like comfort, too much like *home*, and I let go, starting to pull mine away.

'Don't, Dot,' he grasps them tighter, pleading, refusing to let me go. 'Listen to me. *Please.*'

I look back at him suspiciously through damp eyes, already feeling the cold start to cage and harden around me as my instincts look for ways to dull the hurt, to not allow him to add any further to it. Part of me doesn't want to listen to anything else he has to say. Part of me is desperate to hear every word, in case there's the slightest crumb of hope that some shred of it might change things.

I relax my hands, leaving them limp in his as I nod quietly for him to go on.

Theo takes a deep breath.

'You know I didn't decide this lightly,' he starts carefully. 'I've been torturing myself with it for weeks. And I have to give the Diocese my answer at the end of this week—'

'I thought you still had three weeks left?'

'Until the sabbatical's over, yeah,' he nods. 'But they need notice to make arrangements for the sub who's covering.'

'Ah. Admin,' I reply flatly.

Theo sighs, his eyes closed as he feels my shift in tone. After giving himself a second, he opens them again, but this time he doesn't meet mine as he goes on.

'I didn't decide this lightly,' he repeats. 'And I've gone back and forth so many times about it all – the Church, us, my vows, my parish, *this…*'

Theo gestures vaguely around us, lost for a better way to describe what I know he means – the curious circumstance of our respective abilities and the very not-normal succession of side jobs they have the two of us doing.

'But what Hannah said tonight, that confirmed it for me.'

I frown, racking my brains. I don't remember Hannah saying anything about us, or his Vicar gig, or… what on earth did she say?

'You're blaming a ten-year-old for this?'

Theo ignores the quip as he leans forward, eyes boring into mine now, desperate for understanding, for grace, for… validation, maybe?

'This is what I am,' he says simply.

My heart doesn't break, not exactly, not in that second. It just sort of *flops*, defeated, like a poor beached fish flapping about on the sand, knowing it *needs* to be back in the water, knowing it'll die if it doesn't manage it, but with no clue how to even start trying to get there.

'You're a medium,' I remind him softly.

'I'm a Vicar, Dot. I've been a Vicar for more than twenty years. For almost half my life.'

'But you were a medium first.'

'Thirty *years* ago,' he shakes his head sadly. 'And what my parents did to knock it out of me sure as hell had the effect they were going for. Look, you've been doing it this whole time, for all these years, it's all you've ever known.'

'So?'

'So for me, and yes I *know* we were in it together as kids, but this—'

He lets go of one of my hands and moves to reach for his Bible, pulling it across the table until it's literally between us. Seems a bit on the nose, Theo.

'*This* is what I know. My faith, my Church, it's been the foundation of my life for all these years. I can't just give that up.'

This is the most he's shared with me about how it makes him

feel for this whole time we've been together. And I can see what it means to him. The pain in Theo's voice, the tears in his eyes, the *ache* I can feel in his heart: I don't want him to feel like that. I can't ask him to *live* like that.

He shakes his head sadly. 'And I can't be both.'

But I don't know how to let him go. I can't ask *me* to live like *that*.

I'm not sure how I even *can* live like that again; not now I've had a taste of how good life can feel, not now I've had him be part of that life every day. That pure, simple, beautiful, love; that total acceptance of everything I am, flaws – lots of those; god, so many – and all, with no questioning, no exceptions. He loves me so much, I know that, he just *does*.

How can I let him go?

'But I don't want to lose you, Dot,' Theo pleads, his other hand leaving the Book and reaching back for me again, grasping my arm where it lies on the table, pulling me closer to him, his voice choked with emotion, with desperation. 'I don't want to lose *us*. I *can't*.'

I shake my head slowly, lost and confused as I question him with a look.

'But… we've talked about this, Theo,' I shrug hopelessly, my emotions racing back up from the prison of my heart to the open ground of my eyes, filling them with the sting of tears all over again. 'You know if you…'

I can barely get the words out.

'If you go back to being a Vicar, you *know* we can't carry on as we are.'

Theo nods. 'I know.'

Without breaking eye contact, he reaches down under the table, fishing something out of the pocket of his pyjamas. He puts it gently down on the table between us, not lifting his hand from it where it sits beside the Bible.

'What's that?'

Theo keeps his eyes on mine, still, as he takes a deep breath and takes his hand away.

It's a box.

A small, square, black velvet box.

I swallow thickly. This can't be what it looks like.

It *can't* be.

Not for the reasons you might think. Not because I wouldn't want it. Not because it wouldn't be welcome. Not because four months is too soon and we haven't properly lived together yet and we've only had sex once for god's sake because of his stupid fucking vows.

We've talked about it. And talked about it. He knows if he left the Church I'd do it in a heartbeat; I love him, in a way I honestly never imagined possible, and there's not a doubt in my mind that spending the rest of my life with him would absolutely be the best bloody life choice I could ever decide to make. But as a Vicar, he can't be married to a medium. Not an open, practising one, at any rate. If he's going back to the clergy, the only way *that* particular scenario could work is if I wasn't a medium any more.

So it *can't* be what it looks like.

Because he wouldn't ask that of me. He *couldn't*.

'What is that, Theo?'

'Open it,' he urges gently.

Panic suddenly seizes my heart, my brain, every cognitive function of my body. It's *not*; it *can't* be; he *wouldn't*.

I shake my head no.

'Ohhhh-kaaaayyy,' he murmurs awkwardly, '*I'll* open it.'

He does, the lid snapping open with a heavy *click* before he places it gently back on the table again, the open box facing me.

It *is*.

It's stunning, the ring inside. Rose gold, two narrow rows of horizontal, square-cut turquoise stones, either side of a central one with matching shaped diamonds, each row slightly offset from the one beside it, creating a stepped effect. It looks vintage, 1930s maybe – he knows I still prefer to buy second hand – and even though they didn't make rings to fit chubby sausage fingers like mine back in those days, something tells me that if I put it on, this one would slide on there absolutely perfectly.

'It's beautiful,' I tell him, frog lodged in my throat. 'It's exactly what I would've picked for myself.'

Theo smiles warmly. Of course, he already knows that.

'You want to try it on?' he suggests hopefully.

Do I want to try it on?

Christ, what a question.

On one hand… of course I do, duh. A chance of a life with Theo, for the rest of my life? I've never wanted that with anyone, never thought I'd want it at all, but he *knows* I'd love it with him. And it's not like I haven't thought about it. Being only four months in doesn't matter much when you can sort of see inside the other person's head and you *know* what they're feeling and how real it is and how the pure, complete joy of it reflects right back at you.

But…

In this scenario, it's not just the ring. It's what it *means.*

And I'm not talking about commitment, or marriage, or any of that stuff that I could care less about in general terms but in relation to Theo, would be all in for.

He's already made his decision. He's going back to the Church.

Which means I'd be a Vicar's wife.

Never mind the obligation to sit through services for a religion I don't believe in; to support him and his obligations in *preaching* it; helping him minister to his flock, look after his parish; never mind boring bake sales and pestering parishioners. I know the Church has changed, to a point, and I'm sure there are plenty of clergy spouses out there who aren't necessarily still expected to corral the kiddiwinks and fluff up the flower arrangements, and whose individual, independent identities aren't completely defined by their partners' calling.

But there's no way I could still practice as a medium.

All the years I spent hiding it from everyone, hiding *myself*. I've finally got to a point in my life where not only have I actually accepted who I am. I've *embraced* it.

Theo *knows* I'd have to stop all that if I married him as a Vicar.

Is he really asking me to give it up?

'Okay,' he breathes out slowly in response to my silence, taking one of my paralysed hands back in his. 'I know we've talked about this before, and I know why you're hesitating, but just hear me out.'

Maybe he has some miracle plan for how he can be a Vicar, we can be married, and I can still do my thing?

'I know you don't want to stop doing this, but—'

Or maybe he doesn't.

'—Dot, it's getting *scary*.'

Getting scary? Seriously?

I frown at him. 'When we met, you got possessed by a demon. *Now* it's getting scary?'

Theo shakes his head. 'Every new job we take on, we never know what's going to happen,' he starts to explain. 'How serious it's going to get. And the promotion at work's taken so much out of you on top of that. You've been struggling so hard trying to balance them both because of how wiped out you get after sessions, and it's making you stressed, and that's making you miserable, and it's not like you can afford to just give up your *proper* job—'

His words tumble over themselves as they flood out in a sudden gush.

'—and now with this new transference thing, I just keep worrying: what's next? If every other new case you keep getting these new weird abilities that you never had before, where does it end? It feels like it's getting *dangerous*, Dot, and I'm seriously scared something's going to happen to you.'

I squeeze his hand, so warm and familiar over mine as my instinct jumps immediately to reassure him. 'I'm *not* scared. Not of anything like that.'

Theo leans forward suddenly, his free hand on my cheek as he pulls me to him and kisses me. In it, I can feel everything: his transparent, unashamed, total love for me; his fear about all the things he's just said; his *want* for me that he daren't act on, not again; his desperate need to find some way to keep *us*. As he pulls back – only slightly, leaning his forehead against mine – he closes his eyes and breathe out heavily.

'Marry me.'

For a second, I stay there with him, revelling in it, wishing it were that simple, wishing I could just say *yes*.

I sigh sadly. 'In a heartbeat.'

Theo sits up suddenly, hope in his eyes.

'If you quit.'

His face falls. 'You can't ask me to do that.'

I laugh bitterly as I straighten up, and this time I pull my hand away from his. 'But it's okay for *you* to ask *me* to give up who I am?'

He doesn't have a reply for that.

'You've been a Vicar for more than two decades,' I remind him what he told me before. 'It's part of your identity now, part of who you are, you can't just give that up, right?'

Theo just looks back at me, deflated.

'I've been a medium my whole *life*, Theo. As long as I can remember. I've *never* known anything different. It's in every pore of who I am; it's part of everything I do, even when I don't realise it.'

I shake my head, surprising myself with how passionate I sound. I'm not sure I realised I had it in me, not about this. Not about *anything*, apart from him.

'I've spent a *lifetime* being ashamed of it, being embarrassed by it, hiding it. And now, after all this time, now I've finally made my peace with it, I've *finally* accepted myself and accepted that this is who I am, you're asking me to give all that *up*?'

The sheer disbelief must be all over my face.

'You might as well ask me to stop breathing.'

Theo swallows, tears pricking his eyes.

'I'm asking you to spend your life with me.'

I shake my head again. 'No. If we were just two normal people, with normal lives, you'd be asking that. You're asking me to spend my life with you as a Vicar. You're asking me to give *my* life *up.*'

And despite all that, there's a part of me that's tempted. I can't deny it. Give it up, sack it off: if it means bring with Theo, fuck it all.

But I can't deny who I am now. I'd never be able to live with myself.

'You're asking me not to be *me.*'

Theo looks back at me, tears in his eyes. After a few seconds, he opens his mouth to speak, then stops himself. It's not one of those times when he's not sure he should say the thing he wants to. He just doesn't know what to say.

Eventually, he shrugs.

'Dot. I love you.'

I nod back, my own tears starting to sting. 'I love you too.'

I'm grateful that Theo doesn't make the usual joke about Creme Eggs. Instead, he wipes at his damp eyes with the back of his hand. 'I can't give up the Church.'

I shrug. 'I can't give up the dead.'

He laughs flatly.

'So we... you and me... we can't be... we really *can't*... we...' he runs out of words.

'We're screwed,' I finish for him, sighing resignedly.

Theo smiles through tears. 'Are you really making jokes when we're breaking up?'

I can't believe he said the actual words. Out fucking loud.

We're breaking up.

There's a dull ache settling in my chest. I think it's where my heart used to be, before Theo nicked it.

'What else am I going to do? I've never had a love of my life to lose before, I don't know how I'm supposed to— I don't— how— what—'

Now I can't stop the tears. The second they start to fall, Theo instantly closes the gap between us, his arms tight around me as I finally let it out and sob messily into his shoulder.

'I'm so sorry Dot,' I can feel his own tears on the side of my face, joining with mine. 'I can't believe this is happening.'

Neither can I.

But it is.

19

We stayed that way for a while, until our collective tear ducts ran dry and we felt our way awkwardly towards a brief, awkward conversation about practicalities.

We agreed to take turns babysitting Hannah for the next few nights. Not exactly a long-term solution, but in the absence of any more information about her nocturnal visitors for the minute, it's the best we could come up with. And of course, there's the Boldmere job to clear up. We'd already made plans to pay a visit to the church down the road from the house, the one that'd been involved in the incident back in the nineties Theo found details of in the old local paper, so carrying through with that lead seemed to be the sensible thing to do. I got the sense from him that he'd prefer to just sack the job off completely – he *really* doesn't like that bloke – but I explained how uncomfortable I was with the idea of leaving it half done, and of course doing it without him wasn't an option. Theo promised me he'd see it through to the end – as long as that end came before his parish responsibilities started up again in three weeks' time – but that would be the last clearance we'd be doing together.

I didn't even try to think about what I'd do after that.

Going it alone? Doing clearances?

Could I? Did I even *want* to, without Theo by my side?

One shitty situation at a time, please.

Theo insisted I take the comfy downstairs guestroom bed for what was left of the night instead of going back to Hannah's joint-punishing pull-out so I'd at least have half a chance of some decent sleep, and he'd finish supervision duty back up on the airbed. I honestly had nothing left in me to argue so I went along with it, letting him walk me dully to the room and tuck me into the perpetually made Queen bed, giving me one last gentle kiss on the forehead before he disappeared upstairs.

I didn't think for a second I'd actually drop off – how could I, possibly, when I'd just lost the best part of my life? But I did.

At least there were no more nightmares.

And there were none the next morning. Thankfully, the rush to get everyone where they needed to be was chaotic enough that I only saw Becs in passing for about a minute before I headed out to the bus stop, nowhere near long enough for her to clock my awkward avoidance of Theo or my enormous, puffy, red eyes. She was already planning to work from home, so there was no risk of getting caught in her laser beam at the office. Once I got there, after I replied with a smiley face to a quick email from Mags apologising for two weeks of radio silence and promising we'd definitely catch up soon, I cracked on with my interviews. With Bonnie's help – as sub-interviewer, note-taker and write-it-up-and-report-back-to-HR-for-me assistant – I managed to get through all three that were scheduled with maximum efficiency and in record time, allowing me to skidaddle before eleven, giving me a properly solid block of kip time back at the flat afterwards. And solid was the word. Home in my own bed, I finally conked out completely in a beautiful void of darkness, nothing but blissful, empty sleep, until I felt a gentle shake rouse me back out of it a few hours later.

'Dot. C'mon, time to get up.'

Theo.

Somehow I'd expected his voice to sound different to me, now that everything else had changed. I'd expected I'd *feel* different when I heard it. But as it breaks through the glorious fog to rouse me, it still sounds as lulling and anchoring as always, and it still sounds like home.

'What time is it?' I murmur sleepily, eyes still closed, not wanting to come back to this new, colder reality quite yet.

'Just after three.'

Right on time to meet me. The church we're visiting has an afternoon service on a Wednesday, so we'd figured if we could get there when they're due to finish, we might be able to collar the Minister before they bunk off home. Unlike Theo's cushy set-up, this one doesn't look as though it has a live-in property immediately adjacent to it, and assuming they even have allocated housing, we don't know how local they are and how long they'll hang around once they're done for the day.

'Okay. I'm awake.'

I open my eyes. Sitting halfway down the bed, Theo smiles down at me with just as much affection as he does when he hovers closer to bring me coffee on a Saturday morning. He looks a little tired around the edges in the dullness of the room, my curtains still closed against the afternoon sun – it was a long night for both of us, after all – but he's still as handsome as always.

'Kettle's on. You want a coffee while you get ready?'

'That's be great, thanks gorge—'

I stop myself halfway through the endearment.

'Sorry. Force of habit.'

Theo shrugs. 'S'okay. It's a weird adjustment for both of us.'

It feels strange. To have this… familiarity, this automatic, unspoken intimacy that we share, that's become the norm, the day-to-day for both of us for the last few months, and it's still there, but it's… dulled, somehow. It's flat, like all the air's been taken out of it.

Like we're just going through the motions.

My instinct, as always, is to reach for him, to touch him somehow, reestablish that connection, but I know I can't, I shouldn't, because he's not mine to touch anymore, and I have to get used to that.

Then my eyes adjust to the light and I spy it.

His collar.

He's wearing his clerical collar.

Theo registers my surprise and his fingers move up instinctively to touch it where it sits at the base of his neck. 'Oh yeah, this old thing,' he jokes weakly. 'Thought it might help talking to them today if I went fully suited.'

It does make sense, of course. Set a priest to ask another priest weird questions about a haunted house, or something. But after our conversation last night, it's hard not to read a deeper meaning into it. Wearing his collar – his whole penguin suit, in fact, which I now realise he's togged up in – feels like a very deliberate statement.

He's drawing a line. Under us.

Under *me*.

Was there a part of me that actually thought he might still change his mind?

'Good idea,' I nod politely.

Two little words, one uncomfortable truth neatly ignored. And the distance between us grows.

Theo smiles awkwardly back at me, like he doesn't know what else to say. 'I'll sort the coffee out.'

It almost feels easier when he leaves.

At some point as I'm getting dressed again, I notice a steaming mug of coffee on the chest of drawers behind me, Theo having snuck it in quietly when I wasn't looking. I'm grateful for the boost of wake up juice – I needed that extra sleep, but if anything it's made me feel even dozier than if I hadn't bothered at all – and

I sit on the edge of the bed, nursing it as quick as I dare without burning my mouth, giving myself a minute to contemplate how the hell the two of us ended up here.

I love him so much.

And he loves me; I don't doubt that, not for a second.

If he weren't a Vicar.

If I weren't a Medium.

When he took the sabbatical, when he started working with me, the two of us clearing together, I have to admit, part of me forgot it was potentially only ever going to be a temporary arrangement. It felt as though we were just doing what we should've been all this time anyway; I sort of figured that by choosing to do it in the first place, he'd made his decision there and then already, he just needed time to fully see the transition through. I'm not sure I ever really believed he might actually go back. Not after everything we've been through together. Everything we *are* together. Everything we've seen and done. The first inkling I had that anything else might be going on in his head was after my birthday last month, after we – after *he* broke his vows – and I realised that his commitment to the clergy was still calling, telling him something I thought he'd chosen to ignore.

I love him *so* much.

And I know he loves me.

But I suppose sometimes love just isn't enough.

Taking a deep breath, I neck the last of the coffee, leaving the mug on the bedside table to sort later, and dully drag my arse down to the living room where Theo's sat on the sofa, waiting patiently for me as always.

'You ready to go?'

'Yep.'

We head across town in his car this time – he's determined for me to rest as much as possible, so no driving this afternoon –

and the journey's noticeably quieter than it would usually be on our way to a job. Neither one of us seems to know what to say, or how to start a conversation that doesn't somehow end up leading back to the subject of us, so we just don't say anything. At least Theo's car has a working radio, unlike my scrapheap, so we let Trevor Nelson do all the work to fill the silence for us.

It's a gothic-looking thing, the church we arrive at. Far down the other end of the road from Owen's house, it sits at the main junction, taking up the whole of one of the opposite corners. The fascia of the building is dominated by a huge window arch, populated by row upon vertical row of small, rectangular stained-glass panels, all surrounded by lead frames and set back in elegantly sculpted stone. On one side of the structure is a bell tower, a little turret on each corner of its roof, and the large wooden doors at the entrance are topped off with another gothic archway, this one grandly fronted by pale stone steps which sit across almost the whole frontage, except on one side where the modern world has intervened and adapted it into an accessible ramp. Behind the church itself is what looks to be some sort of church hall building – slightly more modern, but not by all that much – and past that, it even has its very own car park. Fancy. As Theo turns into the driveway, only a dozen or so of the plentiful spaces are taken, so he pulls easily into a spot and kills the engine.

'Do you want to take the lead on this one?' I suggest. 'As you got all dressed up.'

Theo shrugs at his clothes. 'Wouldn't want to go to all this effort for nothing.'

'Okay then. Anything I should know before we go in?'

'Such as?'

'You said they're different from your church,' I remind him. 'Anything I need to be sensitive about, that I wouldn't otherwise…' I hesitate, trying to come up with a kind way to describe own my mostly unintentional obliviousness. 'Realise?'

'Not that kind of different,' he smiles gently. 'It's mostly just about the structure. They're sort of more… devolved, I suppose. Less hierarchy.'

'Same beliefs? Same bible?'

'More or less.'

'Anything else?'

'No Vicars.'

'Just priests?'

He shakes his head. 'Ministers. And this one's a woman.'

Nice. 'That's refreshing.'

'We have them now as well, you know.'

'Took you long enough.'

'We've had them for quite a while, actually.'

'What, two thousand years?'

'Okay, maybe not that long.'

It's so easy, being with him, bouncing off him, when we're together like this. When we're *us*.

But we're not us anymore, are we.

So I pack it in, turning to open the door and get back to business. 'Shall we go?'

A few figures drift into the car park as we get out, and from where I'm standing, I see some others milling about on the front steps; mostly past retirement age, although there are a couple of youngish-looking mums with pushchairs and one or two other randoms. Basically the sort of mix you'd expect to see on a midweek afternoon when anyone who doesn't do shifts is likely at work or school or somewhere, anywhere else. Talking with one of the mums is a woman in a light blue tunic with a clerical collar: late thirties, tall, strikingly attractive.

'That's Reverend Rogers,' Theo points her out.

'Catchy name.'

'She's on their website.'

'They have a website?'

'Everyone has a website these days.'

'You don't.'

He frowns at me. 'How do you know?'

'Because I know how to use the internet.'

'Yeah, well,' Theo looks embarrassed. 'There's one now. The sub set it up.'

'So you have a head start.'

It's funny, how we can suddenly talk about him and his Vicaring again – what he's going to have to do when he gets back to his parish – as though everything is perfectly normal between us, and his precious sodding Church isn't responsible for ripping my heart out and stamping all over it.

I gesture up to the Reverend as her conversation partner makes a move. 'She's free.'

We start up the steps, Theo in front. 'Reverend Rogers?'

The woman turns at her name, eyes taking us both in briefly before she nods at Theo, hand outstretched. 'Father.'

He shakes it politely. 'Father Theo Gregory. This is my...'

Theo turns to me, hesitating.

He doesn't know how to introduce me. Not that he ever used 'girlfriend', we're far too old for that, but before he might've used 'partner', even if he just meant in the communing-with-the-dead sense of the word. Now, it has a different connotation, and he flounders.

I step in before his head explodes.

'Associate,' I lean past him, extending a hand to her. 'Dot Miller.'

Reverend Rogers smiles genially as she takes it. 'Are you from the Synod? I wasn't expecting a visit.'

Theo shakes his head. 'Sorry. C of E, I'm afraid. I have a parish in Lichfield.'

She raises her eyebrows. 'You're quite a long way from home, Father Gregory. Has one of your flock defected?'

Funny. I like her already.

'Nothing so scandalous,' he jokes back. 'I'm not technically here on church business. But I am hoping you might be able to help us.'

The Reverend looks between us, amused. 'I'm intrigued. Do you want to come in? My wife'll be trying to drag me into Brownies in a bit. You two would give me an excellent excuse to get out of it.'

I fail to hide my displeasure as a memory comes back to me – along with a wave of nausea – of being forced into a scratchy brown dress around seven years old, despite Grace not being traditionally Christian in any other way. If I remember correctly, they kicked me out about a month later after I refused to recite the Lord's Prayer, told them heaven and hell didn't exist and that Brown Owl's dead grandma knew she'd cheated on her husband and wasn't happy about it. 'Brownies is still a thing?'

'Oh yeah,' she nods back, ushering us inside. 'I remember hating it as a kid. It's a lot more modern these days, of course, but still bores me to tears.'

There's another clergy spouse thing I don't think I could bear. That's it, Dot. Keep doing that. Remind yourself of all the reasons why Theo's have-his-cake-and-eat-it plan would be a massive fucking disaster.

Reverend Rogers leads us through the main church, down along one side of the pews towards the front. There's no pulpit, just a large platform, raised slightly from the floor by a couple of steps, with a lectern off to one side and a big screen tv high up on the wall of the other. Dead centre are the huge pipes belonging to the church organ, a door on either side. She takes us in the direction of the one on the right, opening it into an anteroom set up as a small kitchen, with a couple of aging formica tables, a sink with a rusty-looking hot water boiler above it, and cupboards that look like they haven't been upgraded since about 1973.

She catches my bemused expression as I take in the surroundings and gestures for us to sit. 'We blew five years of budget on the tv system,' she explains drolly, pulling mugs out from a wall mounted cupboard with a fraying melamine finish. 'There isn't much left for amenities.'

Theo nods. 'I can relate.'

'Always enough for the services, never for the servants, right?'

'You can say that again,' he scoffs with a smile.

I try to ignore the pang of jealousy that pokes at me, seeing them joke about a part of his life he's made a point of keeping me apart from. It's a side of him I've never been involved with, and now never will be. I mean, I know I don't *want* to be, but…

'There's a proper kitchen in the church hall next door, but until Brownies starts the Knit and Natter group hold it hostage, and trust me, you do *not* want to cross that bunch.'

I shake off my little moment and laugh politely as I take a seat, Theo doing the same on the opposite side of the table. 'Sounds terrifying.'

'It's always the ones you least expect,' she shrugs amiably. 'But, they do make those adorable postbox toppers you see all over the place, so we tend to let them have at it. Is tea okay? I'd offer you coffee, but I'm afraid the instant seems to've gone a bit solid.' She clinks the jar against the side of the peeling worktop to demonstrate the ugly clump inside.

'Tea's great, thank you,' Theo nods. 'Just milk, please.'

'And you?' The Reverend looks at me quizzically, and I have a sudden instinct that her curiosity has nothing to do with my tea preferences. I'm clearly a layperson, and she wants to know exactly how and why I'm an 'associate' of Theo's on a mission to another church.

'The same, thanks.'

'Both sweet enough, eh.'

Hardly. Maybe I should start taking sugar in my drinks. It might improve my week.

As she finishes up, she hands each of us a mug, turning back to grab her own before she joins us at the table, taking the seat beside mine.

'So. What's all this about?'

I look over at Theo. This is his show.

He clears his throat.

'We were wondering if you – or, the church – might have any information about some…'

I can feel him choosing his words with care.

'…*occurrences*, that happened back in the nineties. At one of the houses up the road.'

The Reverend looks back and forth between us in surprise. 'Occurrences? You mean the ghosts?'

Theo and I both reflect her expression back perfectly as we exchange a quick glance.

'You *are* talking about the big house up on the corner, right?' She points vaguely in the direction where it would be.

'So you *do* know about it?' I ask tentatively.

'Well,' she shrugs, 'not directly, of course. It was well before my time when the church got involved with that business. But everyone locally knows about the Ghost House. Nobody's ever been able to live there for more than a couple of years.'

Theo looks at me, eyes wide, then back to her. 'So it does have a history. Reverend—'

'Ruby, please.'

And I thought just Reverend Rogers was catchy.

'Ruby, is there anything you can tell us? About the house, what happened there?'

Reverend Ruby considers us both for a second. 'You said you're not technically here on church business. So you're not looking into this from a church perspective. What's your interest, if you don't mind me asking?'

It's an entirely polite, reasonable question, but underneath is an implication that the limits of her co-operation might depend on the answer.

Theo hesitates, frowning as he struggles to come up with a plausible response that won't also drop him in it if she decides to rat him out to his Bishop. I mean, she certainly doesn't come across as the tale-tattling type, but you never know, do you.

I decide it's my turn to step in.

'He's helping me,' I tell her quickly. 'I'm looking into the disturbances for the new owner.'

'Why?'

'To make them stop.'

Emphasis clearly on *I*, not *we*. Just because I'm not happy about Theo's latest life choices, doesn't mean I want him to get in trouble. I can't stop loving him and wanting him to be okay just like that.

Reverend Ruby's eyebrows go up. 'Can you do that?'

'Hopefully. With enough information about what's causing it all.'

'Are you a spirit medium?'

I cock my head slightly. 'Just a medium. Spirit medium sounds a bit tosspotty.'

'Hmm. Interesting.'

She doesn't seem especially outraged at the idea, and turns back to Theo.

'What's a Church of England Vicar doing helping a medium get rid of ghosts? That's not exactly out of the Guidebook.'

'Your church tried to help these other people too,' I point out to her quickly before Theo has to come up with an answer.

'That's true. They weren't successful, though.'

'Evidently.'

'But then, they didn't have a medium up their sleeve,' she adds, amused.

'So you *do* know what happened.'

Reverend Ruby hesitates suddenly, taking a deep breath. Her expression grows serious again as she frowns at Theo and I in turn, sipping slowly from her tea before putting the mug down on the table and sighing in contemplation. I look at Theo, not sure if I should say anything else, or if I've said too much already, or what the hell else might be wrong. He gives me the slightest shake of his head in reply, suggesting we just wait and see.

Then the Reverend stands up. We both go to follow her lead, assuming we've outstayed our welcome, but she gestures for us to sit back down.

'Stay put. I'll just be a minute.'

20

The Reverend doesn't keep us waiting long. When she reappears through the door after a few short minutes – during which Theo and I drank our cups of tea in a silence even more uncharacteristically awkward than the one we shared on the drive over – she's carrying an old archive box, one that the numerous scribbled out labels indicates have been used for multiple purposes over the years: 'C̶h̶r̶i̶s̶t̶i̶n̶g̶l̶e̶ ̶e̶q̶u̶i̶p̶m̶e̶n̶t̶', 'O̶r̶d̶e̶r̶s̶ ̶o̶f̶ ̶S̶e̶r̶v̶i̶c̶e̶', 'S̶u̶n̶d̶a̶y̶ ̶S̶c̶h̶o̶o̶l̶ ̶m̶a̶t̶e̶r̶i̶a̶l̶s̶', amongst others. The most recent tag reads: 'House on the corner'. Sounds like the name of a horror film, which seems perfectly appropriate. 'Here we go,' she says as she deposits the box in the middle of the table between us. 'Now, like I said, our involvement was well before my time, of course. That would've been my predecessor's predecessor's...' Ruby pauses for a second to consider. '...*predecessor's* predecessor. I think.' She shrugs, removing the well-used lid from the top of the box and dropping it on the table, sending up a small plume of dust. 'But there've been so many stories over the years, it became something of a hobby for whoever's been in post here to keep track.'

I lean forward in my seat slightly and peek over the rim. There's all sorts of stuff tossed together in there – I see corners of photos poking out from underneath newspaper clippings, some sort of typed pages bundled together, with piles of handwritten notes.

'That's the article I found.' Theo's on his feet already, leaning over the box as he pulls out the newspaper clipping I just had my eye on.

'Yeah,' Ruby nods. 'That was the incident back in '95 or '96,

I think. There are notes in here about how all of that happened, what the family saw, what the Minister witnessed…'

Interesting. 'The Minister actually witnessed it themselves?'

'Oh yeah,' she nods, eyes wide. 'That's the only reason the Church got involved in the first place. And why we've all kept up such an interest in it. It's a while since I read the transcripts, but from what I remember, the family weren't members of the Church. When they first approached Reverend Fowler, he just gave them spiritual counsel, reassuring them, encouraging them in prayer to deal with other problems, that sort of thing.'

'What happened?'

Reverend Ruby smiles mischievously. 'He did a home visit.'

'And?'

'What he saw scared the bejesus out of him, if you'll pardon the expression.'

I look at Theo, but he's still busy rifling through papers, engrossed in the contents of the box.

'What did he see?'

She shrugs. 'Well, ghosts, of course.'

Even more interesting.

Ruby motions for Theo to make space so she can get back into the box, and rummages through the pile, smiling in satisfaction as her hands find the thing she's looking for. 'Ah. Here it is.'

She pulls out an old, creased exercise book, the sort I haven't used since school.

'These are his notes.'

The Reverend holds out the book, unsure as she glances back and forth between Theo and I which one of us she should hand it to. I fight every nosy instinct in my body.

'Theo's the detective,' I finally shrug in his direction. 'I just talk to dead people.'

Theo takes it from her, flashing me a grateful smile as he

flicks through the pages.

'The first time he went,' Ruby goes on, 'it was just noises. Banging, laughing, footsteps.'

Sounds familiar.

'When he went back again, though, that's when he saw them. The ghosts, I mean.'

Theo looks up from the notebook, his eyes fixed on mine. 'Two little girls.'

Ruby nods. 'Yep. That's them. People have reported seeing them for years, at the upstairs window. The one on the top floor, I think. But Reverend Fowler saw them when he was *inside* the house, and he recognised one of them.'

'*What?!*'

Theo and I react in tandem, jaws on the floor.

'Oh yeah, it's all in his notes. She was a local girl, went missing in the seventies, I think,' she shrugs blithely, like this new snippet of information hasn't just turned my and Theo's world entirely on its axis. 'He went to school with her when he was little, that's why he was so affected when he saw her.'

Bloody hell. Theo's too stunned to speak. I'm not much better, but I force out what I can in a hoarse croak. 'What happened to her?'

Reverend Ruby turns to me with a sigh. 'Nobody really knows, not for sure. She was never found. Reverend Fowler went to the police after he saw her – or thought he did – at that house, but they never took him seriously. And besides, the people who lived there around the time she disappeared had been gone for what, probably twenty-odd years by then.'

Theo finds his voice again. I can hear the suspicion in it, the weight of his question, and I immediately know what he's thinking.

'Who were they? The family who lived there when she

disappeared?'

Ruby shrugs. 'Just a normal family. A couple, their two kids, a boy and a girl. They all went to the same primary school in Boldmere, the daughter was friends with the girl who disappeared. I'm sure Reverend Fowler wrote their names down *somewhere* in all of his scribblings,' she muses, reaching to take the notebook back from Theo as she gestures to the other stuff in the box, 'and there's clippings about the girl in here somewhere as well. He was suspicious of the dad, as I recall. Apparently he had a bit of a reputation locally.'

Theo meets my eyes again, the tension in his gaze unrelenting. 'What sort of reputation?'

'A charmer,' she murmurs, frowning as she flicks through the pages, 'especially with the ladies. But not so pleasant behind closed doors. Both the kids turning up at school with bruises, the mom spotted in the local shops in a similar state, that sort of thing.'

Owen said his father could be… what was the word he used? *Turbulent.*

And they moved away… when? Would it fit the timeline?

'And there was talk he could be a bit… *handsy* with some of his daughters' friends.'

Handsy? Seventies' speak for lecherous sleazebag.

Or potential rapist.

That sounds like a motive for murder.

'By all accounts, nobody was sad to see the back of them.' Ruby shrugs, shaking her head bitterly. 'Although of course, despite everyone feeling oh so very sorry for the mom and the kids, it doesn't seem as though anyone back then bothered to do anything about it. Ah, here we go.'

I hold my breath as she scans a page.

'The Morrisons.'

Shit.

Shit.

Could that be it? Did Owen's dad murder that little girl?

And possibly a second one, if the scene I witnessed in the Purple Room is to be believed.

Or is it all just a really weird coincidence?

'You know I don't believe in coincidence.'

The shock of Theo's words takes me by surprise. I guess I figured he wouldn't do that anymore. Not now that we're not… *us.* We're just me and him again now.

'Sorry, what about coincidence?' The Reverend is understandably confused.

'Never mind. Was there ever any actual evidence?' Theo changes the subject quickly. 'Connecting the dad to what happened with this little girl, I mean?'

'No. Reverend Fowler went back and tried to get records from the police, you know, about the original case of her disappearance back from when he was a kid. But there was nothing to find. It was all just gossip and speculation. Plus, from what I understand,' she adds, 'he was some sort of ex-army guy, had friends in the police, and in those days…'

Ruby shrugs again.

I join her. 'The seventies were a different time.'

She smiles wanly. 'Sadly not quite as different as we'd like to believe, I suspect.'

She's not wrong there.

'Who knows how far they even took the investigation. But the family did move out pretty quickly after she disappeared. Pulled the kids out of school in the middle of term, nobody saw anything of them for a couple of weeks, and then the house was just empty.'

'Empty? Nobody else lived there?'

'Well, it sold eventually. But the Morrisons just packed up and went. Left the area, went to…'

Ruby runs her finger down the page.

'Coventry,' I finish for her.

She looks up. 'That's right. How did you know?' Oh, right,' she rolls her eyes at herself, gesturing vaguely above us as she makes the assumption I got the information from the place where all the ghosts live. 'Couldn't they have told you all of this as well?'

'I wish they would. They're tricksy little buggers sometimes.'

She laughs lightly. 'We have similar issues with direct communication.'

There's silence for a minute as Theo and I both take it all in. Then a thought occurs to me.

'Who was the other girl?'

'The other ghost girl he saw?'

'Yeah. Do you know?'

Reverend Ruby shakes her head no. 'He never saw the second one properly. Never saw her face. All it says in his notes is that he thought she was about the same age, but that's it.'

Two girls. The second one *has* to be the owner of the voice I heard in the Purple Room, the one who was chased away.

'The whole thing shook him up massively, seeing this little girl who he'd known. He left the Church not long after.'

'Anyone still in contact with him?' Theo asks hopefully. 'Maybe we could talk to him.'

'*You* might be able to,' she quips in my direction. 'Sorry. Bad joke. Some of the older members of the congregation kept up with him after he left. He passed some time ago.'

Hmm. So who was – *is* – the second girl?

'Any other little girls go missing round here back then?'

'I'm sure there probably were,' the Reverend muses sadly. 'Again, Reverend Fowler had some notes – old newspaper stories of disappearances of all sorts which were reported but never solved, from all over the county. But there's no definitive connection in any of it about who the second girl might've been. *If* he ever even saw her in the first place.'

There's a quiet, gentle dismissiveness in her tone now.

'You don't believe he did?'

Ruby sighs, shrugging slightly. 'Honestly, I never knew the man. I shouldn't make assumptions, I know. But I've read through all of his papers, and it's clear he was already troubled for other reasons. He struggled with...'

Theo and I both wait as she hesitates.

'Honestly, it's not my place to share. Let's just say, back in the nineties, the Church wasn't as... *accepting* as it is now. Of anything that was considered a...'

She looks to the heavens to find the right words.

'...*non-traditional* orientation.'

Poor guy. 'That must've been hard for him. His own church.'

Ruby nods. 'His diaries suggest he self-medicated a lot, mostly with alcohol, and that was *before* he saw the ghost of his dead childhood schoolmate in the house up the road.'

We all fall quiet for a minute, until the Reverend drops the notebook back into the box with a soft thud, her other hand on the rim. 'Anyway, every Minister since has collected whatever scraps they can about the place, but what happened back then was the extent of any direct involvement. People have mostly just kept up with it out of local curiosity.'

'What about you?' I wonder aloud. 'Have *you* ever seen anything there?'

She shakes her head. 'Fraid not. Some of the neighbours nearer the house who come to our services have told me now and then about hearing noises, but I've never seen or heard anything there myself. To be fair, though, I don't have much reason to go wandering past it. We live up in New Oscott, so when we're not doing stuff on site, we're generally not here.'

'You said everyone locally knows the house,' Theo frowns. 'Are there any other stories, anything significant?'

'Not really. It's mostly just hearsay. You know, someone knows someone whose neighbour knew someone who lived there and told them this, that or the other. Nothing solid. Which makes sense for ghosts, I suppose,' Ruby jokes weakly.

Theo changes tack. 'What about the new owner? Have you had anything to do with him?'

'I haven't, but I know he's raised some eyebrows.'

He jumps on it immediately. 'How so?'

'Silly church gossip, really,' Ruby shrugs. 'Lots of speculation about why an obviously single man of his age needs a big four bedroomed house to himself. In all honesty, I think a couple of our local divorcees made a bit of a beeline for him when he first moved in and they weren't too happy when he made it clear he wasn't interested. Apparently, he's quite handsome.'

I catch Theo's irritated eyeroll as he turns away quickly.

'I wouldn't know,' she adds genially. 'Not my personal cup of tea.'

Mine neither.

'Good to see the Church has come on a bit since your predecessor's time,' I smile back politely, giving Theo a second to get over himself.

'A bit,' she agrees, looking back at Theo. 'A bit more than yours, I'd wager.'

Theo cocks his head. 'A bit. At least, I think you have less infighting about it. Progress in general, I mean.'

Ruby's eyes sparkle with glee. 'We're always looking for new ministers, you know. We have plenty of C of E turncoats in our ranks you could swap war stories with.'

Theo laughs. I wonder briefly if they're progressive enough to accept a practicing medium as a Reverend's wife. Although I think that ship's already sailed.

'I appreciate the recruitment pitch, but I'm quite happy where I am.'

Well, never mind then.

He nods down at the box. 'Do you think I could borrow this, go through it properly?'

I. Not *we*.

I know I made a point of saying 'I' before, but I only did that to try and protect him. He's doing it to pull away. Right in front of me. *Ouch*.

Reverend Ruby pulls a face. 'Hmm. I'd rather you not. If you want to sit and go through it here, I'm more than happy to leave you to it, but… I'm just not comfortable with it going outside of here. Sorry.'

Theo looks at me. 'Maybe I should stay for a bit? See if there's anything else in here that might help.'

I frown at him. Is he suggesting I leave? But we came here together. We're doing this *together*.

Aren't we?

He's *supposed* to still be my partner – professionally, if not otherwise – until this job is done with. Are we not even *that* now?

Theo looks away guiltily, as though he saw the thought in my head. Maybe he did. He stares intently at the contents of the box for a minute, refusing to face me. Reverend Ruby looks cautiously between us, conscious of the sudden tension, which is, admittedly, pretty fucking difficult to miss.

'Maybe you could order a taxi,' he murmurs eventually, still not looking up.

A *taxi?* Is he taking the piss?

I'm *livid*.

But we're in company, and I don't want to mess up the chance to investigate the one lead that might actually get us somewhere. So I suck it up.

'Fine,' I croak, trying to sound normal, as though everything's perfectly okay. 'Let me know if you find anything.'

Instead, I turn all my rage inside, pouring it into a single, solitary, booming thought, which I broadcast as loudly and harshly in his direction as my mind will allow.

Fucking coward.

I see him flinch as I turn to leave. He heard that one, all right.

'Nice to meet you, Reverend.'

I sail past Ruby's expression of utter confusion, holding back my tears all the way out of the church. I hold them back for the ten minutes I'm sat waiting on the wall outside for my lift; I manage to keep it up for the whole half hour it takes to get home. The tears don't even come when I let myself in downstairs, when I head up to the first floor, or when I open my front door.

They threaten me a bit more when I walk into the living room, and the light catches something shiny on the coffee table in front of the sofa.

It's his key.

Theo left his key to my flat behind.

Instinctively, I run down the hall to the bedroom, reaching for the chest of drawers and yanking open the middle one. Theo's drawer.

My heart stops as I realise. He must've done it before he woke me up.

Theo's drawer is empty.

Now the tears start. And I'm scared they'll never stop.

21

I didn't hear from Theo that night.

Whether it was late when he finished ploughing through the Reverend's haunted house memory box, or whether he just didn't want to talk to me, I didn't know. And I tried to stop myself from speculating – from spiralling about all the possible scenarios, including the one my brain was least proud of where he didn't call because he somehow spent all night shacked up with a married Minister with less than zero interest in men – but the Overthinking Gods took over, and I had no defences left to stop their noise.

So…

And I'm not proud of this, either.

I tried to have a peek in his head.

Just once. Just for a second, to see where he was, to *feel* him close to me for a minute, however stupid and self-defeating it might ultimately be. Going cold turkey isn't my thing.

I almost made it. Like I said before, what happened at Halloween was exceptional, and I can't do it easily the same way he can get into mine. But I sat there, emptied my head, focused on him, felt myself drift, felt that he was somewhere near, but…

I couldn't get through.

Because I hit a wall.

My wall. The one *I* taught him to use, for fuck's sake.

He'd *blocked* me.

The fact that he did it using tools I gave him in the first place somehow made the slap in the face sting just that much harsher.

It's not like he just unfollowed me on Instagram.

Who I did hear from, finally, was Mags: she texted just as I was on my way to give up on my shitty day completely and slope off to bed.

So sorry matey, I haven't had 2 secs! Are you & T busy this weekend? Fancy lunch?

I didn't know how to reply. It took me a good ten minutes to break my mental paralysis.

Hey mate. I'd love lunch. T & I have broken up though.

I add the big-eyed teary emoji at the end.

Of course, she immediately called. I couldn't bear to answer.

Can't talk about it now, mate. Too much. Will explain when I see you at the weekend.

The three dots of doom hover for a minute. Then a sad face emoji pops up.

I can't believe it?????

I'm so so sorry xxxxx

I'll book us in Saturday lunchtime and text you the details

Do you want me to come over?

Bless her.

No love, but thanks for the offer x

Are you okay? xx

No. No I'm not. But that's not a text conversation.

The dots pop up again.

Sorry, stupid fkg question, of course you're not ok xxx

Look after yourself, tell me if you need anything. Love you xxx

I will. Love you too xx

I stuck the thing on Do Not Disturb for the rest of the night.

When my alarm goes off on Thursday morning – god, I do *not* want to go into work today – and I check my notifications miserably, there's a row of texts from Theo waiting for me, timed half an hour ago.

My heart's in my mouth as I open them.

All quiet with Hannah last night. Got a bit more info from the box about the missing girl. Her name was Debbie Russell, she was eight, vanished without a trace one day, not much else.

Then, separately:

I'm sorry about yesterday. I honestly thought you could use the rest.

And:

But it was cowardly, you're right. I'm sorry.

I missed you. This all hurts. I don't know how else to do it so it hurts less.

I start crying again, then remind myself I have to be in the office in less than an hour and my pasty face needs longer than that for tears to not still be obvious.

I had to tell Rob & Becs as well, I'm sorry, they put me on the spot. She promised not to give you the third degree at work. I'm so sorry. I hope you're okay. T.

That's a lot of apologies.

But no 'Love, T.' No kiss.

And he *told* Becs and Rob? Really?

And how the hell did I forget he was spending last night watching Hannah again?

Shit, that means it's my turn later.

I chuck a few bits in my rucksack ready for another overnight stay and take it with me in the car, preferring the easy option so I don't have to rely on Becs for a lift. Not that I doubt she'd be fine to sort me out when I'm going over to play Ghostwatch with her kid, but if I drive myself, at least I have an easy escape from the Spanish Inquisition. She might've promised Theo she wouldn't grill me at work, but that won't stop her from haranguing me later if she gets half a chance, like once I'm trapped with her in the car.

When I reach the office, I'm fully caffeined up and at my desk before eight o'clock, reviewing Bonnie's super thorough interview feedback to HR yesterday and praying Becs has decided to work from home again.

No such luck.

She shows up just as I'm drafting an email asking HR to invite two of the three back for second interview.

'Morning—'

'It's not true,' she drops into her chair and rolls it beside me, ignoring my greeting. 'Right? Theo was just messing with us. Right? Some sort of weird messed up joke that I clearly don't get.'

Becs frowns at me in vaguely hopeful confusion.

I have to remind myself to breathe as I force the words out. 'It's true.'

Her eyes widen, stunned. '*What?* No, you – I don't – he – but—'

'And he told me you promised not to give me the third degree at work, so leave it alone.'

'Lunchtime,' she replies quickly, in a way that suggests she's telling, not asking.

But I'm in no mood to be told anything.

'We can go down to—'

'I'm not stopping for lunch,' I shake my head, focusing pointedly on the screen in front of me. 'I'm working through. Too much to catch up on from yesterday. Bonnie's picking me something up from Pret on her way in.'

Becs leans in close. 'Dot. Come on. You seriously have nothing to say about this?'

I take a deep breath, gathering myself for a second before I turn to face her.

'I don't want to talk about it, Becs.'

'Not here, okay,' she shrugs, 'I know, but—'

'Not at *all*,' I reply firmly, already feeling my bottom lip starting to wobble as the crack through my voice betrays me. 'I can't. Becs, *please*, I just *can't.*'

She looks back at me sadly, a reassuring hand squeezing my arm. 'Okay, Dot,' she relents at the sight of my panic-stricken eyes, on the precipice of tears. 'Okay. Should you… are you sure you should be in?'

'Yep. Lots to do.'

I turn away from her and pretend I'm proof reading my draft. Chance'd be a fine thing through these tears.

'You can take the day, if you want—'

'*No.* Thanks.' My reply comes through gritted teeth. I know she's trying to be nice, do what she can that she thinks might help, but bollocks am I wasting annual leave just over some bloody *bloke.*

Okay. I know Theo's not just some bloody bloke.

But in my mind, I'm going to have to make him be. I don't know how else I can possibly get through this.

Becs sighs beside me, clasping my arm again. 'Okay. But, just…'

'Hmm?'

'Ignoring it won't help, you know.'

I swallow thickly. 'It's working pretty well so far,' I lie.

In the corner of my eye, I see her nod briefly. 'I know you were supposed to come over tonight for Hannah, but—'

'I'll be there,' I tell her briskly. 'I've got the car, so I won't need a lift.'

'Last night was quiet, maybe you don't need to.'

'Becs.' I turn to face her again, the tears successfully choked back. 'I'll be there. For Hannah.'

Becs nods quickly. 'Okay. Okay, that's great, if you're sure, thanks.' She smiles back, but I can tell she's forcing it, treating me with kid gloves, trying for my sake to play along with the ridiculous pretence that today is completely, perfectly normal.

'Will you be over in time for dinner? I think Rob's doing Bolognese tonight.'

Tempting as it always is to jump at an offer of free food, I'd rather not this time. I'm not sure how long I can keep up a fake happy face in front of the kids. Besides, the longer I spend on Becs' home turf, the more chance there is she'll decide that I ought to talk about the situation for my own good, and she's the one to make me do it. And I *do not. Want. To. Talk. About. It.*

'Thanks,' I reply politely, 'but I'm going to do a late one here, take advantage of the empty office so I can finally get the last of all this shit off my desk. I'll grab something on my way over.'

I can tell Becs is already having to fight back the urge to argue with me. 'Okay,' she breathes eventually. 'You will eat though, you promise?'

'Please,' I scoff. 'Do you know who you're talking to? It'd take a lot more than this to kill *my* appetite.'

Although… the cup of coffee on my desk is the only thing I've had since I got up. I think that might be the first time I've ever skipped breakfast.

'I'll make sure I get to yours before Hannah goes to bed. About eight?'

'She goes up by half past. When she's behaving herself.'

'I'll get there a bit earlier then.'

This time, when I turn back to my screen, Becs wisely decides to leave me to it.

I spend my day with more singular focus than I think I've ever applied during my entire working life. For a warm up, I blitzed through some dinky dictations, rattling off chasing emails to other solicitors. Once I'd cleared my head of the noise – all the *what ifs* I'd had stuck playing on infinite repeat for the last couple of days – I knuckled down to deal with some fiddly jobs I'd been putting off. Prepping for all my teams' performance reviews; updating action points on a shared document for some miserably dull efficiency project I was unwillingly roped into last month; and trawling through multiple Outlook diaries in a determined attempt to find a window where Becs and fifteen other senior partners could all carve out the same two hour gap for a budget review meeting. Thrilling. In the meantime, Bonnie and Becs both took it upon themselves to kindly keep me coffee'd up, Bonnie as a helpful gesture due to knowing how busy I've been, Becs as a sympathetic one knowing the abrupt shift in my personal circumstances. While the others were all off out at lunch, I took bites – little ones – of the baguette Bonnie'd picked up for me, in between working through some file closing admin and covering the phones, and I didn't bother taking a proper break once they were all back, opting instead to sit and breathe for ten minutes in one of the quiet rooms, where I also binned the remaining two thirds of the food that my appetite decided it had no interest in after all. Mid-afternoon, just as HR sent me and the fee earners a set of appointments with the second interviewees for next week, I had a short but sweet email from Mags checking in to see how I was doing and letting me know she'd booked us a table for Saturday lunchtime at The Rectory, a nice little place tucked away in St Paul's Square near The Jam House, which we'd been to a couple of times before after work.

It was nice for once, actually, staying back late. By about half-six, the last couple of fee earning stragglers made a move, and then the building was quiet; peaceful, even. I'd made a massive dent in the backlog, enough to start seeing the light at the end of the tunnel, and I was even hopeful that next weeks' second interviews might end up in a result this time, especially as one of them was temping at the moment so could start pretty much straightaway. I found myself feeling more relaxed than I had since I took on the role.

And of course, my secondary goal had also been successfully

achieved: fill my day with lots of busy important things to distract myself from…

You know.

Just as I'm finally packing up, my bag starts vibrating.

A text on the Batphone. From Owen.

Just wondered if you had any update since last night? It's been quiet here.

God. I'm so not in the mood.

I send a polite reply.

Glad to hear that. Nothing yet, will let you know.

He replies with a thanks and then I turn it off. I know we think we might've found one of his girls, and maybe I should've told him so, but that doesn't feel like a conversation for text and there's no chance I'm getting into a whole thing about it right now. If his house is quiet, good. Let's hope it stays that way until I can figure something out with Theo.

I leave for Solihull at seven. On my way out of the deserted Reception, I blow a kiss past the desk as I've done every day that I've been in the office since we lost her.

'Night, Jackie.'

We had a sweet little memorial plaque put up back there, and I know I'm not the only one who stops and talks to it sometimes when nobody's on duty at the desk.

Mindful of Becs' request for me to make sure I ate, I stop off at the Big John's in Hall Green on the way, thinking some well done chippy chips slathered in bucketloads of salt and vinegar might just be irresistible enough to kick my appetite back into gear, but after I've picked at half a dozen of them, I just start to feel sick. Never mind. They'll be just as good warmed up in the microwave for lunch tomorrow.

When I finally get to the house, Rob answers the door.

'Hi Rob.'

He smiles warmly as I step inside. Out of nowhere, I suddenly feel incredibly conscious of the gentle shift in our group dynamics. Rob's a friend, of course. But in reality, Becs is *my* friend, Becs and Rob together are – were – *our* friends, and Rob is much closer with Theo than he ever has been with me.

'Kids upstairs?' I ask politely, noting the complete lack of squealing and arguing nearby.

'Becs is reading to Adam,' he confirms. 'And Hannah's just gone in the bath.'

I nod quietly, suddenly not sure what else to say.

'Well. This isn't awkward, is it?'

'Not a bit.'

Rob hesitates. 'Dot?'

'Yeah?'

He frowns tentatively. 'Can I give you a hug?'

Aww.

'Of course,' I laugh lightly, relishing how that feels after the last couple of days of absolute bollocks that has become my life as I step towards him.

'I'm not going to bug you with questions,' Rob declares as he wraps his arms around me. 'And I've begged Becs not to as well.'

'Thanks.'

I appreciate the gesture of the hug, as well as the sentiment of his words. But together, they're working to make me a bit sniffly again.

'I'm just…' he searches for the words. 'I'm just so sorry, that's all.'

And getting snifflier. 'Thanks,' I repeat, muffled against him.

'He loves you *so much*, you know that.'

And that's what makes it so much worse.

'I know,' I sigh resignedly, trying hard not to slip into full blown crying.

'He's in pieces about it all. It's killing him, you know.'

'Good,' I murmur stroppily.

Rob laughs. 'You don't mean that.'

He's right. 'Maybe only a bit.'

'Yeah.'

I feel his head shake above me as we just stand there for a minute.

'Dot?' he says eventually.

'Mmm?'

'You smell like chips.'

I pull away from him with a gentle nudge, using my sleeve to give my eyes a quick wipe, thankful for his attempt to lighten the mood as I gesture back toward the front door. 'The rest are on the passenger seat if you want them.'

'God, no,' he slaps his belly. 'I'd love to, but I think I'm already brewing a pasta baby as it is—'

'*NOOOOOO!!*'

A high-pitched, bloodcurdling scream from above us.

We look at each other in shock for about a nanosecond before we both take off running up the stairs.

Hannah.

22

As Rob and I reach the landing – him just ahead of me by virtue of being able to take the stairs two at a time – Adam's hovering nervously outside his bedroom, fear in his eyes as he turns to us questioningly.

'Dad?'

From the bathroom comes the sound of Becs making soothing noises, punctuated by Hannah shrieking.

'It's okay, poppet,' Rob rushes to him, reassuring. 'It's okay. Just stay in here for a minute, all right?'

I give Adam a quick squeeze on the shoulder as I dash past to the bathroom, Rob close behind. I'm not prepared for what greets me as I turn into the open doorway.

Becs is on the floor in front of Hannah, who's curled up against the wall, tucked in the gap between the toilet and the sink, wrapped in a towel, wailing and thrashing her arms hysterically. Becs keeps trying to grab her hands as they flail in front of her, and as she glances over her shoulder towards us, I can see the utter, desperate confusion written across her face.

'I don't – I don't know what's wrong!'

I do.

They're both right there, Bug Lady and The Cryer, standing wordlessly just behind the spot where Becs is crouched, the pair of them facing Hannah, crowding above her. Becs can't see them of course, despite the fact that their combined ethereal presence is literally brushing her shoulder as they edge forward in the tiniest of increments, about to pass right through her as they advance slowly towards her daughter.

'Leave her alone,' I command firmly.

The apparitions stop abruptly.

'*What?!*' Becs thinks I'm talking to her. 'What the *hell*—'

'Not you,' I tell her quickly, not taking my eyes off the pair, somehow even more eerie now that they're still.

Becs frowns up at Rob, whose vision is equally limited to the living.

'Them.'

She swallows thickly, guessing my meaning. 'Them?'

'*Them.*'

Becs looks around the room frantically, trying hopelessly to see what she knows she can't, all the while still trying as best she can to get hold of Hannah and calm her down.

The pair start to turn.

I keep watching them. 'Rob,' I instruct calmly, 'go and take Adam downstairs.'

'What?'

'*Now.*'

'What about Han—'

'Becs and I will get her out. Just *go.*'

Rob and Becs share a pained look, before he retreats back where we came from. 'C'mon, kiddo,' I hear him say, 'Aunty Dot needs us out of the way a bit while she works.'

Their slow rotation completed, both of the girls are staring directly at me now, The Cryer with her unnervingly blue eyes, Bug Lady with her endlessly dead ones. My floaty, incorporeal distant cousins. Jesus.

'Hannah.'

I hold their collective gaze steady as I raise my voice enough to hopefully cut through her panicked cries.

'Listen to me. I'm going to call them toward me, okay?'

'You're going to *what?!*' Becs frowns.

I ignore her.

'Hannah, you're okay. They can't hurt you, I promise.'

Across the room, I hear her start to choke back her sobs, her movements slowing.

'That's it. Good girl. Now, you know your Mom can't see them,' I go on once I'm sure she's paying attention, 'so I'm going to need you to be brave and look up.'

There's silence for a second, nothing but the barely perceptible hum of some unknowable electrical charge hanging in the air. The two unearthly figures continue to stare back at me, utterly still, as though they're waiting, For what, who the hell knows.

'You hear me Hannah? I need you to look.'

Past the eerie stillness of the haunting figures, there's a barely perceptible movement in the corner of my eye as Hannah nods. Fearful, cautious, just a little lift upwards, but it's enough.

'Okay. Good. When I call them to me, as soon as you see them move – I mean the *second* they start in my direction – you and your Mom get out of there and go straight downstairs.'

Becs is still floundering on the floor, bewildered. 'Dot, what—'

'*Not now*, Becs.' I put a hand out to shush her, still holding the gaze of the creepy half-twins on me. 'Just *move* when Hannah tells you.'

I take a breath. Calling them to me is the only thing I can think of to get them away from Hannah, but I'm not quite sure yet what I'm going to do after that. I guess I'll just have to jump off that bridge when I get to it.

'Hans, you ready?'

A choked squeak in response. 'Yeah.'

Okay then.

I take three slow steps backwards, never shifting my eyes from the two figures. Once I'm well clear of the bathroom doorway so Hannah and Becs have room enough to get out past me and both visitors, I call Bug Lady and The Cryer with as much authority as I can summon up.

'Come to me.'

For a few seconds, I think it might not work, as the tightness in the air around us builds.

Then suddenly, they move.

They *drift*.

Slow, but in my direction.

I keep walking backwards. They keep coming.

Hannah grabs her mother's arm and the pair of them scramble up off the bathroom floor, edging along the wall to stay as far from the gently coasting apparitions as possible, not wanting to draw their attention back. Becs – still unable to see any of this, of course – follows her daughter's lead in faithful replication, hesitating when Hannah holds back, moving quickly behind her as she sneaks forward.

'Come to me,' I repeat.

I keep walking backwards, leading them further away.

And they keep coming.

As I reach the opposite side of the landing, the ghostly pair pass the threshold of the bathroom door, moving silently into the wider space between me and them. As they continue to glide closer – clear of the doorway by a foot now, then two, then three – Hannah *sprints* through the gap behind them, yanking Becs with her as they dash towards the stairs and out of sight.

I've got nowhere else to go.

And they keep coming.

Shit. I really should've thought this through.

'Stop,' I command instinctively. 'Tell me what you want.'

But this time, they ignore my instruction.

And keep coming. Closer.

Uh-oh.

Reaching out now, both of them, arms stretching towards me.

'What do you want?'

Closer.

Two feet away. One foot.

Inches. Close enough to feel the *cold* radiating from them.

Eye to eye, barely a breath from my face, they stop.

Well *this* is creepy as fuck.

This close, I can see every detail as my eyes flit between them: the scars criss-crossing Bug Lady's face, sharp lines like razor cuts, harsher and more prominent across her mouth; The Cryer's tears, leaving white trackmarks down the skin of her already grey, pallid cheeks, in such contrast to the bright blue of her eyes, so much like my own; in direct opposition to the empty stare of Bug Lady's blown-out, infinite moons of darkness.

My breath catches as they linger, suspended, directly in front of me.

'What do you *want?*' I croak out shakily.

The Cryer moves her face even closer – barely; the motion is so infinitesimal that I *feel* it rather than see it – and her wide, unblinking eyes search mine.

Show... you...

Just as I feel her face close in on mine, now I feel them *both* as they hover before me, reaching out again, their hands inching toward my arms where they hang at my sides, until their ghostly fingers brush against my skin and—

Cold envelops me.

Darkness *swallows* me.

But it isn't total.

There's something over my eyes. Light – faint, but there – sits somewhere beyond it. I don't understand why; why can't I see, why my eyes are covered – by what? What is it? I can feel it against my face, whatever it is, scratchy and snug and unmoving and I think maybe I can get it out of the way, so I go to reach for it.

My hands.

I can't move my *hands*.

They're tied together. Awkwardly positioned behind my back, something hard and solid keeping them in place. I'm lying on top of the left one, vaguely aware of it aching beneath me, so I must've been this way for a while, I think. My knees are folded up towards my stomach, tucked in tightly, and the moment I register that little snippet, another, even less pleasant realisation hits me.

My ankles are tied together as well.

Wherever I am, it's cramped, it's uncomfortable, and it smells like… bleach. And petrol. And metal.

And it's moving.

Am I… is this a car? Am I in a car?

If I am, I'm in the boot.

That can't be good.

Then suddenly, it hits me.

I've seen this before.

The other night. In Hannah's room. When they touched me.

I only saw a flash of it then, just for a second, and it was mixed in with so many other images that it was hard to tell *what* I was seeing. But it was this. It was a preview of *this*.

Guess tonight I'm getting the full show.

As the utter dread of what that means starts to make itself at home in my brain, I realise the vibration below me is settling.

The car's slowing down.

And now it's stopped.

For a second there's nothing, no sound, no movement, and I wonder if maybe it's over, maybe I'll blink and open my eyes and just be back on the landing at Becs' house, no clearer understanding of how the hell to help these two so they stop visiting Hannah, so they can both move on to where they ought to be, somewhere beyond all of this where they can have peace. But then I feel the *dip* as somebody gets out of the car, hear the slam of the door on the driver's side, the jangle of keys in time with footsteps, and my heart leaps into my mouth with a sickening jolt.

The footsteps pass by, though, stopping maybe a couple of feet away. Another noise: slowly scraping metal, ending in a *thud*. The unmistakeable sound of a garage door closing, an old fashioned, manual up-and-over one.

Where am I. *When* am I?

Who am I? Bug Lady or The Cryer?

Knowing how they both end up, I'm not overly keen on being either one.

It feels like the Purple Room all over again. *Shit*. I thought that whole transference crap was just something particular about *that* room, *that* house, *those* ghosts. I didn't expect it to follow me anywhere else.

The footsteps approach.

And stop.

A thought occurs to me: the first time the transference thing happened – when it was an accident, when I didn't invite them to do it – I snapped myself out of it, didn't I? I told myself I wanted to get out of wherever the hell it was I'd gone, and out I got.

But.

The second time, when I did it on purpose, when I *wanted* to link up with the ghost in the Purple Room so I could find out what happened to her... well, that was a closer call.

That time, Theo was there to anchor me. To bring me out of it.

Shit.

Above me, there's a creak of metal as the boot opens and I flinch instinctively.

'Hmm. You're awake.'

23

A voice above me. Low, male, muffled. Somehow familiar, because of course it is; I'm not me, am I? I'm whichever of Hannah's two visitors it was who ended up in the back of whoever's car this is, and whoever it is, the voice rings a bell for her.

But she can't quite place it. Is he disguising it slightly, somehow?

The man clicks his tongue. 'Have to look at that dose again.'

Dose? Okay, there's another reason it was so hard to move anything. He's drugged her.

I can't see him. But I know – *she* knows – that voice. She's just not sure *how*.

There's a deep sigh. 'Okay. Time to go. I'll top you up inside.'

Hands, then, reaching under me, lifting me – her – out of the boot. Metal clangs as my foot – *her* foot, Dot, it's *not you*, you *have* to remember that – catches on the rim on the way out.

'Oops. Sorry about that, Michelle.'

He *knows* her.

No wonder his voice is familiar to her.

How does he know her? Where from? If I can figure that out, maybe I can figure out who she is. Who *he* is.

Michelle's body is placed gently on top of something high – propped up, just for a few seconds, as he slams the boot shut. There's a rustle of something against the garage floor, before he comes back over and pulls her forward, shunting her smoothly over his shoulder, straightening back up as he moves past the car, her heels bumping against the metal roof. My instinct wants to fight, bound hands and feet and drugs be damned; do *something*, make it harder for him. But I'm just a passenger on this ride. I'm just witnessing what already happened, how she ended up the way she did. I can't do anything because none of it's real, it's just a memory.

Michelle's memory.

So which one of them is Michelle?

He's carrying me now – her; *us* – through a doorway, along a hall, through another doorway, then down.

Downstairs.

And this is when it hits her. This is the moment she realises.

She knows she's going to die.

She knows who he is, and he *knows* she does, even though she can't think clearly, can't put a name to the voice. That's why he called her by her name, with no hesitation. No uncertainty. No doubt.

He's confident. Confident she won't tell.

Because he's going to kill her. And he's sure he'll succeed.

He's done this before, she thinks. I'm inclined to agree with her.

Slung over his shoulder, my front half at his back, whatever's covering my eyes has started to shift with the movement. Only slightly – not enough that I can see much of anything useful, you know, like a piece of post with his name and address on, maybe a proudly displayed family photo or a copy of his driving licence – but hints of the space I'm headed down to. It's mostly dark down there, but I get a glimpse of bare brick wall, dusty concrete floor. Across the room – the cellar, I suppose – he stops, and I can just about make out a surface beside where he's standing, something wooden. A second later I'm moving down as he lowers me onto it, stretching me out flat, hovering silently above me.

I lie there, perfectly still.

And absolutely fucking terrified.

It's not real, Dot, I remind myself quickly. It's not even you, it's *Michelle*. You're just having a piggyback on her memories.

Yeah. Tell that to my blood pressure.

After the longest five seconds of my life he reaches down, picking something up from nearby with a gentle *clang*.

Then he smacks me on the knee with it. *Hard*.

My knee doesn't react, and I barely feel it. I only know it was a hard hit because of the noise it made when it connected.

A *crack*.

Like something in there just buckled.

'Okay. Not *that* awake then, are you?'

He sounds satisfied. Relaxed. Chipper, almost.

Sick fucker.

Who *is* this bloke? How does he know her? Why can't she place his voice?

And if he doesn't care that I know him – arrghh, that *Michelle* knows him – why bother to still keep her blindfolded?

I want to ask him. But of course I can't speak. I can't do anything.

I feel so helpless, so *useless*, and I'm not sure how much of that's Michelle and how much is me. How is any of this supposed to help me help her, or her equally sad dead friend, whoever *she* is? My guess when I met them before was that these two poor murdered girls wanted us to find their killer, bring him to justice somehow, but nothing I'm seeing here tells me enough of anything useful to be able to do that.

'What? You have questions?'

Did my mouth move?

'Oh, I'm sure you do. Always so many questions at work. You never shut up, do you.'

He really, *really* knows her. They work together. *Worked* together. Maybe that might help? Someone called Michelle who was killed or disappeared any time in the last thirty years, find out where she worked, who she worked with… hmm, doesn't really narrow it down much, does it?

'Let's fix that, shall we?'

Oh shit.

Is this it? Is this the moment? Is now when he kills her?

Do I need to get out?

He steps away – not far, somewhere past my head – and there are more noises: what sounds like a drawer opening, a rattle as he picks through its contents, the gentle *clunk* as he shuts it again.

Then silence for what seems like forever as he leans over me.

'Seeing as how you didn't feel that little knee tap,' he muses, 'I'm sure this won't bother you too much either.'

How long do I wait before I get myself the hell out of here? Is there something specific I'm waiting *for?* Something I can actually *use?*

Is there something I'm missing?

Then I feel… not pain, but *pressure*, as he bends over my head, his hands at my face, doing I don't know what, then—

'*Ow.*'

He flinches back, upright away from me again.

'Dammit. Look,' he says with the mildest of irritation. 'Look what you made me do.'

The covering lifts from my face.

His hand is in front of it, waving, palm toward me.

'You just get me too excited,' he sighs creepily, wiggling his fingers at me. A thick, dark streak of red weeps angrily along his left palm, almost across the whole width of it, from near the base of his thumb to just below his little finger, the blood running down in streaks towards his wrist, dripping onto me.

Onto *Michelle*.

'I got a bit carried away.'

I can't see him. He's standing close behind my head now, my head that still won't move, and I can't roll my eyes back far enough to get a look.

Another sigh. 'I suppose I should go and get this cleaned up.'

Every time I hear him speak, he's so… calm. Measured. In control. Even a minute ago, when he chided me for 'making' him cut himself, he didn't *really* sound annoyed. No anger, no fear, no excitement.

Just quietly, completely self-assured.

I'm not sure which part of that is more terrifying.

He moves around the table now, doing something else, moving *me* around. Shit. What now?

'I'll just make you a little more comfortable first.'

Uh-oh. What does *that* mean?

Suddenly, my ankles are unbound. But of course, I still can't move them. I still can't even feel them, not really. Whatever he dosed her with, it's a hell of a drug. Actually, after that whack to my knee, I'm not sure I *want* to feel anything. Maybe it's better that way.

He straightens my legs, moving them slightly apart, and a horrific thought springs to mind, as if this entire scenario wasn't horrific enough as it is.

'Don't want to cut off the circulation,' he murmurs, crouching to my left. Something moves across my body, landing heavily, and as my eyes drift down, the top of his head just barely perceptible in the dark room – I can't even tell what colour his hair is, although he definitely has a full head of it – I recognise something else.

Hinges.

The table. The table from my dream.

So that was what then… *not* a dream? A premonition, in my sleep, of something that'd already happened?

What the hell did those ghosts *do* to me when they touched me the other night?

He stands again, face turned away from me as he leans towards the knee he did god knows what to, and as he fiddles with something, the smell of leather and metal and rust hits me and *it's the strap*, the one from my dream; he's buckling the strap just below my knee. Then he shifts along, doing the same across my hips.

'Now, there's another one of these, but I'll save that for later,' he explains levelly, reaching across with whatever he cut himself on and using it to cut the bonds at my wrists. My arms fall dully, the left one dropping over the open table edge, the right landing with a *thunk* up against the brick wall beside me. He picks up my limp left hand with his – the clean one – and manoeuvres it up, towards my head, until it hovers in front of my own face, clasped tightly under his. 'Want you to see what I got so excited about just now.'

He pushes my fingers up against my mouth for a few seconds, moving them around. Still, though, I feel nothing – and he must know that, so what's the point?

I get it when he lifts my hand again, moving it further up this time, holding it close in front of my eyes so I can't miss it.

My fingers are covered in blood.

My blood. *Michelle's* blood.

He cut up her mouth. Her *face*.

Michelle is Bug Lady.

I try to scream, but nothing happens. I can't do anything that she didn't do then, and she couldn't scream; she was too drugged up, too paralysed. This isn't real; I can't control it, I can't change it; it's already happened. It's a first class window seat directly through the looking glass into the last moments of Michelle's life; the world's most horrific virtual reality experience.

Sick Fucker – I don't know what else to call him, and I reckon that fits – pats me gently on the head. 'I like you better this way,' he says. I can hear his smile in it. 'Quieter. More well behaved. Suits you.'

God, I know I don't believe in you. But please get him away from me anyway.

'I'll be back soon. Need to clear up my mess. Can't leave any of my blood on you,' he muses. 'They hardly need any of it to match your DNA now. It's amazing how fast it's come on.'

Does that give me a timeline? When did blood samples start to be a thing for DNA testing? Late eighties? Nineties maybe?

He drops my hand and I feel empty air as he walks away, towards the stairs, his face turned away from me again. 'Don't worry. I won't leave you for long.'

Take your time, Sick Fucker.

Okay. So I have a first name for Bug Lady. I maybe have sort of a vague-ish timeline. And whoever he is, he must have one huge fucking scar on his left palm, as no way is he off to A&E to get that thing stitched up.

Is that enough? Can I leave?

I want to leave.

Come on, Dot. Time to go.

God, poor Michelle. At least whatever he gave her, she was dosed to the gills enough that she couldn't feel anything. At least *I* can't feel anything.

…and then I start to.

A dull ache in my right knee, nothing much at first. But then it grows, slowly, throbbing, radiating up and down the rest of my leg, and I realise it feels like something's *crushed* inside there, and the ache turns to a boil, getting hotter and hotter, until—

—it's suddenly wiped out completely by the searing pain in my face.

My cheeks, my forehead, my lips.

Cuts, slashes, all across my skin. Searing, stretching, breaking.

Dot, *leave*.

Inside my mouth, too.

My mouth, my *throat* feels wet and slick, and I realise if the pain's coming, the drugs must be wearing off, and if the drugs are wearing off, I can scream.

I don't know where I am, how far I am from anywhere, from anyone else, but I'll scream my lungs out anyway. I know how this story ends for Michelle; I know it's already fucked. What else is there to lose?

But of course, I can't scream.

Not because I'm not Michelle and I can't change this scenario. Not because *she* didn't scream. Not because she didn't *try*.

I try to scream. Michelle tries to scream.

But neither one of us can make a sound. Well, not much of one, anyway. Nothing more than a choked, guttural gasp.

Sick Fucker didn't just cut up her mouth.

He *cut out her tongue*.

Dot.

Dot. *Go*.

Get out, Dot, get out *NOW*—

24

It's still dark.

But it's a different kind of dark. It's *natural.*

It's just late.

I'm on my way home. I finished my shift at the Unicorn nearly an hour ago, and I normally just get the bus back up to campus, but I suppose the snow must've messed up the schedule, because I was stood at Westgate for forty minutes and nothing turned up. I don't like to do the walk this time of night, but it's only half an hour to Darwin, and at least I'll be warmer than I would staying waiting at the stop for a bus that might never show up at all. I don't have enough cash on me for a taxi, and the local firms don't take cards. Besides, in the time I'd have to wait for one, the walk'll get me back, and I could do with a decent night's sleep as I have to do a presentation about Watergate in my American Studies lecture tomorrow morning. I'm nervous enough about standing up to talk in front of the rest of my class without also being completely knackered.

This is all very unnerving to me.

I've never worked anywhere called the Unicorn, I don't know what or where a Westgate or a Darwin might be, and I've never been to a lecture in my life, having not ever gone to Uni.

So… I suppose I'm still not me, then?

I don't think I'm Michelle, either. Whatever this is – wherever, whenever – it feels different to where and who I just was.

Does that mean I'm The Cryer? Oh god, am I about to get a firsthand view of her last hours on this earthly plane as well?

I really don't like this transference business, not one bit. What I *would* like is to return this new gift, please, to wherever it is that all the other gifts came from. I have enough of them already, thanks very much.

But.

I got *something* from my ride-along with Michelle. Not much – her first name, a very rough idea of what decade she was killed, the real reason why she doesn't talk – but it's a start. Maybe this second trip will give me another piece of the puzzle. Enough so I can put it all together and sort this out for Hannah for good. So I let it play out.

And hope that this time, when I *do* snap out of it, this time I go straight back to myself.

I'm walking through a housing estate: suburban, quiet, dark. The houses don't look like post-war, they're too new – a mixture of seventies and eighties, maybe. There are streetlights, but not many, and the light dusting of snow is making gentle halos around the few that work. At the end of the road is a T-junction, with a street sign directly opposite mostly obscured by a hedge; all I can make out is the end of it, 'Something-hurst Close'. At the junction, I head right, towards another sign, this time higher up on a lamppost. This one reads 'University', and beneath that, nonsensically, 'Crab & Wink', the rest of the direction cloaked by the snow. The sign points left, to a pedestrian footpath.

A barely lit, hedge-lined, tree-covered pedestrian footpath, cutting through the back of the estate.

I peer hesitantly down it for a minute.

Well, I don't. *She* does. If I'm nervous about going down there, that must mean she was too.

I look around. There's nobody else about. It's a well-used shortcut up to the Uni campus, this path, but she's mostly used it during the day. It's nearly midnight now, and she has doubts about how safe it is – this late, this dark, no other people. There are a few houses dotted about further down there, but the path runs along the back of them at the end of their gardens, so it's not really overlooked. Anywhere.

I *feel* her gut instinct telling her not to do it; turn around, go back.

But going back means probably ten minutes down to Beaconside, then another half hours' walk up St Stephens, and that's a *big* hill. This shortcut is less than half a mile. It takes five, maybe six minutes. And then she'll be in bed.

She's cold. She's tired. She's already fed up about the buses. The thought of having to trek halfway back the way she came, only to then have a longer, even *more* miserable walk the longer way around – the safer way – is just *too much*. It's been a long night; a long week; a long first term.

So she turns up the footpath.

I already know how this ends.

She's about a third of the way, a couple of minutes along – super alert, walking quickly, confidently, head up, bag tight against her side, keys in hand, sticking out between her fingers, when she stops suddenly.

Up ahead, maybe twenty feet, one of the streetlights is broken. The gaps between each of them are already pretty far apart for them to be of too much use, but with this extra one being out, well, that'll plunge her into almost complete darkness for the next couple of minutes.

She could go back.

She *should* go back.

But she's invested now. She carries on.

Just before the broken light, the tall hedge which runs along the left side of the path has a break in it; only a small one, a foot or so wide maybe.

Something moves in it.

She hears the gentle rustle of the leaves. Sees them shake.

Probably just a cat, she tells herself. Maybe a fox.

Every instinct in her body *screams* at her now: *go back*. For a second, she turns around, looking back the way she came, wondering if she should, feeling unsettled and something else in the pit of her stomach that she can't quite name. But now, from here, the way back looks just as dark, just as threatening, no better of an option.

I feel all of this unfold around me, watching sadly through her eyes, wishing I could change it but knowing there's nothing I can do, hoping that at least bearing witness to it will mean I can make it right.

She carries on.

Past the hedge, past the broken streetlight, walking with purpose, her breath tight in her chest…

…and *nothing*. Just relief.

Halfway there now. She walks on, maybe a little faster.

It's less than a minute later when she hears footsteps behind her. Quiet ones, padded, like trainers rather than shoes.

She doesn't turn to look. She just tightens the keys in her hand, says a silent prayer, quickens her pace.

So do the footsteps behind her.

She loves the Docs she's wearing – they were the first thing she bought when she got here at the end of September, and she's worn them most days since – but she's not sure how well she can run in them; they sit heavy on her feet.

She's going to bloody well try though.

The run she breaks into is staggered, hampered by the weight of the boots, her pace barely any faster. She hopes maybe the footsteps will fall away anyway, disappear into the distance; maybe they'll decide that someone who tries to run is someone not worth the hassle of chasing; maybe they were never actually following her in the first place.

Of course, they don't. Their pace quickens behind her.

They start to close the gap.

The cold is making her chest hurt but she gasps for more air, forcing herself to move faster, pumping her arms now, until—

—hands grab her from behind. One tight around her waist, the other across her mouth, muffling her scream. She thrashes, struggling, trying to fight, but he's stronger and he drags her backwards, towards the treeline on the right, close against him. She tries to hit him with the bunch of keys, but can't reach back enough to get at him with enough momentum for it to mean anything – what a waste of bloody time *that* self-defence tip turned out to be, she thinks – so instead, she manoeuvres her mouth where he's covering it, twisting and whipping her head as he fights to hold on and one of his gloved fingers slips in and she *bites*.

Hard.

He grunts in pain, his hand suddenly away from her face, but before she gets her wind back enough to get out the scream that's waiting to be released, something hits the side of her head.

Also *hard*.

And she goes down – not quite to the ground; he's still gripping her waist – but she *slumps* like a sack of potatoes, woozy and confused and for a second completely forgetting where she is and what's happening to her as the world spins a little.

Come on, Sick Fucker, I think as the scene unravels around me. I know it's you. Give me something: let me see you. And if not, even if I can just remember all the little snippets that have popped from her mind into mine – the place she worked at, what she was studying, where she'd waited in vain for the bus, where she was going, the bits of signs I saw... they might add up to something I can *use*.

'Nice try, Jess.'

A voice rough in her ear.

He knows her.

She has a flicker of recognition – she knows it, she's heard it – but she can't place it, not quite. Someone from the pub, maybe? Someone from one of her classes? From her dorm?

I already knew it was going to be the same bloke – that was the assumption from the start; why else would Bug Lady Michelle and The Cryer always appear together, if not somehow connected in death? But the voice confirms it. It's a little lighter than it was with Michelle, a little higher – a little younger? Did this happen *before* Michelle? – but I know it enough, I've heard it before, and it's definitely *him*.

And he knew them. He knew *both* of them.

This wasn't some stranger, some random, opportunistic thing. Neither of them were. He *planned* this, just like he planned Michelle's death.

He *practiced*.

And I know his voice now.

But what I *really* want is to see his face.

He drags her, dazed, further into the trees, far enough away so that if anyone else *does* happen to wander along the footpath, they'll be well out of sight and hearing. One of her feet catches on a downed tree branch, hitting her hard on the ankle, and that brings her out of her stunned state for a second. She starts to struggle, trying to twist herself out of his grasp, to hit him or kick him or *something*, but he pins her arms back and although she manages to catch his legs once or twice with the heel of her boot, it's not enough to throw him off balance or make him let her go.

'Fight,' he growls in her ear. 'It's so much more fun when you *fight*.'

That chills her blood instantly.

Mine too.

Jess stops. She doesn't want to give him the satisfaction. She doesn't want to give him what he wants. She's terrified of what *else* he might want, what else he might take from her, what he might do to her. She thinks she might die, here, tonight, but she's less scared of that. There are worse things than death.

She thinks she's not going to get out of this.

I know she won't.

She starts to cry quietly.

I'd like to get out of it. And I *can*; I can leave, right now, just fight my way back to my own mind, back to myself. Stop watching, look away. Before it gets worse.

But I want to see his face.

As he pushes Jess to the ground, her side grazes a rock, knocking the wind out of her and with it, the last of her fight. She feels the last of the fallen leaves and dying grass damp beneath her from the snowfall, looks up dizzily at the trees above, their skeleton branches criss-crossing the dark, cloudy sky.

His hands are around Jess' neck now, the weight of him pushing her further into the damp as he straddles her body, bending forward past her head as he uses all his force to join his gloved fingers together at the back of her throat, the smell of his leather gloves all she can think about now. He makes no move to touch her clothes, focused only on slowly squeezing her windpipe tighter, and she's relieved that at least he doesn't seem interested in *that*; he isn't going to rape her. He's just going to kill her.

I *have* to get out now.

I don't know what might happen to me if I'm still here with her at the moment she dies.

But I want to see his face.

I feel Jess drifting now, arms limp, the oxygen draining from her lungs as she tries to gasp for extra breath and fails, unable to fight his hands at her neck or his weight on her chest. She's colder, she's even more tired, and it's been a long night, a long week, a long first term.

She just wants it to be over. She just wants to *sleep*.

The tears continue to flow down her cheeks, the sounds of her crying muffled by his hands.

Her eyes flutter shut.

Out of nowhere, he smacks her across the face. 'No,' he grunts, annoyed.

Hmm. Not as calm as he was with Michelle. Not as *practiced*.

Was Jess his first? Were there others, after her and before Michelle?

'Open them.'

Leaving one hand on her neck, he brings the other up to her face, pulling her eyelids up, forcing them open as his gloves smudge the damp tears on her skin.

'I want to *see*.'

Finally, he leans his weight backwards, sitting full force on Jess' chest, raising his body back up straight. It's dark under the canopy, but there's just enough light above the trees that when he raises his head up, when his hair falls out of the way, I'll be able to see him, to see Sick Fucker in all his sick fucked-up glory, and then—

I'm shaking.

How am I shaking? *Why* am I shaking? Jess isn't.

'Dot?'

A voice, distant, distorted, familiar.

Insistent, pleading.

'Come *on*, Dot.'

Shaking me harder.

No, not now… not yet… five more seconds and I'll have him, I'll *have* him—

'*Dot!*'

25

And I'm back.

No.

No.

All I needed was a couple more seconds. Just a couple more, and—

'Dot? Are you here?'

It's Theo's voice.

I open my eyes, disorientated. I'm lying on a bed that isn't mine, Theo sitting on the edge beside me in his penguin suit, hands holding my arms, frowning as he peers down at me, his face lined with concern.

'*No*,' I groan, defeated.

Theo raises his eyebrows. 'You're not here?'

I shake my head. 'I nearly *had* him.'

'Who?'

'*Him*. Whoever killed them. Michelle and—'

'Who's Michelle?'

'Bug Lady,' I explain, my words tumbling out frantically. 'I saw what happened to her, I was there; he had her drugged in the boot of a car, then he tied her up in a cellar and cut her *up*, Theo, he broke her knee and he cut up her face and he cut out her fucking *tongue*—'

'Jesus.' Another voice.

I turn my head towards it, and as Rob comes into view across the room, hovering in an open doorway, I suddenly get my bearings and realise I'm in the guestroom downstairs.

'Where are they?'

'In the front room. There's no way anyone's sleeping upstairs tonight, Becs—'

'Not them,' I shake my head weakly. '*Them*. Michelle and Jess, Bug Lady and The Cryer.'

Rob shrugs. 'They've gone, Dot.'

'For the moment, at least,' Theo clarifies quickly.

'What happened?'

'Fucked if I know,' Rob replies, confused. 'Becs came running downstairs with Hannah, a few seconds later we heard a bang, so I ran back up and you were on the floor, completely out of it. No ghosts. Well,' he adds quickly, 'it's not like I ever saw them in the first place, but Han snuck up after me and said they were gone. When we couldn't wake you up, I called him.'

Rob nods over at Theo. I look back up at him as he strokes my face gently, his eyes questioning mine like he's worried I might disappear again. Figuratively, of course.

'You scared the hell out of us, Dot,' Rob pulls a face, awkwardly folding his arms as he leans against the doorway.

'*All* of us,' Theo adds softly.

He looks so scared, and sad, and like he wants to hold me, and kiss me, and never let go. I want him to do exactly that. I wish he would.

But he doesn't.

'When did you get here?'

'A couple of hours ago—'

'A couple of *hours?!*' My eyes widen.

'You were out a good hour before he got here as well,' Rob interrupts. 'When he couldn't snap you out of it straightaway, we brought you down here, thought at least then you'd be more comfortable.'

Hours? I figured I'd been out for maybe twenty minutes, half an hour at the most.

'Are we going to have to move house again?' Rob groans. 'I *really* don't want to move house again.'

'I told you before,' I remind him, 'it's not the house. It's Hannah. And no, you aren't going to have to move.'

Theo sits back, surprised. 'Are they gone then? Completely, I mean?'

'Not yet, I don't think. But I know so much more now about what happened. To both of them. We just need to piece it all together.'

'What? How?'

'Well, for a start, that Bug Lady's first name was Michelle. Don't know her surname, but whoever she was, she worked with him at some point. He knew her, she annoyed him at work with questions, that's why he cut up her mouth, and *that's* why her ghost doesn't talk. And the other one, the younger one—'

'The Cryer?'

'Yeah. Jess. She was killed in her first year at Uni. She was on her way back to campus from some job, at a pub I think, and I got the names of some places she was at and I know what she was studying so if we can work out *where* and find out who died or went missing because he knew her too, Theo, he knew *both* of them, they both recognised his voice—'

I break off suddenly, needing to take a breath as I realise that was probably an awful lot of information to share in a single sentence.

'He likes to *watch*,' I go on slowly, my contempt of Sick Fucker plain in my voice. 'He likes to look into their eyes at the moment they die. God knows why. And,' I add, 'after Jess – The Cryer – by the time he killed Michelle, he had a *system*. He was *practiced*. He drugged her, cut her up, took his time.'

Rob looks aghast. '*Jesus*.'

'I'd bet money there've been others. These two just happened to be the ones who managed to latch onto Hannah's frequency, that's all.'

There's quiet for a minute as my update settles in.

'Dot,' Theo eventually murmurs carefully, 'how do you know all this? Like you said, Bug Lady doesn't talk. And last time we saw them, Cryer – sorry, Jess – could barely get out a few random words.'

'They showed me. I was *there*. I saw it, all of it.'

Theo sighs, shaking his head. 'Are you saying this was another transference again?'

'Exactly.'

He pulls a face, jaw tight, and it looks like he's trying not to lose his temper. 'I thought you said that was just a thing at the Boldmere house? In the Purple Room?'

I shrug. 'I thought it was.'

'I barely got you back out of there the last time it happened,' Theo fumes suddenly, 'and now you turn round and *voluntarily* do it here?'

I don't much like his tone.

'It wasn't intentional,' I point out irritably. 'I was just trying to get them away from Hannah—'

'Oh, so now you can just *accidentally* land inside some random ghost's dead subconscious? Terrific. That's *so* much better.'

Theo's not even trying to hide his anger now, and quite honestly, that pisses me right off back. He gave up the right to an opinion on how I use my abilities when he dumped me.

'Don't get pissy with me Theo,' I snap back. 'Would you rather I'd left them to drag Hannah off for a ringside seat to watch a nice cosy bit of mutilation and torture?'

'You know that's not what I mean,' he stands quickly, turning away. 'But this is exactly what I said before about how much more *dangerous* it's getting. The more you can do, the bigger the risk, and you can't control it. What if you hadn't come back this time—'

'But I did.'

'Because I've been sat here shaking you out of it for the last two hours!' Theo exclaims insistently. 'You didn't even realise how long you'd been under, Dot.'

'Guys,' Rob steps forward. 'Keep it down, yeah?'

'Tell *him* that,' I glare back.

'Oh right, I see.' Theo shakes his head, wheeling on me angrily. 'So now I'm not even allowed to *care* what you do to yourself, is that it?'

'If you cared that much you wouldn't be leaving.'

It's out of my mouth before I can stop it.

Theo's face *crumples*, a look of pure, raw hurt in his eyes.

I did that. What a bitch.

I immediately want to take it back.

'Theo—'

'That's what you *think?*'

He takes two paces towards me, his voice cracking.

'That I'm leaving because I don't care?'

'No, Theo, I didn't mean it—'

'Oh, you meant it,' he thunders tightly. 'I know you did. It's been in your head for weeks, that thought; that if I choose the Church over you it means I never really loved you that much in the first place. Does that make it easier for you, Dot? To make me the bad guy, to pretend this is *easy* for me, that it's not *killing* me to give you up?'

'Guys, *please*—'

'If it's that hard then why on earth—'

'I asked you to *marry* me, for God's sake!'

I shake my head quickly. 'You asked me to give up what I *am* for you, that's not the same.'

Theo laughs suddenly, exasperated. 'I asked you to choose a life where you'll be safe, where things like tonight won't happen anymore. And anyway, what do you think you're asking *me* to do by staying, Dot? By asking me to give up being a priest?'

I nearly correct him to Vicar, but thankfully manage to stop that one from popping out.

'You're asking me to give myself up too. Why is it okay for you to ask that but not me?'

There's nothing I can say to that. I know he's right. No matter which way you look at it, for us to stay together, one of us would have to swap the life they have for another they're utterly unsuited to. It's an impossible situation. And if I *really* believe that him not wanting to give up who he is to be with me means he never really loved me that much, well… doesn't that mean if *I* won't do the same for him, then I never really loved him that much either?

But I know that's not true.

I loved him. I *love* him. I can't imagine ever loving anyone else. Not like this. Not like him. I don't want to lose him.

But more than that, I don't want to *hurt* him.

It's bad enough this is happening at all. The last thing I want is to make it even more painful that it needs to be. For *either* of us.

'I know,' I finally sigh gently, hoping to diffuse the tension. 'I'm sorry, Theo. I don't want to hurt you.'

He scoffs back at me, rolling his eyes, and now it's my turn to feel like I've been slapped.

'I *don't*,' I choke out, 'I mean it. I just… I just want *me* to feel less hurt than I do.'

Theo glowers, refusing to meet my eyes. I've never seen him like this. He's usually the chill one of the two of us, the one who calms *me* down; nothing phases him, it's all water off a duck's back. I'm scared I've hurt him in a way I can't come back from.

I'm scared he might actually hate me now.

Rob looks awkwardly between us, checking over his shoulder again that we haven't disturbed Becs or the kids with our argument, pointless in every way other than to hurt each other more.

I sigh, rubbing my forehead slowly. 'Look, let's just… do what we said before. Sort this out for Hannah, finish up the Boldmere job. Maybe try not to make each other more miserable in the process.'

'No.'

Theo says it so quietly that at first I think I've misheard.

'What?'

'Of course I'll do whatever I can for Hannah,' he turns to Rob with a gesture of reassurance. 'Whatever it takes to get that resolved. That's not even a question.'

Theo looks back at me.

'But forget Boldmere. I'm not doing it.'

That stops me in my tracks.

'But – but the client, we—'

'Fuck the client.'

I'm too shocked to speak. Rare for me.

'You *know* if you go back to Boldmere this transference thing is bound to happen again,' Theo shakes his head darkly. '*Both* times we've been over there you've gone under. You go back again it's basically guaranteed at this point, and after you were gone so long tonight, I'm not letting you do it.'

I bristle at his choice of words.

'I'm sorry. *Letting* me?'

Theo stares me down furiously. 'I *refuse* to go back there with you so I can watch it happen again but maybe even *worse*. Maybe next time you don't come back at all. And I *know* you're not so stupid that you'd risk it on your own.'

I'm seething now.

'All right, tonight was an accident, I take your word for that, you didn't expect it. But you know *exactly* what to expect at that house, and I'm not going back there to help it happen.'

He can't *do* that. He can't just go back on what he said.

'But what – what about—'

'I already told you, fuck Owen,' he spits bitterly. 'I never trusted him in the first place.'

'Never mind Owen,' I reply furiously. 'What about those girls? What about putting them at rest? Suddenly that doesn't *matter* anymore? Isn't that half the reason we've been *doing* all of this?'

Theo stops, startled, opening and closing his mouth while his eyes search for something to say.

'You *promised* me, Theo,' I glare back at him indignantly. 'You promised you'd see this through. I could give two shits about Owen and all of his problems. What I *do* care about is putting this thing to bed so those two poor murdered little girls can have some fucking *peace*.'

Theo looks down, sighing deeply as he rubs his forehead.

'Look. I'm sorry. I really am.'

I can't believe this. Is he *really* going to just walk away from this, too?

He shakes his head, slowly meeting my eyes.

'But they're dead, Dot. You're *here*. You're *alive*. And I refuse to stand there and watch while you trade souls or whatever the hell it is with those poor little dead girls and risk ending up just like them.'

How *can* he? How can *do* this? He *promised*. He promised to see this through.

He promised to love me forever.

He promised I'd never be alone again.

Now I want to hurt him.

'Look,' Theo goes on, 'whatever you've learned about Hannah's girls tonight, send it all over to me. I'll do some detective work tomorrow and see if I can track them down. Maybe then we can put these two to rest, at least.'

At least he has the decency to sound ashamed about it. But that's not enough. How dare he go back on his word, turn tail and run away from finishing the job just so he can force *me* off it. He *knows* I can't do it without him.

I'm so angry with him. I didn't think I could ever *be* this angry, not with Theo.

I stare him down, tight-lipped and steaming, fire in my eyes, the slightest shake of my head.

'You are *not* the man I thought you were.'

Cold. Calculated. To punish him, cut him where it matters, hurt him as much as he's hurt me.

I see the anguish flicker across Theo's face as my words hit the target and he swallows, looking back at me with sadness in those big brown eyes that I wanted to stare into for the rest of my life.

Nodding dully, he turns without a word and walks out.

26

I thought I'd feel too guilty to sleep.

I hurt him. I really hurt him.

And I did it on *purpose*.

The fact that I slept like the dead after that for the first time in weeks seems a bit fucked up.

When I finally *do* wake up, the house is silent, daylight streaming through the guestroom curtains. I reach across dozily for my phone where it's charging on the bedside table to check the time, confused.

10:45am.

Shit. That shocks me back to reality. How did I miss my alarm? Why the hell didn't Becs toss me out of bed? I throw the covers off, trying to remember where I left my rucksack and god I need a shower but do I really have time when I'm this late? Then I see a sheet of paper on the floor, just on this side of the closed guestroom door. Like someone slid it through the gap underneath. I swallow thickly as I pad across to pick it up. It's probably a final parting shot from Theo, telling me how glad he is to've dumped me after I showed my true hurtful colours last night.

But then I see the handwriting and immediately know it's from Becs.

Morning Dot. Don't panic, I turned your alarm off. You need a rest, so you're taking today off. Boss' orders, no arguments. Contrary to popular belief, the place WILL survive without you for one day.

Funny.

There's food in the fridge & Netflix etc, help yourself to whatever, or go home if you'd rather. As long as you don't come into work. If I see you in the office we'll have words.

Theo said you've got new info that might help Hannah – that sounds promising?

Oh Christ, of course. I need to email him with it all so he can start looking at it.

Enjoy your rest. xx

PS: Rob told me not to interfere, but he also told me what you said to Theo. I love you, but that was a bit low, wasn't it? xx

I don't know whether to be indignant at Becs forcing me to take a day off that I didn't ask for, or cry with relief at having the choice taken away from me so I don't have to feel guilty about it. As for the other bit…

She's not wrong.

I owe Theo an apology. If he'll even accept it.

So, before I take a shower and decide what the hell to do with my bonus day, I grab my phone and draft two emails. One titled 'Hannah Info', the other just 'I'm Sorry.'

The Hannah one I keep factual and businesslike, just setting out everything I remember from last night that might be any use. Bug Lady is Michelle and The Cryer is Jess, no surnames unfortunately. The killer seemed to know both of them – he worked with Michelle (I have no idea at what), and was somehow connected to Jess when she was at Uni, though whether that was because he was a student there, or a regular at the pub she worked at, or some random bloke who spotted her at the supermarket, I don't know. Jess was in her first year of Uni when she was killed, she was taking an American Studies class as part of her course, she worked at The Unicorn, and I list the names of the places she mentioned and the bits of signs I saw, although I have no idea what it all adds up to. I set out what happened to each of them – how Michelle was drugged and tortured, but Jess was just immediately strangled. How he seemed calmer and more patient and organised with Michelle, like he'd had practice in the meantime, perfected some kind of system. Ick.

I add about how the killer got a deep cut to the palm of his hand when he was… *working* on Michelle – my skin crawls just thinking about it – so might have an obvious, identifiable scar.

I politely ask Theo to let me know what he finds out, and if I don't hear otherwise, I'll assume I'm still needed to take my turn again for Hannah duty tomorrow night. I try and keep it to the point, limited fuss and frills, just giving him details he can use to do all of his searches. Then I send it off, hopefully giving Theo plenty of time to do his detective thing before he has to be back here to watch over Hannah later.

The other message is shorter. But it takes me longer to write.

I'm so sorry for what I said. I was angry at you, and I lashed out. I didn't mean it, and it isn't true. Not a bit.

Then the hardest part. But he deserves the truth.

I said it because I knew how much it'd hurt you. And in that moment, I really <u>wanted</u> to hurt you, even though I said that was exactly what I didn't want.

I'm not asking you to forgive me. But I <u>need</u> you to know I was lying. You're the best man I've ever known, and that's no less true because we're not together anymore.

I was a bitch, and you didn't deserve it. But I really am so sorry.

I debate adding that I love him. And miss him. And don't understand how we got to this.

But I decide against it. It won't help, not now. He's gone. It's over.

I press send.

Okay then. A whole day to myself.

Well, what's left of it. By the time I'm showered and dressed it's ten past eleven, so I have Marmite on two toasted rounds of Becs' fancy sourdough with a soothing cuppa as I contemplate what to do with the time. I think about Becs' suggestion of hanging out here: they have Sky with all the film channels and a bunch of nice snacks, although they keep them in the top cupboards where the kids can't reach which probably means I can't either. But honestly, the idea of bumming around somebody else's house when they're not there feels a bit weird, so if crashing out and doing fuck all is going to be the order of my day, I'd rather do it back at the flat. Catch up on my gaming, maybe? Pick up a big stash of chocolate and binge watch Judge Judy?

The Batphone vibrates. Yet another text from Owen.

Sorry to keep pestering. Any news?

Christ. I'm going to have to call and tell him we're dropping his job, aren't I. Thanks a lot, Theo. How am I going to explain? I don't even know where to start.

Unless…

A tiny speck of a thought occurs to me.

And once it settles, it starts to grow.

With Theo and I officially over – as ghostbusting partners as well as everything else – I have to think practically about how I'm going to carry on doing jobs without him. Clearing houses on my own will be tricky – not because I can't deal with whatever presence might be kicking about on my own, Theo was right about that much – but because as a lone, not especially fit and healthy woman, rocking up to some stranger's house isn't the best idea in the world. You just never know who's going to be a psycho, do you?

I could just go back to doing readings. Proper ones, I mean, one-to-ones, not the half-cocked student scarefests I was doing before I met Theo. I certainly don't plan on ever setting foot in another Spiritualist church again, so working the platform to pass on messages from beyond the grave to rapt audiences is out of the question.

The problem is though…

I *like* clearing houses. I like the feeling that I'm actually helping people – dead and living alike – the feeling that this absurd 'gift' of mine, so useless in so many other ways that matter, actually has some purpose to it. I don't *want* to stop clearing houses, Theo or no Theo.

Maybe I don't have to.

Maybe I could hire someone; an assistant of sorts; not to do medium stuff, but to act as a chaperone, a safety net, make sure I don't end up alone in a sticky situation that I can't get myself out of. Preferably someone who'll work cheap. A student, maybe. An imposing one. Now that I think about it, Penny's shown more than a passing interest in our cases whenever we've caught up with her and Lisa. It's possible *she* might even be up for it, and she can be pretty intimidating when she wants to be.

In the meantime…

Maybe I don't need to call Owen and tell him we're pulling out.

Maybe I *can* just finish this one job myself.

From what Theo texted me the other night, I know the one little girl's name now – Debbie Russell – the girl who went missing, one of the pair we think is haunting the house. That might make her able to communicate without needing to use transference at all; a name can be a powerful thing, from a spiritual perspective. If I can call her, make that direct link, that might be enough. My best theory is still that she and her nameless friend were killed – maybe even buried – at the house, most likely by Owen's dad, if the local suspicions at the time were close to the mark. If she can finally tell me what actually happened, confirm if he *was* responsible for her death, for the other little girl's death as well… that might do it. If it really was Owen's dad who killed them, well, he's already dead himself, so it's not like they'll get justice, not really. But *someone* will know the truth. *I'll* know. And that might be all they need to have peace.

Theo'll be on the case with Hannah's girls today; there's nothing more I can do for them right now. But maybe I can find the answers for the Boldmere girls? I sigh as I consider my options for a minute. You go your whole life waiting for a pair of Ghost Girls, and then two come along at once.

I look down at Owen's text on the Batphone. The I pick it up and text him back.

Might have something. Are you around today?

I put it back down and take another bite of toast.

He's quick to reply.

Yeah, WFH still. Come over whenever.

I hesitate. If Theo knew I was doing this…

But Theo's *done* with this. And with me.

Worst case scenario, I drop into transference again. If I struggle to come back on my own, well, Owen'll be there, won't he? As long as I warn him what to expect, he can snap me the rest of the way back out of it. Last night's extended disco remix version was likely just because what Michelle and Jess showed me was all just so intense; I haven't felt anywhere *near* that far out of it with the Boldmere girls.

Fuck it. Theo wanted to paint me into a corner, stop me from finishing this job because of his own frustrations, his own fears. He wanted to force me into doing what *he* thought was best for me – never mind my opinion, my agency, my *choice*.

It's time to stand on my own two medium feet.

I text Owen again.

I'll be there in an hour.

No time like the present.

27

I get to Boldmere just before one. The sunshine which blazed fiercely enough through into Becs' guestroom that it woke me up earlier had been replaced by dull clouds by the time I left Solihull, and the heavens opened halfway through my drive. As I park up close to the gate, the pre-April shower is in full swing, and I wonder if it's worth waiting a minute before I get out in case the downpour passes and I can avoid a soaking.

The wait is also partly an excuse to check my emails.

In amongst an update on my current Tesco points, a reminder about my car insurance renewal and all the guff I keep meaning to unsubscribe from, there are two replies from Theo.

I open the safe one first, timed about an hour ago, just as I was on my way out of the house.

Thanks. I'll start looking and let you know what I find. Will update later. T.

Short, polite, to the point. Fair enough.

I don't expect the other one will be.

But Theo proves me wrong.

I'll always forgive you. And I'm sorry too. I just want you to be safe. I love you. I wish things were different.

xx

Dammit, Theo. Now I feel like even more of a nasty cow. And I love him all over again; not that I stopped even for a second, not really. And I miss him, and I wish he was here with me to see this through and I feel bad for coming without him. Especially knowing how much he didn't want me to.

I sigh, groaning to myself. Is this ever going to get any easier? And if so, when, please?

At least Theo doesn't hate me. Although I'm not sure if that makes me feel better or worse.

The rain shows no sign of letting up. Well, I'm here now. And I really *might* have a chance of putting this to bed on my own, if my hunch about Debbie is right. Best get on with it. What Theo doesn't know won't hurt him, assuming he's not looking in my head anymore, which I very much doubt considering that he's blocked me off from any chance I might've had to nosey into his. Not that it matters, actually. I'm a big girl, after all; I can make my own decisions thanks very much, and if the transference thing *does* kick off and go in any way iffy, I'll just have to own my choice, won't I? I grab my bag and make a run for it, hurriedly locking the car door behind me, bolting through the gate, down the path and into the porch, which for once is thankfully sitting unlocked. Owen opens the front door almost immediately, vaguely amused at the sight of me dripping all over the tiles.

'Miserable out there,' I shrug as he greets me.

Owen nods, looks around, frowns. 'No Theo today?'

'Not this time,' I reply casually. I think. 'He's got something else on.'

'Hmm. Kettle's just boiled, if you want a drink to warm you up? You can leave your jacket to dry out here.'

Of course he doesn't want me dribbling rainwater all over his pristine house. Might be more excitement than all of the beige can handle.

'Any chance of a tea, please? With sugar.'

'Have a seat in the living room,' Owen gestures as he heads down the hall. 'I'll bring it through in a sec.'

I shuffle off my soggy jacket and shoes, leaving them in the porch as per the previous visits, and shut the front door behind me as I pad through to the room on the left.

Hmm.

Something feels… *funny*.

It takes me until I take a seat on the sofa before I realise what it is.

The house is quiet. Too quiet.

It feels *empty*.

Like the girls are gone. Is that possible?

It can't be. Owen would've said. If they were gone, he wouldn't have texted – again – asking for an update in the first place.

I close my eyes for a second, concentrating.

No, I think to myself then. *They're not gone.*

They're *waiting*.

Waiting for what? For me? To call for Debbie?

Maybe to tell Owen what we – what *I* – think happened, see if it provokes some sort of memory about his dad?

And I still don't know how on earth I'm going to broach that particularly sticky subject.

'Here we are.'

Owen's voice comes from the hall as he wanders in with two mugs and passes one to me. 'I hope you don't mind Earl Grey?'

Ick.

'I thought I had another box of proper teabags, but I've run out. Sorry.'

I take it with a polite shrug. Any port in a storm. 'That's okay. As long as it's hot, it'll do.'

Owen takes the chair across from me, just as he did when Theo and I were here that first night. 'So, you said you might have something. Does that mean there's progress?'

'Maybe,' I nod, wincing slightly as the perfumed taste hits my throat, mixed with a massive hit of sweetness. He seems to've interpreted my request for sugar as an instruction to fill the mug with a metric fuckton of the stuff. At least it's warm. 'We think we've identified one of the girls.'

Owen stops mid-sip, his eyes wide in surprise. 'Really?'

'Yeah. A girl called Debbie Russell, she went missing—'

'—when we were kids,' he leans forward, mug down on the small table beside him. 'God, I remember when that happened. She went to the same school as me and Erica, they were friends.'

I nod slowly. 'Did she ever come over here to play? With your sister?'

'All the time,' he shrugs. 'I think her disappearing might've been what scared my parents into moving, now I think about it. You know, worried something might happen to me and Erica. They never found her, and as far as I know it was never solved.'

'Right.'

I need to tread carefully. It's his dad, after all. I don't want to put his back up accusing the man. I don't need to get thrown out before I even have chance to call Debbie and talk to her properly.

'You're sure it's really her?'

I shrug back. 'As far as we can be. There was a family who lived here back in the nineties who had similar disturbances to yours. The local Reverend at the time, he counselled them, and saw her when he was here. He recognised her.'

'How?'

'Another one of your schoolmates. He was a kid round here when she went missing as well.'

Owen shakes his head, breathing out deeply as he sits back in his seat. 'Wow. Unbelievable.'

He pauses for a second, and I wait for him to go on and fill the silence. Take a leaf out of Theo's playbook for once.

'What about the other girl?' he frowns eventually. 'You seemed pretty sure there were two of them.'

'We still are. But we haven't been able to find out who she is yet.'

Owen frowns, picking his mug back up to sip from it briefly. I follow suit to be polite, necking down a big gulp this time to force the not entirely pleasant taste past my palate faster.

'Unbelievable,' he repeats. 'That's – I really – I mean, that's just…'

'It's a lot to take in,' I reply gently, wondering how I bring up the *really* fun part of my theory.

'But why would she be *here?*' He looks baffled. 'I mean, she – god, I can't remember where she lived, but I think it was the other side of Boldmere. My dad always used to drop her home when she'd been over.'

Did he indeed.

'So it definitely wasn't close enough to walk. We walked everywhere when we were little, you know. Not much parental supervision in those days.'

I can relate.

'Do you think she might be haunting whoever lives at her old house as well?'

There's really no delicate way for me to bring this up, is there.

'Even ghosts can't be in two places at once. Look, Owen—'

Sudden buzzing comes from the handbag at my feet. My regular phone. I ignore it.

'Usually, when someone's haunting a place,' I start to explain carefully, 'it's because they're attached to it in some way.'

The buzzing persists.

Owen considers for a second. 'Well, she was over here a lot. They were really close, her and Erica. Two peas in a pod, you know.'

'That's possible,' I nod politely, knowing it's actually bollocks. Nobody gives enough of a shit to haunt a house once they're dead just because they enjoyed a few good games of Downfall there in the summer holidays.

My phone's still buzzing, and it's starting to annoy me now.

'Sorry.' I reach down quickly, intending to press the big red thanks-but-no-thanks button. 'Let me just get rid of it.'

Just as I pull it out of my bag, it flips to voicemail.

Theo. Shit.

Should I call him back? It has to be important. There's no way he'd call me with things as they are between us unless it was important.

In a minute, maybe. Let's get through the rest of this awkward conversation first.

I leave the phone out, putting it down on the arm of the sofa before I turn back to Owen.

'There are other reasons someone would hang around somewhere, though,' I start carefully. 'Especially if they've passed in… let's say… violent circumstances. It often means the place is somehow… connected. To that death.'

Owen blinks at me for a couple of seconds, looking confused.

My phone pings briefly beside me. Theo's left me a voicemail.

Okay, it *definitely* has to be important.

Owen frowns as he works his way through the implication. 'You mean… you think she died *here?*'

'Possibly. Or was buried here.'

I take another big sip of tea to fill the silence.

'Or both.'

My eyes keep darting to my phone now. I really should check it.

Owen leans forward again, elbows on his knees, his forehead creased in concentration as he tries to figure it all out. 'But I don't… are you… what exactly are you suggesting?'

I need to bring this up carefully, diplomatically, sensitively… none of which is my strong suit. That was always Theo's thing. My throat suddenly feels very dry and I cough, gulping down most of what's left of the tea to try and soothe it.

'You mentioned before,' I start slowly, 'that your dad could be… turbulent. Is there any chance—'

'You think *he* had something to do with Debbie going missing?'

He looks horrified.

And maybe the second girl too, whoever she is.

I really should pick up Theo's message.

'Owen, the last thing I want to do is make any accusations—'

'That's not what it sounds like.'

'But he *was* violent,' I gesture placatingly. 'Other people who were around when you lived here as a kid have said he was known for it, that your mom had bruises, that you and your sister both turned up to school with bruises—'

'Not Erica.' He stands up now, shaking his head forcefully. 'Dad *adored* her. She was the apple of his eye. And I know people talked,' he goes on, pacing the room, suddenly agitated, 'we all heard the rumours, but he never laid a *finger* on her, he would *never*. She was his favourite.'

'Okay, Owen,' I stand up as well, raising my hands in a gesture of peace, wanting to diffuse his reaction. I did say I wanted to provoke a memory… maybe I brought back one too many. 'Look, we're just trying to come up with a reason why she'd be so drawn back to this place to be haunting it for all these years. Theo's just left me a message, though, so it might be that he's got another update. Let me just check.'

I know it'll probably be about Michelle or Jess after what I sent him earlier, but any excuse to get out of the room and give him a chance to calm down. I grab my phone quickly and walk back out to the hall, leaving Owen to breathe and sit with the revelation for a minute, kicking myself as I press on Theo's message and hold it up to my ear.

Well, you handled that one like a pro, didn't you Dot? I think to myself as the announcement plays. *This* is why you needed Theo, remember? Your people skills are for shit.

Theo's voice kicks in. *'Dot?'*

He sounds odd. Off kilter, somehow.

'I've found something. You need to hear this.'

Urgent. Serious. *Worried.* What on earth is it?

'I found your girl. Well, one of them. Jess Adams. She was a first year student at the University of Kent in Canterbury in the early nineties.'

Holy fuck. She's really real.

'That's the place you saw. Darwin is a college there and a dorm as well, student housing. There's a pub in town called The Unicorn, it's been there forever.'

I hear him take a breath.

'She was found strangled off a footpath just before the end of her first term, just like you said. A couple of weeks before Christmas.'

The snow.

'The killer was never found. But Dot – god, Dot, you won't want to hear this, but…'

What the hell is it?

'And it might just be a coincidence. It's possible. But, Dot, you know…'

I don't even need to hear him say it. I know Theo doesn't believe in coincidence.

'On the alumni list for her year. Owen Morrison is listed as one of her classmates, Dot.'

What?

My eyes drift back to the living room where Owen stands huffily, arms folded, watching me carefully.

Owen Morrison.

Oh *shit.*

28

'Like father, like son, I suppose.'

Theo's voice in my ear as I try desperately not to react.

'Call me when you get this message, okay? Please.'

Owen frowns over at me, standing in the living room doorway, as I lower the phone and swipe the message off.

'Well? What did he say?'

I swallow thickly.

Like father, like son, I suppose.

'Nothing,' I shake my head quickly, forcing the words out. 'It was about another case we're working on.'

Technically true.

'Oh. Look, I'm sorry,' Owen goes on, heading towards me with a sigh, 'I didn't mean to get worked up. I just… it's a hell of a lot to take in, you know?'

Oh god. It just clicked.

His *voice*.

That's why it sounded so familiar. It had nothing to do with Michelle or Jess recognising it. *I* recognised it.

Younger, lighter, not quite as gruff. But unmistakeably Owen's.

I recognised it because I already knew it, because I'd heard it before. My brain just didn't make the connection.

I suddenly feel sick.

And very, very scared.

In a flash, I remember how much Michelle and Jess looked similar to me.

Now I'm *really* scared.

'Dot?' Owen hesitates a couple of feet from me, peering curiously at my lack of response. 'Is everything okay?'

He kills women who look like me.

And nobody knows I'm here.

Shit. *Shit.*

Damn me and my stupid ego, determined to prove that I can do it myself, that I don't need Theo anyway. That's what this stupid little visit was *really* about, wasn't it Dot? If you're honest with yourself? To show Theo that whatever he was doing trying to stop you from coming here, wanting you to be safe, no matter how misguided his approach, you know better.

He never liked Owen. Right from the start. Instinctively, Theo never trusted him.

And he was right not to.

'What's wrong, Dot?' Owen asks again.

'Sorry,' I reply quickly, snapping myself out of it. 'I was miles away for a second. Just thinking about this other case.'

He nods, smiling gently. 'You look like you've seen a ghost.'

'Very funny,' I force out, wondering how easily I can grab my bag from the living room behind him and get myself the hell out of here.

Owen shrugs lightly, amused. He looks so normal. So...*beige.* I guess the most effective monsters are the least obvious.

Maybe I can sneakily call Theo back. If I can just get another look at my phone—

'You sure you're really okay? You look a little...' Owen studies me carefully. 'Peaky.'

Yeah. I hear nausea is a side effect of realising you're in the presence of a murderer. Especially one who likes to kill women who bear more than a passing resemblance to yourself.

'I do feel a little sick, actually.'

It's not a lie. I've just remembered that he also enjoys torture. But it's probably that bloody Earl Grey. I shouldn't have drunk it just to be polite.

'I wouldn't worry,' he shakes his head, stepping a little closer.

Too close.

I step back slightly. It's an involuntary movement, a gut reaction, and Owen smiles in response. I'm almost backed up to the front door as he leans towards me.

For a horrible moment, I think that Theo was right, the man really *does* fancy me, and is leaning in expecting a kiss.

Then he redirects to the side, his face lingering close to my ear, voice calm and soft.

'It's probably just from the sedative.'

Oh *fuckity fuck*.

That tea. That fucking godawful shitty tasting *tea*.

Fuck my bag, fuck my keys; I have my phone, I can call Theo, call the police; I just need to get out—

I whip round to reach for the door.

It's locked.

I groan internally. Of *course* it fucking is.

'Don't worry,' Owen whispers close behind me. 'It won't knock you out completely. That wouldn't be any fun, would it? It'll just…'

He hesitates, right up my back now, hands either side of my head up against the door, trapping me in place.

'… take the edge off.'

I can feel it. My head's getting swimmy and spaced out. Whatever it is he's given me must be starting to kick in. I remember Michelle, how it felt being trapped with her in the boot of his car, strapped up to that table when he—

It's only a matter of time before it dulls my senses completely. And then I'm truly *fucked*.

If I can just get away from him for long enough to use my phone. It's still in my right hand; I'm amazed he hasn't taken it away from me yet, until I remember more from my trip through Michelle's subconscious memory about his confidence. His assuredness. He hasn't taken my phone from me because he simply doesn't believe I'll get the chance to use it. So it doesn't matter to him.

My head swims again. It's now or not at all.

I take a breath and swing my left hand up as hard as I can behind me, towards his head, pushing backwards from the door at the same time. The dual movements take him by surprise; I hear a pained grimace as my watch connects with the side of his face and he stumbles back a couple of steps, enough for me to duck through the gap and *run*.

I don't get far.

My legs are like jelly, and I only manage five or six steps before they crumple underneath me. As I feel myself dropping, I try desperately to open my phone, but I can't lift it up to my face and my fingers have forgotten how to use the keypad, and then I'm in a pile on the hall floor and my brain is crying out desperately telling my body to *move* but it can't, it doesn't remember what moving is anymore. The phone slips from my hand and clatters on the tiled floor as everything comes to a slow, dull halt, my head dropping to my shoulder, the rest of me propped awkwardly half up against the pillar at the bottom of the staircase.

Owen walks towards me, rubbing the side of his face with a wry smile, a red mark blossoming on his cheekbone.

At least I got one in.

'You were right about one thing,' he looks down at me, satisfied. 'Debbie did die here. And she's buried here, too. Just downstairs,' he nods towards the cloakroom. 'In the cellar.'

Cellar? There's a fucking *cellar* in this house? How the *hell* did Theo and I miss that?

Owen looks away for a second, blinking like he's just been hit by the spark of realisation.

'Actually, that makes two things you got right, doesn't it? Well done you.'

He crouches down directly in front of me now, flicking casually at my face with his index finger. He checks my neck, my arms, testing for any reaction; he lifts my right hand high in the air, watching with sick fascination as he lets it go and it drops limply back down to the floor. The moment he releases it, I see his open, empty left hand as he holds it there briefly, and there it is. Clear as day.

A thick, diagonal scar across his palm. From thumb to pinkie finger.

Owen follows my eyes. 'This?'

He waggles his fingers at me.

'Occupational hazard.'

Of course. He doesn't actually know that I *know*. About Michelle, and Jess. He didn't drug me because of that. There's no way he *could* know.

All he knows right now is that he's got me. That I turned up on my own, no Theo in tow, and he immediately grabbed that opportunity to make me a drink and lace it with god knows what crap and lock the door so I couldn't get back out of the house, even if I didn't drink enough of it to be properly incapacitated.

He was planning to drug me anyway. This is just the first chance he's had to do it.

'You did get one thing wrong, though.'

He tuts lightly under his breath.

'Dear old Dad was a piece of work all right. I told you he was turbulent; that wasn't even the half of it. Never took much to set him off, either,' he rolls his eyes with a weary sigh. 'Either his dinner was too hot, or his tea was too cold, or Mom or me breathed too loud or looked at him wrong. It was all just an excuse to beat the crap out of one or the other or both of us.'

I sit slumped uncomfortably on the floor, my breathing steady. Whatever he's dosed me with, my body's reaction doesn't seem to be getting any worse at least, so it seems I'm not quite dead yet. Let's face it – I know his MO: he likes to take his time. He likes to watch the light go out of their eyes when he kills them. Somehow I doubt this is going to be a quick, easy, painless way to go.

'But not Erica. I told you, he *adored* her. Never touched a hair on *her* perfect little head.'

Ooh. Do I detect a note of jealousy?

'And yes,' he goes on quickly, 'he was a lech and a pervert and I don't know exactly all of the unpleasant things he did to poor little Debbie, but he definitely *did*. It was because she looked so much like Erica, you see. He never laid a finger on *her*. Although I'm sure he wanted to. So her lookalike friend got to take her place for him.'

Jesus Christ. What a fucked-up family. And pretty much the exact motive for Owen's dad to kill Debbie that Theo and I suspected in the first place.

'Yeah, he was a nasty piece of work all round.'

A nasty piece of work who killed that poor girl. And the other one too; I don't doubt it for a second. Not that I'm ever likely to find out who she was *now*.

'He wasn't a killer, though. Not once he was outside the Army without his tough guy mates and his guns and his *rules*.'

Oh, really Owen? Yeah, right. You keep telling yourself that.

Owen cocks his head, smiling levelly as he leans towards

me again, lowering his voice like he's sharing a secret. Which I suppose he is.

'I was just putting her out of her misery.'

Erm… *what?*

'What he was doing to her, it was messing her up,' he shakes his head thoughtfully. 'Everyone could see it. One time when she was here she climbed into my bed naked, tried to get me to…'

He trails off sadly, not explaining any further. I don't think I need him to.

'Why on earth her parents let her keep coming over here I *never* understood.'

This is… is he saying…

'Mom was too scared of him to do anything about it. Erica was just glad he left *her* alone, I think; some friend she was. And I couldn't do anything about him, I was too young, too small, but Debbie…'

Is he really saying what I *think* he's saying?

He can't be. Surely. He was just a *kid*.

Owen meets my eyes steadily. 'She was smaller.'

Holy Jesus fucking *Christ*.

It was Owen. *All* of it. This whole time. Right back to the beginning.

'Erica was in her room. Dad always had her friends sleep in the spare room when any of them stayed over, you know, so he could have… *access*. At first he just used to watch them through the wall. I don't think he realised I knew about his pervert passageway, I used to call it.'

The thought makes me feel physically sick, and for the first time I'm sure whatever he's drugged me with has nothing at all to do with it.

'But with Debbie, after a while, it was more than that. Too much. This one night, he got loud, it was… bad. After he'd…

finished… he got drunk and went out, who knows where. Mom went out looking for him, thought we were all asleep, I suppose. But I wasn't.'

Owen's laugh is utterly hollow.

'It was a kindness, what I did for her. A mercy killing. So she wouldn't have to suffer at his hands anymore, not like *that*.'

I'm not sure if he's expecting my agreement, my approval, but if he is, he's put me in no position to give it.

'But then Erica just *had* to walk in, didn't she, so I had to deal with her, too. I couldn't let her *tell*.'

I suppose it didn't occur to him at the time that the two dead bodies might've given the game away?

'When she went, when she – you know…'

When she died. When you murdered her? Your own *sister*, you fucking psychopath?

'The look in her eyes, it was…'

Owen trails off, taking a deep breath as he closes his eyes, leaning back slowly, as if he's trying to recapture the memory.

Eww.

'Euphoric.'

Double eww.

'I ran back down to Debbie, to see if it was there in her eyes too, but she was already gone. I'd missed it.' He shrugs nonchalantly. 'Been trying to find it again ever since.'

This is so messed up.

'When I saw the house up for sale, I couldn't resist. I have so many good memories here, with them.'

So *beyond* messed up.

'Of course, neighbours thought it was odd. Man my age, living in a big house like this all by himself. I just told people the same thing I told you two, you know. Space for the kids and the grandkids, all that rubbish. It's amazing how gullible people are.'

He laughs. 'I've never even been married.'

He was lying. From day one. It was *all* a lie.

Theo was right.

I *hate* that.

'But I didn't realise the two of them would actually *still be here*. Damn estate agent never said a word about the history of the place. Lying scumbags,' Owen fumes.

Does he even *hear* himself?!

'I had no idea. When the noises and everything started, I thought I'd made a mistake. It was constant, relentless, I didn't know how to make them stop.'

The man looks genuinely pained, like he's the one who's been hard done by in this whole situation. How outrageous that the two little girls he killed should have the audacity to come back and *haunt* his murdering arse. The very *nerve* of them.

'I was dubious when I heard about you. I thought it was nonsense. But then when you showed up the other night, looking just like them, like *both* of them, how they would've looked if they'd grown up, just like the others…'

Ah. Well, that explains a few things, doesn't it.

Two little girls 'like peas in a pod', to quote the psycho himself. Two grown up women with features so similar they could be distantly related to each other. And to me.

We're his type. All of us.

'It never worked with the others,' Owen shakes his head dismissively. 'And I could never figure out why. I tried, again and again, but it wasn't the same. I didn't *see* it, that thing that I saw with Erica. But with you, coming *here* of all places, back where it all started, well…'

His eyes twinkle as he leans in again, smiling happily.

'I don't usually believe in fate, destiny, all that rubbish. But this just… feels like it was meant to *be*.'

Maybe for you, mate. Not so much from where I'm sitting.

Suddenly, my phone goes again. My eyes – the only part of me that's still able to function – dart towards it where it sits on the floor, inching across the tiles in tiny shifts with every buzzing vibration. Owen glances at it, looking at me with raised eyebrows as he reaches out, turning it right side up where it lies so we can both see the screen.

It's Theo trying to call again.

'I don't think so.'

He taps the red 'decline' icon, then picks it up, fiddling with it briefly before dangling it in front of my eyes so I can see the dark, empty screen before he slips it into his trouser pocket.

He's turned it off.

I'm so fucked.

29

Owen's been gone for a few minutes.

Long enough for my brain to kick into overdrive. Not long enough for the sedative to wear off, more's the pity. Not that I'd expect it would. He's calm, meticulous and organised, as well as ruthlessly opportunistic. He knows what he's doing. After all, he's had plenty of practice.

Debbie, Erica, Jess, Michelle. How many others, I wonder?

At least a couple, I'm certain of it.

I also wonder why Jess and Michelle didn't come straight to me instead of Hannah. Was it because I'd already had my initial run-in with Debbie and Erica and they were already taking up too much of my bandwidth, so to speak? Was Hannah the next most convenient available frequency? The first time they appeared to her was the same night Theo and I first visited this place. Is that what brought them out?

Maybe they knew if Theo and I thought Hannah was in any way at risk, the both of us would do whatever it took to get to the bottom of it.

You see, this is why dead people are so bloody annoying. If any one of the four – *four* of them, for chrissakes – could've just said from the start: 'oh by the way, that bloke who's house you've been to, he's actually the one who killed all of us' – that would've saved everyone a *lot* of pratting about. Not to mention that I wouldn't be slumped like a paralysed lemon on the floor of a fucking serial killer's front hall.

I hear keys in the lock. Sick Fucker's back.

Whatever he was up to, it didn't take him long. Digging a grave for a mostly adult-sized human would've taken him at least double that, surely?

He locks the door back up behind him.

'Right,' he slaps his hands together with glee, dangling a set of keys I know well in his hand. 'That's your car away in the garage. Wouldn't want lover boy spotting it if he decides to come round here looking for you, would we?'

Not likely. Theo has no fucking clue I'm here. Nobody does.

Because I'm an idiot.

I've tried to call him. In my head, I mean. But I can't reach him, and I don't know if it's because his wall's still up or just because in my current drugged-up-to-the-gills condition, I just *can't*. If he keeps trying to call my phone, of course, and keeps getting no answer, it's *possible* he might come looking for me – in the supernatural mind-melding sense of the word. But I can't bank on that. It might be just as impossible for him to tap into me as it is for me to reach him in my current state. Besides, he might just think I'm not picking up or calling back because I just don't want to talk to him at the moment.

'Let's get you settled then, shall we?'

Owen reaches down and grabs under my arms with both hands, pulling my limp body more or less upright against him, before crouching down and awkwardly shifting me over his shoulder.

'God, Dot.' He wheezes slightly as he takes the full brunt of my weight. 'You're a hell of a lot heavier than you look, you know.'

Good. All the better to pop a disc in your back, you murdering creep.

Still, he manages it. Which means he's strong. Theo tried to pick me up for a laugh the other week and nearly gave himself a hernia. So my chances of overpowering him physically are slim to none. Even if I was still in full control of all my bodily faculties.

Owen carries me down the hall, stopping in front of the cupboard under the stairs. Theo and I checked in here that first visit and all we saw was the usual mixture of crap you'd keep in that sort of storage, albeit neat to the point of neurosis. Opening the door, he flicks on the light and as he steps inside, from my vantage point at his back I can see it looks the same as I remember. But then I hear a *thunk* and the sound of wood scraping against brick, and as he turns I feel the drag of gravity and realise he's carrying me *down*.

The panelled section on the left of the cloakroom under the stairs isn't a wall at all. It's another bloody hidden door. And it appears to lead down to the cellar he mentioned earlier.

Oh, well, isn't this just *terrific*.

He has previous with cellars, of course. I remember the one Michelle ended up in. It wasn't in this house, but you know; once you've seen one serial killer's torture basement, you've seen them all.

The smell of damp is the first thing that hits me, followed swiftly by a mixture of more wood, an undertone of something like bleach and the unmistakeable scent of some sort of animal droppings. Mmm, lovely. The combination is too much, and I feel my chest heave, my throat trying to force out a pathetic series of half-coughs through my body's drugged-up fog.

'Sorry about the accommodations,' Owen sighs as we reach the bottom. 'Honestly, I'm not quite ready for you yet, but when you turned up on your own today, well…'

I feel the shrug of his shoulders against my ribs.

'I got a little over eager. Didn't want to miss the chance.'

He lowers me carefully down onto a hard surface – at this point, I'm prepared to bet highly that it's a table: wooden, probably with a hinged drop-leaf – and turns away. Overhead, an old fluorescent strip light blinks into life on the ceiling, its beam dulled by years of trapping dust and dead bugs. I squint, my eyes adjusting to the semi-brightness. Owen's back is still turned and as I shift my eyes towards him, I can see he's standing at an old bureau, flap down as he rifles through its gathered selection of contents that I can't make out. I take in the debris-littered brick-paved floor, the uneven concrete steps we came down, the messy, crumbling walls, half plaster, half panelled with the same thin strips of wood Theo and I saw in the hidden passage.

Then I catch sight of the other wall, the one in line with the bottom of the steps.

It's noticeably different from the others. Well, part of it is.

Smack in the middle is a section that looks completely out of place.

It's maybe five feet square, made up purely of bricks, scruffily aligned within the surrounding plaster and clearly slightly less old than what surrounds it. It sticks out like a sore thumb, and instinctively I just *know* that the two girls are buried back there.

As I look up, Owen's watching me, clearly entertained.

'Have you spotted it?'

I look back at the wall, then back at him.

'You *have*, haven't you,' he grins with delight. 'I knew you were a clever one.'

Not clever enough so as not to wind up on your dissecting table, apparently.

He wanders towards the wall, looking at it nostalgically. 'When Mom and Dad got back, he was *livid*. Beat seven shades out of me, of course. But then…' he sighs wistfully. 'I didn't really react. Didn't cry, didn't shout, didn't beg. I think that *actually* scared him.'

Owen shrugs and heads back this way, stopping beside the bureau again.

'Mom managed to convince him it'd be even worse if *I* turned up beaten or missing as well. So he stuck them in there, bricked it up, kept me out of school and a week later we were off to Coventry.'

Head down, he goes back to whatever he was doing before.

I'm terrified.

Not because he just told me his dad bricked up his sister and her friend in the wall across the room.

Because I just realised that when I looked over at it, I turned my head.

I'm scared to death *he* might've realised it too.

I glance back at him again quickly, but he's utterly engrossed in the contents of the bureau, his head turned away from me.

I can turn my head.

Is the dose wearing off?

He did say I was heavier than he thought. A *lot* heavier. Maybe the dose depended on my weight. If he guessed it wrong – if he thought I was lighter, and gave me less – maybe it wasn't enough? Not to really last, I mean.

Keeping my eyes firmly fixed on him, I try to move my hands.

No good.

But I can wiggle the tips of my fingers.

I'm coming back. Slowly, but I am. Never in my life have I been so grateful for my weight problem.

Then Owen turns around and I lock myself into statue mode.

'Now,' he starts as he approaches, a bundle in his hands just out of my line of sight, 'I'm not going to kill you right away. I still need you to get rid of the girls for me. And I'm guessing you won't be able to do your thing until the drugs wear off, will you?'

I look back at him blankly.

'Thought as much. It'll be a few more hours at least.'

Maybe not quite as long as you think, motherfucker.

'In the meantime, I have things to do, and I don't want to

have to babysit you for the rest of the afternoon. So I need to make sure that if you *do* happen to wake up before I come back that you'll stay put.'

He holds the bundle up to show me.

It's the leather straps. The same ones he used on Michelle.

I think I can see blood on them.

Owen leans over, wrapping the straps in place around me as I lie helpless on the table, using the exact same pattern he used for her. Shoulders, knees and ankles.

I'm shorter than she was though. And my hand isn't so far away from my knees.

'There we go. Nice and cosy.'

I would *really* like to kill him.

'Now, I'm not going to gag you.'

Wow. What a gent.

'When your voice does come back, feel free to scream all you like, nobody can hear you down here. Great sound insulation, these old cellars. I'll be back down to check on you in a couple of hours. Then you can finish your job, and as long as you do, I'll make it easier on you when I do mine. And trust me, Dot,' he leans close down to my ear, 'I can make it harder. Much, *much* harder.'

Don't I know it.

He turns off the light before he heads up the steps and shuts the wooden panel back in place. Not only am I ninety-five percent paralysed and tied to a table in a musty cellar with only a couple of dead kids' bodies hidden behind the wall for company, now I'm in complete darkness as well.

Terrific.

I sigh internally, trying to breathe steadily and not panic. He said himself that he still needs me to finish clearing the house, so I have time.

If there's time, there's a chance.

Okay, probably not a huge one. But there is.

There's definitely some feeling starting to come back, because the hardness of the table beneath me is starting to make my bum ache. And the pressure of the strap across my shoulders is starting to feel heavy on my chest. How much longer might it take to get all of my feeling back, though? Once it does, it's possible I could get out of the straps, but even if I manage that, I'm locked in a fucking serial killer's cellar, in a fucking serial killer's house. Correction – a fucking serial killer's *locked* house, and he's the only one with the keys. My options for doing a bunk aren't looking great. And he's got my phone. Plus my keys that he took to move my car were in my handbag with the other one – the Batphone – so I have to assume he's probably found that as well.

I close my eyes and try again to reach Theo.

Come on, Theo. Please.

But I still can't feel him. There's nothing. Blank, dark, *nothing*.

Bloody hell.

To add even more insult to injury, it's getting cold down here now as well. I can feel it building around me, like a thin fog circling the table. Well, isn't this just the icing on the—

Wait.

This isn't cold. Not *normal* cold.

This is creepy dead ghost girl cold.

The fog reaches the bare skin of my arm and as I turn my head to meet it, I'm greeted by a pool of cold light.

And I see them. Properly, for the first time. Those two poor girls.

Peas in a pod is right. Long brown hair, blue eyes, both a little shorter than Hannah, each dressed in their thin kiddie nighties, staring sadly and lifelessly across at me. Tears roll silently down my cheeks as my heart breaks for them, for the life they might've had, for what he took from them.

For Michelle, for Jess, for however many more I'm sure exist out there but for whatever reason didn't have the strength to reach out like these four did.

For myself.

The girls' ephemeral figures blink up at me expectantly. I know what they want; they want me to finish this, to give them justice; and by extension, let them have the peace they're owed. And I want to, more than anything; I want to punish him, to *hurt* him. Last night back at Rob and Becs', I thought I wanted to hurt Theo, but that wasn't a *real* desire to cause him any pain. *This* is what *really* wanting to hurt someone feels like. I've only experienced it once before in my life.

Last autumn, when some half-soaked tinpot wanker of a demon thought he could torture my Theo and get away with it. And look how that turned out for *him*.

I can do this. I know I can.

I just need a little hand. Literally.

I stretch the part of my fingers that can move as close to the cloud as I can and meet the two pairs of blue eyes with my own.

'Debbie, Erica,' I call both of their names silently in my head. *'Help me.'*

As both girls reach out slowly towards me, I feel my chest tense with anticipation, expecting to find myself back in the Purple Room with Debbie maybe, or plunged somewhere into darkness with Erica. Our fingers touch, and—

There's a loud crash somewhere above us.

An exclamation from Owen.

I haven't gone anywhere at all. I'm still on the table in the cellar.

Another clatter upstairs and a series of loud *thuds*, like furniture falling somewhere. The vibration of the impact is audible nearby, Owen's voice mixed in with it, his words unclear but the shock and panic in his tone unmistakeable.

When I look at the girls, they're both grinning happily. Then unexpectedly and quite suddenly, they're gone.

Although…

…*not far.*

There's a surge through my body – an electric current of energy, light, *strength* – and for an instant, a million thoughts mingle noisily with my own, memories and hopes and dreams, everything that was ripped away from them, devastated into nothing by *him.*

Transference.

But backwards.

This time, they're in *me.*

I feel… invigorated. Bigger, almost. I'm not, not physically, but the sensation of it *feels* like an expansion; not of my physical body but of my mind, my psyche. Whatever well of power it is that exists still untapped within me is suddenly, unequivocally, extremely wide awake. And that's not all.

I can move.

All of me.

I'm abruptly, immediately fully conscious and completely physically unimpaired. Because now, I'm not just me. I'm *them.* Both of them. All of us. I – *we* – feel empowered, focused, utterly single-minded.

Mighty.

And *supremely* pissed off.

While the clamour continues kicking off upstairs, I slide my left hand down past my knee, pulling roughly at the leather binding, forcing it to shift its way along where it's tied around me and the table, until it moves enough that I can reach the metal buckle and undo it. With my arm now fully free, I reach up easily to undo the one at my shoulders, then I sit up quickly and yank the last strap away from my ankles.

A noise at the top of the stairs draws my attention.

He's at the wooden door.

I have to be quick.

I drop off the edge of the table and head straight for the open bureau. The dark of the room doesn't matter now – I have other sources of vision, thanks – and I quickly scan over the collected hoard Owen was sifting through earlier, snatching up a heavy clay plant pot, a screwdriver and a really big knife before I quickly turn and dash past the steps, hugging the wall alongside them just as the door above opens noisily and light streams down from the hall. Carefully, silently, I slip the screwdriver and the knife – pointy side up so I don't accidentally stab myself in the arse – inside the waistband of my linen trousers and crouch slightly, still and silent in the shadows.

Like a leopard at the watering hole, waiting patiently for an unsuspecting gazelle to get thirsty.

'Dot,' Owen's panicked voice starts to descend the steps. 'I don't know what's happening, I need you to—'

He stops abruptly partway down, just feet from where I'm leaning in the dark.

'Dot?'

There's confusion in his voice as he takes a couple more steps, facing the side of the room where the table sits. The light coming in from above doesn't reach far enough into the cellar to reveal my hiding spot behind him, but it illuminates the edge of the table itself, and it's clear that it's no longer occupied.

'What the *hell?*'

I hold my breath as he descends further, unable to accept the evidence of his own eyes. *Not* part of his plan. He finally reaches the floor, and I know I have to make it fast. The only thing on my side – apart from the help of two dead eight-year-olds – is the element of surprise. If he puts that strip light on and turns round, I've nowhere to hide. Silently, swiftly, I tiptoe forward as he walks towards the empty table in bewilderment, his back to me now, and as I catch up behind him, I raise the plant pot over my head and bring it down on the back of his with all the strength the girls have just gifted me.

'Wha—'

As it connects, Owen stumbles, dazed, falling in a heap on the dusty bare floor.

I grab the knife from behind me, the metal flashing in my hand as it catches the light and for a second I really believe I could kill him. Stab him through the heart right now, slash his throat, *gut* the fucker for everything he's done.

No.

The Girls don't want him dead.

They want him stopped. They want him *caught*.

Time to go then. But I need something first.

Taking advantage of his temporary incapacitation, I crouch down quickly, reaching into his front trouser pocket to retrieve my phone. As he swings his arms out dozily, making a half-hearted attempt to grab at me, I swipe across with the knife and he rears back, yelping in pain.

Yeah. Hurts, doesn't it, you bastard.

Phone in hand, *now* it's time to go.

Up on my feet, I trot quickly towards the steps, knife out before me, not taking my eyes off him.

'Dot...'

The plant pot gave me a window, but it's a short one. It's not damaged him enough to keep him down for very long. Edging up the steps backwards so I can watch him still, I make my way up quickly, taking care not to do anything stupid that might send me falling arse over tit and all the way back down.

'*Dot…*'

He's starting to stir as I slip through the open doorway and close it behind me. There's a latch on the cloakroom side to keep it in place, but it's not a big one, and it won't keep him trapped for long. I'm already trying to remember what bits of furniture from the downstairs rooms I could grab easily to block the cloakroom door with as I dash out through it, and—

Carnage stops me dead in my tracks. It *was* furniture I heard being chucked about.

There are shards of debris spilling from the home office into the hall, papers and books and desk accessories. The doorway to the room itself is blocked by an upended bookcase crammed awkwardly in the gap alongside an office chair and a short filing drawer; it's a similar story past the staircase, where I can just about see cushions and part of a coffee table from the living room poking out haphazardly.

'*Dot!*'

Owen yells angrily up the steps, his voice muffled but inching higher.

I run towards the strewn about furniture, trying desperately to switch my phone back on at the same time, struggling to press the right combination of buttons. There's a small sideboard lying face down partway through the living room doorway, and I reach for it quickly. Empty of its contents, it's awkward to move but not too heavy, and it's about the right length that I could prop it under the cloakroom door handle to block him from getting out. For a bit, at least.

'*DOT!*'

He's banging on the cellar door now. I can hear the metal latch rattling violently as I drag the sideboard along the hall, turning it on one end and wedging it under the handle of the closed cloakroom door, angling it so the other end is snug against the radiator on the opposite wall, keeping it firmly in place.

'Let me *OUT*—'

Owen crashes through the first door and I jump back as I hear him land inside the cloakroom with a thud. Almost immediately, he moves the handle of the door in front of me, trying to push the door open, and as soon as he realises it's stuck starts to bang against it relentlessly.

'*OPEN THIS DOOR!*'

Not likely.

I run to the front door, phone back on now—

Passcode. *Shit.*

The cloakroom door thuds again and again behind me as I put in the code, ignoring a million notifications from Theo and dialling 999, holding the phone awkwardly by my ear alongside the knife in my left hand while I snatch the screwdriver from my waistband with my right and attack the screws on the front door lock.

'*LET ME OUT YOU FUCKING BITCH*—'

'Nine-nine-nine emergency, which service do you require—'

'Police please, quick,' I rattle out over the operator. 'He's trying to kill me.'

The screwdriver catches on the first screw and I manage to make a quarter turn, but my hand's shaking and clammy and it slips out, clattering against the metal.

'Police emergency, can you tell me where you are?'

'*OPEN THIS FUCKING DOOR NOW*—'

The banging doesn't let up for a second as he tries to force the blocked door open, and as I glance back over my shoulder, I can see he's made a gap. Not a big one, just an inch, but it's enough to poke his fingers through and he grabs frantically up and down the side of the door as he rattles it over and over.

'I'm locked in a house on Copper Beech Road in Boldmere, it's on the corner of there and Foxglove Avenue,' I babble quickly, trying again with the screwdriver. 'I'm sorry, I don't remember the number and I don't know the postcode—'

'*LET ME OUT!*'

'Okay, we're looking for your location. Can you tell me your name?'

'Dot Miller.' I get the first screw on the move again. 'I've been attacked by Owen Morrison, he owns the house, he drugged me and tied me up and he's trying to kill me—'

The banging reaches a crescendo as he pushes the gap wider, the sideboard shifting out of place in gradual increments.

Shit shit shit.

'Okay Dot, help's on the way. Are you injured?'

'No but he's killed people before, he told me, there are two little girls bricked up in the cellar here and he's locked the door so I can't get out—'

CRASH.

I turn just in time to see Owen as he runs towards me, blood dripping a trail down his face, screaming like a man possessed, arms out as he makes to grab me. Without even thinking, I throw the screwdriver at his head and swerve to the side, running up the stairs as he stumbles, tripping on the edge of the upturned bookcase and crashing up against the front door. The police operator is still talking but the phone's down at my side now, forgotten as my new priority is to put as much distance between me and Owen's murderous rage as possible. Panting as I reach the main landing, wishing I'd bothered to do half an hour of cardio ever in my life, I bypass the doorless spare room and try his bedroom door, but of course it's locked.

Owen's footsteps thunder up the staircase.

No choice. Nowhere else to go. Top floor bedroom it is.

My joints are killing me, but I force my legs as fast as I can up the first set of stairs. I'm partway up the second, cleared now from the chaos of the other night, when Owen reaches the landing below me. He starts upwards, taking the stairs two at a time. I reach the top and slip into the bedroom, slamming the door shut and pulling the drawers across just as he lands there, bashing it partway back towards me.

'Nowhere to go, Dot,' he roars.

'The police are on their way, you murdering arsehole.'

'Then I have nothing to lose by killing you, do I?' he cackles through the gap.

I push back with everything I have – the Girls, too – but I can't hold him off for long.

The window. I could jump.

It's a thirty-foot drop to the garden.

But the roof of the bay window in the home office sticks out just below the next bedroom down. It might cushion my fall. If I can land on it. If not, it could be a nasty hobbling or instant death.

I suspect neither of those options are worse than whatever he's got in mind. Fuck it.

Still pushing all my weight against the door, locked in a tug of war I know I can only lose, I shift sideways on to face the slowly widening gap. Lifting the knife, I bring it down sharply against his hand as he pokes it around the edge of the door, and he snatches it back with a pained yell.

It's enough. Just about.

I slam the door shut again, this time pulling the drawers the rest of the way across it. They won't slow him down for long, and with the rest of the stuff that was trashed the other night all cleared up and away, it's the only thing left in here I can use to block it. But the window isn't far. I run for it and release the catch, pushing it wide in front of me before I climb up onto the sill.

The drawers crash down behind me as my foot reaches through the gap.

Owen grabs me, yanking me away from the exit and I land on my back on the floor, the wind knocked out of me, my phone and the knife both falling somewhere out of reach. He's on top of me immediately, hands flying straight to my neck.

'This is where Erica died,' he hisses as his weight on my chest traps my lungs in a vice. 'This is the exact spot where I killed her. Fitting, don't you think?'

I gasp for air, trying to hit back at him, make him move, peel his fingers away, but it's like a gnat grazing an elephant. My vision swims.

And darkens.

It's like the Purple Room all over again. Except this time, it's real. And it's *me*.

Then suddenly there's someone behind me.

Two people, actually. I can feel them.

Michelle and Jess.

Two pairs of ghostly arms reach down from somewhere back behind my head towards Owen's crouching form, and the Older Girls close their hands around his wrists.

Startled, Owen looks up. His eyes fill with disbelief.

He sees them.

In his fright, he lets go of me, exclaiming in shock as he stumbles over my legs, scrambling backwards, away towards the corner. 'No. *No.*'

Yes, Owen. Oh *yes*.

I gulp down precious air, coughing and spluttering as my hand goes to check my neck, tender from the pressure. As the Older Girls drift past me, aiming straight for Owen, I roll away in the other direction, putting as much distance between us as I can until I can get enough breath back to move properly.

'No! Get away! *GET AWAY!'*

Owen cowers in the opposite corner now, arms swinging wildly, half facing the wall but unable to tear his eyes completely away from the sudden sight of the women he murdered decades before. The closer they get to him, the farther he slides down towards the floor in an effort to escape them.

But he can't.

And they're not all that's coming for him.

I feel a *pull* – like a painless, gentle vacuum sweeping through my whole body – and a sudden sinking sensation, like a part of me is dropping away, falling.

Leaving.

The Girls. The Original Girls.

One final, gentle *drag* of separation and there they are: gone, outside of me again. Heading for Owen's corner.

As I watch them go, still fighting to get my breath, I hear sirens through the open window. I force myself up onto my knees and lean against the wall beside me, summoning up my last reserves of strength – and whatever the Girls might have left behind for me – to pull myself up and onto my feet, reaching for the windowsill again but this time for support as I look outside. Now I can see blue lights, too. And people – neighbours, I suppose, dotted about in dribs and drabs around the road in front of the house, pointing and watching curiously. Bloody hell, it's the middle of the afternoon. Don't these people have jobs?

I lean through, pushing the window as wide as it'll go now, waving frantically.

'Here! I'm up here!'

I think I see Reverend Rogers down amongst the rubberneckers. Aw, that's nice.

In the corner across from me, Owen starts *screaming*. The Older Girls have him hemmed in completely. Then, the Original

Girls reach them and the older pair part like the Red Sea, welcoming the children in between them. As Owen catches sight of them, he goes quiet, still, stunned.

Haunted.

The two little girls stand before him now, holding hands, flanked by their grown-up equivalents.

'Erica?' Owen croaks pitifully, staring up at her, wide-eyed.

His sister takes a step towards him.

He shifts his gaze slightly, frowning questioningly at her little partner as she hangs back.

'Debbie?'

The girl steps forward alongside her friend and the two of them look down at him silently, hovering, waiting.

Outside, there's a clamour of car doors slamming, running footsteps down the path, banging on the door downstairs, shouting that I can't make out.

'Erica? Debbie?'

They don't move.

But Owen does.

Tentatively, he reaches a hand out towards them. It shakes as he holds it in mid-air, not quite touching the fuzzy edges of their eerie combined form.

'I'm— I'm—' he hesitates, words catching in his throat.

The Original Girls stand there without a sound, watching him.

'I'm *sorry*,' Owen says, voice breaking.

He shakes his head, looking down at the floor.

'I'm sorry… I'm so *sorry*…'

The two little ones turn to look at one another, then back to Owen as he murmurs his apology again, over and over. Debbie looks back up over her shoulder at Jess, while Erica mirrors her, looking at Michelle on the other side. The two women step forward then, each taking their younger partner's free hand.

Owen's babbling stops abruptly as the four of them face him down, his expression of dubious remorse replaced now with one of quickening fear.

There's pounding on the door downstairs now.

'I'm sorry,' he mutters again quickly, glancing nervously at the assembled group in front of him, the panic in his voice deepening as his eyes flit back and forth between them.

Behind them, another ghostly fog appears.

It starts small, about the same size as Debbie, with a vague, unformed shape inside; but then it pulsates gently, grows, and a second, larger shadowy outline takes its place beside the first. The cloudy form repeats this cycle – a third time, a fourth, a fifth – until it settles with what look like six undefined yet clearly individual figures within it.

Others. Other victims. The others he's killed, but who couldn't communicate. Who couldn't reach through to our side.

I knew there'd been more. I bloody *knew* it.

The fog shifts forward, billowing out at the ends. The two women reach back into it, clasping unseen hands somewhere amongst the mist.

Downstairs there's a crash, then shouting and more footsteps, inside now.

Erica leans down past her brother's upstretched hand, and gently places her forehead to meet his.

Footsteps and noise heading upstairs, reaching the first floor landing.

The fog glows gently. The Girls – all of them – do the same.

They become part of it.

Through the translucent cloud, I see Owen's eyes grow wide. The glow gets brighter still, surrounding Owen completely.

Within it, his face is a mask of raw, pure white *terror*.

Transference.

As footsteps crash up the last flight of stairs, the shroud and everything in it is swallowed up by a piercing, brilliant light and I turn away, shielding my eyes with my arm. When I look back seconds later, there's a gaggle of confused coppers in the doorway, Owen's in a catatonic heap on the floor, and all of the Girls have vanished.

30

It's over.

As a friendly member of His Majesty's Finest wraps me in a foil blanket and guides me away from the open window, I know The Girls are gone, young and old. All of them. The others too, whoever they were, in that glowing mist. Two more officers crowd Owen's prone form, trying to rouse him, and I have a sneaking suspicion it won't take them long.

Because The Girls never wanted him dead. And they sure as hell didn't give a shit about his pathetic, half-arsed, fear-induced apology.

They wanted him stopped. They wanted him caught.

They wanted him *punished*.

And while I'll probably never know for sure exactly what they showed him, I reckon punishment is exactly what it was. I'd like to think that in those few, dazzling seconds when they were all connected, with him in their midst, they showed him everything he'd ever done... through *their* eyes. A lifetime of evil and torture and death, compressed into an infinite space in his memory.

A little later, watching from the back step of an ambulance as the officers escort him out and put him in the back of an unmarked car, hands in cuffs behind his back, whatever it was The Girls did to him, I hope he felt every fucking second of it.

I hope it haunts him for the rest of his life. Now that they won't be around to.

I told the paramedics there was nothing wrong with me half

an hour ago, but they insisted on checking me over anyway. Someone produced a coffee in a little travel mug from somewhere, and despite thinking I'd never accept a hot drink from a relative stranger ever again, I took it, needing something to wipe the chill from my blood, to steady myself back to some semblance of normality. A maelstrom of activity has been unfolding around me since I've been perched here, as more police go back and forth, carrying clear plastic bags marked 'EVIDENCE' out of the house: the mug I drank from, the knife, my phone.

Shit. I need that back.

'Excuse me, officer?'

I wave frantically to get the PC's attention as they pass a few feet from me and she turns abruptly.

'Yes?'

'That's not his. That's *my* phone.'

'Sorry, love. It's evidence.'

She shrugs and continues on her way.

No phone. No car, either; while one of them was taking my initial statement – I have to go somewhere later to give a more detailed one – they told me it was found in a garage around the back of the house, but I can't have it because they're dusting it for prints, or something. More evidence. No keys, because Owen handled those as well, and no Batphone because it has the records of his calls and texts. Apparently my whole life is evidence now. One of the PCs was going to see if he could at least get my handbag back to me, and they did offer to have someone drop me home and call me out a locksmith. I suppose I should be thankful for small mercies, or something. At least if I had my phone, I could call Becs, or Mags, or even Lisa or Pen. But I don't know a single contact number from memory these days. That's what modern technology's done to me.

There's a sudden commotion at the edge of the cordon that's

been set up around the house to keep the gawking neighbours at bay, and one of the PCs is gesturing to someone on the other side of the tape who I can't see.

'Look, sir, you can't come through—'

'You don't understand.' A familiar voice, measured but insistent, full of concern. 'I'm her—'

'Theo?'

The PC turns to look at me as I shout across the road, unblocking my view, and there he is, standing behind the blue and white tape, penguin suit and all. As he sees me, relief floods his face, and more than that; a tidal wave of emotions.

'You know him?'

I nod, putting the coffee down carefully beside me on the floor of the ambulance. 'He's my... emergency contact.'

That's one way of putting it.

'Hmm.' The PC turns back to Theo, lifting the tape slightly. 'Go on, then.'

Theo immediately ducks under it, closing the distance between the cordon and the ambulance in record time. As he reaches me, he leans down, arms tight around me, wrapping me in a bear hug that almost knocks the wind out of me again.

'I was so worried,' he breathes into my ear. 'I kept calling and calling but—'

'I know,' I tell him, enjoying his closeness. 'He took my phone.'

Theo pulls back then, looking me over, searching my eyes. 'Did he hurt you? I swear, if that fucker touched you—'

'I'm fine,' I reassure him, not entirely truthfully. 'Well, you know, I'm... okay. Under the circumstances.'

I shrug back up at him as he gently strokes my face, my hair, my shoulders, like he's checking to make sure all the pieces of me are still intact. When his fingers reach the bruises on my neck he flinches, sadness and anger and guilt and vengeance all fighting for control of those big brown eyes.

'I got your message,' I tell him. 'Before it all went to shit. You were right about him from the start. You knew something was off about him.'

Theo shakes his head. 'Yeah, but I didn't… I should've realised. I thought he was trying to…'

'Told you he didn't fancy me,' I tease gently. 'Not like *that*, anyway.'

'It's not funny, Dot.'

'It's a *little* funny.'

Theo smiles sadly.

'How did you know to come? I tried to…' I pull a face. 'To *call* you. You know, the *other* way. But I couldn't reach you.'

He turns his head briefly, nodding back towards the assembled crowd lingering in the road. 'Reverend Rogers called me. She saw them bring you out of the house.'

'Ah. I thought I spotted her down here.'

'Apparently a bunch of the neighbours called the police because of the noise,' he explains. 'Off the back of that incident they reported the other night.'

'So someone really *did* call the police about that?'

'Yeah. Why?'

I shrug back. 'Just thought it might've been more of his bullshit. You know his whole my-son-won't-bring-my-grandkid-back-to-the-house story was made up?'

'Really?'

I nod. 'When he was… when I was drugged,' I explain carefully, 'he told me a bunch of stuff. Confessing, I suppose, because he thought I wouldn't be around to…'

I shiver at the memory.

'He said he'd never even been married. Although, who knows. Maybe *that* was the lie.'

Theo shakes his head. 'Why on earth would someone make up a story like that? A whole *life?*'

'Dunno,' I shrug dully. 'Make him seem more... plausible, maybe? More ordinary?'

'But... Dot, that whole room upstairs,' Theo frowns at me, worry lines creasing his face. 'That was made up for a kid. You don't think he was planning to...'

He trails off.

I don't think I need him to say it out loud. I don't think I want him to. My blood's chilled enough just at the thought.

'Maybe.'

'*Jesus.*'

I sigh deeply, closing my eyes as I drop my head, rubbing at it as though the movement might wipe out the sheer exhaustion and disbelief. 'Almost *everything* he told us was a lie. Right from the start.'

Theo shakes his head, thunder on his face. 'Fucker. Are you sure you're really okay?'

I shrug. 'Just glad I didn't have to jump out of the top floor window.'

'What?'

'Never mind.'

He frowns down at me curiously, looking up abruptly as the sound of banging starts in the house. 'Are those girls still—'

'No,' I shake my head. 'They're gone. They're probably making a start in the cellar.'

'There's a *cellar?* How did we miss a whole cellar?!'

'Another hidden door. The Girls are buried there. Bricked up in the wall.'

'*Christ*. So his dad really *did—*'

'Oh no,' I correct him quickly. 'Sorry, I forgot you don't already know. It was *Owen.*'

Theo does a double take. '*He* killed those little girls? But wasn't he just a—'

'A kid, yeah. It was never like father like son at all. It was always just *him*.'

Theo looks too stunned to speak. After a while he sighs, shaking his head.

'You think they'll have enough to lock him up for all of it?'

'If what's left of those girls really is down there, then...' I laugh drily. 'And if nothing else, they'll have him for attempted murder. Of me, I mean. Not even my word against his.'

He looks at me questioningly.

'The whole time he was chasing me round the house, trying to strangle me to death, 999 were on the other end of the phone,' I explain proudly. 'And he wasn't exactly subtle about his intentions.'

Theo peers back at my neck again, his fingertips grazing the marks carefully, featherlight against the tender skin. 'I'm so sorry I wasn't here, Dot. I should've—'

'Theo, it was *my* decision to come here on my own,' I cut him off quickly, my hand over his where it sits tentatively against the bruises. 'This isn't your fault. And anyway, it all worked out okay in the end.'

'*Okay?!* Dot, none of this is what I'd describe as *okay*.'

'Of course it is,' I smile back at him lightly. 'Theo, I did what I came here to do. I found out the truth about what happened to The Girls – to *everyone* he hurt – and I even managed to catch the fucker. I gave them the peace that they needed, and that's what matters.'

Theo shakes his head, unconvinced. 'I still should've been here. I shouldn't have tried to force your hand like that, Dot. I was just so scared.'

'Theo,' I put my other hand up to his face to silence him.

He blinks back at me, beautiful brown puppy-dog eyes all big and sad.

'It doesn't matter now. It's over.'

'What about Hannah? Bug Lady and—'

'They're gone too. Hannah'll be fine now. They won't be back.'

Theo takes a deep breath and pulls me close again. I bury my head in the comfort of his chest as he holds me, kissing the top of my head. 'Thank God. At least now that's the end of it, finally. You're done now, right?'

I hesitate, pulling back slightly.

'What do you mean?'

'With *this*. This is the end of it.'

I look up at him sceptically.

He frowns. 'Right?'

'Well… this is the end of the *job*, yeah.'

Theo leans back so he can meet my eyes properly, his hands moving to my shoulders as he studies my face carefully. 'You're not seriously planning to still do this?'

'What, you mean… clear houses?'

He shrugs.

I pull a face. 'Why wouldn't I?'

'After all *this?!*' Theo exclaims. 'Dot, for chrissakes, you nearly *died. Again.*'

'Because I'm an idiot who got suckered in by a serial killer,' I point out. 'That had nothing to do with the ghosts.'

'Dot, you wouldn't have even been here in the first place if it wasn't for—'

'In fact,' I stand up now as I interrupt him firmly. 'The ghosts are the whole reason I *didn't* end up dead. What those little girls did gave me what I needed to save myself. And *they* were the ones who brought him down in the end, not me. I'd actually *be* dead now if it wasn't for them.'

'But—' Theo hesitates, pleading in his eyes. 'But – Dot, please, think about—'

'What do you want me to say, Theo?' I ask him wearily.

I'm tired of us having this same conversation, over and over again.

'That I'm going to give up being a medium, and marry you and make fucking brownies for the church bake sale every weekend? Is that what you want to hear?'

Theo shrugs back sheepishly. 'Well… yeah?'

I laugh sadly. God, I love him.

'The bake sale's only once a month, if that helps.'

I *really* love him.

But I can't keep going round in circles. *We* can't.

I brush his cheek gently, his scruff tickling my skin, so familiar against my palm. 'Come on, Theo. Is that who I am?'

He frowns down at me, eyes starting to mist up. 'No.'

I reach up with my other hand, cupping his face gently.

'I love you,' I tell him. '*So* much. More than I thought I could ever love anyone or anything—'

'Except Creme Eggs.'

Theo sniffles gently, trying to force a smile.

I shake my head. 'No, gorgeous. Even more than those.'

He laughs half-heartedly. 'I always knew it.'

God, this *hurts*.

'These few months… I've been *so* happy being with you, Theo. I didn't even know I could *be* that happy. But you were right. What you said last night.'

'I'm sure I wasn't,' Theo protests weakly. 'I talk a lot of crap.'

'You were *right*,' I ignore his attempt to deflect. 'For us to stay together now, one of us would have to give themselves up. And neither of us should have to do that. If things were different, I'd marry you in a heartbeat, you know that.'

'But they're not.'

I nod, trying unsuccessfully to choke back the tears as Theo does the same.

'So, this is really it then?'

I wish it wasn't. 'I think so.'

Theo shakes his head. 'I love you so much, Dot.'

'I know,' I reassure him. 'I love you too. *So much.*'

'I suppose it isn't always enough, is it?'

'I suppose not.'

He searches my eyes with his, so desperately sad. 'Could we just, maybe… pretend? Just for a few minutes?'

I nod furiously, sinking into him as he puts his arms back around me again, holding me so tightly it almost hurts.

'I'm so sorry, Dot.'

'I'm sorry too.'

Theo buries his face in my hair as my eyes sting with tears.

'I wish things were different,' he says.

'Me too.'

We stay that way for a while, pretending. That we can carry on, that we can still be us, that everything in our lives isn't about to change completely. After I don't know how long – not long enough, though, I know that much – a sudden cough from over Theo's shoulder breaks the spell between us.

'Er, sorry. Miss Miller?'

I pull back gently in Theo's arms and look past him to find one of the PCs I spoke to earlier, standing holding out my handbag.

'The DI said you could have this back. They've cleared it.'

I lean over and take it from him gratefully. 'Thanks.'

'Also, they don't need these.'

My bunch of keys. Minus the one for the car. I sigh with relief.

'Can't give you back the car key while they're still looking it over.'

'Not much use without the car anyway,' I smile back feebly.

'Exactly. But they've got what they need. At least you can get home now.'

'Thank you.'

Theo carries on quietly holding me as the PC shrugs politely. 'Your phone'll be a bit longer I'm afraid, sorry. Once they've processed it, you'll be able to get it back. Might be a couple of weeks though. They'll be in touch.'

I'm not sure how. But it looks like I'm dragging Mags out phone shopping with me tomorrow after lunch.

'Okay. Thanks for letting me know.'

'No problem.'

As he turns away, I hesitate before I decide to call after him. 'Officer?'

'Yeah?'

'Someone mentioned I could get a lift home?'

He nods. 'Course. I'll get someone over with a car.'

I look back up at Theo as the PC carries on.

'You don't want me to take you?'

He looks hurt. I smile warmly back up at him.

'Easier this way, I think. For both of us.'

'You're probably right. If I take you home—'

'—you'll end up coming in, and—'

'I might never leave.'

'I wish.'

Theo shakes his head. 'Dot, I don't – I can't—'

I reach up on tiptoes and cut him off with a kiss. He returns it immediately, desperately, one hand in my hair and the other round my waist as he pulls me closer, demanding I love him back as we forget the world together for a couple of precious final minutes. When I eventually pull away, I giggle through my tears, remembering that he's in his penguin suit and wondering what

Reverend Rogers and the neighbours must make of the scene.

'Still *so* hot in that costume,' I tease.

Theo laughs back, wiping his eyes. 'You're not so bad yourself.'

I smile up at him, looking into those beautiful brown eyes, tracing his neck with my fingers as I map every crease, every line, every freckle, drinking in the sight of him for the last time.

'I love you, Father Gregory.'

'I love you, Dot Miller.'

As the PC waves me over, I return the gesture and slip my bag over my shoulder before I lean up to give Theo one final kiss on the cheek.

'Bye, Theo.'

I slip past him before he has a chance to reply and head toward the waiting police car, fighting not to turn back as I finally let the tears take over.

It's time to go home.

THE END

www.ingramcontent.com/pod-product-compliance
Lightning Source LLC
Chambersburg PA
CBHW072203130726
47910CB00011B/1803